CODY BONNER WAS KNOCKING DOWN HER DEFENSES IN SHORT ORDER

"I'm sorry for a lot of things, Queen Houston. But not that you came into our lives. Thank you for being there." His thumb traced her chin, and he felt her tremble beneath his touch.

"It was nothing," she said and moved away, uncomfortable with the lack of space between them.

He held his breath, expecting her to order him to take her to the bus. But she didn't ask, and he was afraid to broach the subject of her staying longer. Instead they stood, eye to eye.

Queen was furious with herself and the fact that she cared . . . that she'd made the Bonners her responsibility. When would someone ever care for her?

Also by Sharon Sala

Chance McCall
Diamond

Available from
HarperPaperbacks

QUEEN

Sharon Sala

HarperPaperbacks
A Division of HarperCollinsPublishers

This is a work of fiction. The characters, incidents, and dialogues are products of the author's imagination and are not to be construed as real. Any resemblance to actual events or persons, living or dead, is entirely coincidental.

HarperPaperbacks   *A Division of* HarperCollins*Publishers*
10 East 53rd Street, New York, N.Y. 10022

Cover photograph by Herman Estevez

First printing: November 1994

Printed in the United States of America

HarperPaperbacks, HarperMonogram, and colophon are trademarks of HarperCollins*Publishers*

❖ 10 9 8 7 6 5 4 3 2 1

This book is dedicated to my own families. The ties are long, but they are strong. I know that even if I unwittingly transgress upon their feelings, in the end I will be forgiven, because we share something more than the ties of birth: we share love.

To the families of Vester and Katie Smith and their descendants . . . to the families of Christopher and Mabel Shero and their descendants . . . to the families of Ernest and Agnes Sala, my family by marriage . . . and to my family—my husband, Bill; my son, Chris, his wife, Kristie Ann, and their daughter, Chelsea; and my daughter, Kathryn.

This book is for you. Enjoy . . . and remember the love that binds us all.

1

The night breeze blew against Queen Houston's face, shifting her hair and cooling the sweat that had formed on her brow moments earlier. She hefted the shotgun to an easier position against her ribs and pressed closer against the outer wall of the house, confident, for the moment, that darkness hid her presence.

Her mouth thinned, and her eyes narrowed in anger as she watched the man who was standing in the shadows of the alley between their house and Whitelaw's Bar. She wondered how many times in the past he'd done what he was doing and gotten away with it.

Queen knew it was her sister Lucky's bedroom that had captured Morton Whitelaw's attention. Lucky was probably undressing. Queen mentally ticked off the garments that her sister must be removing by the way Morton Whitelaw increased the depth of his self-gratification. Her finger twitched on the trigger of the shotgun, knowing that it would take less effort to cock the hammer than it took to zip her blue jeans . . . and less time.

A small, distinct noise dampened Morton's lust. The click was loud and ominous and, to a man born to the Tennessee hills, as familiar as his own face. It was the sound of a hammer being cocked on a shotgun. Morton Whitelaw forgot he was at the point of climax as the woman's voice came drifting through the darkness.

"You sorry sonofabitch. If Johnny were still alive, he'd kill you," Queen said, stepping away from the wall of the house.

Morton paled, although his fear was hidden by the shadows in which he stood. It was Queen Houston! Even in the darkness he recognized her by the tangle of wild red curls surrounding her face. He'd rather have been caught by any one of Johnny Houston's daughters but this one. She had a hate for men the likes of which he'd never seen. He knew it would take some tall talking to get away with what she must have been witnessing.

"Step out into the light," Queen said. "I think you've seen enough of the Houstons for one night."

He started to shake. It was the quiet, emotionless tone of her voice that made him afraid. That and the fact that she had the shotgun pointed at his crotch. He looked down, realizing as he did that he was still touching himself; he started to move his hand away when she hissed a warning.

"Leave it," she ordered. "You like that thing so much, I'd hate for it to get cold."

"Now, Queen, you don't understand," Morton began. "It isn't what you think. I was on my way over to your house to bring you girls your money, and I felt nature call. I was just about to—"

"I know what you were about to do. I could hear your groans from here, you bastard. You want to jerk off, you use someone besides my sister for enticement."

"Damn," Morton muttered, and let his hand fall to his side. "What about the money for your property? You're still gonna sell, aren't you?" he asked.

Queen waved the shotgun toward his pocket. "Hand it over and then get the hell out of this alley before I find myself forced to shoot a prowler. I wouldn't be accused of anything other than a terrible accident and you know it. We just buried Johnny, remember? No one would blame the Houston girls for being nervous or for protecting themselves with their father barely cold in the ground."

"You bitch! When you get this money, that house is no longer your property."

"Maybe not," Queen said. "But you're buying the house and lot, not me and my sister."

He sighed and reached for the envelope he'd stuffed inside his shirt.

"No! Wait!" Queen ordered as Morton's hand dipped toward the pocket containing the checks. He did as he was told, frozen by the tone of her voice as well as by the ominous gleam of light on steel as the shotgun's direction was changed. She was now aiming toward his face.

"I'd rather you used your left hand, Whitelaw," she said, remembering what he'd been doing with his right one moments earlier.

He flushed and swore, but it did no good. Queen Houston didn't give an inch. Cursing soundly, he yanked the envelope from his pocket, flung it onto the ground between them, and turned and stalked away, silently willing her to hell and back.

The back door of Whitelaw's Bar slammed, and it was only then that Queen let out the breath she had been holding and bent down to pick up the envelope that Morton Whitelaw had tossed into the dirt. She walked out of the alley with the gun hanging in the crook of her arm, barrel downward, and paused long enough by the porch to read the names on the three cashier's checks inside the envelope. The glow of the red Christmas lights hanging across the front of Whitelaw's—which hung there all year round, regardless of the season— was bright enough for her to see the amount of each check.

Five thousand dollars! She still couldn't believe it. And it was all her sister Diamond's doing. The thought of Diamond's absence made her want to cry, but tears were not a part of Queen's life. Instead she stuffed the checks into the envelope and looked over her shoulder once more just to make sure that Morton Whitelaw was gone.

Remembering the look on Diamond's face as she'd walked out of their lives two days earlier on the arm of Jesse Eagle, one of Nashville's hottest singing sensations, was vivid. She'd left Cradle Creek with stars in her eyes and a dream in her heart. Queen envied her optimism, as she herself had long since forgotten what it was like to hope or dream. She'd been too busy raising her two younger sisters as well as herself.

But now she was holding the first chance she'd had for personal happiness in her entire life. Unfortunately it was inevitable that the three sisters would have to part. Diamond was already gone, and Lucky was inside, just waiting for the chance to leave. She'd had her bus ticket since yesterday and had only been waiting for Morton Whitelaw to pay up.

Queen blinked, unaware that the reason her vision was blurred was because of tears. She wouldn't have admitted their presence, even to herself. Queen Houston never cried.

A pack of dogs bayed far off in the hills, and Queen paused in the darkness and listened. Some locals must be running their dogs tonight. She sniffed the air, half expecting to smell the wood smoke from their campfires, imagining how they'd huddle around it, laughing and telling jokes as the finest of dogs from their packs struck trail. But there was only the thick pall of smoke from the coal mines and the stench of car fumes and cigarette smoke coming out through the open windows as the patrons came and went next door at Whitelaw's Bar.

A man's loud, raucous laugh intruded, reminding Queen of where she was and of her vulnerability there. She thought of the anger she'd just seen on Morton Whitelaw's face and bolted across the porch. She yanked open the screen door, then ran inside, slamming it and the wooden door shut behind her. She turned the lock with shaky fingers and quickly set the shotgun inside a closet beside the door.

"Queenie . . . is that you?" Lucky called from the back of the house, unaware of her part in Morton Whitelaw's downfall at the hands of Johnny Houston's daughters.

Queen leaned against the closet door and wiped her hand across her face. But there was no one present to see her moment of weakness, and when she answered, her voice was as strong and confident as ever.

"Yes, Lucky. It's me. And guess what? I got our money!"

The two sisters spent the next morning sorting through their meager belongings.

Queen stood in the doorway to Lucky's room and

watched as her baby sister flitted from the dresser to the bed and back again, folding and refolding her clothing so that it would fit into a bag that she had purchased at an army surplus store years ago.

"Did you get Diamond's check in the mail?" Lucky asked as she packed the last of her clothes.

Queen nodded.

"She's going to be so excited," Lucky continued, unaware of the tense expression on her older sister's face. "Shoot, I'll bet by this time next year that five thousand dollars will be chicken feed to her. She's going to be famous. I just know it."

Queen's lack of response made Lucky look up. It was then that she realized how difficult this parting was actually going to be. The tears that sprang to her eyes were as inevitable as the sun that came up each morning. Her face crumpled and she started to cry.

"Be happy for me, Queenie," she sobbed, and threw her arms around her older sister's neck. "I won't be able to leave if you aren't."

Queen's arms tightened in reflex as she clutched her sister's body tightly against her. She closed her eyes and willed herself not to think of the coming loneliness. For so many years she'd been the only one who'd cared, the only one responsible for her two younger sisters, and now in the space of a week she was losing them just as they'd lost their father, Johnny Houston, days earlier. The heart attack that had claimed him had been unexpected, just as everything else in his life.

"I'm happy," she said, and hugged Lucky even tighter. "I'm just having a hard time letting go. You know how parents are."

Lucky's tears pooled up again. "That's what's so awful, Queenie," she said. "You're not my parent. You're my sister." She turned away and wiped her face with the towel Queen had handed her. "You never even got to be a child. You were too busy taking care of Johnny and of us. Sometimes I forget you're only four years older than me. You've been the only mother Di or I ever knew." She threw her arms around Queen one more time and pressed a quick, desperate kiss on her cheek before turning away and busying herself with her one piece of luggage.

Queen inhaled sharply. This was what was so scary. These feelings between her and her sisters had always been there, but until now they'd never been voiced. It was the finality of the entire situation that frightened her. What if she never saw either of them again?

"You'll write as soon as you get to Las Vegas," she said.

Lucky stopped and looked up. "And mail it where? You're leaving too, remember?"

Queen paled. She shoved her hands through her auburn curls and paced, trying to figure out a way for the three of them to keep in touch. Finally she remembered.

"We'll both communicate through Diamond. Jesse Eagle gave me his card. I used it when I mailed Diamond her check. There's an address as well as a phone number. We'll mail everything to her, and she can relay the information back to us."

Lucky smiled. It was an answer to the fear. She should have known that her Queenie would think of something. She always had before.

Queen suddenly bolted from the room. Moments later Lucky followed and found her digging frantically through her closet for the shirt she'd worn yesterday.

"I can't find it," she said in a panicked voice.

"You can't find what?"

"The card! Jesse Eagle's card. I had it," she muttered, flinging her meager wardrobe onto her bed. "I used the address at the post office. I distinctly remember . . . Oh, God! Lucky! I think I left it on the desk. I've got to get to the post office. Maybe it's still there. Mayrene never cleans. Surely this once it'll still be—"

Lucky stopped her sister's frantic flight by grasping her arm. "That was yesterday," she reminded her.

Queen shrugged out of her grasp. "I don't care if it was two weeks ago. I can't lose it. How will we ever find each other again? I lost Johnny. We can't lose each other!"

She raced from the house, her long legs covering the distance from porch to gate in three steps.

Lucky followed behind at a slower pace. She didn't want to be there when Queen discovered the loss, but she couldn't let her face it alone. Until now their whole lives had been intertwined by the fact that they were the gambler's daughters. Living down that stigma would have been impossible alone. Together they'd snubbed their noses at the world that had done a royal job of snubbing them.

Queen disappeared around the corner of the street, a blur of denim jeans and faded brown plaid shirt as she raced the five blocks to the post office. Lucky followed, using the time to take one last look at the rural Tennessee town that had been the only home she could remember.

She tossed her long black hair over her shoulder and squinted against the glare of sunshine, wishing she'd worn something to travel in other than the faded jeans and yellow shirt. She'd always dreamed of arriving in Las Vegas dressed to kill. She thought again of her silent vow to go back to the source of Johnny's misfortune—to Nevada, the place where their father had lost the Houston Luck in a poker game, and reclaim that which was theirs.

It was a childish dream that had taken root years ago. And even maturity had not dimmed the need to find the family heirloom, a gold pocket watch, and bring it back to Johnny. That Johnny Houston now had no use for it didn't seem to matter. What mattered to Lucky was fulfilling his dream.

A child cried beyond the doorway of one of the houses as she walked past. She looked away, trying to ignore the slap she heard and the knowledge that sometimes poverty was more than a lack of money: it was a frustration with life that often turned itself inside out and made nice people do ugly things to the ones they loved.

And the poverty of Cradle Creek was inevitable. The main commerce in town was the small coal mining company that clung to existence as stubbornly as the hill people clung to their privacy. Most of the houses were ramshackle and in sore need of a paint job. Their gray, weathered walls blended perfectly into the monochromatic landscape of a coal mining community. What wasn't coated with coal dust was layered in dirt.

Lucky knew that it was acceptable to be poor in a place where everyone was the same. It was not acceptable to live off the weakness of man by gambling for a living. She also knew that acceptance in Cradle Creek came from scraping out a living in the bowels of the earth, not skinning a miner out of his paycheck.

She stopped mere feet away from the post office and watched as Queen stood transfixed on the top step, staring blankly at the landscape as if her answer could be found floating somewhere in the atmosphere.

"It's gone," Queen said. "The only time Mayrene Tate's cleaned the damned post office in a month and it had to be now." Her frustration warred with her fear. She didn't know whether to scream or just sit down and cry. But she was a Houston. She did neither. Instead she walked off the steps and started back toward their house.

"How will we stay in touch?" Lucky asked, unable to look away from the despair on Queen's face.

"It'll be all right," Queen muttered, and slipped her hand in Lucky's. "It has to be. When we get settled, surely we can just call information and contact Diamond through Jesse's record label or something. It can't be all that difficult. Come on," she said. "You've got a bus to catch in less than an hour. And I've got to pack, too. I told Whitelaw we'd be out by tomorrow."

Lucky skipped in step to match her sister's long stride. For the last time, they made the trip home together.

Queen stood in the middle of the street, waving at the back end of the bus long after the dust had settled. The smile she'd fixed on her face slid, turning upside down along with her world. For the first time in her life she was alone. It was terrifying and, at the same time, exhilarating.

It was her time. She patted her pocket to assure herself that her own share of the money from the sale of their home was safe, then headed for the bank. She walked inside and up to the single teller's window, took the cashier's check out of her pocket, and slid it across the counter.

Tilman Harger had gone to school with Queen Houston. By the time they were in high school, she'd become the unreachable goal they'd all strived for. He, like every other boy in their class, had made bets as to who would screw the curvaceous redhead first. He, like every other boy in class, had come up a loser. If Queen Houston had ever dated, she'd done it quietly and chosen someone other than a local. And he, like every other man in town, had hated her for the slight.

"What can I do for you?" he asked, picking up the check and then smirking as he looked back at her. "Or I should say . . . what did you have to do for this?"

Queen smiled.

Tilman shivered in his shoes. The smile wasn't friendly, and he suspected that his raunchy humor had gone awry.

"I want two hundred dollars in cash, and the rest in traveler's checks," she said, ignoring the rude innuendo.

Tilman's eyebrows shot upward. "What would you be wanting with traveler's checks?"

"Traveling," she answered. Along with the expression on her face, it was enough to shut him up.

A few minutes later she exited the bank with an envelope in hand and headed for the gas station that doubled as a bus stop to buy a ticket. An hour later she was in her room, shoving the last of her clothes into a bag. By this time tomorrow she should be somewhere in Arkansas, maybe even Oklahoma. She had no notion of how long it took to get to Arizona, and she didn't care. All she knew was, she was going to ride until she found a place where the sun rose on a clear blue sky and the scent of smoky air and coal dust was nothing more than an ugly memory.

There was one thing she'd left unfinished, however. She didn't relish the thought of facing Morton Whitelaw again, but it had to be done. She picked up the document from her bed. This would be her last trip to Whitelaw's Bar.

Morton glanced up when Queen appeared at the doorway. Looking at him always made her think of weasels—his small, dark, close-set eyes; his sharp, beaky nose; his teeth stained from too many years of chewing tobacco.

"What do you want?" he growled, and slung a grimy towel across his shoulder that he'd been using to wipe glasses. He hitched his pants over his sagging belly and ran his fingers through his thin, graying hair.

"I don't want anything," she said. "I came to give you the bill of sale. I'll be gone by six A.M. tomorrow. Until then, leave me the hell alone, Whitelaw. Don't think just because I'm alone in that house tonight that I'm easy game. I'd hate to think I was the cause of my father having to spend eternity with you laid out beside him on the hill behind the gas station."

Morton blanched at mention of the cemetery and then turned red in anger. "Why you think any man in his right mind would want you is beyond me, you bitch. You're mean as a snake and cranky to boot. Men like to bed women, not females with an attitude."

Queen smiled and tossed the bill of sale on the floor between them much in the same manner that Whitelaw had tossed their money in the alley a few nights before.

"Just remember what I said, Morton. Don't set foot on the property until I'm gone or you'll be sorry."

She left as quickly as she'd come. For a few moments Morton stared at the paper on the floor, half expecting it to detonate. The sudden silence of the bar mocked his fears, and in a flurry of curses he grabbed the paper and stuffed it into his pocket. He couldn't wait for tomorrow to get here. The first thing he was going to do was tear that damned house down. He'd been needing more parking space for years.

He'd already forgotten that it was his own greed that had cost him so dearly. The years he'd spent trying to buy Johnny Houston out for ten thousand dollars had come and gone. And when the gambler who'd spent most of his life at the table in the back of his bar had died unexpectedly, he'd planned on the daughters being so devastated that he would get the place for half the price. When they were at their lowest, that's what he'd offered.

Their fury had been shocking. Just as shocking as Diamond Houston's threat to give the entire house and lot to a fanatic bunch of Bible thumpers. He knew as well as she that it would mean the end of his business. They'd preach him out of house and home in months. He'd been forced to pay three times what he'd offered just to get Johnny Houston's daughters out of his life for good.

The sound of a door slamming made him jump and then made him curse. Just to prove that she didn't call all the shots, he walked to the window and stared out at the house across the alley, giving in to the spite he felt obligated to show. But there was nothing to see but shaded windows and the ever-present, gray, weathered walls of Johnny Houston's home.

No one waved good-bye. It was to be expected. Few had cared. Queen stared hard at the back of the seat in front of her and tried not to think of the hillside behind the bus stop. There was no point in dwelling on the fact that Johnny Houston would now be alone in Cradle Creek, because if the God she'd believed in all these years truly existed, then her father was no longer there, but in heaven.

The bus driver emerged from the gas station, readjusting his belt as he walked toward the bus. Queen knew that it was time. In moments she would be gone. She'd never have to wake up and see coal smoke again. She would never again have to suffer the averted stares and hateful whispers of the people who'd judged her and her sisters as unworthy.

The scent of diesel filled the air as the engine kicked to life and the driver shifted into gear and began to pull out onto the highway. In spite of her determination, Queen found herself staring out the small window beside her toward the sloping hillside, searching frantically for the single white cross on the far side of the cemetery.

The bus began moving, faster . . . faster. In a sudden panic she stood and then crawled onto the seat on her knees, pressing her face against the glass and fixing her gaze on the mound of freshly turned earth that was her father's grave. Her vision blurred, her chin quivered, but tears never came. When the last sight of Cradle Creek had disappeared from view, she sat back on her seat, ignoring the curious stares of the two other passengers in the back of the bus.

She'd said her good-bye. It had not been necessary to say it aloud. It had come from her heart.

Her jacket lay on the empty seat beside her. The map that she'd painstakingly marked with yellow crayon beckoned. Queen unfolded it on her lap and shakily traced the yellow line with her forefinger, suddenly anxious to put as much distance as possible between herself and Cradle Creek, Tennessee.

Today was the first day of the rest of her life.

2

Outside, the scene became a monotonous blur of roadway and greenery. As night fell, Queen lost interest in the fact that she was heading west. The strain of the past week was beginning to take its toll. She didn't even notice when the bus passed through Arkansas and into Oklahoma. But when she woke early the next morning as the bus driver pulled into another stop, she knew that she'd arrived into unfamiliar territory.

The Texas Panhandle looked vastly different from the great Smoky Mountains. It seemed to Queen as if sometime during the night a giant rolling pin had flattened the world that she'd known. Gone were the high, mist-covered peaks and the lush growth of evergreen. Gone were the narrow, winding two-lane roads of rural Tennessee, where there was no place to go except straight up the side of a mountain or straight down into a canyon.

She grabbed the seat in front of her and pulled herself upright, staring transfixed out the window. The land was flat, and brown, and it seemed to go on forever. Queen realized for the first time in her life how immense these United States truly were. And it was then that she thought of her sisters and wondered how they'd ever find one another again in a country where there seemed to be no end to the horizon.

"We'll be here thirty minutes," the driver called as he stood and stretched. "You can disembark, get a bite to eat, and look around. But don't wander off. I have a schedule to maintain and won't wait for sight-seers to come back."

Queen realized she was gawking and quickly closed her mouth as she gave the world outside the bus another glance. Where in the world would one wander to? she thought. There was nothing to see and nowhere to go.

She, along with a large assortment of passengers that had accumulated from various stops the bus had made while she slept, got off and straggled in a slipshod line toward the smell of fresh coffee and frying bacon.

"Y'all come on in," a waitress called out as the first of the group came through the door. "Find yourself a seat, I'll be with you in a sec."

Queen chose a single stool at the bar rather than a booth. It was too early in the morning for socializing, especially with a bunch of strangers she sincerely hoped she'd never see again.

Two cups of coffee and a plate of eggs and hash browns later, she rose, paid her bill, and headed for the door, intent on stretching her legs for whatever time was left. She was too tall to be comfortable on the cramped bus seats.

The air was warm and dry. She turned around and faced the east, letting the rays of the early morning sun shine a welcome on her face. Her ample bust pressed tightly against her thin cotton shirt as she raised her arms above her head and tilted her head from side to side to loosen her stiff, aching muscles.

The bus driver inside the diner paused in the act of taking a sip of his coffee and stared, lost in the sight of her womanly shape. Although she was a beautiful lady, he'd noticed that she rarely smiled. It had been his experience that women who looked the way she did usually appreciated the admiration of the opposite sex. This one seemed to be the exception to the rule.

Her face was striking . . . an unforgettable combination of wide, clear green eyes above high cheekbones, a straight, perfect nose, and a mouth that would have beckoned to be kissed were it not for the stubbornness of her chin and the warning her body language gave. Her dark red hair was long and curly, and in the morning sun it looked like a halo of fire. He shuddered, watching her backside sway as she walked away, and tried not to think of how those long legs might wrap around a man and never let him go.

Queen took advantage of the remaining minutes to brush her hair and her teeth in the ladies' room and wished again for a chance to shower and change. But the driver's warning bellow quelled the thought. It was time to go.

Two new passengers boarded, a mother and her child, and Queen held her breath, hoping she wouldn't have to share the empty seat beside her. She wasn't in the mood for three states of small talk. Fortunately the harried mother chose to sit in the front of the bus with her toddler son.

Three hours later Queen realized she could have saved herself the worry. Ultimately the mother's location was moot, as the toddler had taken free rein of the aisle of the bus. Queen winced at the mother's shrill voice and stared out the window as she listened to her repeated but apathetic warnings to the child.

"Frank! You get on back here now. You hear me? I'll whip your butt if you don't, and I mean it."

It was obvious that Frank, the toddler, had heard that impotent threat too many times before to pay close attention. He paused at Queen's seat and looked up at her, venturing a smile. Then he glanced down at the colorful map sticking half in and half out of her pocket.

"Book?" he said, pointing at the map.

Queen smiled in spite of herself and wondered why the mother hadn't bothered to wash the child's face this morning. Remnants of breakfast hung on his chin and down the front of his grimy little shirt.

"No, that's not a book," she said softly. "It's my map."

"Map." The toddler nodded as he repeated the word, uncertain what it meant but willing to agree, happy with the gentle tone of her voice and the smile on her face.

"Frank! You leave them people alone, and you do it now! Hear me?"

Frank didn't wince. Queen wondered if he was even three. His soft brown eyes were huge, but he was small, blond, and spindly, and his bare belly distended suspiciously over baggy shorts. She'd seen many children of similar situations in her lifetime and knew that most of that look could be attributed to malnourishment and lack of care.

She remembered the small bag of dried fruit that she'd stashed in her jacket pocket yesterday to be eaten sometime during the trip. From the look on the child's face, this seemed to be as good a time as any. She glanced warily across the top of the seats, anxious that she not antago-

nize Frank's mother, but the woman seemed uncon-
cerned about where her child was or what he was doing.

Queen dug into the pocket of her jacket, pulled out
the bag, and motioned for the child to come closer.
Aware that he'd spill it if she just handed him the bag,
she opened it and began handing him a single piece at a
time. He slid onto the seat next to her with anticipation.

The child's fist clutched around the bit of dried peach
as if he'd just grasped a lifeline in a storm-tossed sea.
Unlike some children, he didn't even bother to investigate what he was putting into his mouth. Instead, it went
in, and went down as fast as it had been inserted.

Queen laughed softly. "Here's another. Chew it first,
baby," she said. "Chew, chew, chew." She mimicked the
motion, laughing to herself as the child flashed tiny teeth
and imitated her order.

Half an hour passed as Queen doled out the bits of
fruit and Frank chewed. And then the fruit was gone and
Frank's eyes went from the empty bag to Queen. She
shrugged and held out her hands to imply what was
painfully obvious.

"All gone," she said.

Frank stared and then nodded. He was fully aware of
the word. "Gone, gone," he repeated. And, in a flash, so
was he.

"Where have you been?" Frank's mother asked. Queen
winced as she heard the sharp slap of the mother's hand
on the child's tiny thigh.

What hurt her even more was the fact that Frank
didn't bother to cry. What could that child's life have
been like that he was already so accustomed to depriva-
tion and pain?

Queen had an urge to stomp to the front of the bus
and slap Frank's mother into the middle of next week,

but she knew there was no use. There were thousands just like her, and Queen couldn't save the world. By this time tomorrow she hoped they'd all be in different states. Responsibility had just taken its last free ride on Queen Houston's shoulders. She was through fighting other people's battles and raising other people's kids.

"But when can you get it fixed?" a man asked, voicing the same question the other passengers had been thinking ever since the bus had ground to a wheezy halt in a small town just across the New Mexico border.

The driver shoved his hat to the back of his head and frowned. "Look," he said. "I'm a driver, not a mechanic. I've called the company. They've already dispatched another bus. It'll be here in two, maybe three hours. Until then, we sit tight."

"But I've got to get to L.A. by day after tomorrow," the man went on. "If I don't, I might lose my job."

The driver shrugged and walked away.

Queen sighed. This delay hadn't been part of her plan, either, but at least she didn't have a deadline she was trying to meet. All she had planned was to get to Arizona. After that she'd decide what came next.

Two hours and several angry passengers later, Queen was beginning to change her mind. A small cheer arose in the midst of the weary travelers as they saw a bus pull up and park.

"That's not the one!" the driver shouted before the crowd moved toward the door. "That one's a regular, and he's headed for Colorado, not California."

Groans and grumbles met his remark. Queen frowned and then, on an impulse, went in search of their driver, who'd just made a fast exit out the door.

"Would it be possible to change my route?" she asked. "I think I'd like to take this bus instead of waiting."

The driver frowned. "This one don't go straight into Arizona. In fact, if I'm not mistaken, when he gets into Denver, he'll just do a turnaround and come back south."

"It doesn't matter," she said. "I can always catch another later, can't I?"

He scratched his head and then finally nodded. "I suppose you can do anything you want to, lady. Wait here, I'll tell the driver to wait while I get your bag."

Queen felt a small spurt of excitement. He was right. She *could* do anything she wanted. Less than thirty minutes later she was on her way, leaving the disgruntled and stranded passengers who were still waiting for the substitute bus to arrive. Queen didn't care how long it took her to get where she was going. Anything was better than sitting and waiting.

As they traveled north, she noticed that the rivers they crossed were swifter and deeper, the trees were thicker and greener, and the familiar shape of mountain ranges beckoned in the distance. A small, distinct sign on the side of the highway told her all she needed to know: "Colorado State Line."

Queen looked up toward the distant, snow-capped peaks and felt a tinge of familiarity. They reminded her of the Smokies that had surrounded Cradle Creek, with tops that were constantly lost in a swirl of cloudy mist. She frowned. Remembering Cradle Creek was the last thing she'd intended to do.

The farther they rode, the closer they came to the mountains, and as they entered a small town at the foot of a particularly high peak, the bus began to slow down.

Queen sighed. Her legs ached from inactivity. She would be thankful for the chance to move about.

"All out for Snow Gap," the driver called. "We'll be here about fifteen minutes. It's the last stop before Denver, so make it count."

Queen got off the bus and stretched, then looked around. The geography might be different, but the bus stops were predictably the same. Deciding against riding all night with a greasy hamburger in her stomach, she decided to explore instead and began walking along the small, narrow sidewalk, along a street lined with colorful-looking stores. She would remember thinking later that choosing the hamburger would have been simpler.

A child's cry pierced the quiet of the small town. Another accompanied it, and Queen turned to look at the scene being enacted on the street two doors down. Without thinking she walked closer, noticing that a man in uniform was trying without success to usher three children varying in size and age into a van. She frowned at the sign on its door: "Colorado Department of Human Services." Welfare workers! Because of her own childhood, she had an instinctive distrust of the juvenile system.

"No, Sheriff, no!" the oldest boy shouted as he struggled to be heard. "You've got to listen to me. I swear Dad didn't abandon us. Something must have happened to him. He's never left us alone before. You can't take me away, you've got to help me find him."

"Now, Donny," the man said. "You've got to trust me to do what's right. You three came off the mountain claiming that your daddy didn't come home last night, and you expect me to just let you go back the way you came? You'll have to go with Mrs. Sutter. She'll see that you're taken care of until family comes to get you. It's the best way, don't you see?"

Donny yanked away, then grabbed at the smallest boy, who was crying helplessly in the arms of the woman from social services.

"Let him go!" Donny yelled, taking the child from the woman and wrapping his arms around his little brother's trembling body. The child buried his face in his brother's neck and sobbed.

Queen watched in sympathetic horror as huge tears tracked the face of the third child, who was clinging silently to Donny's leg.

The uniformed man shrugged and stared at the social services woman, as if to imply that matters like this were more in her line than his.

The woman frowned and reached to reclaim the child in Donny's arms.

Queen never knew what made her do it. It could have been the déjà vu of seeing her own childhood reenacted in these boys, or it could have been the look of pure terror and then hope that appeared on Donny's face as he looked past the sheriff and into Queen Houston's wide green eyes and saw a sympathetic soul staring back at him.

"What's going on here?" Queen asked as she pushed past the woman and slipped her arm around the boy's shoulder. She squeezed it gently as she felt his body tremble. "My bus just arrived," she said, improvising as fast as she could. "I was expecting your daddy, not you guys. Where is he, anyway?" Then she turned, smiled sweetly at the man, and extended her hand. "Sheriff . . . ?"

"Miller," he added, and shook her hand without thinking.

Queen nodded and smiled. "My name is Queen

Houston. Donny is my nephew . . . of sorts. It's only by marriage, but family is family, you know."

She turned and looked down into the shock spreading across the oldest boy's face and wondered if she was about to get herself into more trouble than she could handle. And then she saw his expression change to one of relief and knew that he'd made a choice. For the moment she was the lesser of two evils.

"My goodness," Queen went on, ruffling the hair of the two younger boys. "You two have grown so much, I don't know which is which. I bet you don't even recognize your aunt Queen!"

Donny caught on to what she was asking him, and his nimble, thirteen-year-old brain kicked swiftly into gear.

"Will's the one hanging around my leg. This is J.J."

"I would never have known," she said, and knelt to look face to face at Will, who looked to be about ten years old. "You guys are really tall for your age."

"All the Bonner men are big," Donny said quickly. "But my daddy, Cody, is still the tallest."

Queen stood upright and then looked down into three sets of eyes in varying shades of blue and knew that she must have lost her mind for what she was about to do. But she knew as well that she'd lose it anyway if she got back on that bus and left these three boys to face this hell alone.

She made her decision. She'd stay long enough for the wandering father to reappear, read him the riot act, and be on her way. It was only fitting.

"My gosh," she said as she heard the bus driver call out for passengers to reenter the bus. "I forgot to get my bag. Hold that thought, Sheriff. I'll be right back, and we'll figure out what to do next."

Her long legs made short work of the distance to the bus. In no time she had her one bag in hand and was back in the midst of the fray.

"Okay, I understand we have a problem," Queen said. "Where exactly is my stepbrother? He called a few weeks ago and asked if I would come and help out."

Donny felt compelled to explain the real situation, lest his newfound savior make a mistake with her ad-lib explanation.

"She came to help 'cause our mother is dead," he told the sheriff. "We just moved to Colorado a few weeks ago. Dad was hoping for help while we got . . . settled."

Queen hid her shock at his words, but a familiar wave of sympathy and a strong memory of being in the same shoes once in her own life made her shudder.

"At the time, I couldn't come. Family problems of my own. My father, Johnny Houston, died last week. After that, leaving Tennessee seemed to be a good idea."

Sheriff Miller frowned. On the face of things, this all seemed plausible. But he still had a duty to make sure her story checked out. He'd been sheriff in Snow Gap for fifteen years, and the Bonners were obviously newcomers to the area. He knew nothing about their situation or their family ties.

"I don't like this," said the social services woman, who had introduced herself as Edith Sutter. "I think it would be best if you let me take the boys to juvenile until things get sorted out. After all, you can't let children just walk away with strangers."

Queen bristled and slid a protective arm around Donny's shoulder. "My sentiments exactly, ma'am," she said. "But you and the sheriff are the strangers, not me."

J.J. turned from his brother's embrace and looked at the tall woman standing beside his beloved Donny.

"Are you really my aunt?" he asked.

Queen nodded, ignoring the spurt of guilt that threaded her system. Sometimes a lie was the kindest thing.

"I want to go with Aunt Queenie," J.J. said, and unwrapped himself from Donny's neck and slid into Queen's arms as if on cue. He hiccuped and buried his face in her neck, once again hiding from the situation in the only way he knew how.

It was reflex, but Queen's arms tightened around the small child's body. Her fingers slid across the thin little back and the undeveloped bony shoulders that she knew someday would be broad and strong. But for now they were too small to hold the weight of the world.

"And you shall, J.J. Will, too." She reached down and gently brushed a dark wing of hair from the middle child's forehead. His skin felt clammy beneath her fingers and she knew how panic felt. Will was obviously in a terrible state, and his quietness only magnified the fact.

Sheriff Miller sighed. "Just let me make a few phone calls, okay?"

Queen nodded. "Call Cradle Creek, Tennessee. Ask anyone there. They'll tell you we didn't have much, but Johnny Houston's daughters were honest and decent. And they'll confirm the fact that my father is dead. Beyond that, I don't know what else to tell you."

"Got a driver's license?" Sheriff Miller asked.

Queen handed it over, thankful that she'd learned to drive and never let it expire, although Johnny had long ago lost their only vehicle in a card game and had never been able to afford another.

Five minutes passed as she and the Bonner boys

stood on the sidewalk beneath Edith Sutter's glare. The social worker's expression didn't lighten when Sheriff Miller came back, handed Queen her license, and tipped his hat.

"It all seems to check out," he said. "I think it's best to let things ride as they are for now."

"What about my father?" Donny asked.

Queen caught the frantic tone of his voice and realized for the first time that their fear might not be misplaced. Maybe the father did have an excuse, but she was going to reserve judgment until he showed his sorry face.

"I think a missing persons report is in order," Queen said. "Come on, boys. We need to follow Sheriff Miller to the office. You'll have to help me give him the facts. I haven't done more than talk by phone to your dad in years. For all I know, he's lost all that pretty hair. Did it ever go gray? I'll bet he's fat as a pig. He always liked desserts too much."

Will shook his head. "Daddy's not fat. And his hair's still really black, honest."

Queen smiled. Without knowing it, the children were supplying her with a faint but distinct picture of their father. The three boys looked remarkably alike, with their sturdy bodies, pug noses, and stubborn chins. And she didn't think she'd ever seen hair as black or eyes as blue as the Bonner boys had. She suspected that the missing father was responsible for the strong genetic imprint. But what she wanted was his presence, not a mental image. She had just embarked on the rest of her life, and baby-sitting abandoned children was not part of that plan.

An hour later they exited the sheriff's office hand in hand. Donny was worried. He had finally convinced the authorities to look for his dad, but in the meantime he'd done something his father had told him never to do: he'd trusted a stranger.

Queen looked around at the small mountain community and then down at the three boys, who were staring at her. "When did you eat last?" she asked them.

Donny sighed. At least she worried about stuff that mattered. "This morning," he said.

"But only Cheerios without milk," Will offered. "We ran out."

"Dad was going to bring groceries back," Donny said, anxious that no one assume further that his father was not all he should be.

Queen had heard that excuse so many times in her own life that the words didn't even sink in. "Right," she said, aware that Donny was going to defend his father to the death. She patted her pocket, realizing that she was about to spend some of her precious hoard of money on a stranger's children, and ignored the warning her conscience was giving her. "Where do you live?" she asked.

All three boys pointed up the mountain.

"Up there?"

They nodded.

"Far?"

They nodded again.

"Then how did you get down?"

Donny grinned, and in spite of her determination not to become emotionally involved, Queen felt a bit of her resistance melting.

"Donny drove Daddy's pickup," Will said, and pointed to a red truck parked in the alley across the street.

"You drove?" She didn't bother to hide the shock she felt.

Donny nodded. "I've been driving for years."

Queen stifled a grin. "How old are you?"

"Thirteen."

She sighed. There was nothing left to do but deal with the situation one step at a time. And from the interest her earlier question had elicited, that meant food was next in order.

"Know where the grocery store is?" she asked.

Donny nodded.

"Okay, then load up. We'll buy some food and then head for your home. I have no desire to be driving around in the mountains after dark, especially on unfamiliar roads."

When they started to troop toward the car, Queen felt J.J. slip his hand in hers. Her fingers tightened instinctively. She would wonder later if it had been to help him cross the street or an unconscious gesture of not wanting to let him go.

Donny didn't know whether he'd done the right thing, but he had at least maintained some control of the situation. Queen started to pick up her bag when he stopped her with a touch of his hand. Their eyes met, green locked into blue, and an understanding passed between them. Donny Bonner owed her, and Bonners always paid their debts.

Queen straightened and nodded, then headed for the truck parked in the alley.

Donny picked up her bag and urged Will ahead of him. The journey had begun.

"You live here?"

Queen couldn't mask the surprise in her voice. This cedar and shake A-frame home didn't look like the place of a loser. The wide redwood deck that spanned the entire house was about four feet off the ground and gave the house a rather majestic appearance, and on the deck was a nearly new set of matching redwood patio furniture. Queen could imagine the peace of mind that would come with the ritual of watching sunsets every evening from such a place.

"I'm hungry," J.J. said softly.

The announcement broke her reverie. "Then grab a bag and lead the way," she said, ruffling his hair. "I am, too."

Donny took charge, handing a parcel apiece to his brothers, careful to adjust the weight of the sack to the size of the boy. Queen noticed the thoughtfulness, although she knew that he'd done it automatically, not just to impress her. His protective attitude made her think of herself at that age, and that in turn made her angry with the absent father as she automatically assumed he was no more responsible than Johnny Houston had been. Where did this Cody Bonner get off leaving the care of children in the hands of a child?

She grabbed the remaining bags and took the steps two at time, making good use of the reach of her long legs. Suddenly she, too, was very, very hungry. It had been a long time since Texas and breakfast, and in spite of herself she was a little excited at the unexpected adventure.

Once again, the interior of the house was not as she'd imagined. It was clean and orderly, with only a few bits and pieces of the boys' clothes lying about. An extra pair of boots had been placed on the bottom of the stairs, waiting to be carried by the next person up the steps.

Her stomach took a dive, then she inhaled and stared

wild-eyed at the size of those boots. They had to belong to the missing father.

She followed Donny and the other boys through the house toward the kitchen and tried not to think of how big a man would have to be to wear them.

Donny stood alone at the living room window and stared out into the darkness. His euphoria of having managed to keep the family together began to deflate as night fell. He shuddered, swallowed, and blinked rapidly as tears burned the back of his eyes. Resisting the urge to fling himself onto the nearest sofa and bawl like a baby, he chewed the inside of his lip instead. He'd never been so afraid in his life, at least not since the day of his mother's funeral. But even then he'd had his father's presence and his broad shoulders to lean on. Now he had no one . . . unless he counted the redheaded woman.

She was pretty . . . for a woman her age. In Donny Bonner's world, anyone past the age of nineteen seemed middle-aged. He wiped his eyes with the heels of his palms and sniffed quietly, hoping that no one had heard him. If J.J. and Will saw him cry, they'd join in. That would be all he needed.

Queen stood in the doorway and watched him. His posture was stiff, his shoulders thrust back defiantly. She sighed, hoping that his vigil would not be in vain. In her experience, waiting for dreams to come true was a waste of time.

And then she saw his shoulders shake and saw him wipe at his eyes and knew that the young man was doing all he could to hide his own fear. She hurt for him, but there was little she could do beyond what she'd already done.

"Get enough to eat?" she asked.

Donny jumped, surprised that he was no longer alone, and then ducked his head, not wanting her to see stray tears in his eyes.

"Had plenty," he muttered. "Where are my brothers?"

"Taking a bath. I told them to get ready for bed." Realizing that she might have usurped his role, she felt obliged to add, "I hope that's all right."

Donny glanced down at his watch and nodded. "It's fine." He looked up at her and sighed, finally giving in to overwhelming weariness. "It's just fine."

"Where do you want me to sleep?" Queen asked.

Donny thought, then made a quick decision. "In my dad's bed. It's the only extra one except for the fold-out. You may as well be comfortable."

Queen nodded, allowing him to be the "man of the house," certain that staying in control would be what he needed to get through the nightmare into which they'd been thrust.

"Follow me," he said, picking up her bag.

Queen did, and as she took the first step, she eyed and then stepped over the scuffed black boots mocking her by their presence. The farther away she stayed from those empty boots, the greater her peace of mind.

Donny paused beside the first door at the top of the landing. "This is Dad's room. He has his own bathroom. Help yourself, Aunt Q—I mean, Miss . . . "

Queen smiled. "Leave it. I've never been an aunt. I think I kind of like it."

For the first time since the whole fiasco had started, Donny felt as if he'd done the right thing. Impulsively he stepped forward and gave her a quick hug.

"Thanks," he said. "I don't know what I'd have done without you."

Queen tried valiantly to ignore the warmth that had spread through her heart when Donny's arms had wrapped around her shoulders. But it was impossible. For the second time today she'd been hugged by a Bonner. What bothered her was that she was beginning to like it.

3

The sun rose on a new day as Queen dragged her brush through the tangles in her hair, then winced as it caught and snagged. The knot was only an echo of the one in her stomach, and she decided to ignore both.

Sleeping in that king-size bed had not been as easy as it had looked. Every time she'd turned over in the night, she'd imagined that a big angry man was hovering above her, pointing a finger and accusing her of trespass. Her chin jutted stubbornly as she eyed her reflection in the mirror over the sink. When he came back, she just dared the sorry so-and-so to complain. She'd show him what accusations were made of.

Aware that the boys would be stirring soon and wanting food, she made her way downstairs to the kitchen. As she started to assemble the ingredients for pancakes, her stomach growled, reminding her that the boys weren't the only ones who were hungry.

Queen broke eggs and poured milk and measured

flour with absentminded thoroughness. But no matter how smooth the batter became as she stirred it angrily, she couldn't forget that three days was a long time to be gone without an explanation, even for a sorry-ass man.

By midmorning she was beginning to get as worried as the boys. A phone call to the sheriff's office had confirmed nothing beyond what they already knew. The sheriff was out on a call, and the dispatcher didn't know anything about the situation. All Queen could do was leave word for Sheriff Miller to call when he returned.

The older the day got, the more strained and anxious the boys became. Queen knew from experience that there was only one cure for worry, and that was to substitute it with something else.

"Who wants to give me a tour of the Bonner property?" she asked.

The request took them by surprise, and then the two younger ones held up their hands and shouted in unison, "Me! Me!" Clearly they were glad of an excuse not to think of another day without their father.

"How about both of you," Queen said. "That way I won't miss anything."

Donny stood his ground. "I think I'll stay . . . just in case."

Queen nodded. She understood his need to remain close to the phone.

The tour began and ended thirty minutes later. The Bonner property consisted of the house, a barn and a shed, and acres and acres of thick, heavily wooded area that Queen elected not to explore. She didn't want to be that far from the phone, either.

She wondered what to do next until she remembered

the wall unit full of video games in the living room.

"I don't suppose you guys are old enough for Super Mario Brothers?"

The question was, she suspected, a stupid one. At the gas station in Cradle Creek she'd seen children barely tall enough to reach the controls playing video games with great skill. J.J. and Will burst forward into a race toward the deck, yelling that the winner would pick the first game to be played.

Queen smiled, watching them running as if their lives depended on it. She stepped aside as they flew past and accidentally bumped into the old red truck in which they'd driven home from Snow Gap yesterday. It was dented and scratched and clearly had seen better days. She ran her hand absently over the fender and frowned. It didn't fit the image of the house at all.

"Dad just uses it to haul wood," Donny said, answering her question before it was voiced. "I saw a puddle underneath it awhile ago. I ran over a pretty good-size rock on the way to Snow Gap yesterday evening. Do you think I broke something?"

Queen heard his voice tremble, although Donny was doing all he knew how to remain calm in the face of a total stranger. "I could take a look," she said, although to be honest, crawling in the dirt beneath that rickety old truck was not what she'd planned to do for lunch.

"But you're a girl!"

Queen grinned. "Girls can fix cars just like guys . . . sometimes even better. I'm not good at it, but I'm also not the worst mechanic you'll ever find. Does your dad have any tools?"

He nodded and jogged away toward the shed, returning moments later with a shiny metal box.

"Thanks," Queen said. "While I'm doing this, why

don't you go back to the house and keep an eye on your brothers. It's nearly noon. Maybe you could fix sandwiches from that meat we bought from the deli, and there's some—"

"I can handle it," Donny said, cutting her off. He pivoted and started toward the house. "Don't get dirty!" he called over his shoulder with a smile.

Even from this distance, Queen could see blue devils dancing in his eyes. She looked down at the puddle beneath the truck, and then at her clothes, and shrugged.

"Get real," she answered, and grinned in spite of herself when Donny Bonner whooped with laughter before entering the house.

There was no way in hell she wouldn't get dirty. But what she was wearing wouldn't matter. The jeans were old and worn, and her green-checked shirt was faded. Grumbling to herself about the merits of being a Good Samaritan, she knelt in the dust, opened the toolbox, selected a couple of tools, and then rolled over on her back before scooting beneath the truck to survey the damage.

The Blazer was nothing more than a streak of color against the landscape. Cody Bonner drove it just as he'd flown fighter jets—skillfully, with total concentration, and without thought of the laws of speed or gravity. He outran the dust boiling from beneath the wheels of the blue-and-white four-by-four and tried to ignore the knot of fear in the pit of his stomach.

"Dammit to hell." There was little else he could say.

The set of circumstances that had kept him away from home for the last two nights would have been ludicrous if the consequences weren't so tragic.

But laughing off what had happened was impossible. He kept thinking of his youngest boy. J.J. was barely past babyhood. *Had he cried for me?* The thought made him sick. *Was he afraid that his daddy was gone for good . . . just like his mother?* The knot in his stomach turned once just to remind him it was still there.

Will was ten, and tall for his age, but he was too damned quiet for his own good. Cody could imagine what must have gone through his mind.

He cursed as his Blazer bounced across a narrow set of ruts in the road, yanked at the steering wheel, and then pressed on the gas as the wheels straightened.

"Thank God for Donny. He'll have managed," Cody said aloud. *He just has to.*

At thirteen Donny was already close to six feet in height and as reliable as Cody's old red truck. And with the thoughts of the truck came the first sight of his home nestled against the tall backdrop of ponderosa pine and Colorado evergreens.

The stark beauty of the landscape had been his main incentive for moving to Colorado with his boys only weeks earlier, away from the cities . . . and his in-laws. But now the isolation of their home made him think again.

After what his late wife's parents had put him through, early retirement from the military had seemed his only option if he wanted to regain complete custody of his sons. They'd made the move just after school had let out for the summer, and Cody hadn't taken the time to make new friends yet. He'd purposely put off meeting any neighbors, savoring instead the serenity of their surroundings and hoping that it would heal whatever was festering inside him. But now, after this incident, he couldn't get past the thought that maybe it hadn't been such a good idea after all. Anything could have happened to the boys.

Cody's belly gave a jerk as he swerved into the driveway. The house was still standing, but the red truck looked as if it had been moved. Hell, he told himself, I've slept since then. Maybe I'm just imagining things.

He pulled into the yard and frowned as the cloud of dust caught up with him, then bailed out of the driver's seat as panic began to set in. No one came running out to greet him! What if something had happened? What if they'd gotten sick? What if . . . ?

He stopped in midstep, frozen with shock and fear at the sight of a pair of long, jean-clad legs protruding out from beneath the old red pickup.

Oh, Jesus . . . someone's stripping the truck. Damned thieves! But what have they done to my boys? he thought, and started toward the truck.

Ignoring the fact that confronting a burglar unarmed was not wise, Cody Bonner walked toward the truck, his eyes fixed on the long length of legs and the old, well-worn boots. Even from here he could see that one of them had a hole worn nearly all the way through.

"Damn drifter," he muttered. "If you've hurt my boys, I'll kill you."

He reached down, wrapped a hand around each boot at the ankle, and pulled hard, dragging the would-be thief out from under the truck. Dust clouded around them.

"You sorry sonofa . . . "

Queen Houston blinked through the dust settling in her eyes, wiped the smear of oil she felt running down her cheek, then looked down at a matching greasy stain spreading across her left breast.

In disgust she looked up into the bluest eyes she'd

ever seen, recognized the familiarity of facial features
he'd given in varying degrees to each of his sons, and
knew that the errant father had returned.

Ignoring his presence, as well as the rude manner in
which he'd dragged her from beneath the truck, she
calmly got to her feet, tossed the 3/16 crescent wrench
and the pliers into the toolbox, and began dusting herself off.

Cody was in shock. His burglar was a woman? A
curvaceous, buxom, green-eyed redhead? And why
didn't she say something? Why wasn't she trying to get
away? Accusations hovered on his lips, but she beat
him to it.

"So! You finally made it home." Queen fixed him with
a hard green stare.

He flushed in spite of himself and then got angry at
the fact that a total stranger was assigning him blame.
He started to argue, but the words he meant to say died
in the back of his throat as Queen once again ignored
him and began brushing at the accumulated dust on
the backs of her legs and rump. Then she leaned over
and began combing her fingers through her unruly hair
in a vain effort to get rid of the grass and dirt he'd
plowed into her scalp by dragging her from beneath
the truck.

He didn't know whether the sudden urge he had to
bury his hands in her hair was to see if it was as hot as it
looked or just to throttle her and get the ordeal over with
at once. But the notion disappeared when she suddenly
straightened. He stared transfixed as she brushed the
wild mane of red curls back into place and then fixed
him with a piercing glare.

Queen hid her surprise. He wasn't what she'd expected. He didn't look particularly dissipated, and he didn't

look as if he'd been in any fights. But she wasn't one to let good looks get in the way of the truth.

"Where the hell have you been?" she demanded.

Cody's answer, a knee-jerk reaction to her accusation, came out all wrong.

"In jail."

Queen snorted. "It figures," she said, and walked away.

Cody stood where she left him, trying to figure out why he'd just let a total stranger reprimand him for something that wasn't his fault, when he heard her call out, "Hey, guys, your daddy's home!"

Seconds later the boys burst from the house and ran past her with their arms outstretched. In spite of her determination to remain neutral, she turned and watched and then, oddly enough, felt abandoned . . . even forgotten, as they flew into their father's arms.

Tears blinded Cody's eyes as J.J. catapulted against him and clung with the tenacity of a leech.

"I knew you'd come back. I knew it," J.J. said.

"Dad! Where did you go? What happened?" Donny asked as he hugged and patted his father, and then repeated the question and the gesture over and over.

Will didn't speak at all, he just clung. For Cody that greeting was the most telling and the most difficult to face.

"I was so worried about you guys," he said, staring intently into his oldest son's face. "Thanks, son," he said quietly, almost mouthing the words.

Donny nodded, relieved enough now that his father was back to convince himself that he hadn't really been worried at all.

"You have no idea what happened," Cody said. "Oh, God, I've never been so glad to get home in my life." And he hugged and kissed them over and over, ignoring the fact that Donny had been refusing the gesture for nearly a year. "Let's go inside where we can talk. You won't believe what happened."

With J.J. in his arms and Will clinging to his hand, Cody started up the steps, certain that Donny would follow. He'd seen the relief on his eldest son's face and knew that they'd talk later. For now it was enough that they were reunited. Then J.J. turned and looked over his father's shoulder at the tall redhead standing alone in the yard.

"Aunt Queenie . . . aren't you coming?" he asked.

Cody stopped, stared at J.J., and then turned around and fixed her with a piercing stare. *Aunt Queenie?*

Donny spoke up. "I'm sorry, Dad, but you're not the only one with a story to tell. If it wasn't for her, we wouldn't be here to greet you."

"The sheriff tried to give us to a mean old woman. I didn't like her. She wouldn't smile," J.J. said. "And then Aunt Queenie came and took us home."

"The woman was from social services," Donny explained.

Cody felt the old fears swamp him. He looked at his sons and then back at the woman in the yard and sighed. All in all, being shot down in the Persian Gulf hadn't been as nerve-racking as the last two nights had been.

"Please . . . Aunt Queenie . . . do come in," he said, just missing sarcasm with his courteous tone.

It was more order than request, and Queen knew it. There was nothing else she could do. Besides, she was intensely curious about the good reason a man could have for being in jail.

But when Cody Bonner sat down and started talking without making excuses for himself, she wondered if maybe . . . just maybe . . . she'd misjudged him.

"Who the hell are you?" he asked, giving the woman a hard, unforgiving stare.

"Daddy . . . she's our aunt Queenie. Don't you remember her?"

J.J.'s question came without warning, and for a heartbeat Cody Bonner wondered if somewhere down the hellish road he'd been lost on, he'd lost more than sleep. But the flush on her cheeks told him all he needed to know. She was an impostor! Just what the hell that meant to him he had yet to find out.

"My name is Queen Houston. I'm from Cradle Creek, Tennessee. Sheriff Miller checked my background. If you doubt me, all you have to do is ask him."

The jut of her chin and the defiant glare emanating from those green eyes told him more than he needed to know. She obviously had more guts than gumption.

And then he caught her inference. *Sheriff Miller?*

Donny recognized the look on his father's face and knew that he was as much to blame for her presence as she. After all, he'd more than aided and abetted in her false claim of kinship.

"Dad . . . let me," Donny said. "We didn't know what to think when you didn't come home that first night. I thought maybe you'd been in a wreck, or had car trouble, or maybe . . . "

It was just as Cody had feared. They'd coped, but what had happened had left scars. He sighed. He was an old hand at scars.

"Anyway," Donny continued, refusing to voice his own worst fears, "when we hadn't heard anything by noon the next day, I decided to go to the police."

"Oh, God," Cody groaned. The authorities were exactly who he didn't want mixed up in their lives. Not anymore.

"Dad . . . I'm sorry. But what else could I have done?"

"What's the big deal about not telling the sheriff?" Queen asked sharply. "It would have been the first thing to come to my mind, too."

"The police came and took us away once before," Will said, surprising them all by his sudden interruption.

"Why am I not surprised?" Queen muttered.

"No! You don't understand," Donny said. "It wasn't because Dad wasn't a good father. He was . . . he is. But at the time he was still in the military, and . . . " He swallowed once as if the words were too painful to repeat. But, manfully, he continued, "And our mother had been dead for about a year. Our grandparents thought he couldn't take care of us and still be away so much. They filed charges."

"I had a good nanny. We were doing fine," Cody said. "Until . . . " He paused, unwilling to tell a stranger about the hell he'd been through.

"Daddy fought in the war in the desert. He's a hero," J.J. said. And then his voice grew soft, and the tone changed to one of fear. "The bad guys shot at my daddy and made him crash his plane."

"Oh."

A shuttered expression slid across Cody Bonner's face at the mention of Operation Desert Storm.

Queen refused for the time being to allow him any leeway. He still had to explain to her satisfaction where the hell he'd been for three days and two nights. Surprisingly, he started to do just that.

"None of this would have happened if I hadn't stopped in Denver to buy you guys some shorts. When I came out, the Blazer was gone . . . stolen."

"You've been shopping for three days?" Queen couldn't prevent the disdain that colored her question.

She'd heard better excuses from Johnny Houston after a week-long drunk.

Cody sighed. This woman was like a damned bulldog with the only bone in a yard full of dogs. She wasn't giving up, and she wouldn't give an inch. The frustration and fury of the past three days overwhelmed him as he broke one of his cardinal rules . . . cursing in front of his kids.

"No, lady. I didn't leave to go shopping. I went to the base to a goddamned shrink. None of this would have happened if I hadn't listened to a friend's advice. Now if you don't mind, I'll continue."

Queen flushed, and she tried to think of why she should be sitting here listening to a total stranger's weak excuses. He was back. That was all that mattered to her. Now she was free to be on her way, although she had to give him credit. Johnny had never used doctors of any kind as a reason for being gone or broke.

She shifted on her seat, uncomfortable beneath his angry stare. If she had an ounce of brains left, she'd already be on the road to Snow Gap. Then she remembered the isolation of the Bonner house and the distance to town. For now, she'd hear him out. When he was through making excuses, he could take her to town. She couldn't wait to be on her way to . . .

Damn the man. For a moment he'd made her so angry she'd forgotten her plan. . . . Arizona. That was where she was going. And she would, too, just as soon as she could buy a bus ticket.

"Please," she said. "Do continue. I can't wait to hear the rest."

He glared. She stared.

Donny broke the ice. "Wow!" he said. "Stolen! How did you—"

"Let me finish," Cody said, redirecting his anger into mirth as he grinned at his oldest son's enthusiasm for gory details. "Part of it was my fault. I left the keys in the ignition. As soon as I noticed it wasn't where I'd parked it, I went back into the store to call the police. They told me to come to headquarters and file a report. I started walking, and then the strangest thing happened. I hadn't gone more than six blocks when there it was."

"What? There what was?" Will asked.

"The Blazer. Just sitting there. Windows down, the key dangling in the ignition. For a minute I thought I must have lost my mind and forgotten where I'd parked. But then I looked inside and knew that someone had definitely taken it for a joy ride because all the tapes were missing."

"Oh, man! Even my Guns and Roses?" Donny asked with a groan.

Cody nodded and shrugged. "Sorry," he said.

Queen couldn't prevent a grin. Kids really put things into strange perspective sometimes. To heck with the stolen Blazer. The calamity was the missing tapes.

"Anyway, I figured I was lucky it was in one piece and not stripped and burned. I tossed the sack with your shorts into the backseat, crawled into the truck, and simply headed out of town. I didn't think about going to tell the authorities I'd found it, because I hadn't actually filled out the papers to report it missing. I didn't think it would be worthwhile to report six missing tapes, and I still had that last stop to make at the grocery store before coming home."

"We ran out of milk," J.J. said accusingly. "But Aunt Queenie bought us more. She bought lots of good stuff. She's a real good cook."

Cody's gaze centered on the woman's flushed face.

She was a strange one. Coming to the rescue out of the blue, spending her own money on total strangers, taking a strip off of him for what she imagined was neglect toward his children—and reluctant to hear someone commend her.

"Thank you," Cody said quietly.

Queen nodded and looked away.

"But why did it take you so long to get home?" Donny continued.

Cody grimaced. "Here's where it gets good," he said. "I drove about five miles out of Gold Nugget and then was pulled over by a policeman and arrested."

"Why?" Queen asked, intrigued in spite of herself.

"Because the people who stole my Blazer didn't just take it for a ride. They had used it to rob a bank and then dumped it, leaving me to walk straight into a trap as a suspect in the robbery. It didn't matter how fast I talked, or how much I explained, the wheels of justice grind slowly . . . very, very slowly."

"Didn't you tell them you were our dad?" J.J. asked.

Cody hugged his youngest son, trying to remember a time in his life when simply telling the truth had set things right . . . when things had been that simple. "I sure did," he said. "But it didn't seem to matter. The more I talked, the more convinced they were that I was involved. Finally I got smart and shut up."

"You had a phone call coming," Queen said. "Why didn't you use it to call the boys?"

Cody raised his eyebrows. He had to give her credit: she was for the boys all the way. Obviously she still suspected his credibility.

"I did," he said. "There was no answer . . . and unfortunately, the answering machine can't accept collect calls."

Donny ducked his head. "Sorry, Dad."

Cody ruffled his oldest son's hair. "You don't need to apologize for my mess. It damn sure wasn't your fault."

"Why did they let you go?" Queen asked.

"Two reasons. One of my constant complaints was that my children were alone and would be hysterical. Whoever put out a missing persons report on me confirmed that part of my story."

"We did. All of us. Even Aunt Queenie," Will said.

"Well . . . we had to do something," she said, refusing to listen to any more accolades. The warmth in Cody Bonner's eyes was making her nervous. "And what was the other reason?"

"Early this morning, they caught the robbers in the act of repeating the same crime . . . in the same manner . . . with another stolen car. They let me go with an apology."

Cody leaned forward and wrapped his boys in his arms, ignoring the stare of the woman across the room. "But it doesn't matter. I'm home . . . and you're safe. You're all safe."

Queen watched him hold his children and knew that the affection between them was genuine. She sighed. It was just as well. She didn't have time to be worrying about men who had no business being fathers. She had a life to pursue.

And then the phone rang.

Cody dumped the boys from his lap and went to answer it. No sooner did he identify himself than Queen realized he was talking to Sheriff Miller. But the shock and then fury on his face was unmistakable and unexpected. Why should he be angry at a follow-up phone call? She noticed a muscle twitch at the corner of his mouth and his cheekbones streak with flashes of red as he started his good-bye.

"Thanks for calling, Sheriff. Yes, I'm anxious to meet you, too. Thanks for all you did on my boys' behalf and—"

He stopped in midspeech as the sheriff assured him that it wasn't so much what he'd done as it was a good thing his stepsister had turned up like that . . . out of the blue. Otherwise the boys would have been turned over to social services.

Cody looked across the room into Queen Houston's eyes and finally admitted to himself that her presence in Snow Gap that day had saved his world. He nodded once at something the sheriff said, then smiled at her . . . slowly . . . and only once.

But it was enough. Queen felt the air leave her body as if she'd just been kicked. All sense of the world shifted sideways, and she gripped the arm of her chair to adjust to the move.

His smile had done something strange to her heart. She didn't want what she was feeling and hated Cody Bonner for singling her out.

Finally he hung up the phone and cursed as if that moment between them had never existed.

"What?" Donny asked, surprised by the fact that twice in the space of a few minutes his father had broken a hard and fast rule by cursing in front of them.

"It seems that while they didn't really believe me about my children being alone, they still made a report to social services, who did some checking into our background and decided that it was their duty to inform our next of kin . . . on record," he added, simply for Queen's behalf, "that I was incarcerated. The long and the short of it is that your grandparents were notified. That means they'll probably show up soon."

Will blanched and began to stutter. "No, no. I . . . I . . . don't wan . . . want to go wit . . . with them again."

Queen was in shock. What was going on here? Why were the grandparents so feared?

"Will, don't," Cody said quietly, shocked by the recurrence of stuttering that had all but disappeared over the last few weeks. He took the child up in his arms, as if to shield him from what he'd said, but it was hopeless. All he could do was hold him, so he did, hugging him tight against the world and its unknowns.

Will forgot that he'd just turned ten years old. He forgot that he'd been the tallest boy in his class for more than two years running. All he could think of was the fear of losing his father . . . again. He buried his face against Cody's neck, wrapped his legs around his waist, and hung on for dear life.

Cody was overwhelmed by his son's emotional collapse. His arms tightened around Will's thin shoulders until he feared the child could not breathe, yet still Will would not turn him loose. The horror of the past months and the helpless fury of the past three days caught up with Cody Bonner.

His voice reverberated with anger and conviction when he spoke. "I will allow them to come . . . and maybe someday you will learn to enjoy their visits. But I swear to God they will never . . . absolutely never . . . take you away from me again."

The boys seemed to accept his fervent announcement with sighs of relief. Daddy could fix anything. But Queen shuddered. She'd seen the look in his eyes and the soldier inside the man. It had been full of hate . . . and almost ready to kill. No matter what they'd done in the past, she almost pitied the unsuspecting grandparents. They couldn't know what they'd unleashed.

◆   ◆   ◆

Cody stood outside on the deck surrounding his house and stared up into the vast and star-studded night sky. A slow breeze came through the trees and slowly cooled his anger. It was good to be home.

In spite of his vow that Claire's parents could no longer hurt him or his family, he was afraid. He knew them. They'd grab on to this latest fiasco without thought to what it would do to his sons. They seemed hell-bent on replacing their dead daughter with his boys. He sighed and buried his face in his hands. He'd do anything to keep from having to put the boys through another round of the judicial system.

"The dishes are done."

Cody turned and stared at the woman standing in the shadows just beyond his reach. "Thank you," he said. "For everything. What you did was above and beyond the call, lady. You'll never know how much it meant to me."

"I didn't do it for you," she said. "I did it for them."

Cody heard the censure in her voice. Somewhere in her past she'd lost complete and total trust in men. He wondered who had hurt her . . . and why . . . and then wondered why he cared.

"Just the same." He shrugged and turned away, unwilling for her to see his fears. It was the acknowledgment of weakness in him that had started all this mess in the first place. If he'd been a man about the damned nightmares he kept having, none of this would have happened.

"Will you give me a ride into town tomorrow? I need to catch a bus."

He nodded.

"Why did you go see a psychiatrist? Why did your wife's parents try to take your children?"

Cody inhaled sharply and spun back around. He was about to shout, to order her off the place and back to wherever the hell she'd come from, and then he saw genuine concern on her face and bit his lip instead.

"I'm not asking to butt into your business. It's just that the boys are . . . I've come to . . . " She turned and started to walk back into the house, realizing that she'd overstepped her bounds.

"I'm having nightmares. Hellfire-and-brimstone-breathing nightmares. I've had them ever since the night I came to in the Saudi desert after ejecting from the jet and realized I couldn't see my hand in front of my face."

Queen shuddered. The lack of emotion in his voice made the telling of his story all the more horrifying. She could do nothing but listen, because there was nothing left to say.

"I realized moments later that I was blinded by blood, not the accident, yanked the helmet off my head, and cleared my vision. I checked to see if my location trans-mitter was sending. It was. I knew it would only be a matter of time before someone found me. But the longer I waited, the less certain I became that it would be the right side. I could hear as well as see the ground fire. That told me I was too damned close to enemy lines for ground rescue. I started trying to walk out."

"Trying?"

"Broke my left leg."

Queen closed her eyes and swallowed the lump in her throat. So much pain. Why did people have to endure so much pain?

"Were you captured?"

"Naw," he said, and grinned. "But it took our side two days to get to me."

Queen was horrified. He had crashed in the middle

of a war, been left two days without food and water, and had had to walk on broken bones. "And the cops in Denver caught you without a fight." She hadn't realized she'd said the last of her thoughts aloud.

Cody jerked as if she'd just socked him in the middle of the back. He stared into the shadows and then started to grin. And then he laughed. Surprised by the sound of it, he stopped almost instantly. It had been a long time in coming, but afterward he felt a strange sort of relief, as if a few old fears had gone along with it.

"So, you're worried about your dreams," Queen said. "Dreams can't hurt you, Cody Bonner. Only people can hurt you."

"I know that. That's why I'm scared as hell. My in-laws, the Whittiers, will show up when I least expect them. They'll use what just happened, as well as the fact that I'm a single father with no extra help, to prove my lack of parental worth. They'll try to take my kids away again . . . I just know it. Ever since Claire's death, they seem to have lost perspective." He sighed. "It didn't help that I went missing for several days, either. When the war was over, that was the main reason I took early retirement. I suddenly realized my boys had come too damned close to being made orphans."

Unknown to either of them, J.J. had slipped outside and had been standing in the dark, listening. Reacting to the fear in his father's voice, he slipped his arms around one of Queen's long legs and started to cry.

"I don't want to live with Grandma or Grandpa Whittier. I want to stay here with you and Daddy."

Without hesitation Queen bent down and lifted the child into her arms. She hugged him gently. "You're going to be fine, honey," she said softly. "Your daddy is a big, tough guy, right?" She smiled at the urgent nod of the boy's head and couldn't resist pressing a kiss on the crown of his head. "He won't let anyone hurt you, ever."

"Promise?" J.J. asked.

Queen looked across J.J.'s shoulders toward Cody Bonner. "Promise," she said, staring intently into his eyes.

Cody was impressed by the way Queen had held his son, as if she truly cared. With J.J. she was soft and gentle and had openly touched and caressed as easily as she took a breath. He had not known that side of her even existed and suddenly realized why his boys had accepted her so quickly.

It was that thought and the look she gave him that prompted Cody to do something he would later realize was unforgivable. But at the moment he'd have done anything to insure his boys welfare, and having an on-site nanny when the Whittiers made their appearance would help immensely.

"Would you stay?" he asked her, and then, before she could voice the objection he saw on her face, he added, "Just until the Whittiers come and go? It would help my case if I had a housekeeper in residence. I'd pay you for your time, of course. It would be nothing more than a job of baby-sitting, and then you could be on your way."

"Yeah!"

J.J. shrieked and wiggled to be put down. Queen let him go without removing her gaze from Cody's face. When the child had disappeared out of sight and sound, she let her fury fly.

"How dare you? How dare you put me on the spot in front of that child? You knew I couldn't say no in front of him. He's been hurt enough as it is."

Cody stood his ground. "Well? Will you?" He was determined to get what he needed with no regard for what it might cost others.

Queen shuddered and drew herself up to her full height of nearly six feet. Then she came up so close to him that he could feel her breath.

"I'll stay," she said. "But like I told you before, only for the boys. And you know something else, mister?"

He shook his head, wondering if he should be afraid to hear what she thought.

"For a short time earlier this evening, I thought you were different, but you're not. You're no different from any man I've ever known. They'll do or say whatever they have to just to get what they want, and anyone who stands in their way can move or go to hell. For now . . . I'll stay. But after your in-laws leave, I'm gone."

Just when Cody thought she was finished with him, she added a postscript that hit home in a particularly vulnerable place.

"I'll be the housekeeper and nothing else, and don't you forget it. I take care of your boys and their needs . . . not yours. If you so much as look at me cross-eyed, or try to make a move on me, I'll shorten your life span, and everything else that matters on your body . . . and it'll hurt when I do."

She stomped away, leaving an aura of heat and hate in her wake. He shuddered. He'd been right to be afraid after all.

He'd had an instant impression of a cat, hackles raised, claws unsheathed, spitting and clawing at everything within reach.

My God. I must be losing my mind. I just asked a total stranger to stay in our home and look after the most precious thing in my life, my children. And if I'm not mistaken, she just threatened to neuter me if I get too close.

Cody shook his head and then straightened as determination sharpened his features. If he'd been as tough as a man should be and not gone to see the damned psychiatrist, none of this would have happened. But, he told himself, it won't happen again. I won't let it.

Within the space of a week, Queen had gone from the Houston household, which was dominated by females both in number and in strength of character, to an entirely male-oriented one. Everywhere she turned she was instantly reminded that she was living in a whole new world.

Male paraphernalia abounded: jockey shorts and model cars, rubber snakes and comic books depicting musclebound heroes. It would have been laughable if she'd had someone to share the joke with. But the Bonners saw little humor in her offhand remarks and often missed the point of them altogether.

With the return of Cody Bonner, the sleeping arrangements had shifted to accommodate Queen's temporary residence. Donny willingly gave up his room to her and moved in with Will and J.J. The two younger boys in turn offered to share a bed so that Donny could have one of his own. None of them seemed to mind giving up their space, but getting all three to sleep at night had become something of an unending marathon.

Being in close proximity to so many males of varying age and size made something happen to Queen that she hadn't expected. She began to miss her father. Alive, he'd been the bane of her existence as well as a constant source of shame; but suddenly she found herself longing to recapture that part of her old life.

Johnny Houston's death had come without warning, as unexpected as all of his plans had been. He'd gone to Whitelaw's Bar, as he had every day since they'd moved to Cradle Creek, and that night he hadn't come home. He'd died as he'd lived, playing cards.

Burying him had come and gone while Queen and her sisters had been in a state of shock. It was only now, with nothing and no one left to worry about except herself, that she allowed herself to grieve, and as she did, she felt able finally to forgive him for the loss of her childhood.

Queen forced herself to concentrate on the basket of laundry she was struggling to carry. She had plenty to do here without letting her emotions get the best of her. Later, when she was alone, she would let the feelings come and remember Johnny . . . and her sisters. For now there was too much work to do.

She dumped an armful of wet clothes into the dryer and then filled the washer she'd just emptied with another load of dirty clothes. Laundry was never-ending.

"Need anything from town?" Cody asked.

His question, as well as his presence, surprised her. She dumped the soap into the washer, spun the dial, and slammed the lid before she answered.

She thought for a moment about what she was going to ask and then decided that if one of them should be embarrassed, he could be the one. It was his fault she was here. He had to be ready for women and all that came with them.

"As a matter of fact, I do," she said. "Do you want me to make a list, or is your memory as good as your manners?"

"I'm not quite sure how to take that," Cody said, and grinned.

Queen looked away, unwilling to take another of his smiles full force. They did funny things to her equilibrium.

Cody dug a folded list from his shirt pocket and looked around for something with which to write. Queen calmly handed him a pen that she'd confiscated from the pocket of a dirty shirt.

"Thank you," he said. "Fire away, I'm ready."

That remains to be seen, Queen thought. "I need several things," she began. "Deodorant. Environmentally safe, powder-fresh scent. I'm nearly out, and I don't want to borrow. Besides, women shouldn't smell like pine forests."

He grinned and wrote it down.

"Shampoo. Get something with a built-in conditioner."

He thoughtfully eyed the thick mass of her auburn curls as he added shampoo to the list. Her hair wasn't the only thing about her that was hard to manage.

"Now on to feminine hygiene. I need—"

"Wait!" His command came on the heels of a faint flush and a slightly embarrassed expression. "Now we're losing ground."

She grinned. "If you ask me, *we're* not losing anything but our composure."

He tilted his head back and laughed. "Okay, lady, I have an idea. Why don't you go to town and get what you need along with what's on my list while I finish the laundry."

His suggestion left her stunned.

"You'd trust me to come back? Just like that? What makes you think I won't keep driving?"

"Because you gave me your word," he said. "And for some reason, I don't think you do that lightly."

She inhaled sharply and turned away, unwilling for him to see the amazement on her face. She wasn't used to being read quite this easily. It was an uncomfortable feeling.

"So what's it going to be . . . are you going or not?" he asked.

The back door slammed. They both turned at the same time, checking to see which Bonner had come in the house. It was Will, the slender shadow who had quietly accepted her presence with less fuss than she would have expected.

"Who's going where?" he asked.

"Queen's about to drive into Snow Gap and pick up a few things," Cody said.

"You real sure I don't need a guard?" Queen asked. She couldn't resist adding the little dig to reclaim the distance she needed between them to maintain her composure.

"I'll be your guard," Will said, then turned to his father. "I'll take real good care of her, Daddy. Can I go? I won't let a thing happen to her, I swear."

Queen's breath caught at the back of her throat. She pressed a finger across her lips to stop their tremble and blinked rapidly. Will had completely misunderstood her hateful remark. She'd been taunting Cody about the fact that she needed to be guarded so she wouldn't escape, not for her own safety as a precious member of a family.

Cody was in awe. In the three years since his wife's death, Will had been the one hardest to reach. It seemed as if he'd closed himself away from the world as insurance so that it could no longer hurt him. This was the

first time he'd come close to opening up and showing
interest in other people. There was no way in hell he
could refuse the child his request. But what was Queen
going to think about taking along a ten-year-old when
she needed to do some private shopping? He soon realized he needn't have worried. When it came to his sons,
Queen couldn't seem to say no.

"I would love for you to come with me," she said. All
the defiance was gone from her voice and posture. "If
it's all right with your daddy," she added.

Will turned to his father, searching for the nod of
approval. When it came, Will actually grinned and clapped
his hands together as he shouted, "All right!" He charged
from the room, pausing only long enough to assure
Queen that he'd be right back.

She was speechless.

"I'll be damned," Cody said quietly.

"What?"

"That is the first spontaneous thing Will has done in
three years."

"Why? What happened three years ago to make him . . . "
The look on Cody's face told her all she needed to know.

"Oh," she said. She leaned against the washer for support as she realized the responsibility of the trust that
he'd given her. "Oh, my God."

"Exactly," Cody said. "So . . . you understand . . . he
can't be hurt . . . not again."

Suddenly she was furious. "Just what are you expecting me to do to him, dammit? I realize I wasn't raised in
the same social circles that you were, but I think I know
better than you how hurtful thoughtless words can be.
Your children will not suffer at my hands."

"I didn't mean . . . "

He could have saved himself the time and trouble of

trying to apologize. Shaking with anger, she handed him the basket of towels she'd started to fold. Then she walked out of the laundry room with her head held high, her back poker stiff.

He didn't have the nerve to call after her, and even if he had, he wouldn't have known what to say. Minutes later he heard the front door slam and then the unmistakable sound of the Blazer's engine firing.

He dropped the laundry and hurried to the front door, hoping for a chance to wave good-bye. But he was too late. All he saw was the back of the Blazer and the small cloud of dust following in its wake.

He noticed that Will was sitting in the middle of the front seat, not by the door, and tried to ignore the wrench of worry in his gut. She'd already warned him that when she got her chance she would leave. What would that do to Will? How would he react to her absence as well?

"Dammit," he muttered, and slapped the door facing with the flat of his hand.

But for now it didn't bear worrying about. He had more on his mind than whether or not "Aunt Queenie" was a "here today—gone tomorrow" type of woman. The Whittiers were coming. He could feel it.

Queen absently wound the dish towel around and around one palm as she stared through the kitchen window at the scene in the backyard.

She hated herself for looking. She hated herself for even wanting to. But turning away from Cody Bonner wasn't possible. Not anymore. He'd done something no man had ever done in her entire life. Sometime during the past few days he'd gotten under her skin.

To a casual onlooker, what Queen was watching would seem to be nothing more than a father instilling good work ethic in his three sons. Unloading a rick of fresh-cut firewood from the back of the old red truck and stacking it against an outbuilding was not unusual. It only made sense that wood would need to cure before the arrival of winter. But it was midsummer, and even though the air was cooler on the mountain, it was still very warm—so warm that Cody Bonner had taken off his shirt and cap, leaving bare an immense expanse of brown skin. His black hair gleamed, sweat-slicked against his temples, as he moved from truck to woodpile and back again.

Therein lay Queen's dilemma. Should she stand there and torment herself with the sight of shoulders broader than a man had a right to own, a corded belly that looked tighter than a high-strung wire, and arm muscles that seemed to ripple as they clenched, then release with each toss of the wood? Or should she turn away?

"No!" she murmured to herself. But she didn't move away, and the knot in her stomach tightened in answer to a heated yearning lower in her body. "Damn you, Bonner. Damn you."

But he didn't hear her. And if he had, he would have been surprised that she'd even noticed him. Every time he turned a corner in his own house and came upon her unexpectedly, he remembered her warning and gave her the distance she'd demanded. It was the least he could do.

For himself, it was the smartest move he could make. It kept him from thinking of skin so fair that he could see tiny blue veins pulsing with life just beyond the surface. It kept him from wondering if it . . . and she . . . felt as soft as she looked. It kept him from digging his fingers into her hair, tilting her beautiful mouth up to his, and tasting the anger and the passion that was always present. Wisely he kept his distance.

But keeping his distance didn't stop the wanting. Cody tried to excuse his lust as nothing more than normal, unfulfilled needs. It had been a long time since he'd had a woman. Obviously his housekeeper was one in spades. He was just horny, nothing more, and if he told himself that often enough, surely he would begin to believe it. Surely.

Queen watched the scene until the last stick of wood was added to the stack. She watched until Cody yanked his shirt from the truck seat and slipped it on, leaving it open and dangling over his jeans. Then he began to unbuckle his belt, loosening it enough to tuck the shirt back inside. She tried to ignore the spiral of dark hair on his chest that disappeared below the waistband of his pants and knew that would be impossible. That was when she moved.

"Oh, God," she whispered, and turned to the sink, leaning over it and splashing her face wildly with cold running water. But she couldn't wash Cody Bonner out of her system, not that easily. "I've got to get out of here," she muttered. "I can't . . . I won't let this happen to me."

The door slammed open as all four Bonner men burst into the kitchen.

"Queen! Did you see? We cut a whole load of wood. Boy, we're gonna be warm this winter, huh? When it snows I'll show you how to build a fire. I was a Boy Scout. I can build good fires."

Will's announcement dumbfounded her. She buried her face in a towel, pretending to dry it off so they wouldn't see the look in her eyes. By the time it snowed she would be gone. How would this timid, lost child deal with another woman leaving him at this tender age? How in hell had she ever gotten herself into this mess?

"Queenie, I'm hungry. Can we eat lunch early? I worked real hard."

J.J.'s plea did the trick. Food! She could always hide her feelings behind work.

"Sounds good to me," she said, dropping the towel and turning to the refrigerator. Maybe if she left her head inside the open door long enough, the heat on her face would have time to disappear.

"Son, her name is Queen, not Queenie. Why don't you try remembering that, okay?"

By mutual agreement and for the sake of what little truth lay in the reason for her presence in the Bonner household, the title "Aunt" had been dropped from her name; but J.J. refused to give up calling her Queenie, no matter how many times he was corrected.

Once again, Cody's gentle rebuke went unheeded as the boy replied calmly, "No, I like Queenie best. If I had a dog, I'd call it Queenie. It's a good name, I think."

Queen laughed aloud.

Cody caught his breath. Joy completely changed Queen Houston's personality. So rarely did she allow herself the luxury of pleasure that he could only stare. When she smiled, she was absolutely beautiful.

"No, it's okay," she said. "I'd rather be named for a dog than a . . . "

The rest of her sentence trailed into silence, and she dropped her train of thought, unwilling to finish what she'd started to say. But she should have expected what came next.

"Where *did* you get your name?" Donny asked. "It's real . . . different." It was obvious that diplomacy was not a commonplace practice for thirteen-year-old boys.

"Are you a real queen?" Will asked.

Confusion warred with dismay as she struggled with an answer.

Cody wished he'd never started this line of conversation. "Let it go, boys," he said sharply. "It's none of our business what she—"

"It's all right," Queen said quietly. "After all, it's not a big secret. It's just . . . it's so . . . " She sighed and started over. "We all have similar names," she said.

"Who is 'we'?" Cody asked, intrigued that she'd even admitted to belonging to anyone else, let alone a family.

"All the Houston women."

"All? How many Houston women are there?" Cody asked, trying to picture a bevy of redheaded beauties like Queen . . . with matching tempers. He nearly shuddered.

"Three counting me. I'll soon be twenty-nine. I'm four years older than Lucky, who's the baby of the family. Diamond is between us in age."

"Wow!" Donny shouted, and clapped his hands on his knees. "Cool names. Where did you get them?"

"From my father."

"The one who died," Will said softly, and slipped his arm through hers.

Queen smiled and ruffled his hair. "Right. The one who died."

"Didn't you have a mother?" J.J. asked.

Queen nodded. "Once . . . a long time ago. But I barely remember her. She died when I was three, but Johnny had another woman, and another daughter already on the way. That baby was my sister, Diamond. He did marry her, and Lucky was born later."

"So you had a stepmother instead," Donny said.

"Not for long. She just packed up and left one night.

Di and Lucky were real small. They don't remember her. I do."

From the hard tone of her voice, Cody suspected that Queen's memories of her stepmother were not fond ones.

"Who took care of you?" J.J. asked, remembering his own fears when his mother had died.

"I took care of us," Queen said.

My God, Cody thought.

"Was your father a miner like the ones you told me about in Cradle Creek?"

Will's innocent question came without warning, and because it did, her answer was somehow easier to say.

"No."

For a moment Cody thought that was all she was going to say. He turned away and, in doing so, almost missed hearing the rest of her quiet admission.

"He was a gambler."

Queen resumed inspection of the refrigerator's contents. "Who wants roast beef and who wants ham for sandwiches?"

Her answers had satisfied the boys, and her question sidetracked any further response, but it set off a whole new train of thoughts in Cody's mind.

A gambler? How the hell did a man raise three little girls alone, without knowing if or when he'd have food to put on the table or a roof over their heads from one day to the next?

As Queen deftly lifted three plates of food at once from the refrigerator and issued orders to the boys at the same time, he knew he was looking at his answer. She'd done it . . . because she'd been given no choice.

Suddenly, what he'd asked of her shamed him. No wonder she'd been so angry. No wonder she'd accused him of using her. Her father obviously had. What else could she have expected from a total stranger when her own flesh and blood had done the same?

Cody turned away, unwilling to sort through the emotions overwhelming him. He had a sudden, intense need to walk across the room, cradle her in his arms as he did his sons, and shelter her from the rest of the whole damned world forever. But he knew it was a stupid and irrational notion. Even if he'd had the nerve, she would never have allowed it.

"I'm going to wash up and change," he announced. "Don't eat all the roast beef."

"I'll save you some, Dad," Donny said around a mouthful of sandwich. Then he added, "In my next lifetime."

Queen laughed aloud. The sound followed Cody all the way up the stairs and into his room.

Days later Cody woke up with a feeling of impending doom. Waiting for the arrival of the Whittiers was like waiting for the end of the world. It had long been predicted, but no one could say for sure when it would happen.

He swung back the covers and stomped toward the bath with resolve in every step. Let them come. He would be prepared.

"I'm going into Snow Gap to stock up on groceries," he told the boys when he found them in the kitchen. "I don't want to be caught short when your grandparents arrive."

The boys stared into their cereal. Their only response was to chew.

"Anyone want to go with me?" Cody asked.

All three shrugged, none willing to be a participant in preparing for the arrival of the unwelcome guests.

"No big deal," he said quietly, understanding their reticence yet unsure how to cope with it. "Queen, make me a list. The trip won't take long."

She walked to the cabinet and tore a sheet from the pad by the phone. "It's already done," she said. "I've been expecting you to think of this . . . any day now."

He grinned. "Starting to read my mind?"

She shuddered and turned away. Not if I can help it, she thought.

He sighed. It was no use. Every time he tried to be friendly, she refused the gesture in no uncertain terms. He wondered why the hell he kept trying.

"Like I said, I won't be long."

Queen heard him leave as she busied herself with cleaning up the breakfast dishes and the boys went to make their beds and clean their room. It was obviously a long and steadfast rule that needed no reminders from her. Reluctant as she was to admit any kind of admiration for Cody Bonner, she was impressed by a man who made rules and stuck to them.

A loud thump overhead told her that the boys were getting out of hand. She took a deep breath and made for the stairs, once again taking charge before the situation escalated out of control.

"Hey!" she yelled as she burst into the room, surprising the three boys, who were in the midst of a free-for-all scuffle on the bedroom floor. "Let's play ball instead of staying cooped up in here."

Her announcement stopped the wrestling match but brought renewed grumbles from Donny as he unwound himself from the clutches of his two younger brothers.

"Don't have enough players," he muttered. "We're

out here in the middle of nowhere. No malls, no movies, no nothing." He sat in the middle of the floor, his chin resting on bent knees, the picture of abject abandonment.

Queen grinned. "Oh, but we do," she said. "Ever played one-eyed cat?"

Three pairs of blue eyes looked up at her in interest.

"What kind of game is that?" Will asked, curious in spite of himself. He'd been all ready to follow Donny's lead and complain.

"If you're through cleaning your room, I'll show you," Queen said. "'Course . . . you've got to face the fact that I'll probably beat all three of you at once. After all, I'm a whole lot older and taller. You guys can't expect to keep up with—"

"Shoot! Come on, guys. Let's show her. No girl is gonna whip a Bonner, right?"

Her taunt and Donny's cheer had the effect that she'd hoped for. For the moment, boredom, fighting, and unwelcome visitors were forgotten.

They filed out of the house like goslings behind Mother Goose. In no time the game had been mapped out on the front lawn, with a pitcher, a catcher, and a player waiting to bat.

Learning that the entire purpose of the game consisted of hitting the ball and then having to run to only one base before heading back home made it seem easy—too easy, until they tried outrunning Queen Houston's long legs. They hadn't taken into account her lean body or her speed . . . or her willingness to get as dirty as hell.

Whatever it took, she went all out to beat them back to home base. She ate, wore, and spit dirt in an effort to retrieve the ball, then she would spin on a dime and

break into a sprint in a heartbeat, determined to outrun
the runner back to home base and tag him out, thereby
earning Donny's undying admiration as a woman of
merit.

But what won their hearts forever was when Will and
J.J. ran headlong into each other. Blood spurted from
two different outlets—Will's nose and J.J.'s lip—and she
didn't even flinch when she doctored their wounds and
cleaned up the mess.

The entire backseat of the Blazer was full of bags,
some containing food, some containing extras like special soaps and bath powders. Cody knew he'd probably
overdone it, but he'd be damned if he'd be accused of
being lax by his in-laws. While they were here, he was
determined to prove that he could provide everything
necessary for common comfort.

He turned in the driveway leading to his house and
found that the knot in his stomach was starting to relax.
Whether it was because he'd accomplished what he'd set
out to do or because he had something and someone to
come home to was irrelevant. He was ready for anything
now.

And then he saw them.

The play erupted as Donny swung and the ball flew
through the air. Cody watched, spellbound, as Queen
turned and jumped, as graceful as a cat, and caught the
ball in midair. Then he heard their shrieks of laughter as
the race began. She and Donny collided on base in a tangle of long arms and legs. Cody watched them roll onto
their backs, hysterical with laughter, covered in blood
and dust, and knew that he wasn't ready at all.

He parked and got out, wishing that his arrival would

not stop the game. Wishing that he could join in and be the next one to roll Queen Houston on the ground. Before the thought could become deed, he heard the arrival of another vehicle and turned, knowing before he looked who it would be.

"Oh, no."

There was nothing else he could say. They were here. Just as he'd suspected. Just as he'd feared. They'd come at the worst possible time, unannounced, and in the middle of something they'd never understand.

5

It was the unnatural quiet after so much hilarity that first alerted Queen that something was wrong. That and the fact that suddenly she was the only one laughing. Startled by the abrupt silence around her, she began wiping at the dust in the corners of her eyes. Then she looked up.

The two younger boys stood soldier straight above her, their faces strained and pale beneath the grime. Will and J.J. moved aside as Donny bolted to his feet and began brushing at his clothes in an unusually frantic motion.

"What in . . . ?"

Her gaze collided with Cody's stern expression. He was back, but something was wrong. Surely a simple ball game would not cause all this concern. She looked beyond him, and in that moment her heart sank as she watched a stately, graying couple emerge from a Lincoln and gawk in disbelief at the sight before them.

The grandparents were here. And from the expression on the elder woman's face, Queen could tell they were none too happy about what they'd just witnessed.

Nothing like a good first impression, she told herself.

Sonofabitch! The word kept replaying itself over and over in Cody's mind, but he knew that giving voice to it, as well as to his frustration, would not be wise. He was in a quandary as to what to do or say first when Lenore Whittier spoke and the decision was no longer his to make.

"Who . . . are you?" Lenore asked, staring in glacial disgust at the long-limbed, buxom beauty sprawled at her feet in an ungainly fashion.

The tone of her voice hurt Queen; it was an echo from her past, when the gambler's daughters had often been judged unfairly. Anger overwhelmed any embarrassment she might have felt as she reached for the ball bat lying by her side.

Lenore Whittier gasped and took a step backward, as if expecting the woman to assault her.

Queen's eyes narrowed as she read the woman's expression. Lady, for two cents I'd give you a reason to be afraid. But the fear on the boys' faces changed her mind. Something had to be done to end this stalemate.

Her fingers closed around the bat. She gripped it tightly and then tipped it on end, using it cane fashion to pull herself up.

"She's our aunt Queenie," J.J. said defiantly, and then looked away, unwilling to bear the brunt of his grandmother's disapproval.

Lenore's eyebrows rose. Aunt indeed! She gave Cody a look he tried to ignore, and when he would have offered an excuse, Queen saved him from having to lie. She dusted her faded jeans and shirt, brushed the tumbled curls away from her face, and swung the bat up onto her shoulder as she spoke.

"Mr. and Mrs. Whittier, I presume?" Then, without giving them time to affirm her supposition, she continued. "My name is Queen Houston. I'm Mr. Bonner's housekeeper. Boys, get your gear and put it up, then come back outside and help your father with the groceries." She handed Will the bat as she addressed the elderly couple again. "Please, follow me. I'll show you to your room."

For all her dignity, she might have been wearing a black uniform, white starched apron, and hat instead of a bloodstained shirt, jeans, and scuffed tennis shoes. Queen led the way into the house with a bearing as calm and regal as her name.

Cody was amazed at Queen's refusal to be intimidated by someone like Lenore Whittier. He smiled in spite of his own misgivings about their visit. He'd already mentally prepared what he would say about the arrest fiasco. Now he was going to have to face questions about a woman like Queen living in the house with him and his boys.

"Hell," he muttered, and thrust his fingers through his hair.

He watched the seductive sway of her hips as she walked away and wondered what had possessed him to assume that a redhead like her would make his life respectable. He stifled a grin and began carrying in the groceries. God help him, but if he was going to lose what was left of his reputation and sanity, losing it over a woman like that would be the curse of choice.

"Hop to it, boys," he said, handing each of his sons a bag. "You heard the lady."

The boys quickly obeyed, glad to be doing something

besides standing pinned beneath the disapproving stare of their grandmother.

And so the visit began.

"Surely *she's* not sitting down to a meal with us?"

Queen was in the kitchen when she heard Lenore Whittier's gasp of disapproval in the other room as she took note of the places being set at the dining room table.

"Yes, *she* is," Cody said, emphasizing the pronoun in the same manner that his mother-in-law had done. "This is not a formal situation, Lenore. I do not have hired help, I simply hired her to help . . . if you get my meaning."

His voice was low but firm. Lenore Whittier glared at her husband, Allen, for moral support and then frowned when he turned away. She recognized his look. His quiet disapproval of her actions angered her even more.

Queen took Cody's words to heart, blessing him silently for standing behind her when it would have been a smarter move on his part to play up to the grandparents, not alienate them.

Fresh from a shower and a change of clothing, she carried the last of the food to the table, then smoothed a wayward strand of hair back into the clip at her neck and straightened the skirt of her one and only dress.

The purchase had been an impulse during the day she and Will had gone shopping. Short sleeves and a scoop neckline on a calf-length skirt hadn't seemed too daring. Nor had the loose princess waistline and the soft yellow fabric with tiny white flowers interspersed across the design. It had been an unassuming dress until she'd put it on and transformed herself and the garment into stately elegance.

Luckily for the lady in the shop who'd made the sale,

Queen had been unaware of the transformation; she only knew that it was the first new dress she ever remembered owning in her life. She loved the way the fabric moved with her body as she twisted and turned before the full-length mirror, but she had to remember her circumstances and the fact that she had yet to settle into a new life. When she did, then maybe she would be able to indulge in other new clothing befitting her life-style. But until she knew what that was, buying more clothes was not possible.

Queen took a deep breath. It was time. She cast one last glance at the dining room table, just to assure herself that everything was in place, and then walked into the living room in time to hear Cody ending the story of his being arrested.

"I suppose I have to understand your point of view," Lenore Whittier said. "But you must understand mine. How would it look if everyone back home found out that you'd been in jail?"

"But I didn't do anything wrong, Lenore! For God's sake, look at it this way: When I was shot down in the Gulf, how would it have looked if Hussein's army, instead of ours, had gotten to me first? I would have been under arrest there, too, you know. And just as innocent."

Lenore looked away, unable to defend her stand on the issue any further. Her son-in-law was in the clear, and she knew it.

Queen's fingers fairly itched to slap some sense into that woman. How dare she blame Cody for something that wasn't his fault! Then she took a slow, deep breath as she realized what she was thinking. It hadn't been that long ago when she'd been as ready as Lenore Whittier to brand Cody Bonner a rake and a loser. What had changed her mind?

She took a good look at her employer and knew that it was the man himself who'd changed it for her. She had a sudden urge to walk into the room and take a stance beside him. He looked so alone . . . and lonely.

She watched him rise from his chair and walk across the room to speak quietly to his sons, reassuring them in the only way he could that they were not responsible for the antagonism between him and their grandparents. His dress was casual, but fitting the occasion, yet even in his most relaxed moments she still sensed how much of the soldier he would always be. Even out of uniform there was no wasted motion in the man. He moved with grace.

But there would be no more stiff collars and perfect creases in his world. After years of uniforms and rules, the last of the starch was gone from Cody Bonner's life.

Queen knew as she watched him that she was getting in over her head. His face had become almost as familiar to her as her own, and his solid, vibrant presence in the household made getting up every day something to look forward to.

For days Queen had wished for the freedom to trace at will the outline of that proud, straight nose, run her fingers across those fierce black eyebrows of his that hovered above eyes too blue for words, straightening their angry arch with nothing but the touch of her hand. If things had been different, in another time . . . another place . . . she might have given this man her heart . . . if he'd asked. But Queen knew better than to count on dreams. In her experience they had a terrible tendency to shatter. So she did what she'd come to do.

"Dinner is ready," she said.

Cody looked up at her with relief. Their eyes met, and for a moment he imagined he felt something pass between them, a connection—a bonding of something more than common goals. And then he noticed her dress, and the voluptuous body beneath it, and his eyes widened. It was the only indication he gave as to how stunned he was by her appearance.

Queen saw the slight change in his expression and suspected it was gratitude for her interruption. She'd made a promise to stand behind him in his efforts to reassure the Whittiers that he was a good and decent parent. She would do what she'd promised. After that . . . She bit her lip and looked away.

The vague and unknown destination that she had had in mind when she'd started her journey no longer seemed as appealing as it once had. Every day it became more and more difficult for her to think of the time when she'd have to say good-bye.

Cody felt her withdrawal and wished in that moment that they were alone. He wanted that feeling back . . . that sensation of being one with her. For a heartbeat, before she'd looked away, he had felt something he never had before. And when the feeling had left him, he'd felt more alone than he had in years.

Queen stood aside as the group quietly moved past her, into the dining room.

Will looked up and managed a weak smile. Without thinking Queen reached out and gently brushed a lock of dark hair from his forehead and then winked at J.J. and straightened his collar, tickling his neck as she did and teasing a smile into place. The gestures were small but caring, something a mother might do.

Cody caught the byplay between them and tried to tell himself that it wasn't jealousy he felt as he watched her working her magic on his sons. He could have used a special look or touch himself tonight, but it was not to be. When he walked past, all she did was stare at the floor. He had a sudden, intense urge to shake the hell out of her, just to see how long it would take that white-hot anger he knew she possessed to erupt. At least then he'd have some kind of emotional response from her other than being ignored.

And the evening had just begun.

Lenore let the first course come and go before she began firing questions around the table with the skill of an arbitrator, promptly ruining what was left of all the Bonners' appetites.

"Donny . . . do you keep up with your studies? I seem to remember that things don't come easily to you. You'll always have to apply yourself, you know. You can't slack off now, boy. Getting into a good college is so important."

"It's summer vacation, Grandma," Donny said. "School is out."

J.J. sniffed, then absently wiped his nose with the back of his arm as he reached for a piece of bread.

Lenore gasped and touched her throat as if struggling for air. "Jeffrey James Bonner, decent young men don't sniff, they blow. And certainly not at the table!"

"Ss-s-sorry, Grandma," J.J. stuttered, and let the bread fall back on the plate.

Cody took a deep breath and stared at the perfectly groomed matron sitting across from him, wondering what made women like her tick. She was never satisfied, and no matter how hard the boys tried to please her, she always managed to find fault, not praise.

Will stared down at his plate. His shoulders trembled as he waited for the next blow, struggling against the need to cry.

Queen was furious with Cody. How could a father sit and let this happen in his own house? This woman was impossible, and the boys had endured enough.

"Will! You're not eating! You won't get up from this table until you've cleaned your plate, and that's an order!" Lenore announced.

"I—I'm . . . n-n-not . . . hu-hungry," he said.

Lenore frowned. "I see you're still stuttering."

If children could wilt, Will would have expired on the spot.

Lenore gave Cody an accusing glare. "I thought I told you to do something about that. You should take him to a specialist. Children with defects like his will never succeed . . . not in this world."

Queen slammed her napkin down and shoved back her chair as she rose. Her voice was low, her anger barely concealed behind a small smile that never reached her eyes.

"Will doesn't have defects, Mrs. Whittier," she said. "And honestly, until your arrival, I'd never heard him stutter. I'm sure whatever caused it will be gone soon . . . don't you think?"

Lenore was horrified at being called down by mere hired help. And she hadn't missed the woman's subtle attack. How dare she imply that it was her own fault that Will stuttered? She looked to her husband for help, but he suddenly seemed intent on the last bite of roast beef on his plate.

Cody grinned behind his napkin. He wanted to applaud. He was also very surprised by Queen's sudden defense of his boys, although she had only said what he'd been thinking. It made him realize that he was letting the Whittiers make him lose sight of what mattered most.

Suddenly he didn't give a damn whether they liked what was going on here or not. By God, they'd already taken him to court and turned him inside out, and he'd still come away with his family intact. They couldn't hurt him again, not anymore. And it was time they heard it from him . . . not a damned court judge.

"Boys, you may be excused so you can get ready for bed," Cody said. "Take turns in the shower, and don't use all the hot water, okay?"

They nodded and bolted from the table, anxious to escape the strained silence of the room.

"I'll clear the table," Queen said. "If you'd like to move to the living room, I'll bring coffee later."

"Not unless it's decaf," Lenore said. "If it's not decaf . . . I won't sleep."

"I'll have whatever you make," Allen Whittier said suddenly, surprising everyone, including himself, by speaking aloud. "I don't sleep much, no matter what I drink." He gave his wife a rare, pointed look.

Queen left the room with a stack of plates in hand, but not before she heard Cody strike fire.

"That does it," he said. "You came unannounced and uninvited, and that's fine. You'll always be their grand-parents. I won't try to undermine your right to that. But you will, in turn, not undermine my rights. I will not have them badgered constantly, and if they need correcting, I'll do it. Do we understand each other?"

Lenore was furious. "If Claire were alive, you wouldn't dare talk to me like this!"

Cody took a deep breath before he began. What she said was true. And he wasn't proud of the reasons why.

"You're right," he said. "I probably wouldn't. Claire made the rules . . . and I let her. She didn't want to live on base or share any part of my life except the paycheck, so I let her have her way about that, too. And because of that, I didn't get to see my family as much as I'd have liked."

He bowed his head and stared at the tablecloth. When he spoke again his voice was lowered to just above a growl as he fixed Lenore Whittier with a cold, blue stare.

"I'm sorry as hell that a drunk driver cheated my sons out of having a mother. I'm sorry as hell that I lost my wife, and you two lost a daughter. But I'm not sorry that I took my boys out of state. That part of Florida was getting to be a crazy place to live. I'm not sorry that for the first time in their lives they're getting a dose of what it means to be boys. A little dirt and blood never hurt anyone, Lenore. And they grow up so fast . . . why don't we agree to disagree? I'm sick and tired of all this fussing, and so are the boys."

Queen let the door swing shut behind her. The sick-at-heart feeling she'd had when Cody had sat silently through Lenore Whittier's barrage was gone, as quickly as his anger had appeared. For some reason it was important to Queen that Cody not lose face. She didn't stop to decipher why it mattered. Besides, if what she suspected was true, there was something else that needed her attention.

She dumped the stack of dishes into the sink and made a beeline for the back stairs. As she'd expected, all three boys were on their knees at the head of the stairs, hidden by the shadows on the landing as they listened to their family fussing over them.

The imploring looks they gave her were all she needed. It was time for Queen to put their world back in orbit . . . to see how good an astronaut she could be with other people's troubles.

"No fair eavesdropping," she said quietly. "Come on, guys. Let's get ready for bed. If you hurry, I'll read you a story."

Donny was the first to see the wisdom in her request as he glanced down at Will and J.J. They looked ready to cry, and he hated it when they cried.

"Good deal," he said, and took each brother by the arm. "Come on, guys, if you don't splash the floor, you two can share the shower. I'll use Dad's bathroom, and we'll be through in no time. What do you say?"

"Can I pick the story?" J.J. asked.

"No, me," Will said.

"We'll read two," Queen said, settling the fuss before it began. "Now scoot, before I change my mind."

They flew to do her bidding.

The promised coffee never appeared, and the Whittiers, weary from their travels, finally turned in for the night. Cody had considered the idea of giving up his own bedroom, then decided against it. They'd come unannounced and ready to criticize, so they could make do with a roll-away in his den instead.

He sighed with relief as they said good night, and when the door closed between them, the smile he'd pasted on his face slid away.

"Jesus Christ!" he muttered, and headed for the kitchen.

But Queen was nowhere in sight. The dinner table had never been cleared, and dirty pots and pans littered the kitchen. Puzzled, he turned in place, and then his gaze fell on the back stairs, and suddenly he knew.

Taking them three at a time, he made short work of the distance to the second floor. He was almost running

by the time he got to the boys' room. Prepared for the
cries and recriminations he would have to face, he was
stunned by the quiet when he entered the room, lit only
by a single bedside lamp between the two double beds.
The scent of soap and bath powder hung in the air, and
the only sounds he heard were the soft growls of
Donny's gentle snoring.

His anxious gaze raked the shadows, and then his
breath caught as he looked past Donny's bed to the one
against the wall.

They'd fallen asleep in the middle of the story. That
much was obvious. He walked across the room, bent
down, and lifted the open book from Queen's limp hand,
careful not to wake them. He looked down at the title
and smiled. *Robinson Crusoe.* He laid it aside and then
stood, slowly absorbing the serenity of the scene before
him.

She was lying between them, holding J.J. with one
arm and Will with the other. Her long legs were outlined
beneath the soft, thin fabric of her dress, and the boys'
dark heads were resting upon her breasts. Cody swallowed with difficulty, watching as one child sighed softly
and the other shifted in sleep. Unconsciously Queen's
arms tightened around each in a firm, protective manner.

An overwhelming sadness slipped into Cody's
thoughts as he realized for the first time that no matter
how much his boys loved him, they must have missed a
gentler presence in their lives. Even though they were
growing tall, they still hadn't grown too old for a mother's
love.

His eyes watered, and he inhaled sharply and looked
away. When he looked back, Queen was staring up at
him in groggy confusion.

In that moment, caught unaware, he lost his bearings

with this woman. He saw love waiting behind the hard-nosed, fast-talking, quick-thinking Queen he'd come to know. He felt it happening as if in slow motion—the exchange of surprised smiles, the sleepy green eyes locking with his. He wished to hell that he could trade places with his sons and find some peace of his own in her loving arms.

And then she blinked as if coming out of a trance, and the shutters came down between them. Cody felt the wall being resurrected. In seconds she'd removed herself from the bed, deftly shifted the boys to a comfortable position, and turned out the light.

Queen was shocked by the intense longing she'd felt when she'd opened her eyes and seen Cody looking down at her. For a moment she'd forgotten her place, and where she was, and almost . . . just almost . . . invited him into her arms. But sanity had returned in time to save her. She'd crawled out of bed in haste and confusion, aware that he'd moved away. Thinking he'd left the room, she was startled to turn in the darkness and find him standing before her.

She stifled a gasp, anxious not to awaken the boys. For several moments they stood toe to toe, eye to eye, lost in the shock of the moment and the silence of the night. His breath was soft and warm against her face, and Queen closed her eyes and swallowed a sigh.

Cody's sight had already adjusted to the darkness. And when she turned and nearly barreled into him, he almost let it happen, so desperate was he for an excuse to be able to touch her. But something—an instinct—told him not to push her or rush things, so he simply stood, and watched, and wished. And when her eyes closed, he took it as a sign.

He reached out, softly threaded a finger through a

loose lock of her hair hanging over her shoulder, and
shivered as it seemed to curl around his hand like a
clinging vine. It had him ensnared . . . and if he wasn't
mistaken, so did she. Just what the hell he could ever do
about it was another problem altogether.

And then she jerked away, and his hand dropped to
his side, and she walked past him in the dark.

"Sweet dreams, lady," he whispered. But she didn't
answer. Moments later he heard her footsteps on the
back stairs and then the sounds of pots and pans in the
kitchen, and he knew that she was finishing what she'd
been hired to do.

Queen rolled over and sat straight up in bed, her
heart pounding, still trying to decipher what had awakened her so suddenly. Thinking she must have heard
one of the boys cry out in his sleep, she staggered out of
bed and started down the hall, forgetting in her confusion that she was wearing nothing but the nightshirt
she'd had for years.

It was old and faded from blue to near white, and its
shirttail hem barely covered her knees. Her body was
completely bare beneath the thin fabric, which emphasized the feminine outline of her figure in a way she
would have hated had she been aware of the seductive
quality of her appearance.

Ignoring her femininity and refusing to enhance her
beauty assets had been part of her self-protection in
Cradle Creek. In Cody Bonner's house, however, she'd
begun to feel safe and had unconsciously let down her
guard.

She stood for a moment in the dark hallway, straining
to hear whatever it was that had awakened her. And then

it came again, through closed doorways and into her heart in a frightful, chilling manner. It was a low moan and then a high-pitched wail of someone in intense pain, and in that moment she knew.

Cody!

The dreams had returned—the nightmares he'd suffered that had sent him searching for answers the day he'd wound up in jail instead. And with that same thought came the sudden knowledge that she couldn't let the Whittiers hear him or see him . . . not like this.

She tiptoed down the hallway and was inside his room before she had time to think. Quickly she shut the door behind her so that no further sounds could escape, then was at his side in seconds.

The sheet covering his body had slipped far below his waist, and Queen trembled at the sight of so much man and manhood barely covered by the snowy-white briefs he was wearing. He moaned again, thrashing out weakly against unseen restraints. When she saw him so helpless and hurting, she knew that she was lost.

She dashed into the adjoining bathroom, grabbed a still-damp washcloth hanging by the tub, and returned to his bedside. Ignoring the warning her mind was sending, she slid onto the side of the bed and gently grasped his arm. With a soothing motion, she began to wipe his sweat-soaked face and neck, all the while whispering quietly in a desperate hope that she'd be able to stop his nightmare without alerting the rest of the household.

"Sssh," she whispered over and over. "Don't fight it, Cody. Don't fight it. It's over. It's over. You're safe. You're home."

She dropped the wet cloth on the floor and grasped him firmly by the shoulders, trying to shake him awake.

It didn't work. He was still locked into the nightmare playing out in his head.

He groaned in whispers, although in sleep they were shouts. "They've got a lock . . . got a lock! Taking evasive . . . "

His voice trailed away as his motions increased. Queen's stomach jerked in response to what she heard him say as she realized he was reliving his plane being shot down.

"Oh, damn . . . can't shake . . . " All movement of his arms and legs ceased. For a split second in time he seemed frozen in place as his body arched in the bed. "I'm hit . . . I'm hit! . . . going down . . . going . . . Mayday! Mayday!"

Queen's eyes widened as she listened to the muttered coordinates he was giving, and she ached for the panic he couldn't seem to let go.

His body bucked beneath her hands, and a fresh wave of sweat beaded his skin.

"Cody! Wake up! You've got to wake up," she whispered urgently. It didn't happen, and the last word she heard him say before he went still as death was "ejecting."

Queen rose on shaky legs and took the washcloth back to the bathroom. After running fresh, cool water through it, she leaned over the sink and splashed her own warm face, then wrung the excess water from the cloth and hurried back to Cody's bedside. Now that he was still, she had no further fear that the Whittiers would hear him. For tonight the dream was over.

But she knew that there had been other nights before this one . . . and feared that there would be many more before this would end.

"No more," she whispered as she wiped his face and neck. "No more dreams . . . just sleep . . . sleep."

The cool washcloth was all there was between her hands and his body, and for one insane moment Queen had the notion to toss it aside and let her hands roam at will across the muscled breadth of his chest.

But sanity returned as quickly as it had left. She stood, laid the washcloth on the marbled top of the bed-side table, and walked quietly from the room.

Within a heartbeat Cody woke, as suddenly as one did when falling from dream sleep into consciousness. He felt the bed shift and knew when she stood, and he imagined that she could hear his heart knock against his chest from the shock of her presence.

When had she come into his room? How long had she been on his bed?

A memory returned of a soft voice and a soothing touch and something cool coming through the heat of the crash. He turned his head and saw the washcloth wadded on the bedside table and knew that tonight had been different from the others. Somewhere during the hell of his dream, Queen Houston had come inside and shared some of the pain and, in doing so, had somehow lessened its impact.

The bone-shaking fear that he always had upon awakening was gone. He felt weak, spent from the effort of the nightmare, but this time there was an odd sort of peace within him.

He stared at the closed door, trying to absorb what had just happened. Sometime during the night, when she'd thought no one could notice, she'd come and cared for him as she would have his sons. She'd been so tender and gentle, he wished to hell that he'd been awake in time to touch the woman he'd glimpsed walking out of his room. Queen Houston had already touched his life when she'd stepped in to care for his sons, and now she'd just touched his heart.

"Ah, God, lady," Cody whispered into the darkness. "I want more from you than I think you're willing to give."

With that, he rolled over on his belly and tried to ignore a sudden and unwelcome pain as his manhood hardened and then throbbed between his legs.

"Just what I need," he muttered as he buried his face into the pillow. "Another damned ache that won't go away."

6

The aroma of fresh coffee, sausage, and pancakes permeated the rooms downstairs. Allen Whittier packed the last of his things into their suitcase and watched with a jaundiced eye as his wife put on her makeup. Every morning it was the same. Whether they were alone in their own room or a thousand miles away from home, she didn't budge until her face was perfectly applied.

Methodically and artfully she added layer upon layer to enhance her features and her complexion, yet she couldn't hide the dissatisfaction lurking in her pale gray eyes or disguise the permanent frown lines at the corners of her mouth and eyes.

"There." She eyed herself coolly, checking her silver pompadour and patting down the collar of her navy two-piece suit. "I'm ready." She turned to face her husband and frowned. "Are you wearing that?"

"Yes, Lenore, I am. I like this shirt, and the slacks are

comfortable. We have a long drive ahead of us today. I don't intend to do it in a suit."

Recognizing that he was in one of his assertive moods, she decided to move on to other topics. She sniffed the air, then frowned. "Just what I suspected. Fried foods. Claire would never have allowed that."

Allen inhaled slowly, mentally counted to ten, and then decided to speak up in defense of the son-in-law he'd always admired.

"Claire would not have cooked it because Claire did not get up before ten A.M., and we both know it," he said. His sarcasm was faint but unmistakable as he continued. "The boys had already had cold cereal and gone about their business by the time she said hello to a day. I don't know about you, but whatever is cooking smells wonderful and I'm going to go beg my share."

He walked out of their makeshift bedroom, leaving her alone. His chance to interject his own opinions and personality into their marriage had come and gone, but it did not save him from regrets that he'd let it go.

Allen stopped just outside the kitchen door, pausing long enough to watch the housekeeper as she stood at the stove, flipping pancakes and turning sausage links with consummate skill. He observed with undisguised male interest the way her long legs and slim hips filled the old blue jeans she was wearing. Her long red hair was loose, providing a stunning contrast to her oversize green T-shirt.

Queen turned around, and Allen took an unconscious step backward at the warning look he saw in her eyes. Recognition changed her expression to one of welcome, but in the split second before she'd masked her thoughts, he knew this woman would give nothing to no man.

"Mr. Whittier . . . I didn't hear you come in."

He flushed, wishing himself into the next county for what he'd been thinking. "I didn't mean to startle you," he said quietly, and then waved his hand in the general direction of where she was working. "It's just that everything smells so good."

She smiled, and when her face lit up he realized that she was younger than he'd first imagined.

"If you'll take a seat in the next room, I'll bring your breakfast," she offered.

"If you don't mind," Allen said, "I'd rather eat in the kitchen. It's cozier."

Queen shrugged and turned away to fill his plate.

When Lenore finally made her way to breakfast, she found her husband and grandsons seated in the kitchen, sharing a meal and laughter as Allen regaled them with a story of one of their mother's childhood stunts.

"Don't tell the children such things," she said as she sat down. "It'll only give them notions."

Allen rolled his eyes and made a face at Will and J.J. before he spoke. "Not unless the boys suddenly decide to wear lipstick and face powder. I was telling them about when Claire was five and got into your makeup."

"She looked like a clown," J.J. said, giggling.

Lenore almost smiled. "And ruined a perfectly good dress," she felt compelled to add, and then stared pointedly at Queen. "I'll just have juice and coffee. I don't eat fried foods. It's bad for my cholesterol."

Queen bit her lip to keep from arguing. Lenore was subtly condemning her care of the boys, and she knew it.

"It's not pork sausage. Actually it's turkey sausage," Allen said. "And the pancakes aren't fried in oil. Queen uses a nonstick griddle, and egg substitute in the batter instead of hen fruit." He grinned and winked as the boys giggled at his foolishness. "But the syrup is the real thing. Maple . . . sweet and thick, just the way I like it."

Queen tried not to smile, but it was impossible. She thought it was a shame that Lenore Whittier wasn't as nice a person as her husband.

"What's sweet and thick?" Cody asked as he walked into the room.

Queen blushed as she looked away to tend to the pancakes on the griddle. Last night had changed things between them, even if only in her own perception. She'd gone from paid employee to caregiver. From taking care of his house and sons to taking personal care of him. Try as she might to ignore it, the feelings that came with it were making her crazy.

"Way to go, Dad," Donny drawled, eyeing his father's bare feet and the fact that Cody looked as if he'd just crawled out of bed and into the jeans and T-shirt he was wearing. "I thought you were gonna sleep all day."

Cody busied himself with getting a cup from the cabinet and pouring some coffee before he answered. "Just overslept, I guess," he said. "I didn't think to set the alarm."

"Do you want two stacks?" Queen asked, waving a plate laden with hot, steaming pancakes beneath his nose.

She had interrupted on purpose. Changing the subject had been instinctive, just like her concern for him last night. She caught Cody's grateful glance and looked away, unwilling to share anything with him, even something as simple as a thank-you.

He took the plate, sat down at the table, and even talked his mother-in-law into trying a single cake with only a thin smear of syrup. Cody tried not to grin when she took a second helping along with two links of sausage. Queen had done the impossible. She'd silenced Lenore Whittier, because at the moment her mouth was too full of food for further complaints.

But when it came time for the Whittiers to leave, Lenore resumed her attack on Cody's abilities as a proper parent.

"Boys, give your grandparents a good-bye kiss," Cody urged, knowing that it would not be offered unless he insisted.

Lenore held out a cheek and took each kiss as her due, all the while fussing with the boys' clothing, hair, and manners in turn as they followed their father's orders.

Then they lined up beside Cody and stood on the deck, watching nervously as their grandfather carried the bags to the car and their grandmother lingered at the bottom of the steps with a look on her face that they'd come to recognize meant trouble. And they were right.

Lenore took a couple of steps toward her husband, who was waiting for her at the car, and then stopped and turned. Her lips firmed and her eyebrows arched contemptuously as she spoke.

"Don't think that just because you've moved so far away, I won't know what's going on," she warned.

Cody's gut wrenched. He should have known. She'd been playing games with him all along, trying to get him to let down his guard long enough for her to pounce.

"I don't know what the hell you mean," he said softly.

She glared past him to the woman standing quietly in the doorway behind them and then smirked. "I think you do," she replied. "At any rate, be forewarned. You do anything to endanger these boys' morals, and I'll take you back to court and prove you're an unfit father. I'll do whatever it takes to protect Claire's children."

Donny paled. J.J. started to whimper, and Will clung to Cody's leg in silent terror.

Queen couldn't believe what she was hearing. The woman was a witch. She smiled out of one side of her face and threatened from the other.

"No, that's where you're wrong, Lenore," Cody said. "You take one step over the line of grandparental boundaries and I'll see that you never visit them again. Do you understand me?" His nostrils flared and his chin jutted in anger. "And another thing. Don't you ever—by God, ever—threaten me again."

With that, he turned and ushered his sons into the house. Queen stepped aside to let them pass. Even though Cody was silent, she could feel his fury.

Allen Whittier was disgusted with his wife. Queen could tell it from the way he walked and the cold anger with which he escorted her toward their car. But he didn't speak up in Cody's defense, and to Queen that in itself was unforgivable. Before she could stop herself, she was off the porch and at the car just as Allen opened it to seat his wife inside.

"What do you want?" Lenore asked, angry at the housekeeper's audacity.

"You know something?" Queen began in an almost conversational tone, ignoring the woman's rude question as though it had not been uttered. "When I was little, I always thought that my sisters and I were missing something in our lives by not having grandparents. In my mind, grandparents would always be good for extra hugs and kisses, for making cookies and taking me places." She leaned closer until she was nearly face to face with Lenore Whittier. "But I see now that I was wrong. If you are an example of how grandparents are supposed to act, then I'm glad I never had any. In fact, I must have been lucky as hell."

Queen turned and started to walk away, ignoring the angry sputtering she heard behind her; then she remembered the fear on the boys' faces and turned.

"And one other thing." Her voice rose with each word as she pointed her finger at Lenore. "If you bother Cody Bonner or try to hurt his boys again, you'll come through me to do it."

Allen started the car and put it into reverse before Lenore had fully closed the door.

"For pity's sake," Lenore said, shocked beyond words at Queen's threat. "How dare she talk to me like that?"

Allen looked at his wife with something akin to loathing and wished he had the guts to do what that redhead had just done. "Buckle up," he said instead. "It's a long drive."

Queen hit the front door with the flat of her hand and then slammed it shut behind her. Her breasts were heaving, and her breath was coming in short, shallow gasps. Her eyes flashed green fire, and if someone had crossed her path at that moment, she probably would have taken them apart blindfolded.

Then she blinked and inhaled slowly and looked at the Bonners, who were staring at her in shock.

Cody had heard only the last few words that she'd flung into the space between yard and house, but it had been enough to give him hope. *Come through me to do it*. Those were fighting words if he'd ever heard them.

He would have liked to think that she'd included him in that pledge, because he had a sudden flash of insight as to what he wanted from Queen Houston, and it was much more than protection.

The passion on her face was unmistakable. Even though it had been born out of anger, it was proof that she was capable of great love as well. Only someone who hated so fiercely could love so deeply. That was what he'd seen, and that was what he wanted. He wanted Queen and her love.

And she wanted a bus ticket out of Snow Gap.

"Boys, go to your room," he said quietly.

Queen felt herself go limp as the anger slid out of her body. She leaned against the door and covered her face with her hands. My God! What did I just do? she thought as she heard the boys' footsteps on the stairs.

"Are you all right?" Cody asked.

She nodded, too embarrassed to face him.

"Queen . . . "

His voice compelled her. In spite of her reluctance, she looked up and then swallowed nervously at the expression on his face.

"I'm sorry I—"

He caught her apology before it was finished, stopping it by pressing the tip of his forefinger against her lips. "No. I'm the one who's sorry. I'm sorry I put you in this unforgivable position. I'm sorry I dumped you in the middle of my personal problems."

The touch of his hand against her lips stunned her. Her mouth was on fire.

And the fact that she'd left it there stunned him. He'd half expected her to slap it away. When she didn't move, other than to stare up at him with those wide green eyes, he knew he was on shaky ground, but he couldn't stop himself from finishing what he'd started.

"I'm sorry for a lot of things, Queen Houston. But not that you came into our lives. Thank you for being here . . . and for last night." His thumb traced her chin and felt it tremble beneath his touch just before she moved.

So he had known! She'd thought he was still asleep when she'd left the room. Now her face truly burned.

"It was nothing," she said, and moved farther away, uncomfortable with the lack of space between them. "I was afraid you'd wake the boys."

He nodded. "Just the same . . . "

"Forget it," she said.

His eyes narrowed. He held his breath, almost expecting her to order him to take her to the bus. Would she remind him that she'd upheld her part of the bargain and now it was time for him to uphold his? But she didn't, and he was afraid to broach the subject of her staying longer. Instead they stood, eye to eye, quietly assessing each other's anger, not realizing that the anger they felt was not with each other, but with the situation.

Queen was furious with herself and the fact that she cared . . . that she'd made the Bonners her responsibility. She stomped past him into the kitchen and began banging pots and pans. She didn't want to care about anyone else. When would someone ever care for her?

The euphoria of having quelled the Whittiers' front-line attack faded, and along with it went Cody's appetite. His moods swung dangerously, and Donny watched his father with a nervous eye, alerting Queen to the fact that Cody's behavior was not normal. One day everything and everyone got on his nerves, the next day the house could have blown away and he'd never have noticed.

Queen watched until she felt she could no longer remain a silent observer. It had been a week since the Whittiers had come and gone, and Cody had done nothing but go from bad to worse. And he was continuing to experience restless sleep, plagued by nightmares. She knew it was time to intervene. She waited until the boys were in bed and Cody had retreated to the deck outside to brood.

All he can do is tell me to get lost, Queen told herself. She smoothed her hands over the front of her shirt and took a deep breath before pushing open the screen door and slipping outside into the darkness to join him.

Cody heard the hinge squeak. It was Queen. He didn't have to turn around to know. The air around him changed, charging with an electricity she seemed to emanate.

"Something wrong?" he asked.

There would be no easy way to approach this subject. But Queen had never taken the easy way out of a problem yet, and tonight was going to be no exception.

"You tell me," she said.

He closed his eyes and smiled, confident that his expression was hidden by the darkness. He'd never known a woman as straightforward as Queen.

"You aren't sleeping. When you do, you have that same dream . . . don't you?" she asked.

A soft curse slid quietly into the night shadows between them. "Let it go," he told her.

"It doesn't have hold of me, Cody Bonner. You're the one with the monkey on your back."

He vaulted from the chair, angry that she'd said what he already knew. He braced his hands against the rail of the deck and looked up into the night sky and the heavens in which he used to fly, and he felt anchored to earth by the terrible weight of fear he couldn't lose.

"Dammit, you don't understand."

"No, I think it's you who doesn't understand," Queen

said softly, and slid her hand up his arm in a comforting gesture. "I think you need to go back to the base and make another visit to the doctor . . . don't you? What did you say he called this thing that was happening to you—delayed stress syndrome? How can you get better when all you're doing is heaping more stress onto yourself?"

His shoulders slumped, and then he turned and leaned against the railing as he crossed his arms and stared intently at her silhouette, wishing he could see her more clearly.

"If I start something like that, it would mean constant trips back and forth to the base. Don't forget what happened the last time I left the boys alone for the day."

His answer hung between them, and Queen suddenly knew why he was suffering alone. He wouldn't start what he couldn't finish . . . because of her. Because she'd promised to stay only until the grandparents came, and they'd been gone for days.

She took a deep breath, worrying her lower lip between her teeth as she contemplated the easiest way to tell him of the decision she'd already made.

"Yes, but that was before I came," she said. "I'm here now. I'm not going anywhere. Why don't you give the doctor another try?"

Cody couldn't believe what he was hearing. She'd just offered to stay . . . indefinitely. His heart pounded, and he had a sudden urge to gather her in his arms and hold on to the solid comfort of her body. But touching her was probably the worst thing he could do.

"You know what you're saying to me?" he asked.

"Oh, yes," she said, and laughed softly into the space between them. "And don't think I haven't given myself a very good tongue-lashing for the decision, either."

"That's what I mean," Cody said. "You'll be staying out of guilt. And that will only make my guilt worse, don't you see? I've already coerced you into something you didn't want to do. How do you think this makes me feel . . . knowing that once again I'll be taking advantage of your good nature for my own needs?"

"Maybe that was so the first time," she said. "But there's no one but you and me to hear what's said between us now. I'm not being forced to stay. I'm offering. This time it's by choice, not design. Okay?"

"Oh, God, lady," Cody said, and took a step toward her. "I don't know what I did to deserve you coming into our lives, but I'll be forever thankful that you did."

He reached out, but she was no longer there. He heard the hinge squeak, and then the click of the latch, and then he heard her call softly from the darkness.

"Good night, Cody. Go to bed and try to get some sleep. You'll see . . . tomorrow is a brand-new day."

And so the trips began. The days turned into weeks and the weeks moved toward autumn, and Queen forgot about her plans to go to Arizona and "find herself." There was too much to do every day for her to worry about herself. As time passed, Cody's laughter could once again be heard throughout the house and from the woods as he and his sons continued to gather firewood for the coming winter.

Queen learned not to jump whenever he came too close and often managed to return his smile when they'd pass in the hallway. But things between them were the best when they shared laughter at something the boys had said or done. Yes, those were the best of times. The worst were yet to come.

○   ○   ○

Cody dug through the pile of clothing on his bed and then lifted it into his arms and carried it downstairs.

"Hurry up, guys," he yelled. "I want to get to Snow Gap before noon."

"What are you doing?" Queen asked as she walked into the living room and stared at the stack of clothing he had just dumped on the couch.

"Getting rid of some old clothes," he muttered. He walked back to the stairs and yelled again, "Come on, I'm leaving you guys here if you don't hurry up!"

When he turned around he saw Queen sifting through the clothes he'd pulled from his closet, laying a garment or two aside as she searched.

"What are *you* doing?" he asked.

"Why are you giving these away? They're still like new." She held up a couple of sweaters and a heavy suede coat lined with sheepskin.

"Because I've gained weight since I mustered out," he said. "My flying weight was about twenty pounds less than what I am now."

Queen squinted her eyes, trying to imagine less meat on his immense frame, and shook her head. "Then you were too thin," she said.

"The fact remains that I can't wear those clothes."

"If you don't mind my asking . . . may I have them? I don't mind wearing hand-me-downs. They were all Johnny ever brought us," she said, and then felt compelled to add, "I wouldn't want all of them, of course. But I could wear these sweaters . . . I know it." She held one up in front of her and stretched out the arms in measurement against her own. "See? Only a little bit too long. I could push them—"

"You can have anything of mine you want, lady," he said quietly, trying not to imagine her body inside his clothes. Or her breasts pushing against the soft cable knit, restructuring its lines into those of womanly shape and form.

He was shocked to think that she would willingly wear something that had once belonged to someone else. Once they were a year old, Claire wouldn't even wear her own clothes, let alone someone else's. And then he had a flashback of the first time he'd seen Queen lying beneath his pickup truck—the old, faded jeans and the boots with the soles worn nearly through. He realized that he knew little to nothing about her life before she came to live with them. In fact, he couldn't remember if he'd ever heard her mention any "Johnny" before.

Queen smiled with delight and turned to dig through the pile on the couch. Cody watched her excitement as she slid her arms into the coat sleeves and then turned back and forth in front of the living room window, using the faint reflection as a mirror.

"It's not bad. Not bad at all," she said. "With layers of winter clothes beneath it, it should be just about right. What do you think?"

"I think you're one hell of a woman, Queen Houston. That's what I think. And I also think you better get a move on if you're coming with us."

She didn't hear the break in his voice, and it was just as well. Shows of emotion always bothered her. Instead she grinned, almost dancing as she ran from the room with the sweaters over her arm and the coat still on her back.

Shame for what he took for granted overwhelmed him. Cody dropped onto a chair and sat with his elbows on bent knees, staring wordlessly at the floor and trying to imagine Queen as a child, wearing other people's cast-off clothing. The image made the backs of his eyes burn, and it was with relief that he finally heard the footsteps of his sons on the stairs.

"It's about time," he said. "Donny, carry that stuff to the car for me, will you? Will, get your jacket. J.J., tie your shoe."

"Wait for me!" Queen shouted as she came running down the stairs.

Cody looked up. There was a smile on her face, lighting the green in her eyes to that of fresh-mown grass. Her hair was loose and bouncing as her long legs took the stairs two at a time. She was wearing a nearly new pair of jeans, the burgundy sweater she'd just inherited, and the same old boots.

Wait for you? Lady, I think I've been waiting for you all of my life.

But the thought was never voiced, and it was just as well. Queen wasn't ready to hear it, and Cody wasn't ready to say it. Not yet.

"Cool! Queenie's going with us!" J.J. yelled. "Sit by me, sit by me."

"No dice, men," Cody said. "She's sitting by me. Now move."

Queen's heart did a little hip-hop of its own. It was almost . . . just almost . . . like being part of a family. She grabbed her purse and headed out into the clear, crisp day. She had a mission. Today, when they reached Snow Gap, there was something she needed to do. She'd put it off long enough, and delay was only making her nervous. The balance of her five thousand dollars was going into her very first, very own bank account.

"Got everything?" Cody asked once just before he backed out of the yard, and then he noticed that Queen was the first to look as she quickly checked and rechecked the contents of her purse.

"I'm ready," she said, settling back onto the seat. She shoved the sleeves of her sweater up to elbow length, pushed back a curl that fell across her nose, and grinned in spite of her determination to remain calm and cool.

Cody couldn't help wondering about her excitement, and he had a single moment of fear, thinking that today might be the day she announced she was leaving. Just for a moment he thought of making an excuse and turning around so he could go back to the house and lock her inside, never letting her out of their lives. But he couldn't, and he didn't. Instead he stared straight ahead as he drove, ignoring the knot in his belly.

The boys soon became immersed in hand-held computer games, and Cody tried to think of a way to start a conversation with Queen without turning it into a fight; yet that's just what he felt like doing. He was scared half out of his mind at the thought of losing her.

"So . . . what are your plans for the day?" he finally asked.

Queen looked startled, and then she clutched her purse a little tighter against her lap and fiddled with the catch. "Oh . . . things," she said, and then pointed out a window. "Look! Geese! They're going south for the winter. Johnny always said that—"

"Queen . . . who's Johnny?"

Her mouth dropped, and her eyes widened. For a moment she was too surprised to answer. "Why, he was my father," she finally said. "Haven't I ever mentioned him?"

Cody's sigh of relief was hidden behind a slight grin of embarrassment. "Not his name. Why did you call him Johnny, anyway? Why not Dad?"

Queen's answer came without taking time to think. "Because he was never much of a father, I guess," she said. "But he was always Johnny, if you know what I mean."

Cody didn't, not really. But the more he learned about this woman, the more intriguing she became. And they drove all the way to Snow Gap before he realized that he still didn't know what had put that gleam in her eyes.

7

Cody stood on the street corner across from the bank and tried to look occupied. It was not an easy task, because his entire attention was focused on the fact that nearly half an hour earlier Queen had disappeared into that same bank and had yet to emerge.

He kept telling himself that she must be waiting on a long teller line to cash the paycheck he'd given her. He kept telling himself she hadn't slipped out the back door and was somewhere in Snow Gap, waiting for a bus to take her away. If he said it often enough, he might start to believe it. But he still wasn't convinced.

A black-and-white police car pulled into the parking space in front of the store where Cody was standing. A uniformed officer got out, adjusted his hat and his holster, and then started toward Cody as if on a mission.

"Just the man I've been wanting to see," the officer said as he walked up to Cody and extended his hand. "I thought it was about time we met face to face."

Cody eyed him with surprise and confusion.

"Sorry," the officer said, and laughed at Cody's blank look. "I guess I've got the edge. Your picture came in over the fax after we filed that missing persons on you. I'm Abel Miller, sheriff of Snow Gap."

A wry grin slid across Cody's face. "So . . . Sheriff Miller, we finally meet." He accepted the other man's handshake. "Queen and the boys talk about you often. I can't thank you enough for what you did for my family."

"Like I said before, it wasn't so much what I did as what your sister stopped from happening."

"She's not my sister."

Cody's denial was so vehement and so sudden that it surprised even him.

Sheriff Miller frowned. "Now I was given to believe—"

"No, no," Cody interrupted. "Wait, before I accidentally get myself in more trouble. That's not exactly what I meant to say. What I mean is . . . we're not really related at all, at least not by blood. Only by consequence." That was as fair an assessment of their relationship as he could give and still look himself in the face.

Abel Miller grinned and shoved his hat on the back of his head as he propped himself against the storefront with one hand. "Oh, yeah, I already knew that. I guess I didn't make myself clear, either." And then he grinned. "You've been standing here for nearly half an hour, staring at the bank across the street. What are you doing? Casing the joint?"

Sheriff Miller's laughter was loud and hearty, and Cody felt himself flush, although he was able to laugh at the joke at his expense. "No," he replied. "I'm just waiting for Queen. She had to . . . uh, she had some business to—"

"No big deal," Sheriff Miller said. "I was just kidding. Shoot. This is Saturday. They may actually be busy today. Snow Gap is small, but we do a fairly good tourist trade, and we're not too far from some good ski trails." He sighed and pushed his hat back down in its proper place. "But that'll be later . . . when it snows. That's when it gets hectic. It's the outsiders that usually cause the most trouble around here."

Cody started to comment, but his attention was caught by the sight of Queen emerging from the bank, her hand nestled in the crook of another man's arm while she stopped and looked up and down the street.

"Your sist . . . I mean, Queen . . . makes friends fast, doesn't she?" Abel Miller asked.

"Obviously."

There was nothing else Cody could say. But the feeling that took hold in the pit of his stomach and began worming its way up his belly toward his chest was as unexpected and as unwelcome as the man coming across the street with Queen.

I'm jealous!

Cody didn't have time to analyze the realization before they reached him and Sheriff Miller.

"Sheriff Miller," Queen said, greeting the officer nervously. She still had visions of being hauled off to jail for lying, although the time had long since passed when that might have mattered.

He smiled and tipped his hat, missing nothing of the cold look Cody Bonner was giving the man escorting his sister who wasn't a sister.

"What took you so long?" Cody asked, staring pointedly at Queen's hand caught between the other man's elbow and rib cage.

"Oh! Right!" Queen said, and the smile on her face

transposed her natural reserve into vivid excitement. "Cody! You'll never guess. I was standing in line at the bank waiting to conduct my business when . . . "

Cody lost his train of thought. That was right: he still didn't know what her business in there had been. His mind wandered, as it had off and on for the past thirty minutes. Maybe if he broke his leg, or got a bad case of the flu, she would have to stay longer.

" . . . enrolled for the year."

Queen stopped talking, and Cody realized that he'd completely missed everything she'd been saying.

"Umm, what was that last part again?" he muttered, embarrassed that he had to ask.

Queen rolled her eyes and dropped the man's arm as she stepped in front of Cody and waved her hand across his face as if checking to see if he were conscious. "Yoo hoo," she drawled. "Is anybody home?"

He laughed. It was so unlike her to tease him. "Sorry, Queen. I was lost in thought. I guess I was still worried because Sheriff Miller here had just accused me of casing the joint." He pointed to the bank across the street and then grinned.

Queen looked once at the sheriff and then back at Cody and started to smile. "Caught in the act?"

He nodded. "Something like that."

He watched the laughter dancing in her eyes, although she never broke a giggle. He wished he knew what it would take to make Queen not take herself so seriously.

The sheriff cleared his throat and kicked at a pebble on the street. Queen's face turned as red as her hair, and Cody couldn't think what to say. There was nothing to be said but the truth, and that was that they'd forgotten anyone else was present.

"Sorry again. You must think we're idiots. But it's not

lack of brains that keeps me from introducing myself, it's lack of manners." Cody offered to shake the hand of the man who had accompanied Queen across the street. "I'm Cody Bonner."

"Cody, this is Stanley Brass," Queen said. "He'll be the boys' principal here in Snow Gap. He was just telling me about the early pre-enrollment day available for new students. I thought you'd like to meet the man who'll be in charge of your sons."

The knot in Cody's stomach promptly untied itself. Thank God! He was just the school principal.

He took a second look at the man and decided that he didn't look so menacing after all. In fact, he looked absolutely nondescript. He was probably pushing at least thirty extra pounds and fifty years of age. His hair was thinning, and even though he had a nice smile and twinkling eyes, the best thing about him was the wedding band Cody suddenly noticed on his ring finger.

"Mr. Brass. It's a pleasure. After you meet my boys, I hope you can say the same."

They all laughed, and the tension passed. Within minutes Queen left the trio on the street corner to continue making acquaintance. She had other things to do.

"Meet you at the restaurant in an hour, okay?" she whispered just before she walked away.

Cody smiled and nodded as he continued to talk to the other men. To the casual observer it would seem that he was entirely committed to the conversation at hand, but it wasn't so. He didn't miss where Queen went or the intent way in which she was walking. If she was about to run, he was going to be right behind her.

o   o   o

"Gee, Dad. Didn't you ask her where she was going?"

Donny's plaintive question was echoed by Will and J.J., who were impatiently awaiting Queen's arrival so that they could all go to lunch.

Cody shook his head and tried not to give his imagination full rein. He'd already mentally ticked off the places she wasn't. He'd looked in every corner of the shops along the main street while his boys were still occupied at the video arcade. But his surreptitious surveillance had come to a halt when they'd arrived at the appointed time and place, anxious for pizza.

"Tell you what," Cody said. "You three go on inside and get a table. If you're too hungry to wait, order some garlic bread and sodas until I get back. I'll run on down the street and hurry her along. I'm sure she's just dawdling in some dress shop. Okay?"

The suggestion was met with approval as Donny took charge and herded his younger brothers into the pizza parlor. Cody watched until they were safely seated inside before he made a break for the street corner where he'd last seen Queen.

The day was clear. Sunshine over the Rockies colored the blue sky with a white-hot glare. It would be a nice day for traveling. And that thought scared him to death.

He went up one street and down another, staring in windows, peering inside doors. He didn't miss a store in four blocks, and there was still no sight of Queen.

"Hey," he said to a man who'd just exited a pharmacy. "Where would someone go to buy a bus ticket . . . or catch a bus in Snow Gap?"

The man paused for a moment and then pointed. "I think the bus still stops at the café on Turner Street. But I'm not sure if they sell tickets there."

"Thanks," Cody said, and was down the street in a flash, his long legs making short work of the distance.

He turned the corner the man had indicated and then stopped and watched in horror as a long gray bus pulled out of the café parking lot and onto the highway, moving at a fast clip through the two-lane traffic on its way to somewhere else.

"No!" Cody didn't know he'd shouted aloud until he saw a woman eyeing him strangely. "God . . . no," he whispered, and ran a hand through his hair. He hadn't been able to find her anywhere else, and he'd been too late to stop the bus to see if she was on it.

His shoulders slumped as he turned in a slow circle, like a lost soul trying to get his bearings. And that was just exactly how he felt. He'd lost his anchor.

An ache started around his heart and began to spread in a twisting, winding pain. It hurt to breathe, and he was having trouble focusing on the street sign above his head. He looked up at the sky, then closed his eyes and swallowed several times until he thought he was able to go back to the boys without losing control of his emotions. And then he heard someone calling his name.

She was almost running, and smiling as she came nearer. Her hair fanned around her face, and she had her purse in one hand and a small paper bag in the other.

"Where were you going?" she asked as she came to a halt and clasped her hand against her breasts as if to hold back her heart, so winded was she from her sprint. "I thought we were having pizza."

Cody could only stare. Every nerve point in his body went on alert. He saw a pulse throbbing wildly at her throat and imagined he could hear her heartbeat.

Vibrant heat radiated from her tousled and windblown curls in such force that he imagined the skin on his face was scorched. His gaze raked the questioning glance in her wide green eyes and then down to the slight gap of her lips where she was slowly drawing in long drafts of air.

"Oh, hell, lady," he said, and yanked her into his arms.

It was hard to say who was the most stunned—Queen because she was suddenly pressed against a wall of muscle and a wildly beating heart or Cody for having brought her there. One long moment passed before either moved or spoke. And then, when they did, it was Queen who moved and Cody who started talking, and fast.

"I'm sorry," he said, holding up his hands in surrender before she could take offense. "Don't misunderstand what just happened."

Queen stepped back, clutching her purse and sack against her chest. "What did just happen?" she asked nervously.

Cody groaned and wiped a hand across his brow. "You don't want to know."

"Oh, but I do, Cody Bonner. I not only want to know, I have to know what made you grab me like I was about to fly awa . . ."

The question died on her lips. She stared at the receding panic in his eyes and then at the bus stop behind him. Realization dawned. He'd thought she'd run away!

He turned around and stared blindly at the café, silently discussing with himself the merits of confessing the truth and giving her ideas she didn't already have, or lying through his teeth and hoping she bought the whole nine yards. He looked back and, as it turned out, didn't have to lie because she'd already guessed the truth.

She doubled up her fist and punched, connecting in a halfhearted blow above his belt buckle. "Damn you, Cody Bonner. I don't deserve that."

He took the gesture as it was meant to be given and had the good sense not to argue when he saw the fury on her face.

She spun around and started to walk away, blinking furiously to clear her vision from a sudden burst of angry tears.

"You're right, lady," he said quietly, "you don't."

His admission of guilt was the only thing that would have stopped her, and it did. But all the joy was gone from the day. In a single second she'd gone from imagining herself an honorary member of his family to someone he didn't even trust to keep her word.

When she stopped walking, his hand slid across the back of her neck, and she felt him move around to face her. He was only inches away from her, and still she would not look up . . . could not look up and see the doubt and know that she was nothing in his eyes.

"Oh, God, honey, don't shut me out," he whispered, and dropped his hand to his side, completely ignoring the fact that they were standing on a fairly busy side street in broad daylight, as near to an embrace as two people could be without actually touching.

Queen finally looked up, her eyes swimming in tears, and then could do nothing but shake her head and look away. The pain was too fresh . . . too deep . . . for words.

"I'm sorry. So, so, sorry. All I can say is . . . I panicked. You said an hour. It's been closer to two. I looked and I looked. I couldn't find you anywhere."

She muttered something.

"What? I didn't hear what you said."

"I said," she shouted, suddenly too angry to hold back, "I was getting my stupid boots half-soled. It took longer than I expected."

She kicked at his shoe with the toe of her boot, drawing his attention to the new, shiny black soles shining on the sides.

"Soles . . . on your boots? You were just getting your boots fixed?" The tenor of his voice rose with each word until he was somewhere between laughing and shouting.

Before she knew it was coming, he'd swooped her up into his arms and was dancing a little jig in the middle of the sidewalk. A woman smiled at them from behind a store window, and another giggled, but Cody didn't care if the whole damn town was watching.

"Put me down," Queen sputtered, and yanked at the tail of her sweater, which had ridden above her waistline. Her cheeks were as red as her hair, and a small sprinkling of freckles that hardly ever showed had suddenly sprouted into plain sight across the bridge of her nose. "What will people think?"

"I don't give a tinker's damn what anyone thinks," Cody said as he put her back on her feet. "All I care is that you're still here. I don't even care if you're mad enough not to speak to me for . . . oh, hell . . . at least a week."

The grin on his face was contagious. Try as she might, she couldn't stay mad. She looked up and bit her lower lip to keep from smiling. "Well . . . comb your hair," she ordered, smoothing hers back into place. "We can't go eat pizza with you looking like that."

"Yes, ma'am," he said, and dug in his pocket for a comb as he began following her down the street.

"And when we get to the pizza parlor . . . for God's sake don't tell the boys what an ass you just were," she added. Then she thought of something else. "You haven't already scared them to death, have you?"

"No way."

"At least you had that much sense," she muttered, and resumed her march toward the pizza parlor with Cody half a step behind.

Cody swallowed hard and fixed his gaze on a spot just above the level of her right shoulder, telling himself that if he concentrated on something else, he wouldn't notice the sway of her slender hips beneath the loose hem of his sweater. But it was no use. She was too tall and leggy for him to ignore, and she was too justified with her anger to ignore him.

Just before they went inside, she turned and jabbed a forefinger into his chest, punctuating each word of her last order.

"Smile. Don't act as if anything is wrong." A small smile of her own came and went, but it was enough to give Cody hope that sometime he might be forgiven.

"And I don't like anchovies or black olives on my pizza," she announced as if nothing had happened. With that she pushed open the door and left Cody on his own to decide if he wanted to follow.

He did.

In less than a month school would start. Cody stood on the deck behind the house and watched the boys playing their favorite new game, Queen's now famous one-eyed cat. They ranged so far apart in age, he feared that when school started they would slowly grow apart, especially Donny, who was now an official teenager. He just hoped that the basic closeness between them didn't diminish during the years.

"Who's winning?" Queen asked.

Cody turned and grinned. "No one. Everyone. That's the beauty of that game, isn't it?"

Queen nodded. "My sisters and I always played it. Partly because we didn't have anyone else to play with, and partly because there wasn't room in the backyard for more than one base."

"Do you miss them?" he asked.

She bit her lip and looked away. "More than I thought possible."

"You could always call them. I wouldn't care about the bill. You know that, don't you?"

Queen remembered how carefully he'd been treading around her feelings since that day in Snow Gap, and she nodded. "I know. It's just . . . Lucky and I have no way of contacting each other at all. And I did try once to reach Diamond, but all I got was the runaround."

She frowned, remembering the disdain in the secretary's voice at the offices of the record label under which Jesse Eagle sang. She couldn't really blame the woman. They probably got similar calls constantly from fans with an unhealthy devotion, and they had to protect Jesse Eagle's privacy. "For all I know, I may never see them again," she said, trying to disguise the tremor in her voice by clearing her throat. But it was difficult to hide the pain of saying her worst fears aloud.

"Why?" Cody asked. "I always imagined you were close."

"We were . . . are," she corrected herself. "But when Johnny died we no longer had a home. Not in Cradle Creek. And we were all going different directions in life. There's no longer a center in our lives."

"Why? Because you sold your house?" He knew bits and pieces of her life, but not enough, he now realized.

She sighed. "It was an impossible situation. If we'd stayed, we would not have survived."

She walked into the house, leaving him to make what he would of her answer. Although she never let on, he decided she must often get lonely for her family.

He turned back to watch his sons' ball game and remembered his own childhood. Cody had been an army brat and an only child. He'd grown up with no roots, attending a new school every year or so, depending on where his father was relocated next, and he accepted it as a way of life. In his second year of marriage to Claire, his parents passed away within months of each other, but by then he'd already learned to give everything possible to his work, and what little was left over went to his family.

As Lieutenant Colonel Cody Bonner, squadron commander assigned to Fifty-ninth Fighter Squadron, Eglin Air Force Base, state of Florida, his was an impressive rank with an impressive group of men. He was a damned good officer but an on-again, off-again, father. And after Claire's death, it had nearly cost him his sons. Now he knew that nothing was worth that loss.

He sighed, shoved his hands in his pockets, and followed Queen into the house. Sometimes the most difficult thing in life was just the living of it.

Night came. The boys, exhausted from their wild game of ball, inhaled their food, slopped through their baths, and fell into bed with less than the usual amount of argument.

Within a few hours the house was silent and only the sounds of distant thunder from a faraway storm could be heard. Now and then a floorboard creaked as it settled against the night, and dry leaves from the trees surrounding the yard rolled outside beneath the legs of the deck, rustling along with the wind, crackling like paper being consumed by a wild, gusty fire.

Queen kicked restlessly and turned to pull an extra cover over her shoulders. She had almost resettled into that comfortable spot on the edge of her pillow when she heard the cry. It was high-pitched and heart-stopping, and she'd heard it before.

Without thought for the chill of the floor or her scant clothing, she was out of bed and down the hall in a flash, opening and then closing the door to Cody's room, anxious to stop the dream before he woke the children.

"Oh, Cody," she whispered as she ran to his bed. "I thought this was behind you."

Held in the throes of the nightmare, caught in the twisted covers of his bed, he lay on his back, arms outflung, legs jerking against the linen confinement. Although the night was chilly, he lay bathed in sweat from the exertion in his mind.

Queen slid onto the bed beside him and took his face in her hands. "Cody! Cody! You've got to wake up!"

But nothing stopped the progression of the nightmare.

Stroking the sides of his face with the palms of her hands in a slow, comforting motion, she felt the tension in his jaw as it clenched and reclenched beneath her touch.

He groaned, muttering unintelligible words. Queen's hand slid from his face to his chest, and unconsciously her fingers splayed across it, feeling the heartbeat beneath. It was rapid and irregular, and when his body arched, she threw herself across it in a desperate effort to keep him from falling.

The movement had been instinctive. Of course he couldn't fall. He was flat on his back in bed. But she'd sensed that he'd reached the point of his dream in which he'd ejected from the plane, and the instinct to catch him and keep him from falling was immediate.

"Oh, God, Cody, wake up. Wake up," she whispered, and laid her face against his chest.

She slid her arms around him, closed her eyes, and knew only that when he came out of the dream, she couldn't bear for him to think he was hurt and lost as he had been in the desert. She had to be there, in body as well as spirit, and this was the only way she knew how to let him know he wasn't alone. She held on for dear life . . . and for Cody.

He shuddered. The last thing he remembered was blacking out after hitting the ground. He groaned softly and reached out, trying to lift the weight from his chest and clear his eyes. But this time something was different. It wasn't tight bands of straps he felt across his chest. It was a woman. He could feel her soft skin and gentle curves and could even smell the scent of shampoo. He wondered why no one had ever told him that when you died and went to heaven, angels would smell and feel this good.

When his arms moved upward to lift the helmet from his face, it wasn't there, just a fine webbing of angel hair spread over his cheeks. His fingers slid over the hair and then downward. Clutching a fistful of curls with each hand, he sighed and opened his eyes.

She knew when it was over. He became still, and his body went limp. But before she could move, he'd entwined his hands in her hair. She was caught, trapped where she lay by a man filled with pain. She lifted her head, and in the shadowy darkness of his room, their eyes met. And just for a moment before he blinked and looked away, she imagined she saw into his soul.

"Queen . . . it's you." He dropped his head back to the pillow, released her hair, and covered his face with his hands. "What the hell happened?"

She resisted the urge to caress his face. Asleep she'd been able to touch him, awake he was out of bounds.

"You had another dream," she said, and started to rise.

He didn't even know he was going to do it until his hand closed around her wrist and he held her beside him with desperate force. "Don't," he begged, and then loosened his hold and let his hand slide slowly up her arm, coming to rest at the slender curve of her neck below her chin. "Don't leave me, lady."

Queen's heart pounded. Her stomach tightened as an answering coil of want began to spiral low in her body. He'd asked something of her she wasn't ready to give.

Their eyes adjusted to the darkness between them. Cody could see the slender outline of her body through the old, soft fabric of her gown. His own body hardened and rose, aching with a need he'd long been denied. Queen not only had awakened him from the dream, she'd awakened another part of him that he'd tried valiantly to ignore. But the want between them had been too close to the surface for too long.

He reached out and cupped her breast, molding the fabric against it until she looked to have been carved of marble. He felt a shiver of longing so deep inside him, he shuddered from the need.

She covered his hand with her own, and for a long quiet moment he was caught between her body and her touch.

"I can't," she finally whispered, and could have wept when his hand slid away and dropped onto the bed beside her.

"Why? Because you don't trust me? I wouldn't hurt you, lady. You mean more to me than any woman has ever meant in my entire life. I know you think I'm crazy, but—"

"Don't!" Her hand covered his mouth before the words could be finished. "You're not crazy. You're a survivor, that's all." Her voice softened, and he strained to hear her continue. "You're a survivor . . . just like me."

Cody held his breath, sensing that she was about to reveal more of herself now than in all the time he'd known her. "But you don't trust me," he said softly.

Queen shuddered. "I don't trust anyone. Not even myself."

She buried her face in her hands, and for a moment Cody thought she was crying. But then her head jerked back, and she dropped her hands into her lap. When she spoke again, her voice was quiet but strong.

"We had nothing. We were nothing. Nothing but the gambler's daughters. Johnny loved us, but he didn't know how to care for us. All my life I've felt like I was on the outside looking in. We never belonged . . . my sisters and I . . . except to each other. We were judged and found lacking so many times by so many people that I grew up believing it. And by the time I was old enough to know that the fault was theirs and not ours, it was too late. Oh, God, Cody! Don't you understand? I don't know how to trust, because I don't know how to love."

Her heartbroken cry brought him upright, but it was not in time to catch her flight. She was off his bed and out of his room before his feet hit the floor. And by the time he thought about following her to her room, he realized the futility of it all. She'd just told him all there was to be said. It was now up to him to decide if she was worth fighting for, because he didn't think she would walk across that imaginary line in her head on her own and fight for him and the chance for love.

It didn't take him long to make a decision. But soldiers had a way of knowing the thing that had to be done to survive. And Cody Bonner was a survivor. He'd already proved that, to himself as well as everyone else.

He went back to his bed and lay down, staring up at the ceiling with single-minded intent until the ache in his body finally subsided and exhaustion claimed him.

8

Cody soon realized that the easy camaraderie between him and Queen was gone. The relationship that had taken months to develop had been destroyed in the space of a night. Only with the boys was she still the same. For Cody she was, once again, the woman he'd dragged from beneath his truck on the day that they'd met. When they spoke to each other it was in single sentences and answered with monosyllables. Whenever they could they dodged each other and made weak excuses to the boys and to themselves as to why being alone together was no longer an option.

But it didn't change the past. Neither could forget the memory of that night and how close they'd come to stepping across that invisible line. Of how easy it would have been to lie down in each other's arms and forget, if only for a while, that there were nightmares within each of them that wouldn't turn loose.

Cody's hell was one born of a single incident in his

life. Queen's hell had been created from a lifetime of incidents. She wouldn't let go, and he didn't know how to make her. And so they hung, halfway between love and loss, and wished that life had been kinder to them both.

When the day came for new beginnings, it was not for Cody or Queen, but for the boys: their first day of school in a new environment.

Queen wasn't the only one who was dreading the change. Will and J.J. had dogged her every step all morning and looked ready to claim sickness with little provocation.

And then it was time to go, and there was no time left for procrastination.

"Are you going to be lonesome while we're gone?"

J.J.'s plaintive question pierced the silence in the hallway as the boys got ready to leave. Queen heard more in the question than nervous excitement about a new school. J.J. was afraid she wouldn't be here when he came home.

Queen smiled and knelt as she helped him button his jacket. "I might, just at first," she said. "But I'll stay busy and the time will pass, and before I know it, you guys will come running up the driveway from the school bus, yelling for something to eat. Right?"

He grinned. "Right."

She stood, brushed at the wayward lock of hair that wouldn't stay out of his eyes, and knew that he'd gotten her message.

Will slipped up beside her, as always, a quiet shadow of the other two boys and their ebullient personalities.

"Will, do you have your lunch money?" She caressed the soft skin on the side of his cheek.

He nodded, his eyes beseeching her to comfort him.

"It will be okay," she said. "You and J.J. are going to the same school, remember?"

He nodded again and then slid an arm around her waist and quietly leaned against her. His head came to just above her belt buckle, and she felt his reluctant sigh through the fabric of her shirt.

Queen hugged him gently, then turned him loose. It would have been too easy to never let him go. "I'll make brownies," she offered.

Will smiled. And because it was rare, it was all the more precious.

"They'll be fine," Donny said. "We all ride the same bus. And my school is just across campus. If they have a problem, I can be right there."

His words came as no surprise to Queen. Cody's oldest son was already quite a man in his own right, even if he was only thirteen. He surprised himself as well as Queen when he dropped his backpack and gave her a big, impulsive hug.

"But it's good to know that when I can't handle everything"—he grinned to make his point, a silent reminder of the day in Snow Gap when she'd come to their aid—"you'll be around. Right, Queenie?"

She made a face and pulled his nose. He knew she hated being called Queenie. He also knew she'd never tell them stop. "Right. Now hit the road, guys. Your dad is waiting. Thanks to him, you get a ride this morning, but you'll come home on the school bus this evening. Have a good day. Make lots of friends. And remember, come home hungry. Brownies . . . and me . . . will be waiting."

"Yeah!"

The trio's sentiments echoed in her ears long after they were gone. She walked to the window and watched them barrel toward Cody, who was waiting patiently by his Blazer. In minutes they were buckled up, with Cody behind the wheel. Once she thought she saw him look toward the house, then convinced herself that she'd imagined it as he backed up and drove away.

Queen turned and stared at the rooms. The house was silent. Listening. Waiting. Just like her.

But it felt different from their house in Cradle Creek had when she'd been the only Houston left. That house had been waiting to die. This house was full of life. For the moment, it was only resting.

Queen took a deep breath, refusing to dwell on the uneasy state in which she and Cody existed, and headed for the stairs. She had a list of chores a mile long that had been waiting for a day like this. There were closets to clean, windows to wash, and, later, brownies to be baked. No time to dwell on the fact that she was already lonely and more than a little isolated from civilization.

Cody parked on the main street after circling the block twice. He was surprised by the number of four-by-fours and Jeeps in Snow Gap, then remembered what Sheriff Miller had said weeks ago about ski trails and tourists. Although it had yet to snow, it looked as if the season had begun.

He got out of his Blazer, zipped his coat against the sharp chill of the early morning air, and checked twice to make certain that he'd locked the doors and that the keys were safely in the pocket of his new down jacket.

Even though he was no longer a stranger in town and would not be mistaken twice for a thief, he'd learned his lesson about unlocked vehicles and parked cars.

"Hey, Mr. Bonner! Yoo hoo!"

He turned and saw the lady who owned the crafts store across the street waving at him. Wondering what she could possibly want with him, he headed toward her shop.

"I'm glad I saw you," she said, stepping aside to let him inside. "Brr, but it's chilly today. Come in, please."

Cody did as she asked and then waited for her to tell him why she'd called. She dug beneath the counter as she continued to ramble, somehow assuming he would know what she was talking about.

"I have Queen's order. It came in yesterday. And since it's already paid for, I thought you might like to go ahead and take it home with you. She's been waiting patiently for it for weeks." She thrust a rather bulky package in his arms. "Tell her I'm sorry it took me so long to get it. But she was so insistent on this color, and I didn't have it in stock. I had no choice but to order it, you see."

She smiled, darted around him, and opened the door, then stood aside, waiting for him to leave as abruptly as he'd arrived.

Cody complied and found himself back outside in the brisk breeze, package in arms, wondering what could possibly be under the thick brown wrapping; then he shrugged. If it was so important to Queen that it had to be special ordered, then the least he could do was see that she got it as it had arrived—wrapped.

He told himself he'd know soon enough what was inside and headed across the street to lock it in the car. There were a couple of errands he needed to attend to before he returned home. And the longer he took to finish them, the better off both he and Queen would be. There weren't too many places to hide in his own home, and being alone with her every day while the boys were at school was going to be pure hell.

The front door slammed. Queen looked up, surprised by the noise, and then glanced at the clock on the mantel. It was almost noon. Where had the morning gone? She looked down at the meager assortment of pictures scattered about on the coffee table and knew where it had gone. It had been in Cradle Creek, along with Queen's memory. And then Cody came in.

"You bought a new coat!" she said.

Cody nodded and handed her the package. "Mrs. What's-her-face from the crafts shop sent this to you."

Queen smiled in spite of her determination to keep Cody at arm's length. "Her name is Mrs. Eller."

"Whatever," Cody said, and hung his coat in the closet. When he turned back, he expected to see Queen tearing into the package, but she'd simply set it aside. He sighed. She hadn't offered to share her secret, and he didn't know how to ask. He noticed the pictures arrayed across the table and slipped onto the couch beside her before she could argue. Then he started a conversation before she could move.

"What are these?" he asked, picking one up. It was a snapshot of three women standing side by side beneath a tree.

He recognized Queen by the auburn cast to her thick, loose curls, evident even beneath the shade of the tree. Next to her was a tall blonde and then a dark-headed woman with similar features to the blond one.

"Pictures of my family," she said. "I found them when I was cleaning closets. I'd forgotten I'd tossed them in the bottom of my bag when I left Cradle Creek."

"You're all so beautiful," he said softly, and turned from the picture to her and then back again. "Different . . . but beautiful."

Queen held his words to her heart but did not comment other than to add, "We all have Johnny's eyes."

Cody's gaze caught hers. Time paused, and then Cody was the first to look away. "Emerald green when you're mad as hell, spring green when you're happy," he said.

Queen nearly gasped at the tenderness of his voice and took the picture from his hands, thinking it would stop this intimate interchange. She put it down on the table, only to watch him grin and pick up another.

It was old and bent at each corner, as if it had once been mounted in an album. A man and three children caught in time by the click of a shutter and the blink of an eye. "You have your father's smile, too." His eyes lingered on the curve of her mouth as he added, "When you bother to use it."

"I didn't fix lunch. I wasn't sure if you'd be back," Queen said abruptly.

Cody looked back down at the picture. She always seemed to live with a fear of revealing emotions. Later he would wonder how he'd had the guts to do it. But when it happened, it was so natural, it would have been impossible to stop.

In the space of a heartbeat he leaned forward and stopped the apology on her lips with his before she could say anything else. As first kisses went, it was frightening. No one ever expects lightning to strike at the first touch. No one ever warns about hearts stopping and bones feeling as if they're melting. But lightning did strike, and it didn't go away.

Cody's sanity fell by the wayside, and his lips

demanded, turning hard, along with other parts of his body that had no business getting into the act. The kiss was but a taste of the heat that burned between them.

Queen's mouth opened instinctively, and then, when it would have closed the same way, the insistence of his lips made her cease and desist and simply wait for whatever would come. And it did.

His mouth, firm and cool from the brisk outdoors, moved across her lips, which were soft and warm to match what was heating inside her heart. A small moan slid from him to her with little effort as her tongue moved across his lower lip in a tentative but taunting foray.

She shuddered. She hadn't meant to do that . . . to taste him so intimately. But it happened before she thought. Fear became a living thing as sanity intruded into the act. And both knew that it would take little tinder to start something neither could control.

They stopped as if on cue, both releasing contact and moving back in unison. Her eyes were wide with surprise, and his were the color of stormclouds. He ached. She trembled.

Queen saw the moisture still shimmering on his lower lip and knew that it had come from her. She wanted to look away but found herself impaled by a look she was too cowardly to decipher.

"Please," he finally whispered, "learn to trust me. I need you, lady, but I won't push. And I promise I won't let you down."

He got up from the couch and left the room without looking back. Seconds later Queen heard the front door open and shut. Her heart skipped a beat. Had she angered him so much by remaining silent that he was walking out on her? But her question was answered moments later when she heard the door reopen and heard him call out as he headed for the kitchen.

"I brought pizza," he called. "No anchovies. No black olives. Hurry up! I'm hungry as hell."

Her legs moved of their own accord. She was too overwhelmed by what had just occurred to realize that once again Cody had changed the menu of their relationship. She was about to get a demonstration in how one went from passion to pizza in one easy lesson.

She would have smiled. But it might have stayed on her face too long and given someone the wrong idea. Instead she simply followed his lead, played cool when she was nearly at meltdown point, and fixed them something to drink.

Less than a month into the new school year, it snowed. A light dusting that didn't entirely cover the ground. But it was enough to send spasms of joy throughout the Bonner household. For kids who'd spent most of their life in Florida, snow was a rare thing to see.

For Queen it was like a whitewash over old wounds. A fresh beginning for her as well.

"Can we stay home?" Donny asked during breakfast.

Cody laughed. "Not on your life, buster. School first, play later. Besides, by what I hear from Abel Miller, you'll get more than a bellyful of snow before it's over."

Cody and the sheriff had become good friends and had even gone hunting together once, using the afternoon excursion as an excuse to traipse over his heavily wooded property with someone who'd keep him from getting lost. They hadn't even taken their guns off of safety, but they'd traded enough stories and theories to know that they were two of a kind.

Donny grinned at his father's answer as he and his brothers left the kitchen to get their coats and backpacks. He knew it had been a stupid question, but being the kid that he was, he had felt compelled to ask.

"Had to give it the old Bonner try," he said, and laughed and ducked when his father swung at him with a sofa pillow.

Excited by the advent of snow and the fact that their father had tossed the first blow, the other two boys promptly joined in, pillows swinging, shrieks bouncing off the walls in the rooms below.

Queen stood at the head of the stairs and looked down at the melée of male arms and legs and the bodies rolling wildly around on the living room floor, and she wished she had the guts to join in.

Even Will had cut loose and was giggling hysterically as he tried unsuccessfully to unwind himself from beneath the pile-up.

"It's almost time for the bus," Queen said, and then ducked when a pillow came flying up the stairs at her, striking her in the belly. She looked down in shock and saw Cody brushing at his hair and clothes in an effort to remove the bits of foam and feathers that had escaped the pillows.

"Sorry," he said, grinning, "it was a misguided missile."

"Oh, sure." She tossed the pillow back onto the sofa and gave him a sarcastic look, then went down the stairs and started pulling coats from hooks and assembling books and bags.

"Tuck in your shirts and comb your hair," she said, eyeing the boys' disheveled state.

"Yes, ma'am," they all said in unison.

Queen tried not to grin at the fact that Cody was playing along, acting the child by complying with her order along with his sons.

In a flurry of giggles and belated pokes and punches, the boys ran out the door. Cody watched them flying down the driveway as the roof of the big yellow school bus topped the hill below his house.

"They'll just about make it," he said, and then turned and stared at Queen, who was leaning against the door with a faraway look on her face. He cupped her face with shaky hands and wiggled her chin to get her attention. "Where were you, lady?"

She looked up at him in confusion.

"Just then, where did you go? Don't tell me nowhere, because I saw you leave."

She stepped out of his arms and looked away, trying to think of a safe way to answer. With him, there was none.

Cody saw her shudder. "Queen?" Concern deepened his voice.

"They're so lucky," she said.

"What do you mean?"

She stared down at the floor, absently noting that feathers had collected in the small crack against the baseboard. Time and silence hung between them, and still he waited. She knew she should have expected it. Cody Bonner wasn't the kind to give up.

Something inside her cracked, and then broke, and she felt an anchor around her heart tug and turn loose. She straightened, tilted her head, and looked directly into his eyes.

"Meaning . . . they're lucky because they have you," she said, and walked away.

Yes, and you could, too, if you'd give it half a chance, Cody thought. But he didn't have to say it. It was obvious that she already knew.

Enough snow had accumulated by the weekend for the boys to play in it. Drawn by the pristine whiteness of the powdery fall and their pleas, Queen found herself in the middle of it all, dusted with remnants from snowballs, numb from the wet and the cold, and having the time of her life.

She would wonder later if coming to Colorado had somehow shifted her center of gravity. It seemed that on Cody's mountain she was doomed to be flat on her back whenever meeting a man.

The boys were in the middle of a snowball battle and had disappeared to the backyard and the thicker cover of trees behind which to hide. Queen was in the midst of making her fourth snow angel when the shadow crossed her face.

She looked up, imagined that she saw a man in uniform silhouetted against the brilliant sky, and blinked rapidly, trying to clear her vision enough to see if she was hallucinating. Then she heard his voice and knew he was real, and she thanked God that at least this time she hadn't been beneath a truck leaking oil.

She tried unsuccessfully to crawl out of her angel without ruining the shape. "Good Lord," she muttered as a large glob of snow slid down her boot.

"Need a hand?" he asked.

Queen heard the laughter in his voice and knew it was long past the time for graceful exits from her situation.

"I'd appreciate it," she said, and extended her arm.

She was propelled up and out with speedy finesse and no further damage to her art. Embarrassed by her predicament, she began brushing vigorously at the snow on her clothes and hair.

"I came to see Colonel Bonner, but I think I'd like to change my destination. If you have an opening on the next flight to heaven, I'm your man."

Queen's mouth dropped. His audacious statement and the reference to her angels were too much to ignore. She laughed long and loud, and that sound was what drew Cody out onto the deck.

When he saw Queen with the man below, he couldn't think and couldn't move. All he could do was stare in astonishment. Queen had done something with a total stranger that it had taken her weeks to do with him: she was laughing . . . and at a level that could almost be called bubbling. He vacillated between shock and jealousy, and jealousy won out.

Then the man with Queen turned and looked up, and the smile on his face broke even wider.

Cody sighed. He should have known.

"Macon, you asshole, get out of my yard and quit bothering my lady."

Queen looked up into Cody's eyes and felt the world spin beneath her feet. A flush suffused her face. Cody had just laid claim to something neither of them had even admitted to themselves, let alone to someone else. She stood there, unable to move, while the tall officer stomped up the steps into Cody's rough embrace of welcome.

It took Queen some time to assemble herself and her thoughts. By the time she'd made it to the back door, dumped her wet clothes and shoes, and scurried up the back stairs, the men had gone from greetings to guffaws and she knew it was too late to undo what Cody had done. Not that she wanted to, it was just that she felt obligated to tell someone besides Cody that she was *not* his lady.

She slipped into clean, dry sweats, relishing their warmth, and after a glance in the mirror over her dresser made a beeline for the living room. She stopped just outside the door, smoothing her hair and adjusting her sweatshirt before making her entrance. Then Cody saw her and ruined it before she had time to proceed.

"Queen, I'm glad you're here. There's someone I want you to meet."

"I was just coming to see if there was anything you wanted, Mr. Bonner."

Cody grinned. "Can the 'Mr.' stuff, honey. This is an old friend. You don't have to be formal with him."

Queen glared. She'd been trying to be formal with Cody, not the friend. She was still irked by the way he'd laid public claim to her in front of the man, and he was ruining it again by treating her like a member of the family and calling her "honey."

Then she stopped herself, wondering what in the world was making her so angry. Wasn't this what she'd wanted all along? To be considered a member of the family? Then what in the world was she so worked up about? She threw back her shoulders and tilted her chin in a defiant gesture, determined to regain her footing within this mess.

Cody's eyes narrowed, and the smile died on his face. She looked as if she were about to go to war. He already knew that what he'd said had shocked the hell out of her. He'd seen that much before he'd taken Dennis Macon inside with him. He wondered if he was about to get his comeuppance . . . and if he would survive it.

Queen walked into the room, her hand extended. "We've already met . . . sort of," she said, and gave both men a dazzling smile.

Cody forgot what he'd been going to say.

"As I was about to say before we were so rudely interrupted," Dennis Macon said, wiggling his eyebrows at Queen to make his point, "I'm Lieutenant Colonel Dennis Macon, late of Eglin Air Force Base, Florida, and as of two days ago stationed at Lowry Air Force Base, Denver, Colorado."

"That's where Cody goes," Queen said, and then caught herself, uncertain whether or not Cody had admitted to his friend that he'd made visits to the base psychiatrist.

"Yeah," Dennis said, and punched Cody lightly on the shoulder, "so he was telling me."

Then she remembered she hadn't identified herself, and it was obvious that Cody was not going to do it properly. His lady indeed!

"I'm Queen Houston . . . Cody's housekeeper," she said, and extended her hand.

The look on her face and the glint in her eye dared either man to make jest of the fact or deny it. Cody knew better, and it didn't take Dennis Macon long to get the message, either.

"Pleased to meet you, angel," he said. "Very pleased indeed." And I wish to hell I'd seen you first, he thought.

Cody frowned. Angel!

"Queenie! Queenie! Donny's nose is bleeding!"

Will's frantic shout brought everyone running into the kitchen. It didn't take long for her to establish that the bloody nose wasn't life-threatening, but that it had come from the direct hit of an icy snowball.

"No more snowballs," Queen ordered, propelling

Donny backward onto a kitchen chair. "At least not until the snow is fresher. It's getting too icy. Someone will get a black eye next time . . . right, Cody?"

The nervous plea in her voice was all Cody needed to hear. No matter how casually he or the boys would view a black eye, Queen seemed horrified by the thought. He backed her up and saw her sigh with relief as she pressed an icebag against Donny's nose. She combed her fingers through the boy's hair in a gentle motion, pushing it away from his eyes and out of the oozing blood.

"You need a haircut, mister," she said, using the excuse to touch him when what she wanted to do was sit down and cry at the sight of all that blood and his swiftly swelling nose and lip.

This was much worse than the little scrapes they'd had when playing ball. Even though she kept telling herself that boys would be boys, it didn't help, especially when she saw tears in the corners of his eyes.

Cody handed her a fresh compress and then sent the other two boys upstairs to change into dry clothes while they dealt with his eldest's latest bump of life. He watched Queen's tender ministrations toward Donny and tried not to envy the attention his son was receiving.

She was not only his lady and the best damned housekeeper he'd ever had, she was also quite a mother. He wondered how his boys would react to her care on a permanent basis and thought he already knew the answer. When Donny had gotten hurt, hers had been the name that they'd called.

Dennis observed with interest their not-so-casual glances and their careful-not-to-touch-each-other moves. He sighed and gave up whatever wayward thoughts he'd been having about the pretty redhead before they became too painful to ignore. It was as obvious as hell that she was already taken. What was also obvious was that she had yet to admit it—to herself or anyone else.

9

The snowfall during the night had been heavy, but sometime between the midnight and early morning hours it had stopped. The trail of footprints leading from the rural, unpaved, snow-packed road was impossible to ignore, as was the fact that for the first time in thirty-one years, Patrick Mooney, the man who carried the mail to the outlying areas of Snow Gap, had failed to show up for work and wasn't answering his phone.

It hadn't taken long for his concerned co-workers to make a report that sent Sheriff Miller toward the Mooney home, which lay nestled just above the foothills of the mountains around Snow Gap.

Abel Miller didn't expect a problem other than the fact that he could very possibly get himself stuck in a snowdrift. He'd been roused and sent on the call before the road crews would have had time to get on the job.

He gunned his four-by-four up a gentle incline and

then found himself having to pull over to let Snow Gap's school bus pass on its morning route. He grinned and waved as he recognized several familiar faces, including those of the Bonner boys, who were sitting at the back of the bus. He now had a passable set of ruts in which he could drive, thanks to the bus's wide dual wheels.

Abel pulled into Mooney's driveway and then turned and waved as another vehicle passed and honked. He recognized Cody Bonner and tipped his hat as he climbed out of his police vehicle.

"You're out early!" he yelled as Cody drove by. "Did you miss the bus?" He laughed loudly at his own joke when Cody grinned and waved before driving on.

It was Abel's opinion that Bonner was a good man with a lot on his plate. These days it was hard enough to raise a family, even with a complete set of parents. Doing it alone would be doubly difficult. Then he remembered the pretty sister who wasn't really a sister and figured there was a lot more between them than the welfare of three boys.

He turned back to the business at hand and started toward the house. The first inkling of trouble hit when he saw the door slightly ajar and a double set of footprints—one set going in, the other leading out of the house.

He walked onto the porch and then stood for a moment and looked around at the flat area around Mooney's house. Though the footprints had come from the road, they went away from the house into the forest in the distance.

"What in hell?" he asked aloud as he walked toward the open door. "Surely old Pat didn't have some kind of spell and just wander off?" He pushed the door open a little farther and leaned inside. "Hey, Pat. It's me, Abel. You in there?"

No one answered, and a sick feeling began twisting at the pit of his stomach. He walked inside and then stopped short and quickly pulled his service revolver as adrenaline kicked in. He started a silent sweep of the scene and had a sudden suspicion that he might wish he'd skipped breakfast before he made this call.

Abel Miller had seen a lot of things in his fifteen years on the force, but the last time he'd seen anything this bad had been in a village in a Laotian jungle just after a bombing.

Furniture was overturned. Pictures were knocked off the walls. Phones had been yanked from their jacks, and half-opened packages of foodstuffs littered the floor. The plaque that Patrick had received for twenty-five years of on-the-job excellence with the postal service was broken and lying in the fireplace.

Abel cursed beneath his breath and accidentally kicked an unopened can of tuna lying beside the wall as he started toward the back of the house. But he didn't have to go far to find out why Patrick had been late for work. What was left of Patrick Mooney lay in a pool of blood half-in and half-out of the doorway to his bedroom. His head rested at a crazy angle to the rest of his body, and it was obvious that whoever had done this had been sick as hell and in a blinding rage.

"Damn it, old buddy, it was a bad way to go," Abel said as he knelt and gently touched the bare flesh above the victim's wrist. It was cold and rigid, and Abel knew it was going to be hard to get a good fix on time of death, because the cold air had probably interfered with the body's natural rate of morbidity.

He stood abruptly and walked out of the house much

faster than he'd come in, heading for the radio in his unit. It didn't take long to say what had to be said. Now all he could do was wait for the coroner and the boys from the crime lab.

Minutes later the mobile phone in his police car rang and he grabbed it, surprised by the sound.

"Hello?"

It was his dispatcher. "Sheriff . . . I think you need to hear what just came in over the fax."

"Can't it wait until I get back to the office?" Abel asked, trying to block out the image of Patrick's body from his mind as he swallowed the bile at the back of his throat. "And why the hell are you calling me on the phone? Why didn't you just use the radio?"

"Because of the scanners all the big ears out there probably have on," the dispatcher said. He was referring to the way the locals liked to tune their scanners to the police band so they could monitor the activity in their area without leaving the comfort of their homes to snoop. "I don't think you'll be wanting this to be broadcast . . . and it may have something to do with what you just found."

Abel inhaled sharply. "Let 'er rip, then."

The dispatcher began to read verbatim the fax that he'd just pulled off the wire.

"Virgil Stratton, white male, fifty-four years of age, six feet three inches, two hundred and forty pounds. Brown eyes, gray hair, and balding. Identifying marks: spider tattoo on his left cheek below his eye. Escaped from Denver while en route to another holding facility at fourteen hundred hours yesterday. Believed to be traveling south. Survivalist background. Must be considered armed and dangerous and believed to be traveling toward area in which he was raised."

"Oh, Lord," Abel said, and rested his forehead against the steering wheel while he contemplated this news. "Where did this Stratton grow up?"

"A little community up in the mountains called Nugget that no longer exists. It was once an old gold mining town, and it was played out in the late sixties." The dispatcher drew a breath before continuing. "Sheriff, I checked. Nugget was somewhere in the mountains between Denver and Snow Gap. I think we've got a problem."

"Okay! Then alert the proper authorities to the possibility that Stratton might be in this area, and get me some more men up here fast. We've got us a killer on the loose, that's already a fact. If it's this Stratton, then we've got ourselves another problem. If he knows the area and is a trained survivalist, it'll be hell pulling him out of these mountains in this goddamned snow."

"Yes, sir," the dispatcher said.

"And keep this quiet about Mooney. The last thing I need is a bunch of gawkers up here messing with my crime scene."

"Yes, sir."

"But . . . we've got no choice about issuing a bulletin that a killer is in the vicinity, whether it's Stratton or someone else. Get on the horn and contact the proper people. I don't want to have to investigate any more crime scenes like this one, you hear me?"

"Yes, sir!"

The line went dead, and Abel sighed. In his business it didn't take long to ruin a good day. He crawled out of his vehicle and headed for the tracks that he now knew belonged to the killer.

That the footprints still existed told Abel Miller that Patrick had died after the snowfall had ceased. The imprints left in the snow were still clean and sharp around the edges, although they'd already started to deteriorate from the wind and the glare of early morning sun. He stared into the tree line and then shuddered.

Cody grunted as he continued to shovel the last of the snow from the steps and then made his way across the yard, creating a small path to his Blazer in the process.

He'd become adept at traveling on snow-packed roads but had accepted the advice of locals and purchased a set of chains for his tires so that he would have less chance of being stranded during his periodic trips back and forth to Lowry Air Force Base.

Just thinking about the trips made him feel guilty. He knew that Queen was under the assumption that he was still seeing the base psychiatrist, although he'd been released some time ago. In actual fact, he'd been working on a project Dennis Macon had proposed weeks ago, on the day of his visit.

He had yet to accept the offer of heading the project, but the temptation to do so increased daily. Being in charge of the operation, and one so close to his home, was highly appealing. But he could not in all conscience give his word that he'd do it without the knowledge that his family would be well cared for, and that rested entirely on whether or not Queen Houston stayed. He was afraid to broach the subject, certain that it would only be adding yet another layer of responsibility on a woman who deserved better.

His shovel hit ice, jarring his shoulder, making him curse lightly as he repositioned and then scooped up another load of snow.

He figured that any way he turned he would be doing her an injustice. He lost sleep just thinking about making love to her and then lost more sleep thinking of the consequences of the act. How could he ask a woman to love him and commit herself to raising his sons when this was the kind of responsibility she had been running from?

Granted, the chemistry between them was explosive. There was no mistaking the ache in his body and the want in her eyes. He'd been around long enough to recognize lust when he saw it. And the difference in their ages bothered him. There was a big gap between forty-two and twenty-nine.

At this point, asking her to give up the rest of her life when she had yet to experience the first of it was more than he could bring himself to do. So he procrastinated and time passed as the trips to Denver continued.

He shoveled a path up to the door of the Blazer, then dropped against it with a weary sigh, resting while his legs quit shaking and his lungs quit burning. The early morning sun was so bright that the cold had been deceptive and he'd shoveled at too fast a pace.

He looked up, gauging the contents of the sky, and then decided that even if another front blew in, it wouldn't come before evening. That gave him time to still get to Denver and back before dark. He pushed himself away from the truck and walked back to the house using the narrow path he'd just dug.

Queen saw him coming and hurried away from the window, unwilling for him to know that she'd been watching him work. The power of his body was evident by the deep bites his shovel took in the snow and the speed with which he'd worked. Yet she feared that he wasn't hurrying for any reason other than the fact that he'd be leaving again. She'd come to recognize the signs before he ever announced his intentions and had convinced herself that she was partially to blame.

She'd already decided that he didn't like to be alone with her in the house. And after Dennis Macon's unexpected visit, she'd decided that he was sorry he'd taken early retirement from the service, that he missed flying and the camaraderie of his fellow officers.

Talking out what was going on would have saved both of them a lot of needless worry. But they hadn't, and judging from the way the subject was avoided altogether, it was unlikely to happen.

Cody stopped at the front door to clean his boots, carefully sweeping snow from the sides and tops before coming into the house. Queen had the hardwood floors gleaming with a mixture of oil and polish, and he had no desire to ruin her hard work.

She came into the hallway as he shut the door behind him, and she couldn't help staring at him in all his male glory. His hair was so black that it shined, his eyes so blue they burned, and he had an expression on his face that she'd come to dread. It was anticipation, and he got it every time he was planning to leave.

"Leaving so soon?" she asked, and then felt her stomach tilt at the guilty expression that swept across his features.

"I thought I'd run up to the base for the day. I might see Dennis. He called last night, remember?"

His gut wrenched. The look on her face made him sick. It was somewhere between accusation and acceptance. It made him mad as hell that she suspected he wasn't telling her everything. He shouldn't have to explain; after all, it was his damned life. And it hurt him like hell to think that she would stand there and take whatever he dished out without questioning or fighting. He had no idea that Queen Houston had fought her entire life for the right to simply exist. Asking for more had been beyond her ability.

So she stood and waited, letting him talk, unwilling to aid him in the lie she felt coming. She'd heard Johnny's lies all her life and told herself that this was just another man doing the same, that it shouldn't hurt. But it did, and she tried not to think of why it mattered.

She didn't want to love this big, dark-haired man and all that went with him. But she was afraid that it was already too late for what she wanted. Facts were facts, and what was in her heart was impossible to deny.

"Weatherman says more snow is coming," she said. "Be careful." With that she turned and walked out of the hall, leaving him standing in a puddle of melting snow with a knot of guilt growing in his belly.

He wiped his feet across the mat, then bolted after her, unwilling to leave on an awkward note. He caught her at the door to the kitchen.

"Do you want me to bring anything back with me? If you need something special . . . anything . . . I'll get it and damn the embarrassment."

She smiled at his offer, remembering months earlier when she'd given him a list of personal items he'd sent her to get instead. "No, I'm fine," she said. "There's nothing I need."

He grabbed her by the arm and pulled her toward him. She felt trapped in the intense stare of his eyes.

"But is there anything you want? All you have to do is ask and you'll have it."

Queen caught her breath and would have looked away, but breaking away from his gaze was impossible.

She'd heard the hidden message behind his question, she just didn't know if she had the guts to answer him truthfully.

She bit her lower lip and took a slow, deep breath. "Wanting and having are two different things, Cody. I learned long ago to never want what I couldn't have."

"Who says you can't have it, lady? I don't hear anyone around here telling you no. In fact, if memory serves, you're the one with the negative attitude. Am I right?" His voice had risen with each accusation until he was almost shouting.

"Oh, God, just let it be," she said, and buried her face in her hands. "You don't understand. I can't be casual about things like this. I can't just go with my feelings and then pick up what's left of them later and move on. I don't live on urges and promises."

"Neither do I, honey." Sorry that he'd lost his temper, he pulled her into his arms. "Neither do I. I just don't know how the hell to prove it to you."

With that he hugged her gently, kissed the top of her head, and walked out of the room.

"I'll be home before dark," he called back. "Take care."

He went upstairs to change. Minutes later he was gone as he followed the school bus down the mountain to Snow Gap and beyond, leaving Queen with nothing but her own fears.

The day felt crooked to Cody . . . somehow off center. From the moment he'd left with the argument hanging heavily between them to now, as he drove through the heavy-falling snow, he knew he should have stayed. He'd tried to get back to Snow Gap before school was out and had even been too late for that. His intention to catch the boys and save them the long bus ride home was futile, as traffic was beginning to pile up because of the snowstorm.

His radio was a mass of static and squawks, and he absently punched the seek button, hoping it would tune in on a station clear enough to hear, but in these mountains, in this weather, it would be unlikely. And then a station came in just in time for him to hear the last bits of the broadcasted bulletin.

" . . . must be considered armed and highly dangerous."

He frowned as the announcer finished and for a moment felt anxious that he hadn't heard it all. Then he reminded himself that there was never anything broadcast but bad news and promptly tuned it out, certain that it could not possibly pertain to anything concerning him or his.

By his calculations, he figured he had about eight miles of snow-packed road left to negotiate before he reached his driveway, and he thanked God for the friend who'd advised getting chains. They made all the difference.

As he negotiated a curve in the road, he was surprised to see the road ditch lined with emergency vehicles as well as several police cars. He frowned, fearing that someone must have had an accident.

Patrick Mooney's yard was full of cars and trucks, and Cody suspected that they'd used it as a central turning place to remove the victims. An officer stepped out from between two vehicles at the side of the road and waved him down.

"What happened?" Cody asked. "Did someone have an accident?"

"May I see some identification?" the officer asked.

Cody began digging his wallet from his pocket when Abel Miller walked up.

"It's okay," Sheriff Miller said, waving the deputy away. "I know this guy. He's shady, but I think we can let him pass."

Cody grinned, but something told him that the smile Abel gave him was forced and that something was terribly wrong.

"What's going on, Abel? Someone have an accident?"

"Not exactly," Abel said, and then scratched his chin, wishing he'd taken time to shave this morning. His whiskers itched like hell. "Patrick Mooney was murdered sometime early this morning. We have reason to believe that the perpetrator might be an escaped convict out of Denver. The guy's a wacko. One of those survivalist nuts."

Cody's belly lurched. He looked down at his watch, calculating the time it would take before his boys got home, and thought of Queen all alone in the house. "I've got to be going," he said. "I want to get home before dark."

Abel nodded. "We've been broadcasting warnings all day. I think everyone in the area knows what's going on and has taken the proper precautions . . . but you can't be too sure about something like this. I'd like to think the sonofabitch is on his way straight up the mountains and out of everyone's way."

Cody slammed the Blazer into gear and drove away, barely giving the sheriff time to step out of the way. Suddenly the instinct he'd been ignoring all day began to renew itself tenfold.

"Please, God, let her be all right," he said aloud. "Please let her be all right."

He turned on the windshield wipers, increased his speed past the point of safety, and focused on the road through the snowfall. The dry, squeaky swipe of the wiper blades against frozen glass and falling snow were a taunting and repetitive reminder that he might be too late . . . too late . . . too late . . . too late . . .

When Cody drove away, Queen was left with a sense of foreboding, which she promptly told herself was nothing but her unhappiness over the fact that she couldn't bring herself to take a chance. To simply let go of her childhood fears and just love the man . . . to let whatever would come, come.

By early afternoon the snowfall had resumed to the point where it was often difficult to see past the front decking. She paced the house, going from busywork to doing nothing but standing silently at the windows and staring down the long empty driveway, hoping that the boys would make it home safely and that Cody would be right behind.

She kept telling herself she was being silly, that she was only feeling isolated because of the snow. But in her heart she knew that wasn't it. If she'd been home, her sisters would be laughing at her as they often did when Queen got one of her notions. Suddenly she wished for the sound of their voices teasing her into a different state of mind.

Television was not an option. The reception was bad, even on a clear day. In weather like this it was awful. Cody had promised for weeks to look into buying a satellite dish, but he'd let it slide, and installing one in this kind of weather would have been nearly impossible.

She turned on the radio in the kitchen and then

promptly walked away, leaving it playing low enough to be nothing but background noise. She was not in the mood for songs about failed love affairs and no-good men. But the feeling of dread increased as the snow continued to fall.

Thoughts of the boys who would be coming home prompted her to go to the kitchen, where she soon lost herself in the act of baking cookies. For a time she forgot her nervous concerns until the sound of running footsteps on the front porch interrupted her work. She looked at the clock and knew that it was too early for the boys. It could only mean that Cody was home.

"Thank God!" she muttered, dusting the flour off her hands as she hurried toward the front door.

The smile of welcome died on her face with the force of the blow as the door was kicked inward. It flew back, taking her with it. She hit the floor and slid, her head striking the baseboard with a resounding thump, and knew that it wasn't Cody who'd come inside. She looked up, dazed by the blow to her head and the cold blast of air that followed behind the intruder.

The man loomed over her, a hulking shadow in baggy denim, his face half-hidden by a hooded parka pulled loosely over his head. Ice had frozen on his mustache and beard, and snow still clung to the shoulders of his coat and the cuffs of his pants.

"Aren't you going to ask me in?" he said, and then laughed, a deep, ugly sound that came out like a growl.

Queen screamed, struggling to get to her feet and away from him, then fell back when his boot connected with her belly. The scream died in the back of her throat as she struggled for breath instead. Pain shot upward, and the room turned black, and she wondered if she was on her way to spending eternity with Johnny.

Virgil Stratton hadn't planned on another break-in. But the stupid bastard at that house this morning didn't have half the stuff he needed to get where he was going. He'd gotten clothes and some staples and canned goods, but he needed guns . . . and ammunition.

His eyes narrowed and his mouth pursed so that it made the spider tattoo on his cheek look as if it were crawling. He stared at the tall redhead laid out at his feet and then came to a sudden decision. He reached down and squeezed her breast and then groaned as his groin burned and another kind of hunger began to build.

He'd been in the penitentiary for twelve years. It had been too damned long since the ass he'd had was female. Maybe he'd just take her with him. If they got far enough up the mountains before full winter set in, they'd never find him. By spring he'd be long gone into Canada. He nudged her body with the toe of his boot and then grinned. By spring she'd either be used up or fed up. It didn't matter to him. Either way he would be through with her.

"Ooooh."

Queen's groan was soft, but Virgil didn't miss the sound. He knelt on one knee, wrapped a huge, beefy fist in her hair, and yanked sharply. "Wake up, bitch! I need you to help me pack. We're going on our honeymoon."

His laughter was shrill and raucous, and it was the first thing Queen heard as she swam out of the dark miasma of pain in her head. Her stomach roiled and the bile clogged her throat, but somehow she managed to keep everything, including her panic, down. Sixth sense told her that staying alive meant cooperation. And Queen Houston had an overwhelming need to live.

She opened her eyes, stared up into a face filled with

dissipated evil, and tried not to faint. His hand slid across her body, squeezing and pinching, groping at every curve and indentation. She shoved away and kicked at him.

He laughed. "That's good, bitch," he whispered, yanking her to her feet and thrusting his face into hers. "Fight me. Go ahead and fight me. That's the way old Virgil likes it. Hard and mean."

Queen's eyes were wild, her hands doubled into fists and her legs braced as she stood toe to toe and dared him to make another move.

His eyes narrowed at her defiance, and he had a moment's thought that she might be too much trouble to bother with, that he should just wring her damned neck, get what he needed, and be on his way.

"Just get what you want and get the hell out," Queen said, and knew that she was taking a risk by challenging him in this manner.

He grinned, her words an echo of what he'd just thought, and dumped the idea of killing her. It would be a waste of too much fun.

"What I want," he growled, grabbing her by the hair and yanking her off her feet, "is clothes and guns, some food and a fuck, and not necessarily in that order." He laughed again and pulled.

Tears shot to her eyes as he dragged her down the hall by her hair. But Queen would have died before crying. And then she knew that it could very well happen. This man was so crazy, she could be dead before a teardrop fell.

Within minutes the house was in shambles. He'd confiscated a shotgun from Cody's den and a handgun from a locked drawer in the desk. He'd cursed roundly about the lack of ammunition, other than the rounds already loaded in the guns. No matter how fiercely he threatened, there was no more to be found.

"I told you," Queen said, speaking calmly as if to a child, "I don't know a thing about guns. I'm only the housekeeper."

He backhanded her, slapping the words from her lips, and then snarled in her face, "Then you'll come with me. I need my house kept."

His breath was thick and rancid, and Queen tried not to gag at his innuendo. She closed her eyes against the fear and held her breath, unwilling to inhale any more of his malevolence.

"Open your eyes, bitch. We're ready to travel. Get your coat. When I bed you, I want hot and wet, not a frozen ass."

Queen grabbed her coat as he yanked her out the back door of the kitchen. For the first time in her life she wished she'd never left Cradle Creek. At least there she'd known who and where her enemies were.

The snow came down, soft and constant, blanketing her face and cooling the hot, swollen knot on her jaw, peppering her vision until she had to squinch her eyes to see where they were going.

She looked back once and saw their footsteps disappearing swiftly in the new-falling snow, and knew that even if help came, it would be too late. No one would be able to track them.

She thought of Cody. In that moment she lost her composure and struggled, trying to break away from Virgil Stratton's grasp. But he was too strong, and she lost her footing in the snow and fell. His boot slammed into the side of her ribs, and his curses filled the air.

"Get up, dammit!" he yelled as he pulled her to her feet. "And you by God better stay on your feet, because the next time I find you flat on your back, I'm gonna pump some sense into you—the old-fashioned way."

His ugly threat, accompanied by a high-pitched giggle and his hand angling toward her crotch, told her all she needed to know. There could be no more defiance. Not with him. All she could do now was pray for a miracle and hope that a time would come when she'd have a chance to break and run. Until then, she would have to be patient.

10

Cody's pulse accelerated as the roof of his home came into view. He steered the Blazer through a drift, braked as he swung into the yard, and exited the vehicle before the engine had stopped turning. The path he'd so diligently shoveled that morning was already filled. He looked up toward the house and whispered, "God, please let her be all right."

His heart hammered against his chest as he squinted through the falling snow, trying to tell himself that there would be a good reason for the fact that his front door was ajar. Fear lent strength to his legs and he started to run, staggering only once in the deep snow.

He raced up the steps and across the snow-covered decking, then stopped in midstride at the door to stare in shock at the splintered wood on the side of the facing and the black imprint of a boot centered across his front door. His fingers raked across the stain, as if that touch alone would tell him what happened. He paused only briefly and then bolted inside, to be met by the chaos Virgil Stratton had left behind him.

"Jesus!"

There was nothing else left to say, and from the looks of the place, it was already too late for prayers. Panic set in as he ran through the living room, stumbling over broken furniture, stepping on food that had been scattered throughout, and calling her name.

"Queen! Queen!"

But no one answered, and when Cody began to absorb the meaning of the silence and the condition of the house, he realized that he didn't want to find her at all, because if she was still there, she would be dead.

The kitchen was in shambles. He checked it only briefly before charging throughout the rest of his house, bolting up the stairs, shouting her name in frantic half breaths, searching for something he was afraid to find. Phones had been ripped from the walls, clothes from his closet strewn across the floor.

"You sonofabitch," Cody whispered. "I'll kill you for what you've done to her!" He began to shake from the overdose of adrenaline that had coursed through him.

He took the stairs down in three leaps and stood for a moment in the middle of the hallway, trying to get a sense of what to do next. Cold air funneled from left to right across his face. He shut the front door and then retraced his steps, suddenly aware that he might be able to trace their flight in another way.

A chilly draft still moved across his boot tops. Cody shook off the maybes that were making him crazy and started to search for the knowns. It was an old military trick he should have remembered earlier. Deal only in givens and leave the possibilities to others.

He turned, following the draft to its source, and was surprised to find himself back at the kitchen. He stopped in the doorway and looked around carefully, nearly missing the fact that the kitchen door leading to his backyard was standing slightly ajar.

"Hell!" he muttered, wishing he'd seen it on his first round of searching and not wasted precious time.

He ran outside, stopped at the deck rail and then found what he'd been looking for. A trace of Queen.

There across the space leading into the woods were tracks. And because of the snowfall, they were disappearing swiftly. He was off the deck in seconds and dropped to his knees in the snow, touching the place where Queen had fallen, grabbing a fistful of snow where her knee had dragged, and squeezing it in silent anger until it turned to water and ran through his fingers.

It was obvious by the shape and length between strides that the man who'd taken her was tall and that most of the time Queen was being dragged rather than walking.

Fury overwhelmed him as he accepted the ramifications of what had happened and what could still happen to her. The rage that came with the acceptance was unmistakably that of a man whose boundaries had been crossed and whose mate had been taken.

Cody stared once more at the snow and the tracks and made his decision. He bolted back into the house, into his bedroom once again, praying that what he needed had not been taken or destroyed along with everything else.

It was there! Just as he'd hoped. The cordless phone was still behind the bedside table where he'd knocked it off that morning as he'd reached to shut off the alarm.

The base was still in one piece on the shelf below, somehow missed in the moment of destruction. If only the handset hadn't been off the base too long and lost its power, he might be in luck.

He was.

Swiftly he punched in a number. As he counted the rings, he dug through his closet, grabbing at a duffel bag on the top shelf and then tossing it onto the bed at the same moment that Abel Miller's dispatcher answered the phone. Cody opened the bag and thrust his hand inside until it closed around the semiautomatic pistol and the loaded clip.

"This is Cody Bonner. Tell Sheriff Miller that the man he's looking for, the one who murdered Patrick Mooney, was at my house. Tell him that Queen is missing and the house is a wreck. Tell him to get the hell up here with his search team fast."

The dispatcher's voice seemed disjointed, and several times their connection went bad. But Cody could hear enough to know that while the dispatcher had gotten his message, he was now trying to tell Cody to wait for the sheriff's arrival.

"No time," Cody shouted. "Snow is covering their tracks. If I wait, I'll lose them. Tell Abel to head up the mountain directly behind my house. I'll be ahead of him . . . and hopefully right behind them." He inhaled sharply and closed his eyes for a moment against the hell of what he'd witnessed and what was yet to come. "Please. Tell him to hurry."

With that he disconnected and the dispatcher was left with no alternative but to relay the message and hope that help arrived in time. If not, there might be more than two victims before the night was over. If Virgil Stratton didn't get them, the snowstorm would.

*   *   *

Tears burned Queen's eyes—not from pain, but from the bitter snow stinging and swirling constantly in her face.

She'd long ago lost her bearings in the thick forest of trees. She'd become adept at dodging low-hanging limbs, heavy with the weight of the snowfall, only to find herself walking into smaller bushes whose slender, bare limbs slapped sharply across her face instead.

Her lips were cold and dry, and she licked them gingerly, aware that it would only increase the chaffed condition yet unable to stop herself. A silent moan was all she could manage as the salty taste of blood came away on her tongue.

Twice since they'd left the house Virgil had slammed her against a tree trunk with a short, vicious order not to move, and during that time she'd watched him take out a compass and a small, hand-drawn map.

While he was otherwise occupied, she tried to assess her own surroundings, but she could see nothing beyond ten or twelve feet away. The snow swirled thickly beneath the cover of trees, lifted in tiny vents and updrafts by the wind on the mountain. She struggled with hysteria, knowing that even if she eluded him, she'd probably perish in the storm. She had no earthly idea of where she was, only that she was lost . . . and a very long way from Cody, and from Cradle Creek.

Watching Virgil's careful calculations, she suddenly realized he had a destination in mind and wasn't just wandering aimlessly through the woods in an effort to get away from authorities. That knowledge, coupled with his braggadocio comments and threats, increased her panic. If he reached cover with the dried and canned food that they had, it would be weeks before he would have to surface for more. Knowing that made her even more desperate to escape.

"Come on, bitch, move!" Virgil yelled above the sound of the wind, and grabbed at her coat sleeve.

Queen balked, and in that instant Virgil staggered from the unexpected jolt of her immobile body and fell backward against an overloaded limb. Snow shifted, instantly blinding him by the miniavalanche that fell across his face.

Queen bolted. It was now or never, and dying in the snow was preferable to dying at this man's hands. Her long legs sank deep, struggling as she ran to get out of sight before his vision had time to clear.

The bullet slammed into the tree beside her head. She stopped in midstride, sinking to her knees in weary defeat as he fired one more round to emphasize his point before he started forward.

"Oh, God," she moaned, and covered her face. She hadn't made it, and he'd already warned her what he'd do if she tried such a stunt.

The thought of a bullet to the head was suddenly an attractive alternative to what was about to occur, and Queen tried to crawl forward, hoping that he would simply shoot and get it over with. It didn't happen.

Anger burned in Virgil's brain. Sanity disappeared behind the need to control and dominate. He shifted the rifle to his other hand and reached down, yanking Queen from the snow only to slam her down onto her back. He kicked viciously, and when she dodged and returned the action, it only made him laugh. He liked the fight. He liked the pain. It was what made him hard. It was what made him come.

"I think it's time," he said. Anger warred with the

need to make her pay. It made him careless. He dropped the rifle behind him into the snow and started fumbling at the front of his pants. Just thinking about sinking himself into her hot, wet depths blinded him to all but the deed at hand.

Queen saw his hands moving across his crotch and kicked again, only this time she connected with flesh and bone. Virgil's knee buckled, and he roared wildly with anger and pain as he struggled to stand. Furious with the fact that she'd drawn first blood, he grabbed the handgun from his jacket and aimed at her head.

Flat on her back, Queen stared up through the swirling snow into the barrel of the weapon. This wasn't the way she'd planned to die. She closed her eyes and prayed he was a good shot.

Cody's lungs burned from inhaling the cold. His eyes watered constantly, forcing him to swipe at them continuously with his bare hands, trying to keep his vision clear and his focus on the swiftly disappearing tracks before him. He ran until he could no longer feel his legs, and then he switched into the same mode of semiconsciousness that he'd used when he'd walked out of the desert on a broken bone. If one didn't think of pain, it would become nonexistent.

Snow quickly covered the black cap of his hair and then just as quickly melted from his escaping body heat, running down across his face and into the neck of his coat and shirt.

Every few minutes he would stop and listen intently, his eyes trained on the landscape and the thick trees, ever searching for additional clues that would tell him where they had gone. The wind moved across the floor of the forest, constantly shifting and changing the surface of the cold, blowing snow. He cursed, refocused on the obliterating tracks, and started forward, again on the lookout for something to give him hope.

The shot came without warning. It was loud, and it echoed over and over beneath the heavy cover of trees until Cody was so disoriented, he couldn't tell its original location. And then the second shot followed, and for a moment he lost all hope.

"Oh, God," he muttered, tried not to think of the implications, and started running as a fresh spurt of adrenaline shot through his system.

The tracks were gone. All he was doing was running on instinct, moving through the snow with nothing but guts and determination to guide him.

And then he heard her scream and took fresh heart. At least she was still alive. He couldn't consider the conditions. He could only hope that when he found her, she'd still want to live. He'd seen what the madman had done to his house. Queen had obviously put up a terrible fight before being overcome. He didn't want to think of the repercussions she might have suffered because of it.

He burst into the clearing on a run and then staggered as he came to an abrupt halt between two towering pines, staring at the scene before him.

The man was huge and seemed even more so because of the hooded parka and the layers of clothing he wore. He loomed over Queen, who was lying stretched out on the snow. Cody groaned, calculating the distance between them to be just under fifty yards. Using a handgun in this low visibility was going to play hell with his odds of helping her in time to prevent further injury.

And then he saw her in the snow, silent, unmoving, and he started forward, afraid that he'd found her too late. He kept telling himself that surely God wouldn't . . . couldn't . . . let him get this close only to find that he hadn't been able to stop the inevitable.

He realized that they were unaware of his presence. He saw the man kick at Queen and then drop a rifle into the snow as he began fumbling at the front of his pants.

A rage exploded, blinding Cody to all but the sight of a man in the act of violation. He shoved his hand into his pocket, pulled out his semiautomatic pistol, and aimed as he began to run.

He fired two shots in rapid succession and stopped the progress of everything, changing the texture of the world around them. Now something more than fear had been added to the drama. Death had come calling and was waiting to see whom it would claim as bullets ripped through the air between the two men.

Cody drew a deep, shaky breath and stopped just inside the clearing, only yards from the man, who had bucked from the bullet's sudden impact. He had been hit. Expecting to see the man stagger and fall, Cody was shocked to find that it only seemed to enrage him further. The man roared, and then picked up his rifle and shook it above his head in a taunting gesture as he began to run toward Cody, who stood his ground and continued to fire.

Virgil had forgotten he still held the rifle. He'd didn't know there was a shot in the chamber he'd forgotten to fire. All he could think of was getting to the man and removing that look on his face. He put one foot in front of the other and kept slogging through the snow, unaware of the snowflakes that were beginning to coat his face and beard, giving him the appearance of a yeti, a mythological half man, half beast, dressed in human clothing.

The second shot hit Virgil high on the shoulder. He screamed in pain as he heard the bones break. The rifle fell from his useless fingers, and still he ran. The third shot hit him in the leg.

He paused and staggered, and for a moment Cody thought he'd finally stopped the brute. But it was not to be.

Virgil threw back his head and shouted an obscenity that was lost in the howl of snow and wind. The hood of his parka fell off his head, and for the first time since the ordeal had started, Cody stared into the face of the devil.

Even from this distance he could see the spider tattoo and the black and broken teeth, bared in a growl of rage. He shuddered, wondering how Queen had fared at this man's hands.

It was that thought that made what came next possible.

As a soldier, Cody had fought many battles during Operation Desert Storm, but never on the ground, always from a distance, in the air. He'd never seen his enemy's face . . . until now.

Virgil inhaled, relishing the cold influx of air into his lungs, and ignored the pain. Moving on nothing but adrenaline and rage, he once again started toward the man with the gun.

"Sonofabitch."

There was nothing else Cody could say to express his shock at the fact that the man had resumed motion. By all rights he should be dead on his feet. Cody looked down at his gun and then up at the man only a few feet away and knew that this shot had to find its mark. It was his last. He aimed and curled his finger around the trigger as it jerked beneath his grip.

Cody squeezed but didn't consciously hear the shot.

Yet he realized the finality of its impact as shards of pink and red stained the snow behind Queen's abductor.

The hole was neat and round and just above his nose. Virgil Stratton stared, but he didn't see. His last conscious thought had been one of rage, and the last thing he'd seen had been the hole in the barrel of the gun. His huge body wavered and then fell backward with a resounding thud, sending up a white cloud of snow upon impact.

"My God," Cody muttered, resisting the urge to collapse as Virgil had. His legs were shaking so hard, he didn't think he could remain standing. And then he looked past the man's body to the woman in the snow and knew that he had farther yet to go.

Queen's body ached, and her head throbbed. And she was cold . . . so cold. She reached out, thinking she was home in bed, and struggled to find the covers that must have fallen at her feet. And then she heard his voice, felt his touch, remembered wanting to die, and was suddenly glad she hadn't.

Cody had found her!

She opened her eyes and stared up into a world of cold and snow and then focused on a blue so intense that it made her burn.

"Cody?"

"Thank you, God," he muttered, and lifted her from the snow and into his arms. He closed his eyes against a wall of threatening tears and began pressing tiny, reverent kisses across her face.

With her arms wrapped around his neck in a desperate need to feel life, Queen cried as Cody praised her courage and promised her things she would never hold him to, and she knew that she was loved.

Sounds of approaching motors broke the moment, and minutes later four snowmobiles burst into the clear-

ing, matching red-and-black steeds of motors and steel.
Each carried two riders, who came with guns aimed
toward the pair enfolded in each other's arms in the center of the clearing. In the blinding storm they were
unable to tell who was holding whom.

Abel Miller was afraid to look. If he had a hostage situation, that meant Cody Bonner either didn't make it
through the snow or was already dead. And then he saw
broad shoulders and black hair and knew that for once
the good guys had won. The right man was still standing.

He remembered Patrick Mooney's body and the state
of the Bonner household, which he'd seen before starting up the mountain, and he shuddered. It was a justified, bona fide miracle.

"Bonner! Is she alive?" Abel Miller shouted.

Cody looked down at the woman cradled in his arms,
at Queen's bruised and battered face, saw her trying to
smile around the cuts on her lips, and wrapped his hands
in her hair, pulling her head closer against his chest
before answering. He still needed to feel her just to
know that the nightmare was over.

"Yes, she's alive," he said as Abel knelt at their feet.
He pointed toward a snowdrift and the body that was
quickly disappearing beneath the falling snow. "But he's
not."

"Fine by me," Abel said, and touched Queen's arm in
a silent gesture of thanksgiving.

She shuddered and turned away, hiding her face
against Cody's coat, for the time being unable to face any
more of the world than what she'd already seen.

Abel's eyes narrowed, and he resisted the urge to
curse as he saw the extent of her suffering at Virgil Stratton's hands; yet thanks to Cody, it was minor compared
to Patrick Mooney's suffering. He sighed. Her body

would heal long before her mind. For the victim it was always so.

"Radio the men at base," he called to the others. "Tell them to tell Bonner's boys we found their daddy . . . and we found their Queenie. You be sure to tell them that they're both fine . . . just fine."

Cody's heart quickened. In that moment he realized that he'd completely forgotten about everything and everyone in the world except the lady lying in his arms . . . his lady.

"Come on, Bonner. We'd better get you two off this mountain. Snow's coming down right nice. It'll be good skiing when this one is over, I betcha, or I don't know my mountains."

Cody nodded, understanding Abel's offhand remark about the weather. It was time to put the horror behind them and get on with the business of living.

"Baby, can you stand?" he whispered, and cradled her face in his hands, unwilling to turn loose of her yet aware that they needed to get to shelter fast.

Queen nodded and then bit her lip and groaned in pain as she began to stagger to her feet, aided by Abel Miller on one side and Cody on the other.

Cody cursed the dead man's soul to hell as he watched her trying to walk. In one angry motion he scooped her off her feet, ignoring the fact that minutes ago his own legs had felt like lead, and began carrying her toward one of the snowmobiles.

"Cody . . . you came," Queen said, and started to shake at the onset of intruding reality. "I didn't think you'd find me. I thought I was going to die."

"I will always find you, lady," he said, whispering against her cheek in short, angry breaths. "I don't give up what's mine."

She sighed and relaxed against him, too sore and weary to get past the exultation of being alive. There would be time later to think of the fact that Cody had laid claim to something she had yet to offer.

Hours had come and gone since the time they'd returned to the house to be reunited with three very frightened boys.

Cody had talked to them, but to no avail. The boys weren't convinced that their Queenie was truly all right until she'd told them so herself.

Upon her arrival she'd been whisked away to her bedroom and examined by waiting paramedics who'd been summoned by Abel Miller and his search team. Although exhausted beyond belief, she'd suffered no lasting trauma to her body beyond that of severe bruises from his beatings, scratches from their trek through the forest, and some minor frostbite.

Statements had been given and Cody had suffered handshakes all around from the authorities assembled as they'd praised him for what he'd done. He had a hard time accepting praise for killing a man but had no problem with the fact that it was Virgil Stratton, not Queen Houston, who was dead.

He prowled the hallway outside his bedroom, listening for her voice should she call out in need, and then saw Donny slip out of the boys' bedroom and come toward him.

"I thought you guys were asleep," Cody said.

"I just couldn't, not yet. Dad, are you sure she's going to be okay?" Donny's voice cracked on the question, and he stuffed his hands in his pockets and tried not to cry.

Cody pulled his son into his arms and hugged him. Somehow, tonight, he'd been unable to stop holding the ones he loved, because for a time today he'd been uncertain of ever getting another chance to do so.

"I'm sure," he said. "Physically she's in good shape for what she went through. But I have to be honest with you . . . and I think you're old enough to understand. Mentally it was hell, son. You guys are going to have to be real understanding and not give her any grief for a while. Do you know what I mean?"

Donny bit his lip and nodded, then shuffled his feet before continuing. "Dad?"

Cody waited. He could tell there was more to Donny's concern.

"Did he . . . did the man . . . uh . . . did he . . . "

"She wasn't raped," Cody said.

Donny's mouth curved into a slight smile and he looked away. "Good. I would hate to think of our Queenie going through anything like that. I was afraid if she had been, that she would hate us."

"Why on earth would she hate us, son?"

Donny shrugged. "You know . . . because we're men . . . like him."

"Hell no, we're not like him," Cody said, and then swallowed his rage. It did no good being mad at his son. Donny was as innocent as Queen. "That wasn't a man who killed Mr. Mooney and kidnapped Queen, it was an animal . . . and don't you forget it."

"Yes, sir," Donny said. He looked at the closed door to his father's bedroom, then sighed. "I think I'll be able to sleep now."

"Good night, son," Cody said, and then added before Donny disappeared, "I love you."

Donny grinned and gave his dad a thumbs-up sign.

Right now, answering him back might have made him cry, and Donny had seen enough tears tonight to last him a good long while.

Cody watched him until the door was shut, and then he turned to his own bedroom door, contemplating only a moment before opening and entering.

She was still in the bath. He could hear her moving around. "Are you okay?" he called, and listened when everything went quiet. Finally she answered.

"Yes. I'll be down in a minute."

"Right, just checking." Cody started out the door.

"Cody!"

Her voice was just the least bit frantic and stopped his progress instantly. He ran toward the bathroom door and stopped just outside. "I'm right here."

"Would you wait for me until I'm through? I don't want to be in here alone."

"Take your time, honey," he said quietly. "I'll be here when you get out. We'll go downstairs together, okay?"

"Okay."

The single word came on a sigh and a sob, and Cody spread his hand across the outside surface of the door, wanting to touch yet unable to reach the woman behind it who was in need. He shook his head at the futile gesture and then dropped onto the corner of his bed, trying valiantly to quell the rage that swept over him. But it was no use. His lady had been hurt, and if he had the chance, at that moment he'd have killed Virgil Stratton all over again.

11

Queen stared at herself in the mirror, tracing the bruise below her eye with the tip of her finger and then jerking back at the sudden pain, sending a hairbrush flying to the floor. It clattered on the tiles, and moments later Cody burst through the door.

"Are you all right?"

The fear in his voice was all it took to keep her from being angry that he'd come in without knocking. Too many things had happened today for her to worry about propriety.

She sighed and picked up the brush with a rueful smile. "Just clumsy." She turned too fast and winced, grabbing her side as she carefully laid the brush back on the vanity. "And a little bit sore."

Cody's gaze went from her face to her near bare body, concealed only by the bath towel she'd wrapped around herself. But it wasn't desire that made him look, it was the size of the bruise on her thigh and the ones across her back and down the side of her arm. He got sick just thinking of what she'd endured at Stratton's hands, then worried about what he couldn't see concealed beneath the towel.

He reached out a hand and then yanked it back, needing to hold her but afraid to touch her. Rage shattered his control.

"The sonofabitch."

Cody spun around and stalked out of the bathroom, coming to a halt at the edge of his bed, unable to stop the venomous flow of curses coming out of his throat.

Queen followed him to the bedroom. Before she thought, before she knew it, she'd wrapped her arms around his waist and laid her head against the middle of his back, holding on to him in a futile effort to stop the flow of his anger.

"Don't, Cody, don't," she whispered, and held him tight.

His body shook from the emotional outburst. She closed her eyes and in that moment let herself imagine they were about to make love. Her bare breasts flattened against his shoulder blades as her hands slid around his chest, unable to clasp across the widest breadth of him.

Cody got hard, instantly, and with an ache he knew wasn't going away, as her breasts crushed against his back and her body aligned itself with his. Her touch sent his imagination into overdrive, letting him think how it would be if they were about to make love, not peace.

Jesus Christ, lady. Either stop or never let go....

He covered the back of her hands with the palms of his own, pressing them against his chest, letting her feel the thunder of his heartbeat, wanting more from her than he knew he was going to get.

"Stop it. Don't let what happened today do this to you," she pleaded. "That man wasn't worth it."

"That man . . . as you call him . . . wouldn't have hurt you if I'd been here."

There. He'd finally said aloud what he'd been thinking ever since he'd driven up and found the front door open and his house in shambles. He didn't have the nerve to look up and see the agreement on her face.

"If you'd been here, we'd probably both be dead."

Her rebuttal shocked him. He spun around, pinning her to the spot with a look she couldn't ignore.

"What do you mean?"

"I mean . . . I don't think Virgil Stratton was looking for hostages, Cody. I was an afterthought. If I hadn't been alone, he probably wouldn't have bothered."

It was hard to hear, yet he realized that for the most part she might be right. It just didn't make it any easier for him to accept the fact that he'd left her alone when his conscience had told him not to.

"Still . . . ." He couldn't give up the guilt so easily. The need to protect was ingrained within him. It was part of who he was and why he'd entered the military.

"Still nothing," she said. "It happened, and because of you I survived it."

She fidgeted beneath his gaze, unable to get past the fire in his eyes, uncertain whether it had come from anger or something else. She looked down at her nearly nude body, aware for the first time of their intimate surroundings and the fact that if she dropped her arms and inhaled, the towel would be at her feet.

"It seems I forgot my gown."

Cody walked to his closet, pulled down a white, full-length terry-cloth robe, and held it open, waiting for her to come in.

Queen smiled, a little embarrassed but aware that what had happened today had changed what lay between them.

She slid her arms in the robe, then turned her back to him, letting the towel she'd been wearing drop to the floor at her feet as she wrapped the voluminous folds around her instead.

Cody tried not to look at the towel at her feet, tried not to imagine what lay beneath his robe, and turned her around to face him, fussing with the tie as he would if he were dressing one of his sons.

"Here, let me," he said, and looped the ends of the belt, pulling them gently but firmly to hold the oversize folds in place. Her hair, still damp from her shower, was caught in the neck of the robe. He lifted it out and let it fall loosely across her shoulders, where the thick terry could absorb the rest of the moisture.

"I'll be downstairs if you need me," he said, and left her alone in his room.

Hours later Cody was still on his easy chair, sitting in the dark in front of the fireplace, staring blindly into the flames, trying not to relive the events of the past few hours yet unable to let them go.

A sound on the stairs startled him and sent him bolting out of his chair. In seconds he was in the hallway, thinking it was one of the boys, afraid that they would awaken Queen. The last thing he expected to see was her standing on the stairs, her arms wrapped around her middle as if in pain, still wearing his robe.

"Honey . . . are you all right?"

His gentle voice was her undoing. Her chin trembled. The tears she'd been fighting all night came without warning. The explanation she'd planned to use was lost in the sob that came up her throat. She shook her head.

Cody didn't stop to ask. In seconds he'd crossed the space between them and lifted her from the steps and into his arms. The moment he touched her, her body went limp and she started to shake.

Queen wrapped her arms around his shoulders and buried her face against his neck. She had no strength, no knowledge of how to fight the terror. And then Cody's arms tightened around her, and she splayed her hand across his chest, feeling the power beneath it and the steady, reassuring rhythm of his heartbeat, and knew that this was a man she could lean on. No longer did she have to be the strong one in the family. No longer would everyone look to Queen to fix what couldn't be fixed. Cody Bonner protected what was his. For tonight, Queen needed to let herself believe that that included her.

"I couldn't sleep," she said, and tried to stop the tears. "I kept seeing spiders . . . and hearing his laughter . . . and his screams of rage. I don't know how to make it stop."

"Sssh. I do, baby. I know how. Thanks to my repeated trips to the base shrink, I'm a damned expert. Just let it go. There's no one but me to see you cry, and I swear to God, if it matters to you so much, I'll never tell that it happened."

The gentleness in his voice and the depth of his understanding undid her. The sobs she'd been denying wrenched out of her as Cody wrapped her in his arms.

"I thought I was going to die."

Her plaintive cry was nearly his undoing. He rocked her in his arms. "I know, darling. I swear to God, I know. I've been there, remember?"

It was that connection and his understanding that made everything else okay.

He carried her to the couch, sat down with her still in his arms, and then pulled her across his lap, cradling her head against his shoulder, burying his lips over and over in the tangle of her curls against his face, planting tiny, gentle kisses she never felt.

He held, and rocked, and promised. And when the sobs had finally disappeared and the trembling in her body had lessened to a single, occasional shudder, her lids drooped, and her body relaxed, and she slept, held in Cody's arms, revered in his heart.

Sometime during the night the snow had stopped. When morning broke, the world outside was covered in a new, undisturbed blanket of white. Towering pines stood tall, their stately limbs covered in dollops of vanilla ice, weighted low to the ground. Bare branches on leaf-less trees were coated with more of the same in careful and pristine perfection. The day awaited.

Queen rolled over and then came awake suddenly, wondering how she'd gotten to bed, remembering where she'd fallen asleep. She smiled and stretched, then groaned when sore muscles and aching joints protested.

"She's awake!"

Queen heard the whisper outside her door and grinned. She sat up, plumped her pillows behind her, and reached for the hairbrush on her bedside table. It would seem she was about to have guests.

"No, she's not. She just turned over, you goof!"

"I'm not a goof. You're a goof."

Queen smothered a grin as she crawled out of bed. She reached for Cody's robe, wrapped it around her, and went to the door.

"Hi, guys," she said as she looked down at the two boys framed in the doorway.

The argument they'd been enjoying died in the middle of a sentence. Last night's fear slid back on their faces as Will and J.J. looked up into their beloved Queenie's face and saw the results of Virgil Stratton's damage.

"Well, aren't you going to come in?" she asked.

They flew into her arms.

"We were so worried!" they shouted in unison, and then J.J. pointed toward her face.

"Does it hurt?" he asked.

She nodded. "But not much."

Will's hand slid into hers as she ushered them toward her bed. With little urging they joined her as she crawled back beneath the warmth of the covers, using the headboard for a backrest.

With a boy beneath each arm, their heads resting on her stomach, Queen began to reassure them and calm their fears.

"That man was mean . . . really mean," J.J. announced, and patted Queen's leg.

"Yes, he was, J.J. But he's gone. He can't hurt anyone ever again."

"Daddy killed him. I heard the sheriff talking," Will said.

Queen frowned, hearing the horror in the child's voice and uncertain how to explain without making it worse. She wasn't sure Cody had even wanted the boys to know the intricate details of her rescue. Obviously the decision had been taken out of his hands by what they'd overheard. She sighed. It was to be expected. Last night had been hell.

"Your daddy saved my life," Queen said softly, and ruffled Will's dark hair, burying her nose in its thick, soft texture. She thought how much like their father they were. "The man was trying to hurt us. Your daddy was just defending himself . . . and me. Do you understand?"

Both boys nodded in relief, accepting her word as gospel. Will sighed and wrapped his arms around Queen's waist.

"We made you breakfast in bed," Will said, suddenly remembering why they'd come upstairs in the first place.

"I helped," J.J. added.

"Then bring it on," Queen said, glad of the change of subject. "I'm starving."

"You won't be when you see what they made," Donny said, grinning from the doorway.

Queen looked up at the man/boy, who was looking more like his father every day, and smiled. "Oh, yes, I will," she said, defending the younger boys' instant objections and silencing the impending argument before it erupted.

The phone rang downstairs, and Donny rolled his eyes. "Not again," he said.

"What?"

"It's like this, Aunt Queenie. You made the news. Everyone in Snow Gap has been calling to see how you are . . . and wish you well."

"You're kidding!"

"Why are you so surprised?" Donny asked. "Everyone likes you a lot, even us."

"Thanks . . . I think," she said, and tossed a pillow at him to hide her pleasure at the words. And then she thought for a minute, trying to remember what day it was. "Why aren't you guys in school?"

"Can't get there. Or the bus can't get here. Whichever. There's too much snow."

"Yeah," J.J. said as he bounced out of her bed. "And after we feed you, we get to go out and play in it. Dad said."

"Then feed me! I'd hate to be the cause of postponing so much fun."

Her room cleared, but her vision did not. She had a sudden attack of fresh tears as she sat and absorbed the news. She'd spent her entire life in Cradle Creek, and in that time less than half a dozen people had ever cared what happened to her. And of those who had, three of them had been family.

"Well, well," she said quietly, and laid her head back on the pillow behind her, letting the tears seep out from beneath her lashes as she contemplated the news. "I had to survive Virgil Stratton to find out I'm loved. It makes almost dying worthwhile."

"Nothing would have been worth that," Cody said as he entered the room and dropped a handful of messages into her lap for her to read later. "Nothing would have been worth losing you, lady."

He bent down and kissed the corner of her mouth, then straightened as he heard the boys coming up the stairs, not giving her time to react to the embarrassment of facing him after last night's emotional outburst.

"Prepare yourself," he warned.

It was impossible. She hadn't gotten over the kiss when the boys burst into the room. Will had the tray laden with food, J.J. was carrying a glass of milk in one hand and a glass of juice in the other.

Her eyes widened at the dripping culinary disaster. But she managed not to laugh and made decent inroads into the plate of toast, peanut-butter-and-jelly sandwiches, slightly burned, slightly cold, but still warm from the love with which it had been prepared.

*   *   *

The next morning Queen was allowed out of bed. She got downstairs in time to listen to the boys' moans of regret that the snowplow had gotten through. School was in session.

Cody had the boys firmly in hand, unrelenting in his efforts to give her space and recovery time. She smiled as he ushered them out the door and down to the bus stop, calmly ignoring their comments, reassuring them that he'd be here with Queen when they got home.

Yet as she watched the four march off the deck and down the short driveway, she knew another problem lay ahead of her. She had yet to face Cody and the consequences of her feelings.

The sleeves of her oversize blue sweater, one of Cody's cast-offs, were too long. She turned up the cuffs and then absently shoved them up her arms. But she wouldn't have traded it for a new one with a better fit. Today she needed to be as close to Cody Bonner as possible, and inside his old clothes was a good place to start. She ran her hands across the soft, faded fabric of her blue jeans, then unsnapped the top button to ease the strain across a sore spot on her hip. Comfort, not style, was the order of the day.

She heard a commotion outside and hobbled toward the living room, taking possession of Cody's favorite chair before he returned, snuggling into its overstuffed depths, careful not to bump anything sore.

"Come on in," she heard Cody say, and realized with a start that someone else was coming in with him. But the shock of who it was and what they were carrying was more than she'd been prepared for.

"Surprise!" Mrs. Eller said, and hurried over to

Queen, planting a swift kiss on her cheek before dumping an armload of presents in her lap.

Queen was speechless. She and Mrs. Eller had passed many enjoyable conversations in her craft shop, but the fact that she'd actually come to see her was more than she could comprehend.

Abel Miller was next, carrying two potted plants. He stood in the center of the room with a silly grin on his face, waiting for someone to unload him.

"The one with the posies is from all of us at the department," he said, bouncing the pink chrysanthemums in one hand. "The ivy thing is from the guys down at the firehouse. You met some of them the other night—the paramedics, remember?"

Queen nodded. How could she forget?

"And don't think this is all," Mrs. Eller said. "I know for a fact that several people will be here off and on during the next few days with food. You don't need to be trying to feed this brood until you're feeling back to par."

"I don't know what to say," Queen said, trying not to cry.

"That's a first," Cody said, teasing her into laughter instead of tears.

"I never imagined . . . I didn't think . . . No one ever . . ." Queen bit her lip. Her chin quivered. She was unable to continue. All she could do was stare up at the assembly while the tears finally slid down her face.

Abel Miller shoved his hat to the back of his head and cleared his throat before he spoke, unwilling to let anyone see how moved he was by her joy. "I don't know why you didn't expect this. You've become a heroine to all of Snow Gap. You survived a real ordeal, little girl. And we're all real glad that you did."

"Well, open your stuff," Mrs. Eller said. "That's why we brought them."

"I need help," she whispered, and picked up the first package with shaky fingers.

"You've got it," Cody said as he knelt at her side and began sorting through the presents. And then he added softly, so that no one else could hear, "And I need you, lady. Don't you ever forget it."

His hand brushed across her fingers as he handed her the first gift. It could have been an accident. It could have been nothing more than a friendly touch. But Abel Miller saw past the action to the emotion and knew that the sister who wasn't really a sister had come into her own.

The streets of Snow Gap were busy. The small motels and bed-and-breakfasts were booked into spring. The "snowbirds," the nickname the locals applied to the people who came to party and ski, were in rare form, spending money like crazy just for the pleasure of sliding down mountains on pieces of waxed and polished wood. It was a crazy but lucrative business, and it was what kept Snow Gap from dying out like so many other small towns across the United States.

A small, nondescript man shivered as he slipped into the phone booth on the corner across from the pizza parlor. He closed the door behind him with a quick snap, anxious to shut out the sharp burst of wind. His overcoat hung loosely on bony shoulders, and his shoes were snow-packed and soaking wet. He kicked them against the wall of the booth to loosen the snow and shivered, wishing that his job had taken him south, not north, for the winter.

A woman walked past, her eyes narrowed against the buffeting wind, and almost missed the wink the man in the phone booth gave her. Her mouth dropped, her eyes widened, as he grinned. His close-set eyes, long, pointed nose, and wide, thin mouth made him seem almost like a caricature. She flushed and hurried past. Strangers in phone booths couldn't be trusted, especially those who had the misfortune to look like Ichabod Crane.

Wally Morrow was harmless, but the woman didn't know that and didn't care to find out. And Wally wasn't the type to pursue someone who saw him coming. His job was based on deception and covert observation. Wally Morrow was a private detective who didn't come cheap.

He dug through his wallet, pulled out his calling card, and slid it in the proper slot, then punched in a series of numbers and waited for his party to answer.

"Hello."

The woman who answered had a voice that matched the weather in Snow Gap. Frigid.

"It's me," Wally said.

"What do you have?" the woman asked.

"Nothing you'll want to hear," he said.

"How do you know? I'm not paying you to read my mind. I'm paying you for information. Please continue."

Wally resisted the urge to hang up on the bitch and pretend later that their connection had been broken. Sometimes he absolutely hated his clients. But he wasn't in the business to make friends. He was doing it to make money.

"Okay. Here goes." He pulled out a notebook to remind him of all he'd learned and began going down the list, ticking off the notes he'd made to himself earlier.

"As of yesterday evening, Cody Bonner is the hero of

the hour. Single-handedly killed an escaped killer who'd murdered the local postmaster earlier the same day and who had later taken a local woman hostage. One Queen Houston, to be exact."

The woman made what sounded like a snort in his ear. He continued as if he hadn't heard.

"As for the woman in question . . . Queen Houston has a good reputation in this town. Everyone who knows her likes her. They think she can do no wrong. And after surviving being kidnapped, she's high up on Snow Gap's list of saints. There's more. Are you interested?"

"Not if it's more of the same," the woman said sharply. "Keep digging. Something has to turn up. I won't believe that all is as it seems."

"Yes, ma'am," Wally said. "I'll call you next week, same time."

The woman disconnected in his ear without saying good-bye. He shrugged and hung up the phone. With what she was paying him, he didn't have to like her attitude. But he damned sure liked her cash.

Bubbles from her bath floated up around Queen's nose as water lapped at the nape of her neck. She stretched full length in the old-fashioned tub, testing her toes against the spigots, and reveled in the warm, soothing water easing the lingering sore spots from her week-old ordeal.

The weekend had come and gone along with a continuous stream of visitors. She had not had a moment's peace or a minute to herself to worry about the change in Cody's behavior toward her. Where he'd once given her a wide berth, he now hovered. She didn't know whether she felt honored or cornered.

She lifted a foot from the water, noting that her once smooth skin had begun to prune, and decided that she'd soaked long enough. Using her toe for leverage, she flipped the switch on the drain, then crawled out of the tub ahead of the swift, receding bubbles.

Shivering now that she was out, she hurried through the rest of her toilette, drying herself and then dusting with body powder in record time. After the last week of visitors and gifts, she had an unusually large assortment of loungewear from which to choose. The sweatpants and matching shirt in a soft shade of blue would serve perfectly. She put them on and made her way downstairs before she had time to change her mind.

It was a heady thing, having a choice of what to wear. Although she'd replenished her own meager wardrobe slowly over the months she'd been with Cody, the luxury of vivid colors and stacks of clothing was beyond her wildest dreams. The ski resort mentality of the residents of Snow Gap had colored their choices of gifts to the point where she would be years wearing out the sweats and sweaters and soft knit house shoes. But more important than the gifts that they sent was the fact that they'd cared.

She plopped down on the bottom step and began putting on her socks. The phone rang, and before she could move to answer it, it had stopped. She figured Cody must have answered it. Surely no one would hang up so abruptly. Leaving her shoes on the stairs for later, she walked across the hardwood floor in search of him, her silent footsteps giving no warning of her approach.

When she heard him talking she started toward the living room with a smile on her face, anxious to greet him and the new day.

"Dammit, Dennis, I don't care," Cody was saying.

"It's no use arguing. I've been over and over this with you until I'm blue in the face. I'm not going to leave my family again . . . not even for Uncle Sam."

Queen swallowed the greeting she'd been about to give, stepped silently into the room, and did the unforgivable. She eavesdropped.

"Yes, she's fine, no thanks to me," he said.

Queen frowned. She thought they'd been all through this the night of her rescue. Obviously she was wrong. It sounded as if Cody still blamed himself for being gone when Virgil Stratton had arrived. And what else wasn't he telling her? What was it that Lt. Colonel Dennis Macon and the United States government wanted from Cody Bonner that he wasn't willing to give?

She knew he still went to the base occasionally. His counseling sessions regarding his nightmares were ongoing, though on a less frequent basis than before.

She listened intently, certain that her welfare, as well as that of the Bonner boys, rested on what she would learn.

"Yes, I'll tell her you called," Cody said. "But I don't want to discuss the project again."

A combination of frustration and longing colored his voice, and Queen knew that regardless of the subject, it was time to interrupt. She suspected it had everything to do with his constant visits to Lowry AFB before her attack and the fact that he'd refused to set foot off the mountain since. It was time to find out the truth.

"I want to discuss it," Queen said as she walked into the room.

Cody pivoted, the phone still close to his mouth, and knew that she'd heard a lot. "Not now, honey," he said, and then realized he was still talking into the phone when Dennis decided to play along with his faux pas.

"That's what you say all the time," Dennis whined in a falsetto voice. "If you're sick and tired of our relationship . . . then just have the decency to say so."

"Dammit, Dennis. I wasn't talking to you and you know it."

Dennis laughed loudly, enjoying the joke at Cody's expense.

"What's going on?" Queen asked. "Who's on the phone? Is it Dennis?"

Cody frowned and turned away as he tried to end the phone call. "Look, I can't talk now. I've said all I need to on the subject. Just get—"

Queen came up behind him and took the phone from his hand before he was finished. "Dennis? Hi, this is Queen."

"Hey, angel," he said, his voice softening as he thought of the pretty redhead and what she'd endured. "Long time no see."

"Yes, it's been a while. Dennis, can Cody call you back?" Cody reached for the phone, and she neatly sidestepped the motion.

"Anytime," Dennis said, and caught the fact that she'd probably overheard enough to make her curious. He hung up, hoping that she'd be the one to change his friend's mind. Cody was perfect for the job at hand, if only someone could change his attitude.

"He hung up," Queen said, calmly handing Cody the phone. "Said for you to call back anytime."

Cody slammed the receiver onto the base and then tried to glare. But it was hopeless. The light in her eyes was familiar. It was the look she got just before doing battle.

"I think you owe me an explanation," Queen said.

"I don't know what you—"

"Dammit, don't!" she shouted, her anger hot and instantaneous. "I don't deserve the bullshit, Cody. I think it's time you told me the real truth behind your visits to Lowry."

Cody turned away as he answered, aware that if he looked into her eyes, he would not be able to hide his thoughts. Then he turned back to face her with a deadpan expression. "I was asked to head a project. I turned it down. No big deal."

"What project? Where? And I better not be the reason you said no."

The warning tone in her voice was enough to make him look away in guilt. It was all she needed to see. She pummeled him with her fists in halfhearted thumps, frustrated and angry with the stubbornness of the man.

"Dammit, Cody Bonner! How many times do I have to say it? You weren't to blame. You couldn't have stopped—"

He yanked her into his arms, stopping her angry tirade with his mouth. His hands spread across her breasts and then slid around behind her back, cupping her rear, molding her to him with a rocking thrust. It was a moment before shock sank in and he realized what he'd done.

Queen moaned and then leaned against him in silent submission as her hands sought warm flesh and familiar territory.

At the time it had been instinct, something to stop her from digging too deeply into his secrets. But when her hands slid beneath his sweater and raked across his back in a tender but compelling gesture to continue, he forgot that he'd started this to prove a point, not drive himself crazy.

"I didn't mean for this to happen," he said, pulling

away from her mouth, and her hands, and the look on her face. "And I can't tell you what's been going on without asking more of you than I already have."

Queen shuddered as she tried to regain her self-control. Then she closed her eyes and sighed. This had been waiting to happen.

"Yes, you can tell me," she said as anger shook her voice. "And if you don't, I can promise you . . . I'll find out anyway, and then you'll be wishing you'd been the one to tell it."

"Dammit!" He hit the desk with his fist and then spun around, the decision taken out of his hands by her threat. "Okay, you wanted to know. So listen."

She dropped onto a chair, folded her hands in her lap, and waited.

"They asked me to head a project that would be based up the mountain on government-owned land only a few miles from here. Because of my background and experience, they want me to spearhead and train units of men who are more maverick than military in survival techniques. Each unit's ultimate purpose would be search and rescue. It's a good idea, but it would entail periodic bouts of being gone all day every day for several weeks and sometimes even overnight. And I just can't do that. I can't leave the boys alone, and I can't ask you to be any more responsible for me and mine than you already are."

"Why?"

The single word stunned him. It was a full minute before he could form the answer, and then finally, when he did, it came quietly and with a sudden sense of defeat.

"Because I've already asked too much and nearly gotten you killed. Because of me you interrupted a journey you'd dreamed of making all your life. Because of me you were saddled with more children and more responsibility when you'd just gotten free of a lifetime of the same. Because of me you're snowbound, and I'm scared as hell for spring to come. Because I'm not ready to face the fact that one day you'll walk into a room and tell me you want to leave . . . and I won't want to let you go. That's why."

Fury sent her rocketing out of her seat, wondering why men were so dense and couldn't see past the end of their noses.

"My God! You still don't understand. Since the first day, I've been here by choice. No one made me get off that bus. No one made me take three lost boys up a mountain and wait for a no-good man to come wandering home. No one made me stay. It's been my choice."

Her eyes were green and wild with anger, and her hair had come loose from its clasp. He couldn't tell whether she wanted to slap him or kiss him. He shivered, almost afraid to hope she meant what she said. And then all the fight seemed to go out of her as she continued.

"If you want to head that project, then don't use me as an excuse. Because I don't want to leave. I couldn't if I tried."

She slumped onto the chair and leaned forward, ashamed that she'd humiliated herself to the point that he now knew how she felt about him, and buried her face in her hands.

And then he tilted her face, pinning her with a look from his burning blue eyes that promised more than she dared to hope for.

"I love you, Queen," he said softly. "I don't know whether you're ready to hear it or not, but I've kept it inside me too damned long as it is."

"Then I think it's time you proved it," she said. "Because I've been waiting for a sign that would tell me I mattered in your world, Cody Bonner."

He stood, pulling her to her feet, and into his embrace. "It's been there all along, lady," he whispered. "You were too afraid to look."

12

Queen sighed in Cody's arms, trying to think of a way to respond to his words as he swept her off her feet and carried her into his bedroom.

"Oh, I saw the signs. But I couldn't bring myself to believe them. And it's not that I don't want you. A woman would be a fool not to love you, Cody Bonner."

She tilted her chin, aware that she was leaving herself open to all kinds of rejection just by the admission. "It's just that I never expected anything to come of it."

"Why the hell not? I've done everything but take out an ad in the paper about how I feel about you," Cody said.

"Because of who I am . . . and who you are. You only know me now, the woman who was on her way to somewhere else. You don't know the gambler's daughter from Cradle Creek, Tennessee. You don't understand what a gap there is between your world and mine.

Where I lived . . . " She trailed off, her lips tightening at
the old, ugly memories. "You don't know how I lived . . .
what we had to do to survive. You fly high-tech planes
with computer systems I could never understand. I
cleaned house for the owner of the coal mine back
home."

"You think that changes how I feel about you? You've
got a bullshit opinion of me, and men in general, don't
you, lady?"

Her face crumpled. Cody should have known, the
moment he'd gotten angry, that it had been the wrong
thing to do.

"Oh, hell," he said, raking his fingers through his hair.
"Don't cry. For God's sake, don't cry. If you aren't ready,
I'm not insisting. The last thing I ever wanted to do was
hurt you. I never was any good at saying the right thing
to a woman."

It was the fear on his face that made the difference. If
he loved her enough to back off, then she had to be
brave enough to take that first step and do something
she'd sworn never to do . . . trust a man.

"You already said the right thing, Cody. You said you
loved me."

"Then what is it, honey?" he asked, wanting to touch
her but afraid to move. "I'll do anything to make you
happy. If this feels wrong . . . if you're not ready for this
. . . then please, don't turn away from me. Just tell me.
As much as I want you, I'd rather stop right now than
take the chance of losing you."

She started to cry.

"Jesus!" Cody said. He started forward but was
stopped by the look on her face. "Baby . . . don't." He
held up his hands and started backing out of the room.
"Look! I'm leaving. No pressure. No problem."

"So help me, God," Queen whispered, "if you walk out on me now, Cody Bonner, I'll never forgive you."

He stopped in midstride, stunned by the impact of her words. He'd imagined it was fear that had made her cry, not joy.

"Hell, lady," he growled, starting toward her, "you scared me half to death. I thought you hated my guts."

"Only once," she whispered, taking his hands and guiding them beneath her sweater, "right after you dragged me through the oil and out from under your old red truck."

He grinned at her audacity and then inhaled slowly and in wonder at the intoxicating, satiny texture of her breasts and the life racing just beneath the surface of her skin. His fingers splayed across her, cupping, caressing, and he felt himself getting hard in response.

Queen moaned, her knees weakening as the wanting of Cody Bonner came upon her. She slid her fingers along the waistband of his jeans and started a search of her own, smiling at his swift intake of breath and the belly that tightened beneath her touch.

Cody couldn't believe what was happening. Moments ago he'd been afraid of losing her, and now he was afraid he wouldn't get her soon enough to satisfy her hunger. He shuddered as he realized he wasn't the only one who knew how to play with matches.

In one smooth motion he lifted her sweater up and off, leaving her bare except for the plain cotton bra restraining her curvaceous body. When he would have removed it, too, she stopped him with a shake of her head, raking his chest lightly with her fingernail, tapping at the buttons on his shirt in a gentle reminder that she wasn't in this alone.

Cody got the message. Queen was calling the shots,

and it was fine with him. In seconds his shirt was off and his boots went flying. He waited, a questioning look on his face, as if asking her what came next.

She smiled and unfastened her bra, letting herself fall free and reveling in the flush that swept across his cheeks as he looked his fill.

He swallowed, groaning at the restraint it took not to touch her, and began unsnapping his jeans, delighting in the way her eyes opened wide and then slid nearly shut, heavy with passion. His body throbbed, reminding him that when he came out of the jeans there'd be no way of denying how badly he needed her. His hands dropped to his sides, and he took some slow, calming breaths, waiting for the next passage in the sexual symphony to begin.

He'd understood. Queen smiled, her green cat eyes widening in appreciation, her body humming beneath her skin. She looked at the sculptured perfection of his shoulders and belly and at the spiral of dark hair on his chest that disappeared beneath the wide white elastic on his briefs. She sat down on the edge of the bed, lifting a leg and waving a sock-covered foot in his direction.

"I need help," she said softly.

"I think I'm the one who's going to need help," he said with a grin. Then he stepped forward, straddling her legs and gently pushing her backward onto his bed.

His hand encompassed her foot, stroking and then lifting it gently as one sock came off with a yank and then the other followed. He crawled onto the bed, pulling gently at the buttons on the front of her jeans. One gave way . . . then another . . . and another.

Her eyes widened and her breath shortened as she watched him coming toward her, but there was no time to think as he stretched out beside her and covered her lips with his own. She reached up, her arms tightening around his neck and back, holding on to what was being offered, sighing with pleasure as her fingers found firm flesh.

His mouth took everything from her including sanity, grazing lightly across the curve of her lower lip, taking it into his own and sucking gently before moving across it completely and staking claim.

His tongue ventured forward, tracing the edge of her teeth, then the roof of her mouth, then rocking in and out in an indecent proposal she could not refuse. Aching in places she couldn't reach, Queen guided his hand instead, begging him without words to make it better.

Following her lead, his fingers moved across the flat plane of her belly and then slid beneath the elastic on her underwear to the pleasure beyond. His own needs increased to the point of pain as she sighed and arched, moving toward his touch, begging him in ways as old as time to release the tiger that he'd teased.

His fingers swept across the soft petals of her flesh and slid into the folds, then stopped, aware that things were moving too fast. He shuddered in response to her moans of pleasure and then moved his attention back up her body in a desperate attempt to regain control.

Her breast felt lush beneath his hand, and when he covered the soft brown areola with his lips, then rolled the nipple between his teeth, the tiny pain made her cry aloud.

"More . . . no more," she whispered, unaware that she'd asked for two different things.

He raised his head. She stared up into a blaze of blue and got lost on the way back. His lips were moving, saying things on which she could not focus, promising things for which she dared not hope.

Instinct prompted her to hold on to what was hers. She reached up and cradled his head between her hands, urging him to fulfill the promises he was making. His hair was black and soft beneath her fingers as she gripped thick handfuls of midnight in the full light of day.

The ache between her legs was worse, the heat higher. She felt herself melting and knew from the look on his face that it had only just begun.

"Lady . . . my lady," he whispered, and loved her with a look that made her hunger for more.

Queen moved, and then her hands slid between their bodies, her fingers tugging at the soft white band of his briefs.

"Oh, God . . . baby wait! Let me . . . "

He rolled away enough to allow her access to free him and then a heartbeat later wondered if he'd gone mad by doing so when she took him in her hands.

"No . . . let me," she whispered, and encompassed the hard thrust of his manhood, sliding satin over steel in one smooth motion.

"Queen!" The cry came from his heart. He closed his hands over hers and guided her actions until he lost track of everything but the feel of her hands upon his body. Shuddering, he shut his eyes against the urge to give himself up. But he'd dreamed of this too long to let it happen this fast.

She stroked him to the point of combustion. Cody was going blind and didn't care. In a matter of seconds it would be over unless he regained control.

"No, you don't, lady. It's not going to end like this." He groaned and rolled away from her touch.

Lost in the pleasure that loving him was giving her, Queen didn't expect his retreat. Before she knew it, she was devoid of the rest of her clothing and lay bare to his gaze, awaiting his pleasure . . . and hers.

Cody fumbled in the bedside drawer, slid fully out of his clothes and into protection, then rolled back on top of her before she had time to get cold.

Queen inhaled, closed her eyes, and let her hands roam at will across the body of the man who had staked his claim. His weight pressed her down onto the mattress as the hard thrust of his sex pressed against her legs. She moved, wanting him closer, needing the empty place in her body as well as her heart to be filled.

Cody relished the feel of her beneath him, aware that for the moment he had total mastery over her body, and then knew when she opened her eyes and looked up at him through a green veil of tears that he was the one who was bound. Bound by love and the goodwill of a Queen.

"No more waiting," he whispered, and slid a knee between her legs, opening the way for him to come in.

She sighed. He was right. It was time.

He paused, stared down into the eyes of love, and then moved with a smooth, powerful thrust, sliding through as swiftly and surely as if it had happened a thousand times before.

She arched beneath him in reflex and shuddered at the feel of so much man within her.

"Cody?"

It was a question as well as a plea.

"I'm here, baby," he whispered, and braced himself above her, unwilling to burden her any longer with his weight. "I won't let you down . . . and I won't let you go. I swear."

With that he began to move, slowly at first to allow her body time to accept him. He swallowed a groan at the hot, tight fit and knew that few, if any, had gone before him. But the clutch of her hands on his arms, and then across his back, urged him forward . . . deeper . . . faster.

Pleasure came first. The knowledge of being loved, the feeling of a need being fulfilled. And then pleasure gave way to compulsion as their bodies began moving on instinct, no longer able to control the inevitable.

Her blood felt thick, pushing itself through her veins in a constant but building pressure as he moved within her. And then in a sudden and blinding flash of need, it no longer became possible to think of what was coming because it was here. Instinctively she wrapped her legs around him, a subconscious effort to stay on firm ground when she knew she was about to fly.

"Let it happen," Cody begged. "You won't be alone . . . I'm with you all the way."

It was all she needed to hear. The last vestige of her restraint shattered along with her sanity as the flashfire of pleasure exploded.

And just as he'd promised, Cody groaned and then, with a single last thrust, spilled himself inside her and collapsed across her body, shuddering from exhaustion.

As she lay beneath him, he felt her body tremoring in the dying throes of spent love. He raised up on his elbows and stared intently, yearning to see past the body to the soul inside.

Her hair was an auburn fan of thick, damp curls that spread across his arms as well as the pillow beneath her head. Her eyes were wide with dissipating shock, as if she still couldn't quite comprehend the magnitude of their joining. And her body still held him, unwilling to lose what had given so much pleasure. But it was the look in her eyes, and the tears that ran freely, that moved him beyond words.

He leaned forward until their foreheads were touching, cradled her face within his hands, and pressed constant but fleeting kisses across her cheeks, her eyelids, and her mouth, telling her in the only way he had left that she meant everything to him . . . that she was everything to him.

Peace had come to Queen suddenly, without searching, without warning, in the guise of love, at the hands of Cody Bonner. She sighed. It had taken so long, and she'd come so far. But if she'd known it would be this easy, she might have gotten here sooner.

"I'll be right back," he said, and rolled away, headed into his bathroom. Moments later he crawled back into bed with her.

"Cody . . . "

"No pressure, remember," he whispered, and slid an arm beneath her neck and pulled her against him. "Rest. There'll be plenty of time to talk later. Right now I just want to feel the love."

Feel the love. What a simple yet overwhelming way of expressing what had come and gone between them. Queen smiled, dug a place for herself in the bed beside him, and let the feeling roll over her, too. Just before she dozed off she remembered thinking that he'd been right. The love *was* there, if you knew where to look.

She'd been awake forever, just watching him sleep as he lay flat on his stomach, one arm sprawled out across her upper body, the other tucked beneath his pillow. She leaned on an elbow, brushed away a wing of black hair from his forehead, and kissed a small scar on his shoulder while marveling at the strength and length of him. She smiled to herself, remembering that her first impression of him had been of his boots, abandoned on the bottom of the stairs.

I was right. It took a big man to fill them.

She looked at his legs, so strong and lean, and thought of a time when he'd been hurt and broken. She could have wept at the idea of him in pain. Then she remembered how fast he had traveled through the snow to come after her, to rescue her from Virgil Stratton, and of how he'd never stopped or given up his pursuit even though he must have been exhausted.

He moaned in his sleep and shifted, his arm sliding lower from her breasts to her waist, then tightening in automatic response to the move. Even asleep he wouldn't let her go.

His hands, so broad and strong, yet gentle with his sons and so loving with her, had killed for her. She would never get over the feeling of waking up in the snow and hearing his voice and feeling his hands on her body and knowing that God *had* heard her prayers.

This man . . . her man . . . was worth fighting for, worth keeping. If she could get past a lifetime of doubts and remember that not every man was like Johnny Houston, then maybe . . . just maybe . . . they could make it work.

"I love you, Cody Bonner."

But he didn't hear, and later when he woke, she didn't repeat it. It had been hard enough to say when she'd known he wasn't listening.

It took hours for them to get out of bed and dressed. And the single most obvious need for doing so was his three sons, who were running up the driveway from the bus stop, tossing snowballs and verbal assaults back and forth as they came.

Queen spun from the doorway in sudden fright. "Don't tell them," she said.

Cody nodded. He didn't have to ask what. And he didn't have to ask why. What had happened between them was too new and fresh to share with anyone. Besides, what would he say? "Boys . . . today I slept with your aunt who's not really your aunt." Or better yet, "Boys . . . today I made love with the housekeeper, the woman who bakes your cookies." Not exactly the sorts of things a father tells his sons, especially when the woman in question is not their mother.

Queen sighed with relief, uncertain of what she'd thought he would do but happy that he agreed with her enough to pretend nothing had happened.

They could have saved themselves the time.

Donny burst into the house ahead of his two younger brothers, eyes bright with laughter, cheeks glowing from the sharp wind, and headed for the stairs to dump his books before razing the kitchen for an after-school snack.

"Hi, guys," he yelled as he ran past. Then something struck him as odd, and he turned on a dime and stared back at the pair who were standing on opposite sides of the room.

He backtracked into the room with a slight grin on his face, ignoring Will and J.J., who raced in behind him, slamming the door and barreling into the kitchen to lay claim to their snacks. Donny had suddenly realized there were more interesting things to do than fight for food.

"So . . . what's new?" he asked, and dumped his books on a chair.

"Not much, son," Cody said. "And I think that's supposed to be my line. What's new with you?"

Donny shrugged and turned his attention to Queen, missing nothing of her high color or the way she carefully avoided his father's slow gaze.

"Boring day, hunh? What with this snow and all, I bet you never set foot outdoors, did you?"

Queen blushed furiously and then realized that they were falling into the little wretch's trap.

Donny grinned. "Hot damn!" he shouted, clapped his hands together, and then started out of the room.

Cody rolled his eyes and shrugged. He should have known they would be helpless in the face of teenage ingenuity.

"Donny!"

Queen's sharp tone stopped him in place. Thinking he was about to be reprimanded for his vocabulary, he sighed and turned.

"You forgot your books," she said.

He grinned and wiggled his eyebrows Groucho Marx style, his favorite new thing to do. "Yeah . . . right." And then he was gone.

"It's not my fault—" Cody started to say.

Queen held up her hand. "Don't bother apologizing for anything," she said. "It's no one's fault. And we should have known we can't hide hormones . . . not from someone with an overabundance of them."

Cody burst out laughing. The description of his son was perfect. And she was right. He could no more hide what he felt for her than he could stop breathing.

"Shall we dine?" Cody asked, making fun of the fact that they were about to referee snack time in the Bonner household.

"No, I think I'll leave the pleasure to you," Queen

said. "Surely I've got some mending . . . or patching . . . or something that needs my attention. I think you should join your sons and have a time of sharing. It will be good for you."

He rolled his eyes. When those three were together there was no such thing as sharing; it was always more of a "go to your corner and come out smiling" sort of time, and she knew it.

"Thank you for the honor, my lady," he said softly as she left the room.

She turned and smiled at the look he gave her. On the surface she knew he'd been teasing her for the fact that she'd dumped the care of his sons in his lap, but on a deeper level she also heard him thanking her for more than here and now. He was thanking her for the past few hours they'd spent in each other's arms.

"It was my pleasure, sir," she said. "My pleasure indeed."

He stood for a long time, staring after her, and thought, No, that's where you're wrong, love. The pleasure was entirely mine.

As always in the mountains in winter, night came swiftly. Weary boys struggled through lessons and protested little when bedtime came. And as children will do, they sensed the change in their home without understanding it. Clinging to Queen as if she might suddenly disappear, Will and J.J. insisted on a nighttime ritual they'd almost forgotten: a bedtime story.

"How about me, guys?" Cody asked, seeing Queen's exhaustion in the dark shadows beneath her eyes, remembering that a short time ago she'd suffered a severe emotional and physical trauma. He also remembered what they'd put each other through only hours ago.

"No . . . we want Queenie," J.J. said, and then grinned at his father. "She does the sounds along with the story."

"She does? Then maybe I should listen, too. I like stories with sound effects."

"Yeah!" Will said. "You can sleep with Donny. We get Queenie."

Queen flushed. There was no way she was going to look at Cody's face. She knew him well enough to know that he'd be enjoying this greatly and at her expense.

"It's fine with me," she said. "I don't care who listens, but they'd better be quiet."

Cody knew that last jab was meant for him but wisely made no comment.

"And remember the rules," she continued. "One story and then lights out."

It took forever to get the boys settled. Even though she'd warned them, the war still came when it was time to choose the story. They argued until Cody was about to step in and settle it his way. Queen intervened—as always, the peacemaker.

"How about if I tell you a story instead?" she asked.

The novelty of the idea was enough to make everyone curious and quickly get in place, waiting for the show to begin.

Queen took a deep breath, suddenly certain of what she would say. She needed to tell her story . . . in her own words . . . and to the people she'd come to love. They had to know her world just as she'd come to know theirs. And they had to accept her for who she was, as well as what she'd become to them.

"Once upon a time . . . ," she began.

Cody grinned, unaware of the importance of the impending story until he saw the expression on her face and heard a tremble in her voice.

Donny sensed that more was about to happen than a little-kid fairy story, and he quieted instantly, shushing his brothers with a hiss and a look that brought silence to the room.

And then there was only Queen and her deep, husky voice, telling in a slow Tennessee drawl the story of the gambler's daughters.

" . . . in a tiny town . . . far away in the Tennessee hills, there lived three little girls and their father, who was by trade a gambler."

Cody caught his breath and tried not to stare at the sheen of tears in her eyes. If she cried, he would not be able to keep his hands off her, and he knew that she had to tell this story alone.

The boys listened, their eyes widening when she told them how the children were often hungry and many times never knew where they would sleep. And how they moved from town to town with their father, who was always in search of a better deal and a little luck, who would bet anything and everything he owned at the turn of a card. She told how the girls would whisper in their single bed, making plans for the day when they'd be grown and leave this awful life behind. Go somewhere to a faraway place where the air was clean and no one knew that they'd been poor.

"And the years went by, and the girls grew up, and a funny thing happened."

"What? What?" J.J. and Will echoed each other's questions, drawn to the story by the idea that three little girls had been motherless just like them.

"Just listen, and you'll find out," Queen said, gently hugging them against her. "Well! As much as they'd hated their father's life and the way that they'd been raised, they found out that they couldn't leave him as easily as they'd imagined. The tables had turned. They were still tied to him as they had been when they were children. But now it wasn't because they were small and poor. They couldn't leave him now because he was growing old, and he would have been alone. You see, along with the bad things in their lives, they realized that they'd had something very, very special as well. They'd had love. It held them together long after they were grown. And it held them together until the old man died."

Will sighed. "My mother died," he said.

"I know, sweetheart," Queen said. "But she loved you a lot, didn't she?"

He nodded.

"Then that's what you have to remember. Her love."

Cody couldn't look at her. He was too overwhelmed by her story to do anything but stare up at the ceiling above Donny's bed and hope to hell that no one saw him swallowing tears.

"What happened next?" Donny asked.

Queen's lips trembled, but she smiled and continued. "Let's see . . . where was I?" she asked.

"The gambler died," Cody said.

Queen nodded without looking at him. "Right. . . . The gambler died. And when he did, the sisters realized that now they were free."

"Did they leave?"

Queen nodded. "They sure did. As fast as they could travel. One followed her heart and a man with a hatful of promises. One followed the bright lights and the old gambler's dreams."

"And what about the other one? Where did the last one go?"

Queen sighed. "She was the lucky one. Because when she left, she didn't know where she was going. She was just running. What she didn't know was that there was a special place and some special people just waiting for her to find them."

"Did she live happily ever after?" Will asked.

It was then that Cody looked up and held his breath, awaiting her answer as anxiously as were his sons.

Queen lifted her head and stared straight into his eyes. "Yes, honey, I think she did. Now . . . it's time to sleep. Tomorrow's a school day."

She slipped out of her nest between the boys, leaned over, and kissed each of them on the cheek before covering them up, then stepped aside when Cody came over to tuck them in.

"Night, Queenie. Night, Dad," they said in unison.

"Good night, guys," she said softly.

"What about me?" Donny asked as she started out the door.

Queen was surprised. Donny never allowed hugs and kisses unless he was the one offering. Cody stood aside as she slipped in between the beds and bent over the boy.

"Good night," Donny said as she kissed him on the cheek. "I'm really glad you ran to us," he added quietly.

She couldn't speak, only nodded her head in agreement as Cody turned off the lights.

They left the room together, closed the door behind them, then stood for a moment in the silence of the hall and looked at each other without speaking. And then Cody opened his arms and she walked into them, sighing with the peace that comes when you've been lost and finally find your way home.

He hugged her, rocking her within his embrace until her trembling stopped, and her arms came around him, and she turned her face up for the kiss she knew was waiting.

13

A sound intruded into Cody's sleep, yanking him rudely into consciousness. Without taking time to decipher what he'd heard, he rolled out of bed, pulled on a pair of jeans, and began buttoning them as he stepped into his sneakers. An impulse to hurry frightened him. The only thing he could imagine was that one of the boys was sick or that Queen needed him.

In seconds he'd gone from his room to his sons' room down the hall. It didn't take long to see that all three were in place and deeply asleep. That left Queen.

She was gone. Her bed was empty, the covers thrown back as if in a hurry. Her robe, the one he'd given her, lay across a chair where she'd tossed it. Her gown was on the floor at the foot of the bed.

The bathrooms were empty, the hallway in shadows, lit only by the glow of the quarter moon hanging just above the treetops. The house was cool, almost chilly, and he absently turned up the heat as he passed the thermostat.

The stairs creaked in several places as he came down them, and he stopped and listened between sounds, hoping once again to pinpoint what it was that had awakened him. Ignoring the darkened rooms, he walked with unerring aim through the house toward the kitchen. And then he saw her through the open door.

He recognized the sweater she was wearing as an old one of his by the fact that it hung nearly to her knees, noticed that her legs and feet were bare as she stood on the decking outside, staring out into the night. The wind tossed her hair and pressed the sweater against her body with constant persistence.

"What in the world?" he muttered, and went out the kitchen door to where she stood sentinel at the rail.

"Queen, baby . . . what's wrong? And where the hell are the rest of your clothes? You'll freeze."

She spun, startled by the sound of his voice, and then put her fingers to her lips and shushed him.

"Listen! Cody . . . what is it? What's making that sound?"

He listened, and then he heard . . . coming down the mountains, dancing across the treetops, sliding through the hollows, and racing toward the valley below. He tilted his head and felt its breath and shivered responsively at its power.

"Chinook."

To a lady from Tennessee, it was an unfamiliar term.

"Is it a storm? I heard water dripping off the roof of the house by my bedroom window and thought it was raining. And then the wind rattled the windowpane."

Cody slipped his arms around her, pulling her backside snugly against him, and rested his chin against the curls blowing across his cheeks as they faced the wind.

"Don't you feel it?" he asked. "Close your eyes and tell me what you feel."

Safe in the shelter of his body, she obeyed and then seconds later cried, "It's warm!"

"Right!" Cody said. "A chinook is a dry wind, a warm breath from the west that comes down the Rockies during winter or early spring. Look at the trees."

Queen peered into the moonglow and then gasped. "It's melting! Cody! The world is melting."

He laughed softly at her excitement. "No . . . the world's not melting, but the snow damned sure is, and I can't say I'm sorry. This was an early snow, even for Colorado. I'm afraid our winter has barely begun."

Queen shivered within his arms. "I don't care. As long as you're here, I'm not afraid of anything."

Her admission left him speechless. He tightened his grip and felt her relax against him. The trust that she gave so willingly made him humble.

"Lady, you take my breath away."

"That's just the wind," Queen teased, and smiled to herself as she felt his hands sliding up the outside of her sweater.

She closed her eyes and sighed with pleasure as he cupped her breasts in his palms and then moved against her from behind in a slow, side-to-side motion that she knew was meant to entice and excite. Within seconds it had served its purpose as his hands slid down her front and splayed across her belly and lower, marking their place in increments of heat.

"Cody . . ."

He heard her say his name, felt her muscles jerking in spasms beneath his hands, and knew that the chinook had warmed up more than the snow.

"It's too cold out here for this," he said, and urged her toward the door.

"Not if you don't stop," she whispered, turning in his arms. She moaned softly when his hands slid around to her backside and cupped her hips, pulling her closer, too close, not close enough, to the hard bulge of him beyond the fly of his jeans.

"Come upstairs with me," Cody said. "I want to feel you beneath me when I come."

His words were a seduction in itself. She shuddered, remembering the powerful thrusts of his body within her and the ensuing burst of pleasure and passion.

She moaned as he shifted her sweater to caress her bare flesh beneath. "I can't walk that far, Cody Bonner. I'm already too far gone. Help me, because I can't help myself."

He couldn't think past the whispered admission in his ear. But he could feel her body trembling, and her honey on his fingertips, and knew that one of them had to act before motion became impossible.

"Oh, God," he groaned, and moved without thinking, aware only of the woman about to combust and the need he had to burn in her fire.

He yanked at the buttons on his jeans, let free the swollen jut of his manhood, and then with one smooth motion lifted her up and then let her down . . . on him.

She locked her arms and legs in place and fell face forward on his shoulder as his arms held her firmly upon him.

Words were impossible as sensation became the only sense she could remember. He filled her.

Cody braced his legs, tightened his hold, and tried not to explode as her muscles contracted around him in tiny tremors of motion. "Come with me," he begged, and began the act of love.

She did as she was told.

Minutes later Cody shivered, but from exertion and emotion, not from cold. Somehow he managed to pull himself together and stagger to a deck chair, where he and Queen collapsed in each other's arms.

She snuggled against his chest and curled her feet and legs into his lap, unwilling to give up the closeness of what they'd just shared. "Oh, Cody," was all she could say.

"I know." A moment later his heart crashed against his chest as he realized what they'd just done. "My God, lady! I just made love to you without protection."

Queen turned and drew her knees up on either side of his legs as she straddled his lap. She placed both hands squarely on his shoulders and looked him straight in the eye.

"I know what we did. And I don't care," she said. "The question now remains . . . if . . . if anything happens . . . will you be ready to suffer the consequences or will you be buying that bus ticket for me yourself?"

He shook her, overwhelmed with anger at her doubt of his love. "Goddammit! Don't put words into my mouth, lady! I was concerned for you, not myself. In my heart, you're already a part of my family. We've just never discussed adding to it, that's all."

Queen sighed and leaned forward until her lips were inches away from his face. "You don't understand what you mean to me yet, do you?" she asked. "In *my* heart . . . you already protected me. In *my* mind . . . you'll do what's right no matter what the cost. With you, I always feel protected . . . and loved. Whatever comes from that will be wanted and welcomed."

Their lips met. Soft meshed with firm, cool with warm, sighs blended and changed into reluctant moans as they drew apart.

He lifted her into his arms and then stood and headed for the door. "Come with me, honey," he begged. "This time we do it my way."

"Whatever you say, Cody. Whatever you say."

The next morning, less than an hour after the boys had left for school, Cody was already downstairs when he heard a familiar but unexpected sound.

Queen came out of the boys' bedroom with a handful of dirty laundry and then stopped at the top of the stairs and watched Cody dart from the living room out the front door. It was then that she, too, heard the noise, dropped the laundry, and started to run.

It came out of the sun, its propellers making a popping noise that echoed back and forth between the mountaintops as it circled above them and then began to descend, coming down toward the wide-open space in front of the house like a bee aiming for the open petals of a blossom.

"What in the world?"

Cody turned at Queen's surprised comment and shrugged, trying not to frown at the spectacular appearance of Lt. Colonel Dennis Macon. "It's Dennis."

Queen grinned. "I knew you should have called him back." She ignored Cody's muttered obscenity as Dennis climbed out of the helicopter and sidestepped what was left of the melting snow as well as the puddles it had created.

"Got any coffee left?" he shouted as he bounded up the steps. The helicopter's rotors were still turning, lifting Queen's hair and Cody's temper.

"What the hell do you want?" Cody asked.

"Come on in," Queen said. "I'll see."

Cody glared, aware that he and his comments had been entirely ignored, and followed the two inside.

Dennis Macon wasn't the type to stand on ceremony. He took one look at Queen and then embraced her. "Angel . . . it's good to see you smiling."

Queen flushed and wiggled out of his hug as quickly as possible. She'd seen the look on Cody's face and had no desire to make things worse between the men. She sensed that Dennis somehow held the key to Cody's ultimate satisfaction with himself.

"Thanks," she said. "It's good to still be here and able to do it."

Dennis shook his head, marveling at what she had endured and the strength of character it must have taken to survive it. And then he remembered who had been ultimately responsible for it happening and grinned.

"Hey, Coda-man," he said, slipping back into the vernacular the men had used when serving together, "so you've gone and made yourself a hero again. That's good . . . real good. Getting you in practice for the real thing, right?"

"Dammit, Dennis. I told you I—"

"Cody . . . "

Queen called his name quietly, firmly, and with warning. He frowned, caught the look on her face, and sighed, knowing that she'd never forgive him if he turned this down now.

"Why are you here?" he asked Dennis.

"Because the snow melted enough for me to show you the project sight. Thought you might want to take 'er up yourself on the trip over. And because you didn't call me back and tell me not to come."

Cody's eyes, bright with a mixture of reluctance and desire, told Queen everything she needed to know. She'd seen the interest . . . and she'd seen his need. Flying was in his blood. She'd already accepted that. And forty-two was too young an age for a man like Cody Bonner to retire.

"I'll get Dennis his coffee while you're changing," she said, and walked out of the room.

Cody watched her leave and knew that she'd given him more than her blessing. She'd given him back his life . . . and everything that mattered in his world.

"Quite a woman," Dennis said.

"Yes, she is," Cody replied. "And just so you don't forget . . . she's all mine."

Dennis cocked an eyebrow and grinned at his buddy's friendly warning. "Like I didn't already know," he said as Cody disappeared up the stairs.

Minutes later Cody came downstairs to find Queen calmly entertaining Dennis and feeding him banana bread and coffee. Cody watched her, suddenly remembering her fears of being unable to compete in his world. She needn't have worried. She didn't have to do anything but exist and she had men eating out of her plate . . . and hands.

Queen looked up. Dennis's words faded into the background as she focused on Cody. His blue gaze raked her body with a look that made her tremble. Her hands shook as she quietly replaced the empty plate upon the table between Dennis and herself. She remembered being impaled upon Cody's body only hours earlier and felt herself go weak. From the look in his eyes, he was remembering the same thing.

Dennis stuttered to a halt as he noticed that he was the only one having a conversation. He half turned on his seat to see Cody waiting at the doorway.

"Hey! I didn't hear you come in. Why didn't you say

something?" He set down his coffee cup and got to his feet.

"I was talking to someone else," Cody said, and watched Queen blush.

"But I didn't hear you . . . " Dennis stopped. Suddenly he got the message of what was, and was not, being said. "Okay." He sighed. "Maybe I do hear you. For God's sake, let's go before someone catches on fire here." He turned and gave Queen a wink. "Unfortunately, I can tell it won't be me."

Queen grinned, ignoring his playful complaint as she walked with them to the door, aware of the excitement Cody was experiencing.

"We'll be back in the early afternoon," Dennis said. He dug into his pocket and handed her a card. "And if you need to get in touch with Cody before then, just call this number. They'll patch you through to us anytime."

"Thanks, man," Cody said. This unexpected gesture had suddenly released him from his last vestige of guilt at leaving her alone. If she had a way of contacting him, she would not feel totally abandoned.

"Thank you," Queen said. "But don't expect to hear from me because I don't expect any problems. In fact, I have all kinds of projects planned that definitely require that I have my space."

Dennis tipped his hat and went out ahead of Cody, giving them their own space in which to say good-bye.

Queen brushed at a wayward strand of dark hair across Cody's forehead that seemed destined to stray and resisted the urge to cling to him. He'd become so important in her life that she couldn't imagine it without him.

"Be careful," she said. "And look at this project with an open mind, not old fears. We can't be happy if you're not happy, Cody."

He nodded and then opened his arms. She stepped inside. "I love you so much, lady," he said, and pressed a quick, passionate kiss across her mouth before she had time to argue or answer.

In seconds he was gone, and she watched from the deck as he crawled into the chopper, belted himself in, and then lifted off with a wave and a smile.

She watched until the small black speck disappeared into nothing. She tried not to mind that he had a love other than her, then told herself she was crazy for being jealous of motors and wings. When he was with her, they had their own way of flying.

"I love you, too, Cody," she said. "And one of these days you'll be around to hear it."

She entered the house, locked the door firmly behind her, and went straight to the hall closet to pull out the package that Cody had brought to her days ago from the craft shop.

She tore it open and sighed with pleasure, smiling as the skeins fell across her lap in royal profusion. The yarn was precisely what she'd ordered—ten skeins—and the exact color of his eyes. The knitting needles she'd asked for had been poked safely into a thick skein of the deep blue wool, and the pattern book was at the bottom of the pack, just as she'd hoped.

"You gave me one of yours," she said, fingering the wool and remembering the sweaters that he'd outgrown and passed on to her. "I'll give you one of mine."

She ran through the house, quickly setting things to rights and starting the laundry she'd abandoned earlier. In no time she was through with the hasty cleanup and ready to sit down and begin her own special project.

She could hardly wait for it to take shape as she started

a chain, knitting with quick, sure flicks of the needles, then turning at the end of the chain and beginning the purl back across. When Christmas came he was going to be so surprised.

The days fell into a calm routine. The boys went to school. Queen took care of the mundane details of the house and, when the mood struck her, drove into Snow Gap in Cody's Blazer to go shopping. Dennis and Cody dealt with the project at hand.

And gradually, Cody's sweater, and their lives, began to take shape.

"Are you gonna tell Dad?" Will asked J.J.

"What if it makes him mad?"

A sigh accompanied the snort before Will's comment. "He won't get mad, stupid. He always told us not to talk to strangers, remember?"

"Yeah, but we didn't talk to him. He talked to us, remember? We just ran away, right?"

There was little Will could say in argument to J.J.'s rebuttal. "I know, but if we hadn't run, what would that man have done? Maybe he'd have snatched us like that bad guy did Queenie. Then what, stupid?"

J.J. got quiet.

Queen's heart skipped a beat at the tone of their conversation. She stood in the hallway and continued to listen to the boys' conversation, unashamed of eavesdropping when their safety was at stake. What on earth had been happening to the boys that would make them not want to tell Cody? She'd never known them to be reticent with their father before and couldn't imagine what would be at the root of their fears. Then she got an answer she didn't want to hear.

"But if we tell him the man asked about Queenie . . . what if he makes her leave so the man won't bother us anymore? Then what, yourself, stupid?"

Queen sighed and buried her face in her hands. Oh, God! Who on earth could be asking questions about her? And why ask them of children who knew little to nothing about her past?

And then a thought occurred to her. Maybe it did not have to do with her past in Cradle Creek, but with the present. A swift vision of Lenore Whittier's angry face and bitter words crossed her mind before she knocked once and then pushed aside the partially opened door.

"Hi, guys. Get through with your homework yet?"

"Yeah, we're through," they replied together.

"Where's Donny?"

Will shrugged. "Maybe playing Nintendo . . . we don't know."

She sat down on the edge of the bed and wished Cody were there. "So, what's new with you?" she asked. "School going okay?"

They both looked away. "Fine, I guess," Will said, unable to completely ignore the woman who'd filled his life with peace and comfort.

"Making many new friends?" Queen asked, persisting in the hope that they'd open up to her instead.

"Some," J.J. said. "There's a neat guy who sits next to me in homeroom. He can burp anytime he wants. All you have to do is ask him . . . he'll do it for free."

"Wow!" Queen smiled and tried not to laugh, remembering the purpose of the conversation.

"That's stupid," Will said, poking J.J. on the arm.

"It's not, you're just jealous 'cause you're bigger and you still can't burp like Weeber."

"Weeber?" Disbelief colored Queen's voice. "Is that his real name?"

"Yeah," J.J. said. "Weeber . . . Michael Weeber."

"Oh." She'd forgotten about the male thing to call peers by their surnames instead of their given names. It was a whole new world every day just waking up in a house full of men, no matter their ages. "Well, maybe he can come out and play with you sometime," she offered, and then added, "If your daddy doesn't mind."

"That'd be cool!" J.J. said.

The boys got quiet. Queen saw a quick look pass between them.

"Did your daddy ever tell you not to talk to strangers?" J.J. asked her.

"He sure did," Queen said. "And we didn't . . . ever. Not me. Not any of my sisters. They might hurt you."

Will nodded. "See, I told you so."

"Why?" Queen asked. "Has someone been bothering you?" She sensed J.J. withdraw, and yet she persisted. "You can tell me," she said. "I'll understand. Besides, that's what grown-ups are for . . . to fix what little guys can't."

J.J. gave in. "There was this man at school . . . he asked me my name, and when I told him, he asked me if I knew you. He asked me if you were nice. I ran away." J.J. ducked his head. "I didn't answer him. But if I had . . . I would have told him yes. I would have said you were nice, Queenie, honest I would."

She hugged him, angry beyond words that someone had interfered in a child's world enough to terrorize him, however innocent it might be. "Did he touch you?" she asked.

"No!" Will intervened. "We were inside the schoolyard. He was outside the fence. He can't come in, right?"

"He's not supposed to," Queen said. "Did you tell your teacher?"

J.J. shook his head.

"If it happens again, you must run and tell your teacher that a man is bothering you. Will you promise me that?"

J.J. nodded. "I promise," he said, relieved that he'd been given a solution and that no one was angry.

"What did he look like?" she asked.

He shrugged. "Just a man. But all weird."

Queen frowned. A child's version of weird might be quite different from an adult's. "Weird, how, honey?"

J.J. thought. "Well . . . he had on a long droopy coat, you know . . . the kind like Columbo on TV wears? And he had a big pointy nose and a real funny mouth. And the goofiest thing was his throat poked out when he talked."

Queen listened, absorbing his description and realizing that it was, for a child, quite thorough, even down to the description of an oversize Adam's apple that bobbed as he spoke. "Did he tell you his name?" she asked.

"Naw . . . I ran away too fast."

"Good boy!" Queen said, and hugged him, including Will in her praise. "Now promise, if it happens again . . . what do you do?"

"Tell the teacher!" they shouted in unison.

"Right! Now, if you're through with homework, I left a snack on the kitchen table. Don't make a mess . . . and don't fight. There's plenty for two, okay?"

"Okay!" they said, and burst from the room, leaving Queen alone on their bed, absorbing the news.

"Oh, Lord," she muttered. "Cody . . . where are you when I need you?"

But she knew where he was, at Lowry AFB completing the last of the proposal for the building site of the survival training camp. All she could do was wait for him to come home, and she already knew that it would be tomorrow at the earliest before he would.

She walked into her room, dug out Dennis Macon's card from her dresser drawer, and fiddled with it as she tried to decide if this was emergency enough to call Cody home.

Minutes later she decided that first things came first. Tomorrow she'd go to the school herself and talk to the principal, warn him that a man was lurking around the schoolyard. Then when Cody came home, she could tell him what J.J. had said, and what she'd done, and let him take it from there.

With the decision made, she went in search of Donny to tell him what she'd learned and ask him to be on the lookout as well. It wouldn't hurt to have extra body-guards for a trusting seven-year-old.

Donny Bonner had inherited more than looks from his father. That night, after his talk with Queenie, he went to bed with a whole new attitude toward his two lit-tle brothers. They'd gone from being little pests to pre-cious possessions. No one was going to bother *his* broth-ers. Not if he had anything to say about it.

Long after the boys had gone to bed, Queen sat star-ing into the embers of the dying fire and tried to remem-ber her life before Cody and his sons. The more time passed, the harder it became to remember the ugliness of Cradle Creek and the mean, unforgiving way in which she and her sisters had often been treated. Her life was being filled now with something she hadn't known exist-ed until she'd met the Bonners. Trust.

They trusted her to take care of them and, in turn, loved her for it. She loved them for the fact that they trusted her to do it. It was a good deal all the way around.

The phone rang, startling her out of her musings. She picked it up on the second ring and waited to hear the sound of his voice.

"Queen?"

She forgot she hadn't answered. "Hi," she said, and laughed softly. "I knew it was you. I forgot to say hello."

He chuckled. "As long as you don't forget about me, we're okay."

"I think you're safe," she said.

"If I were there, you wouldn't be," he said, and sighed as he heard her breath catch. Just listening to her talk made him hard. "Anything new?" he asked.

Then she remembered. "Yes, there is," she said. "But I think it can wait until you get back. You're coming home tomorrow, aren't you?"

"You've got my promise," he said, and then he thought about the hesitancy in her voice. "Are you sure you don't need to talk? The boys aren't sick. You're not afraid, are you? If you are, then I'll—"

"Cody, I'm fine, they're not sick, and what I need to tell you can wait. Okay?"

He sighed. "Okay. But I hate like hell not being there when things like this happen."

"You'll soon have everything in working order, and things like this *won't* happen. Besides, I can take care of *things* all by myself." She felt compelled to add, "Most of the time. Remember, that's why I'm here, so you can be there."

"No, lady. That's not entirely true. You're in my house because you're in my life. I love you, honey. Sleep tight. I'll see you tomorrow."

"'Night, Cody. I love you, too."

She hung up before he had time to answer and then smiled. That hadn't been nearly as difficult to say as she'd imagined. Of course, the fact that she hadn't had to face him when it came out had influenced the decision.

The phone rang. She picked it up with a grin.

"Damn you, woman. You wait until I'm hours away and the only connection between us is a telephone line? My God, my lady . . . do you know how long I've waited to hear you tell me that?"

Cody dropped back onto the bed and stared up at the ceiling, aware that if wishes could fly, he'd already be airborne.

Queen closed her eyes and absorbed the texture of his voice as it wrapped around her soul. "No, but if you hurry home, I might be tempted into saying it again . . . sometime soon."

"Ah, Queen, my heart is already there," Cody said, and disconnected as suddenly as he had called.

14

An unwelcome sensation of déjà vu came over Queen as she entered the principal's office at Snow Gap Elementary School. She took a seat in the outer office and absorbed the ambiance. Schools seemed to have one thing in common, a lingering odor of chalk dust, floor sweep, and the sweaty bodies of children hard at work and play.

But this one differed drastically from the school in Cradle Creek that Queen and her sisters had graduated from. It was clean and updated, and she could hear the purr of electric typewriters in an adjoining office as well as a copy machine kicking out paper with smooth regularity.

She closed her eyes, remembering vividly the day she and her sisters had gone to enroll at Cradle Creek and the fear of rejection that had accompanied her.

That day had been a turning point in Queen's life.

She would never forget Jedda Willis's kindness. The principal of Cradle Creek had been an extremely sensitive woman, one who'd immediately seen the defenses twelve-year-old Queen was struggling to maintain. Mrs. Willis had let Johnny Houston's daughters maintain what dignity they could in the face of their adversity.

"Miss Houston?"

The secretary's voice startled Queen. She stood with a jerk, fumbling for her purse, smoothing down her hair and clothing in a sudden fit of anxiety, and then she remembered that she wasn't in trouble. J.J. was the one with problems. But in Cody's absence, it was up to her to fix them.

"Yes," Queen answered. "I'm coming."

Stanley Brass looked up in pleased surprise at the woman who entered his office. He stood up and came around his desk with an outstretched hand. "Queen Houston, isn't it? We met at the bank."

Queen smiled. "Yes, we did. I'm glad you remember me. It makes my visit here easier."

Stanley nodded as he ushered her to a seat. "Now, what brings you to my office? Are the boys having problems of which I'm unaware?"

"You could say that," Queen said. She began to repeat the boys' conversation that she'd overheard as well as what J.J. told her.

Stanley's expression grew serious. He fiddled with a pen and made periodic notes as she continued to talk, pausing only now and then to interrupt to clarify the description she was giving him.

" . . . and that's about all he would say regarding the man's description," Queen finished. She leaned back on the chair and sighed, relieved to have given part of the responsibility of this problem to someone else.

Stanley frowned. This wasn't the first time something like this had occurred. With the influx of strangers in town every year during ski season, they often had an oddball or two pull such stunts. Unfortunately, when it involved children, it involved him. The world had changed drastically since he was a child, and he often felt a sense of helplessness in relating to it.

"I can't thank you enough for coming to me with this," he said. "I'll take instant precautions, of course. I'll meet with my teachers this evening after school. And . . . I'll notify Sheriff Miller immediately. He will need to be on the lookout for this man. He could be preying on other children outside the school system."

"I know that you'll do all you can," Queen said. "But my concern still rests on the fact that the man was asking about me. I can't help but feel responsible."

Stanley shook his head. "No, Miss Houston, I tend to disagree. I learned long ago in this business that you can't be responsible for other people's shortcomings. You do what you can when the opportunity is presented, and then mourn for what you can't. But you never . . . absolutely never . . . feel guilt. You can't heal the world. Remember that."

Queen nodded and stood. "And I'm sure you'll be hearing from the boys' father just as soon as he returns. I didn't think I was stepping out of line by coming to you in his stead. I felt this was too pressing an issue to wait."

"I think you were right," Stanley said. "And thank you for coming. Please keep me informed of any developments from your end; I'll do the same."

Queen left the office with an entirely new appreciation for Stanley Brass. What had been most assuring of all was that he'd taken her seriously, treated her as a respected citizen, and believed her implicitly. It was a new and heady experience for her.

She walked down the hall and was about to exit when the bell rang for classes to change. She stood aside as children swarmed out of the rooms like drones in a hive, hunting for the next place in which they needed to be.

J.J. spotted her instantly. It would have been impossible not to. She stood heads above the children and most of the teachers, her vivid coloring and height a beacon to any who chose to look her way.

"Queenie!" His shriek of delight was heard by several other children as he broke ranks and ran toward her.

She grinned and caught him on impact, ruffling his hair and pulling at his collar as he danced around her feet, thrilled that someone special was available to show off to his friends.

"This is my Queenie," J.J. said as his teacher came through the crowd.

Queen smiled at the woman who had come to check on her wayward pupil. "Mrs. Barrett, isn't it?" she asked. "I'm Queen Houston. J.J.'s—"

"Oh!" Lisa Barrett's face broke into a wide, infectious smile. "Miss Houston! I'm so glad to finally meet you. J.J. talks of you constantly. It's Queenie says this and Queenie says that. You've made quite an impression on this young man, no doubt." And then on a more serious note, she added, "And may I say we're all extremely glad that you came out of your ordeal unharmed."

Queen's eyes filled with unexpected tears as she nodded, then looked down at the unabashed adoration J.J. was giving her. Her hand slid gently across his forehead, then came to rest on his shoulder.

"Well, he made an impression on me, too. I'd say the

feeling is mutual. Actually, the entire Bonner family has pretty much claimed my heart." She blushed the moment she said it. "I mean, the boys are special . . . you understand . . . "

Lisa Barrett grinned. "Oh, don't bother to explain. I met their father. I know exactly what you mean." She rolled her eyes and sighed. "Well, I'm happily married these last fifteen years, but if I weren't . . . and if . . . " She laughed. "You know what I mean."

Queen grinned. There was no need to reply.

"J.J., say good-bye to Queen, and quickly, please. You need to get to your next class," Mrs. Barrett said. "Miss Houston, it's been a pleasure. I hope we meet again soon. We have a yearly tradition of Halloween parties in the elementary. If you would like, we always need sponsors to bake—"

"Queenie can make anything," J.J. piped up. "She's the best cook in the whole world."

They laughed.

"It looks like I've just been invited to a party," Queen said. "I'll talk to you later about details."

And then she knelt and took J.J. by the arms and pulled him close so that none of the other children passing by could hear. "I talked to Mr. Brass about the man, J.J. He's going to take care of everything. You just remember what we talked about last night. If you see him again, you tell Mrs. Barrett, or Mr. Brass, or any of the other teachers who might happen to be close by, okay?"

Lisa Barrett frowned as she overheard part of what Queen was telling her student. "Problem?"

Queen nodded. "Mr. Brass will fill you in later, I think. I'd better go so you can get back to work and J.J. can get to class." J.J. seemed reluctant to turn loose of her. "Pizza tonight," she promised. He left with a smile.

"You're very good for those boys," Lisa Barrett said.

"No . . . quite the contrary," Queen said. "They're very good for me."

She left the school with a lighter heart than she'd had in weeks and felt pleased with the fact that she'd made the right move. But there were a few more items on her agenda before she could leave Snow Gap, and she needed to hurry and finish them before Cody came home. She made a run for the Blazer and was soon headed back toward the shopping area of town.

She turned the corner and, as she did, saw that classes were changing in the high school on the opposite side of campus. It didn't take long to spy Donny's familiar dark head and lanky figure in one of the groups of boys walking from one classroom to another.

She honked, then grinned at Donny's exuberant response as he waved and whistled while she drove away.

"Hey, hey, hey, Bonner," one of Donny's friends remarked, and added his own brand of wolf whistle to Queen's retreating vehicle. "Who's the babe? You been holding out?"

Donny glared. "That's no babe! That's Queen, the lady who takes care of us. And don't get any fresh ideas. If my dad's half as smart as I think he is, she'll be my new stepmother any day now."

The boy whistled beneath his breath. "She's still a knockout, Bonner. Looks real hot."

Donny punched his friend on the arm. "You don't know hot from hopeless, Marv, and we both know it. So save it for some girl who's stupid enough to fall for it . . . and you."

The group laughed and went on their way, leaving Donny with a new awareness of his soon-to-be mother. His overprotective mode kicked in, and he renewed his efforts to be on the alert for the pervert she'd warned him about last night. That was all they needed—some guy trying to outdo that Virgil Stratton nut and hurt his Queenie or his little brothers.

He hurried on to class and hoped that when he got home this evening, his father would be back. Responsibility was a heavy load to carry alone.

Thanks to the abrupt change in weather, Wally Morrow had shed his trench coat for a rather weedy-looking sport coat and donned neat round sunglasses that unintentionally hid his small, close-set eyes and did their part in minimizing his beaky nose. The old soft-brimmed hat was worn more to hide his thinning hair than for style.

It was this small change in wardrobe that saved him from Queen's notice as she walked out of the pharmacy and back toward her vehicle.

She might have missed him, but Wally didn't miss a thing about her. It was his first up close and personal sighting of the woman he'd been hired to investigate. The description that Lenore Whittier had given him did not do justice to her beauty. He suspected that it was sour grapes as much as anything.

Wally turned his back to the Blazer at the curb and used the store window as a mirror in which to watch Queen Houston's next move. She tossed a small sack onto the seat, locked the door, and then made a dash across the street between traffic to a dress shop on the opposite side.

"Okay," Wally muttered to himself, taking the opportunity to make notes unobserved. "Been to the school, to the doctor, to the pharmacy, and now going shopping." He dotted the *i*'s and crossed the *t*'s and privately thought that Lenore Whittier was spitting into the wind.

He'd been on the job for weeks and had yet to hear one negative thing about the lanky beauty under observation or see her do anything suspicious. But he had his orders, and they were to stay on the job until he found something Mrs. Whittier could use against Cody Bonner to prove him an unfit father.

He slid his notebook inside his jacket, stuffed his hands in his pockets, which made his pants sag even more across the rump, and shuffled down the street to hang out on the corner with a few ski bums who were waiting for a bus to take them to higher ground.

The chinook that had come and gone had left them with no powder on which to schuss, no moguls to attack, no place on which to execute perfect snowplows that would show off their highly defined thigh and buttock muscles.

Wally Morrow stuck out like the proverbial sore thumb in the crowd of young men bursting with vitality and joie de vivre. But it didn't matter. As long as no one actually recognized him, he was satisfied.

Queen entered the store with one goal clearly in mind, and that was to add to her wardrobe of sweatsuits, sweaters, and jeans. Today she wanted soft and feminine. She wanted to look pretty for Cody. And the dress in the window would do the trick, if they had it in her size.

Minutes later she was in a dressing room, stripped down to nothing but her bra and panties. The dress she'd picked from the rack was a deep, dark, cranberry-colored knit that would hug her body in soft folds. Her fingers caressed the fabric, and then anticipation had her fumbling with the zipper as she quickly pulled it off the hanger and slipped it over her head.

It was better than she'd hoped. The color didn't clash with her hair as she'd feared; quite the opposite—it enhanced the nut-brown undertones and auburn highlights to perfection. The sweetheart neckline was low enough to taunt an observer's gaze to wander toward her generous bust and just high enough to remain sedate. The princess waistline emphasized her slender waist as well as the soft, gentle flare of her hips. And the fabric from which it was made molded against her shapely legs as she walked.

"This is the one," she said, and in no time had dressed in her old clothes and paid for her purchase.

Minutes later she was back out on the sidewalk, her purchase in hand, a smile on her face that would have stopped traffic had the drivers been looking.

But only one person was watching her exit, and he wasn't driving. Wally Morrow stared, blind to the fact that the crowd of young men in which he'd been hiding all got on a bus and left, leaving him alone on the street corner with his lust in high gear.

"Oh, my," he muttered, feeling a strange stirring in his nether regions that hadn't bothered him in months. "Oh, my," he repeated, and watched her breasts bounce enticingly and her hips undulate in rhythm to the long strides she was taking.

Queen started across the street toward her Blazer, still thinking about Cody's reaction to her dress, and almost missed seeing the man on the corner. In fact, if a car hadn't honked for her to hurry across, she might not have looked up. But it did, and she saw, and something about the way he was standing, and the solemn, intent way in which he was watching, caught her attention.

Wally Morrow jerked as he suddenly realized she was staring back at him. "Oh, shit," he muttered, and turned in a complete circle, so caught off guard by her attention that he forgot everything he'd ever learned during his fifteen years as a private investigator. Don't call attention to yourself, and don't panic. He'd just done both.

He looked around wildly and then darted into the first open doorway he came to, afraid to look back and see if she was still staring. He had a sudden flash of insight as to how the people upon whom he'd spied over the years must have felt and likened it to that of targets in a shooting gallery.

Queen's stomach turned. Another car honked, and she looked around in shock, realizing that she was still in the middle of the street, and made a run for the other side, where the Blazer was parked. She had a sudden urge to get home and lock herself in—and the world out—until Cody came home.

Something told her that the man's observations had not been all that innocent, especially after the way he'd behaved when he realized she'd seen him. And in spite of his funny-looking sunglasses, she would have sworn he had a sharp, pointy nose, just as J.J. had described.

Cody felt for the jeweler's box tucked safely inside his pocket, as he had more than once during the trip from Denver.

"I'm hurrying," Dennis said, and grinned at the look on his buddy's face.

"I didn't say a word," Cody said.

"You didn't have to. It's called reading your body language, Coda-man. You're as antsy as a green flyboy on his first scramble."

Cody leaned back on the seat and tried to relax. Dennis was right. He felt just as he had the first time he'd been involved in an all-out alert—only the rush the pilots made to get to their jets and get them in the air was nothing compared to the rush of adrenaline shooting through his system now. He had a gut feeling about the odd message Queen had given him regarding a "problem" at home, and the feeling wasn't good.

He sighed. Maybe he was just inventing trouble. All he needed was to get home and see Queen's beautiful face, dig his fingers through her hair, and feel her wrap herself around him. Then he would be fine.

"Nearly there," Dennis said as he topped the last hill.

Cody grinned. "Thanks for the ride. Next time, I'll drive."

"No, next time we'll have your own car ready, compliments of Uncle Sam. A gray, government-issue special."

"Oh, great."

Cody's sarcasm was not lost on Dennis Macon, and his easy laugh filled the interior of the car as they took the last turn toward home.

"Here we are," Dennis said as he drove into the yard and parked.

"Sorry you can't stay," Cody said, making his point with a sharp look he dared Dennis to contest.

"Oh, Lord, but you've got it bad," Dennis said. He looked up in time to see Queen exit the house and stand above them on the deck, waving down in happy anticipation. "And I can't say as how I blame you."

Cody didn't answer, and Dennis didn't wait around to

see if he would change his mind about the invitation to come inside. He knew when he wasn't wanted. And he also knew that if it weren't for Queen Houston, he wouldn't have Cody Bonner heading this project. Priorities being what they were in the military, he decided to take what he could get.

Cody met her at the top step and laughed with joy as she hurled herself into his arms. My God, but I've missed coming home to this, he thought. And then he recalled his life with Claire and realized that he'd never come home to this. She'd always been at some social function or didn't want her hair or makeup mussed. He wondered what he'd done to deserve this kind of love, and this kind of woman, this late in his life.

"I missed you," Queen said, feeling a surge of response from his body as he moved against her.

"I think it's pretty damned obvious that I missed you, too," Cody said, then took her upturned face as an offer to kiss.

Her lips were soft and tasted of strawberries. He wondered what she'd been cooking and then wondered why he cared. The last thing he wanted now was food.

Queen took in the scent and the feel of him, glorying in the fact that she could make him ache in all the right places with nothing more than a look or a touch. His mouth raked across her face, centering on her lips, and then insisted on staking a claim she would never deny him.

She groaned, and his hands slid behind her, cupping her hips and grinding her gently against the ache she'd created. "Cody, I—"

"Come inside," he whispered, and lifted her off her feet.

"But we need to—"

"I know what we need, my lady. It's each other."

"Yes, but—"

"No buts. Besides, I distinctly heard you say 'yes.' Am I right?"

The wind caught in his hair and ran playful, gusty fingers through the raven-dark mane. His eyes, as blue as the sky behind him, dared her to argue with forces beyond their control.

Queen sighed with defeat and smiled in answer. She knew defeat when it came. And she was no match for the passion between them. "Yes, my love, you're right, as always."

Cody whooped with joy, carried her through the door, and kicked it shut behind him, careful to turn the lock before carrying her up the stairs.

Within seconds of entering his bedroom he started to remove their clothing, first his, then hers, one step at a time, increasing the need between them in slow increments.

"I seem to remember you telling me something special last night," Cody said as he laid her on his bed and slid himself upon her. "Something I've been waiting a long time to hear."

Queen feathered her fingers through his hair, combing the texture over and over in gentle strokes. Her eyelids grew heavy with passion as his body grew hard. The feel of his weight and his need, and the hard, rhythmic thump of his heartbeat against her breasts started a low and constant throbbing down deep in her body.

She moved, her legs shifting apart as her hands slid down the length of his back, and, when she'd made room for him, urged him in by digging her fingernails lightly across his backside and arching herself upward to meet the thrust she knew would come.

He couldn't resist her offer and slid inside without conscious thought, moving on instinct. The groan that slipped out of his tightly clenched lips was one not of pain, but of ecstasy, and when she began to move beneath him, he knew that it had only begun.

"Oh, Cody!" she gasped, and then tried to focus when the movement inside her changed from controlled thrusts to a pounding need. One minute she'd known what she was going to say, and the next thing she could remember was an overwhelming rush of sensation that swept everything from her mind except the surge toward completion.

She clutched him, holding on for dear life as the world within her mind splintered, and knew as he wrapped his arms around her and laid his face against the curve of her neck that his sanity had shattered as well.

He shook, shoulders heaving from exertion and spent need. His hair was damp beneath her fingertips, and his breath against her breasts was short and uneven.

"I love you, you know," she whispered, and held him as he grew still.

He lifted himself up, bracing on elbows that were barely steady, and stared down into a world of green that was wild and deep enough for a man to get lost in. He pressed his lips against her mouth in a fervent thanksgiving and knew that for him it was already too late. He was lost as hell and didn't give a damn about finding his way out.

"Thank you, my lady," he said, and kissed the smile on her face. "For giving me everything a man could wish for."

Queen heard a clock chime downstairs and sighed. "You're going to get a lot more than you wished for if you don't let me up and let me get dressed. The boys will be here before you know it. And I don't think they're quite ready for this scene."

Cody grinned, remembering the jeweler's box in the jacket lying somewhere on the floor. "Oh, you'd be surprised," he said as he rolled away and reluctantly let her up, watching her nudity with undisguised appreciation as she struggled back into her clothes. "I think they're ready for more than you give them credit."

She smiled and then remembered the problem that Cody didn't even know existed. "When you get yourself together, come downstairs. There's something you need to know."

Moments later she was gone, and it was the tone of her voice and the look in her eyes that sent him scrambling out of bed and into his clothes, the jeweler's box for the moment forgotten.

The work island in the middle of the kitchen was between them when he walked into the room. From the nervous gestures of her hands and the way she kept looking away, he knew it wasn't good.

"What?" he said. "And for God's sake, honey, please don't be afraid. Whatever it is, you can always tell me."

The knot in the pit of her stomach began to unwind. She'd known it. She'd just needed to hear him say it. "Some man was bothering J.J. at school. He wasn't going to tell, but I overheard him talking to Will about it."

"Oh, hell," Cody said, and raked his hands through his hair. It was a parent's worst nightmare—the thought of a pervert touching their child. "What did you do?" he asked.

"I hugged him. After that, he told me everything,

even down to the fact that the man's throat 'poked out' when he talked."

Cody managed a grin. "Thank God you were here."

"I went to the school today and told Stanley Brass. I didn't think this should wait until you got home."

Cody covered the space between them in seconds and pulled her into his arms. "Thank you, Queen. You did the right thing."

He kissed her cheek and tilted her face toward him, needing to assure her by action as well as words that she had his full support in whatever had to be done regarding his sons. If his plans went on schedule, before long they'd be her sons, too.

"There's more," she said, pulling out of his arms. Until she finished the story, she couldn't accept his gratitude when it might later turn into regret.

Cody waited.

"The man who bothered J.J. . . . . was asking about me."

Cody jerked. She felt his shock even though they were not touching. "What do you mean?"

His voice deepened, his posture changed. Queen could see him going on alert. "I mean, he was questioning J.J. about me, Cody. And today, after I left the school . . . I thought I was being followed."

"Damn!"

Cody spun, slamming his fist against the counter in a gesture of fear and frustration. Fear that once again Queen had been threatened, and as before, he'd been absent when it had occurred.

"Don't be mad," Queen said. "I couldn't bear it if you were. . . . "

"Oh, honey." His voice was thick with regret as he slid his arms around her shoulders and rocked her against him. "I didn't mean that the way it sounded. I wasn't mad at you. I was mad at me. Every time someone I love is in danger, I'm not around."

She sighed. "I can't say I felt threatened. The man I saw ran away when he realized I had noticed him."

Cody's eyes narrowed, then grew cold. His mind began to race over all the possibilities. Could Virgil Stratton have had family that wanted revenge? Could someone from Queen's past . . .

"Queen?"

She looked at him, hearing the question coming before it was voiced.

"Did you have any enemies back in Cradle Creek? Was there someone who held a grudge against you or any member of your family? Someone who might have—"

"No. I've already thought of that," Queen said. "And honestly, by the time I left, there wasn't one person in Cradle Creek who seemed to care about me one way or the other."

He shook his head, puzzled by the reason for this latest event.

"Cody, I don't think it was someone from my past."

He turned and stared at her. There was something in the way she said it that told him more was to come.

"I think it was someone from yours."

"The hell you say! No one from my past even knows you, honey . . . except Dennis Macon, and I—"

"Your ex-mother-in-law hates the sight of me."

Cody grew still and then pale, and then when he could face her, she knew from the expression on his face that he'd just accepted the possibility.

"If she's behind this, I will personally wring her god-damned neck," he said. "How dare she frighten my sons? How dare she try to frighten and intimidate you because of me?"

"Now, Cody, I'm not saying it's true. It's just the only thing I can think of that makes any sense. Remember, J.J. didn't say the man tried to touch him or hurt him. He was just asking him about me."

She began to pace the floor between the table and the counter. "And today, when the man saw me, he didn't try to attack me. On the contrary, he ran like hell. I think I'm just under . . . what do you call it . . . observation?"

"I'm calling Abel."

Queen caught him before he could leave the room. "I think Stanley Brass has already done that."

"Then why the hell are you telling me, Queen? So we can just let it drop? Because if you are, I can tell you right here and now, I'm not about to let anyone come between us, and that includes any snoops Lenore might have hired."

"I'm telling you that we don't know anything for certain, and until we do, I suggest you not make a bad thing worse, that's all."

She wrapped her arms around his waist and laid her head against his chest. For a long moment neither moved. And then she felt Cody sigh and felt the anger slide slowly from his body.

"Okay, my lady, for the time being, we do this your way. But so help me—"

"I already know what you're willing to do for me, love," she said. "I'm living proof of your promise to love and protect. I'm not likely to forget it . . . or Virgil Stratton."

He groaned and held her tight.

Soon they heard the boys' footsteps as they ran into the house.

"Yay! Dad's home!" They had seen his bag sitting by the door where he'd dropped it when he'd carried her inside.

He smiled down at Queen, kissed her quickly on her upturned nose, and then went to meet his sons.

15

"*I'm taking the boys* to school," Cody said.

Queen nodded. She'd expected it, as well as the reaction she'd had last night when she'd told him about the man.

"Why don't you come with us?" he asked.

"No, I'll be fine. I have things to do while you're gone. And I did all my shopping yesterday."

Cody paused, wishing he had a good excuse for making her come. He didn't want her out of his sight.

"They're going to be late," Queen said.

He got the message.

Donny came through the door with his backpack in one hand and his jacket in the other and took a good long look at Queen, suddenly remembering his friends and the sexual innuendoes they'd made regarding her.

She'd absently piled her hair into a topknot, and some wayward curls were dangling around her face and neck.

She had on one of his dad's old sweaters and a pair of blue jeans nearly worn through at the knees. On her feet she wore no shoes, just socks, and she still had a smear of flour across her knee from the pancakes she'd made them for breakfast. He stared long and hard and even squinted his eyes and took a step back, as if assessing her from a different angle.

"Something wrong?" Cody asked, noticing Donny's intent gaze.

Donny flushed and shrugged. "Naw," he said. "Just thinking." He put on his jacket while Queen held his backpack. When she handed it back, he leaned forward and kissed her on the cheek. It was a quick peck, but unexpected.

"What was that for?" Queen asked, pleased but surprised by the gesture. She'd learned to expect Donny's affection to come in the form of teasing.

Donny wiggled his eyebrows. "One of my buddies thinks you're a babe. I was just checking to see if he knew what he was talking about."

Queen's face turned red, and her mouth dropped open. "He said I was a what?"

"Babe. You know, hot . . . good-looking, whatever it is you old guys call sexy." He grinned.

"Dammit, Donny. You tell that—"

Donny laughed aloud at the anger and jealousy on his father's face. "Oowee. I was right. I told them not to get any big ideas. That you'd already scored too many points for them to have a chance."

Now Cody was at a loss for words.

"Oh, man! What do you think we are, Dad . . . lame?" Donny asked, seeing his father's blank stare.

"Yeah . . . lame?" Will and J.J. echoed their big brother without catching the innuendoes in between.

Queen started to laugh. "Well, you tell your friends I said thank you . . . but no, thank you."

Donny grinned. "I already did."

Cody yanked them through the door and pointed toward the car, issuing orders without words in the manner of a true military officer. Then, before she could speak, he turned and gathered her in his arms, kissing her hard and drawing more than the breath from her body in the process.

"So . . . 'babe,' will you wait for me while I'm gone?" His eyes crinkled at the corners as he gave her a mock leer.

She laughed and closed the door in his face.

As soon as she heard the motor start, she made a run for her room and pulled the partially finished sweater from beneath a pile of quilts and resumed knitting where she'd left off.

In two short weeks Halloween would be here. It had to be ready by Christmas. That didn't leave her much working time to complete Cody's surprise. Her fingers flew, up one row and down another, as the yarn took on a different shape. And so her morning passed.

"Abel, I want to talk to you."

Sheriff Miller looked up, caught the angry glint in Cody Bonner's eyes, and waved him into his office. "Been expecting you," he said, motioning for Cody to take a seat.

"Queen said—"

"I know all about it," Abel said. "Stanley Brass called me from the school yesterday."

"Yes, but do you also know that Queen thought she was being followed yesterday? She saw a man staring at her, and then when he noticed he'd been caught, he broke and ran like a thief."

"Well, hell, Cody. Your sister . . . who's not a real sister, mind you . . . is a looker. I'd think lots of men stare at her."

Cody glared.

Abel sighed. "I was just joshing you, man. I've already done some checking. There is a man in town who's been asking questions. But they haven't all been about Queen. Some of them pertain to you and your boys."

"Pertain how?" Cody asked.

"Like, do they run wild? Do you take good care of them? Do you and your . . . do you and Queen," he amended, "ever act like there's more between you than there ought to be."

The flat of Cody's hand hit Abel's desk. "Damn if she wasn't right on target," he muttered.

Abel frowned. "Did I miss something here?"

"Queen thinks that my ex-mother-in-law is behind this. They came for a visit a while back and didn't like anything they found, including her."

Abel nodded. "That would be the Whittiers. I remember their names from the report your boys filed when you went missing."

"So, what can I do about this?"

Abel shrugged. "It isn't against the law to ask questions, Cody. And if that's all the man does, you can't do a thing."

"So help me God, if he goes back to school and frightens my boys, I will do something, and you can count on that."

"No, I'll be the one doing something about it," Abel warned. "You'd be well advised to stay out of it. If the Whittiers are trying to get something on you, then starting a fight will be playing into their hands."

Cody cursed.

"My sentiments exactly," Abel said. "How about a cup of coffee?"

Cody stood and shook the other man's hand. "No, I'll take a rain check. I want to get home. I don't like to leave Queen alone."

"She's a fine woman. Be a shame to lose her."

Cody stuffed his hands in his jacket and had started to walk away when something made him change his mind. He stopped and turned. Now was as good a time as any to start letting people know that she wasn't actually related to him.

"I don't intend to lose her," Cody said. "I intend to marry her."

Abel grinned. "Then it's a damned good thing that she's not really your sister, isn't it?"

"For an old man, you're a real smart-ass, aren't you?" Cody asked, and watched the smile spreading across Abel Miller's face.

"My wife thinks so," Abel said.

"My sympathies to your wife, Abel," Cody said, and shut the door behind him with a sharp click.

Abel dropped onto his chair, laid his head back, and started to laugh, slapping his leg now and again with glee as he remembered the look on Cody's face, then laughing all over again at the memory.

"It's me."

Lenore Whittier inhaled. "What do you have?" she asked.

Wally Morrow stared at himself in the mirror, testing the tender territory above his nose with a fingertip. "Other than a black eye, not much," he grumbled.

"I don't pay you to get into trouble," she snapped.

Wally rolled his eyes. "About the report," he said, interrupting the woman before she got started on another tirade. The last two times he'd called she'd been furious when he'd hung up. He couldn't figure out what the hell she wanted him to do—make something up?

Lenore sighed. "Continue."

"Not much to report that's different, other than the fact that Miss Houston has visited a pharmacist and done the odd shopping around the town."

Lenore heard the sarcasm in his voice and wanted to scream. This wasn't getting her the results that she'd hoped for.

"And," Wally added, "my questions are starting to raise notice. Yesterday when I asked a local if he knew anything about her, he punched me in the nose. People around here like her, I tell you. And although it's fairly busy during the tourist season, Snow Gap operates on small-town mentality. They don't like strangers butting into the business of one of their own."

Wally was amazed at what he was just about to suggest. He'd never thought he'd turn down business, but something told him he'd just about worn out his welcome in Snow Gap.

"Look," he said, "why don't we just call it quits? It's fairly obvious that they're a model family. I even heard someone say"—he paused for effect—"understand this is unverified, but I heard that Cody Bonner was getting married. Now what can be more normal than that?"

Lenore gasped. Rage filled her breast at the thought of that woman in complete control of her grandchildren and their futures. "Find out!" she shrieked. "Find out if it's true!"

Wally gulped, suddenly aware that he'd unleashed

the bitch he'd been trying to contain. "Yes ma'am," he said. "But it may take some time. I need to lay low for a while, maybe change my appearance."

"I don't care if you have a complete face lift!" Lenore shrieked. "Just do what I said, and call me as soon as you know."

"Yes, ma'am," Wally said, and then winced when she disconnected sharply in his ear. "You old bitch," he added, just to make himself feel better, fully aware she couldn't hear.

"Now what?" he asked himself.

It was hard to hide his face, his features being what they were. He hadn't shaved since Queen Houston had spotted him on the street corner. But the blond, scraggly three-day growth of whiskers didn't hide a damned thing. And Snow Gap wasn't exactly brimming with stores selling special effects.

He grabbed his sunglasses, slid them up his nose to hide the worst of his spreading bruise, and traded his slouch hat for a baseball cap. But he only had the two coats, and the October wind precluded eliminating either. He'd have to take a chance on no one spotting him, he thought as he slid his arms into the droopy trench coat. He had a new mission. Was Cody Bonner about to pop the question, or was that simply another small-town rumor about a pretty woman and a virile, attractive male?

Cody parked the Blazer and then went around to open the door for Queen, who had accompanied him into town.

A cold front was moving in, and some intermittent snow was being predicted for the next few days. She knew it might be her last opportunity to get out of the house for some time and didn't want to miss the trip, as well as the chance to be with Cody.

He helped her out, taking the time to fasten the top button on her coat and let his gaze linger on the rosiness the sharp wind had spread across her cheeks.

"Sure you don't want me to come with you?" he asked.

Queen smiled. "And sit and fidget while I try on shoes? I don't think so."

He grinned and shrugged. "I'd do it for you."

"My hero," she said, and couldn't resist squeezing his arm, although public displays of affection with Cody made her nervous. Especially since half the town thought that she was his sister and the other half suspected she wasn't.

But Cody had no qualms about letting people know what he thought of her; he bent down and kissed her with a gentle, lingering caress.

"Cody! What will people think?"

"They will think I love you," he said. "They will be right."

She rolled her eyes. When he was in one of his obstinate moods, there was no stopping him. She patted her pocket to make sure she had her list and started to walk away.

"Do you have enough money?" Cody asked. "I deposited your paycheck directly to the bank a couple of days ago, as usual, but if you're a little short, I can—"

"I have my own money, remember?" Weeks ago she'd finally confided to him that she'd opened up a bank account with her share of the sale of their home in Cradle Creek.

"That's your money. What I give you, you earn."

She looked away, and he could tell by the way her jaw tightened and her shoulders stiffened that she was uncomfortable with what he'd just said.

"I don't feel right about taking your money anymore," she said. "Not since we . . . not since I . . . "

"Look, honey," he said, and grabbed her by the arm before she could escape. "The fact that our emotional relationship has changed does not change the fact that you still earn every cent that I put in the bank for you."

She glared at him. "It makes me feel kept."

He laughed. "That's a good one. How do you think I feel? You're the one who's been keeping us, lady. You kept my family from being taken away. You kept me from losing my sanity when the nightmares wouldn't stop. And because of you . . . I may even still believe in Santa Claus."

The laughter was rich in his voice. He teased her into a smile by poking his fingers at the corners of her mouth and then pushing upward.

She couldn't resist him, and it didn't surprise her. She'd been unable to tell this man "no" almost from the start. "Okay," she said with a sigh. "You win. And to answer your question, no, I don't need any extra money, and I will meet you back here in time for you to buy me lunch."

"Yes, ma'am," Cody said.

"Don't pretend that you aren't happy you just got your way," Queen said. "Lying doesn't become you." She made a face and walked away.

Cody watched her until she stopped at the corner, turned back, and waved. She was smiling. It was what he'd been waiting for.

He stuffed his hands in his pockets and started across

the street to the diner. If there was one thing he knew about women, it was that their shopping expeditions lasted longer than some wars.

Cody alternated between cradling his cup of coffee between his fingers and staring up at the clock on the wall of the diner. She'd been gone almost two hours. How long did it take to pick out shoes? Either they had them or they didn't.

He suspected it was beyond the male psyche to understand about things like compromising on color when one had been set on a certain thing.

He remembered last night, and the way that her eyes changed colors when they made love, from dark to bright, from wild to sleepy. And then he groaned softly, wishing he'd thought of something else.

The ring. That was a safe topic on which to ruminate. It was safely tucked away, waiting for the right moment at which to present it. Cody smiled to himself. He could just imagine what she would do. And if she cried, he was going to delight in kissing away every single tear.

"Hey there!"

Cody looked up and then smiled a welcome as Abel Miller entered the diner.

"Mind if I join you?" Abel asked.

Cody shook his head. "Got any news for me?"

"Naw. I think whoever it was that was snooping is long gone. No one has reported seeing him in a couple of days. I don't know what the bugger is up to, but he's cagey, I can tell you that. I've yet to set eyes on him myself, and the descriptions I keep getting vary enough to make me think that people might be seeing shadows that aren't there anymore."

"No one hopes that more than me," Cody said. "My family has gone through enough. We're due some comp time."

Abel nodded. "So, have you popped the question yet?" he asked, and then relished the glare Cody gave him. "Hmmm, from the look on your face I suppose not. Or . . . you asked her and she told you no. Which is it?"

"I think I made a mistake in telling you before I asked her," Cody said. "You're worse than a mother hen."

"So. You haven't asked her yet. What's holding up the process, cold feet?"

"No. Just waiting for the right time," Cody muttered, and stared down at the coffee grounds settling in the bottom of his cup.

"How about her birthday?" Abel asked. "It's coming up soon. That would be a good time."

Cody looked up in shock. He'd just realized he didn't know when her birthday was. "Why the hell do you know when her birthday is and I don't?" he grumbled.

"I've seen her driver's license, remember? Oh, that's right," Abel said, and tried not to grin. "I guess that was when you were in jail."

"Dammit, Abel, for a sheriff, you're a real mean-tempered man. Do you know that?" He sighed and raked his hand through his hair. "So . . . how come you remember it . . . and when is it?"

"I remember it because it's the same as my wife's, October the twenty-eighth. I always tell my wife she just missed being a little witch. She don't quite see the humor in it, but I tell her so, just the same."

Cody grinned. It was hard to stay irked with a man like Abel Miller. The twenty-eighth? That was only a few days off. And it would be the perfect time.

"Thanks, man," he said. "I think I'll just do that—that is, if you don't spill the beans and tell her for me."

Abel held up his hands. "Oh, no. I make it a practice never to meddle in other people's business."

"Yeah, right," Cody said. This time he was the one who laughed. Long and loud.

The waitress came to fill his cup and take Abel's order, and they sat, waiting for Queen to return.

Within minutes of the arrival of Abel's order, Cody saw her turn the corner and start down the street opposite the diner. "Finally," he said, and pointed.

Abel turned to look.

It was hard to say which man reacted first. But within a heartbeat they were both on their feet and out the door, bolting across the street, dodging traffic, on their way to rescue Queen from a murder—Wally Morrow's, to be precise.

He'd been nothing more than a shadow in the corner of her eye. A figment, she kept thinking, of her own imagination. When she would turn to look there would be no one staring, no one noticeable, no one even coming her way.

But the feeling persisted, and the instinct that had kept her whole and sane while growing up in Cradle Creek prevailed.

Queen knew, as well as she knew her own name, that she was being followed. Now it was simply a matter of letting the man think he was successful in his pursuit and then catching him at his own game.

Lingering longer than necessary inside the shoe store, she realized that the clerk's patience as well as the assortment of shoes in her sizes had come to an end.

"I'll take those," she announced, pointing to the second pair she'd tried on and ignoring the clerk's pained expression.

Exiting the store minutes later, she adjusted her coat against the sharp wind and swung her head in a small, sharp jerk, supposedly to toss her hair from her eyes. That was when she first saw him, darting between buildings, startled by the sudden, unexpected movement of her gaze. Using the reflection of the shop window as a mirror, she stared at him.

To a casual observer, it would seem she was intent in her perusal of the store display. In the vernacular of his own business, Wally Morrow never even knew he'd been made. But when she saw him, the sharp jolt of reality that surfaced made her furious. How dare some total stranger play peek-a-boo with her life? How dare he snoop, and creep, and in the process frighten children who had unknowingly been thrust into the fray?

Queen turned away from the window and began walking down the street, her eyes ever forward, her walk slow and casual. Her brain was in high gear as she sorted through the options open to her, and she wished she hadn't encouraged Cody to wait behind. If he was here now, there'd be no discussion as to how this man would be dealt with. The only question would have been whether to hit him first or call Abel Miller and let him handle it. Knowing Cody, Queen was sure he would have opted for the former.

Her stride increased slightly, anxiety overwhelming her as she realized that the man might not be as harmless as she'd first supposed. What if he was a stalker of the Virgil Stratton variety? She didn't think she could endure another episode like that.

"Oh, Cody, where are you when I need you?" she muttered, telling herself not to run.

The light turned red, and she had the most overwhelming urge to turn and look, just to assure herself that he wasn't right behind her with a knife or a threat she couldn't ignore. But she didn't turn, and when the light finally changed she nearly bolted across the street, using the onset of traffic in the opposite direction as an excuse for running.

Wally Morrow cursed. It was impossible to keep up with a woman who had legs that long. Either he kept her in sight or he stayed secluded, proceeding at a more careful rate, and lost her in the rush. Remembering Lenore Whittier's angry order, he made a decision that he would later regret. He stepped out into the main flow of traffic and started following along behind, at what he thought was a safe and undetectable distance.

Thank God—the diner! Queen turned the corner, saw the Blazer still parked where they'd left it, and prayed that Cody would be inside, nursing a cup of coffee.

In her haste she stumbled and, as she did, grabbed on to the side of the nearest storefront for stability. In that moment, in the window's reflection, she saw him only mere steps behind her.

Something snapped. A rage swept over her that she hadn't felt since the night she'd walked into the alley with Johnny's old shotgun and witnessed Morton Whitelaw in the act of self-gratification. She dropped the bag with her new shoes and spun around.

"Why don't you take a good look?" she yelled.

And before Wally Morrow saw it coming, she'd grabbed him by the collar and slammed him bodily against the window, rattling it to the point that it was near to shattering down upon them.

"Let me go!" he screeched, aware that the knee in his groin had upped the level of his speech several decibels. "You have no right!"

"No," Queen whispered, her breath hot and angry as it swept across his face. "You're the one who has no right!"

Cody was in a panic. He couldn't believe that she'd actually taken the initiative and tried to subdue the man. That it was the man they'd been looking for was obvious, right down to the beaky nose and the long trench coat. He ran like a man possessed, certain that Queen would be mortally hurt before he could reach them and pull her away.

"My God, Queen, get away from him!"

The shout startled her, and then she recognized the voice and felt Cody's hands on her shoulders as he pulled, sending her staggering backward into Abel Miller's arms.

Just when Wally Morrow thought he'd been saved, he looked up into a pair of eyes—wild, blue, and blazing mad—and knew that whatever Lenore Whittier was paying him was not going to cover the hospital bill that was bound to ensue.

"Turn him loose, Cody."

The calm, even tone of Sheriff Miller's voice penetrated Cody's rage. He shuddered, loosening his grip around the man's neck, and then airmailed him to Abel Miller's feet.

"Oooh, I'm hurt," Wally groaned as he landed, and then rolled onto his side, certain that his tailbone would never be the same.

"Not as much as you could have been," Abel said. He

yanked the man to his feet, dusted off the front of his coat, and then pinned him with a hard stare. "Now, do you want to start talking here, or wait until you're booked?"

"Oh, God," Wally groaned. "You don't understand. I wasn't doing anything wrong. Since when is it against the law to walk down the street?"

"When you interfere with someone's privacy to the point of scaring the hell out of them, then it becomes my business," Abel said. He pulled back his coat and let the sun glint on his badge.

Wally groaned again. This was only getting worse. "I didn't do anything wrong, I can prove it."

"What about scaring my son? What about frightening a woman who'd just survived a kidnapping only weeks ago?"

Cody's anger was barely contained, and Wally knew he was in deep trouble. Suddenly he decided he didn't want the sheriff to turn him loose after all. "Take me to jail," he said. "I'll call my lawyer."

"That's fine with me," Abel said. "And while you're at it, tell him you're being charged with stalking, loitering with intent to molest a minor—"

"I was just doing my job," Wally protested. "I'm a private eye. I was just doing my job."

"Who hired you?" Cody asked, and grabbed the man by the coat collar, readying for a fight if he didn't get an answer.

"That's my business and also privileged information between me and my—"

Cody lifted him off his feet. "What I'm about to do to you will be my privilege," he warned. "I want an answer, dammit!"

"Don't, Cody," Queen begged, aware that they were

creating quite a scene and that Abel was close to arresting them all just to get them off the street. "He's not worth it. Let Abel take care of him. Besides, think of the boys."

The urgent manner in which she tugged at his arm, as well as the plea in her voice, got through the red rage that he was struggling to overcome. Once again, Cody let the man drop. This time Wally caught himself with both hands and then fell backward, gritting his teeth in pain as his elbows took the brunt of his fall. He couldn't have borne it if his rear had taken any more punishment.

"Come on, Cody, you owe me lunch, remember?" Queen bent down and picked up the bag containing her new shoes.

Abel grinned as he handcuffed Wally and helped him across the street to the police unit.

Cody stared down in amazement at the glow in Queen's eyes. "You can eat? At a time like this?"

She grinned. "I haven't felt this good since I pulled a shotgun on Morton Whitelaw."

Cody gawked. "Pulled a . . . Who the hell is Morton Whitelaw?" He went all still, just thinking about the hell in her life before she'd had him to protect her.

"Feed me and I'll talk all you want," she promised.

He sighed, wrapped his arms around her in a grateful hug, and let her lead him where she might.

Exactly who and what have I fallen in love with? he asked himself. He had sudden visions of a female Rambo and started to smile. By the time they'd made it across the street and sat down at the booth that he'd vacated only minutes earlier, he was laughing aloud.

Queen smiled, took a menu, and began to choose, suddenly hungry, suddenly happier than she'd been in months. Finally everything was going to be all right.

But there are none so blind as those who will not see. And Queen and Cody would have realized that, had they taken the time to think about the reaction of whoever had hired Wally Morrow when it was discovered that he was no longer on the job.

16

"*I don't see why I* couldn't go to town with her," Will grumbled as he stood at the window, watching the Blazer disappear around the curve in the road beyond the house with his beloved Queenie behind the wheel.

"Because she didn't need help today," Cody said. "Besides, as soon as Donny and J.J. come downstairs, I have something I want to ask you guys."

"I didn't use your razor, Dad, honest."

Cody laughed. So that was what had happened to the last of his shaving cream.

Will slumped onto a chair. He'd told J.J. they would get caught, but J.J. had been so certain that no one would notice they'd borrowed the razor, especially since it was minus a blade. They hadn't taken into consideration explaining how a full can of shaving cream had suddenly gone empty.

"J.J. did it, too," Will added, and sighed.

"That's not what I want to talk about," Cody said, and gently tugged a lock of his son's hair before walking to the foot of the stairs. "Hey, you guys, hurry up. We've got to talk."

When Cody came back into the room and sat down on the couch, Will moved to sit beside him. Cody grinned as he hugged his son and then started a wrestling match that soon evolved to the floor.

"I thought I told you kids not to do that in the house," Donny said. He grinned at his father's expression as he caught them in the act of rolling beneath the coffee table. "Just practicing for when I'm a parent," he added.

Cody got to his feet, allowing Will to have the last punch, and then settled back onto the couch, motioning for the others to find a seat.

"How come I miss all the fun?" J.J. asked, and flopped onto a chair beside the couch, sorry that he'd missed out on the roughhouse tumble. It was his favorite thing to do with his dad.

"Listen," Cody began. "I have something serious I need to talk to you guys about."

Donny frowned. He knew that the guy who'd bothered J.J. at school had been arrested. Surely something else hadn't come up that his father hadn't told him about.

"Like what?" Donny asked, and waved for his little brothers to be quiet.

Cody leaned forward, resting his elbows on his knees, and stared intently into three pairs of matching blue eyes, very much like his own. They were so dear to him, and what he did in his life affected them as well. Yet he couldn't bear thinking about his life without Queen in it. God . . . what if they don't go for this?

He took a deep breath and then blurted out the first thing that came to mind. "How much do you remember about your mother?"

The question shocked all three boys. It wasn't something they thought about often. It had been more than three years since she'd been missing from their lives. There were lots of things that came to mind . . . and, surprisingly, plenty of things that didn't. Silence filled the room as they considered the question.

"Donny, what about you?"

Donny bit his lip and tried to ignore the odd pain around his heart. Now that he was growing hair on his chest, he'd come to the mistaken conclusion that he shouldn't want to cry.

"Well . . . lots of things. Like her favorite foods, and how she used to laugh herself silly at Chevy Chase movies, and how she hated to cook and was always trying to talk you into taking us out to eat . . . just stuff." He shrugged. "You know."

Cody nodded. "Will, what about you, son? What do you remember most about Mom?"

Will's mouth trembled, and he looked everywhere but at his father's face. "Sometimes . . . " He took a deep breath and then let everything fall out, as if it were something that had been bothering him for a long, long time. "Sometimes I forget what she looked like." His expression was at once distressed as well as apologetic. "But I remember things we did. And I remember always going with her to the base to get you when you'd come in from a mission. And . . . I remember when we all went to the zoo and Donny threw up in the gorilla pit."

Donny rolled his eyes. Why did they always have to remember the bad stuff?

Cody smiled gently. He hadn't realized how much Will had been bothered by the fact that his memory of Claire was fading.

"It's okay that sometimes your memory is a little

fuzzy. You know that, don't you? Remember, you were only seven when she died," Cody said.

Will nodded, relieved that he wasn't in trouble for forgetting something as important as his mother's face.

"J.J., what about you?" Cody asked. "Do you remember anything at all about your mother? And . . . if you don't, don't feel bad. You were only four when she died."

"I remember!" he crowed. "I remember that she smelled good. And that sometimes she would rock me when I was sick. And I remember her hair was short and curly and she wore red lipstick. I remember her lipstick real good."

Cody pulled J.J. into his lap and scooted Will beneath his arm. His gaze caught Donny's intent stare, and he swallowed nervously, at that moment almost afraid of his own children and their possible reaction to what he was about to say.

"So . . . sometimes do you miss having a mother? You know that your real mother can't ever come back . . . but do you wish that there was someone else who would take care of you like she did?"

Will shook his head. "No! Not anymore!"

J.J. shrugged. "Me either. Not anymore."

Cody's heart dropped. *Oh, God, I was afraid of this,* he thought.

"But why not?" Cody asked. "Wouldn't you like to have someone who would be here when you get home from school and who would take you places when I was busy? And what about the special days like birthdays and Christmas . . . a lady does those kinds of things lots better than me, right?"

Will gave his father a disgusted look. "But we don't need that, Dad. Not since we have Queenie. I don't want anyone else but Queenie." His chin jutted out, making him look like a smaller version of Cody when angry.

"Yeah, Queenie takes real good care of us. We don't want anyone else," J.J. said, and did his best to imitate Will's defiant stance.

Thank God!

Donny grinned and leaned back on his chair. "So . . . Dad . . . when are you going to just spit it out and get your misery over with?"

Cody would have glared, but he was so damned happy at what they'd just said, he didn't quite know how to show it.

"So you think you know what's on my mind?" he asked Donny.

"Oh, heck, Dad. I've known what was on your mind since day one. Remember, she's quite a 'babe.'"

Cody laughed and hugged his sons. "So, what you guys are telling me is that you'd have no objections if Queen lived here forever."

"Right," the younger ones echoed, wondering what all the fuss was about. They couldn't understand why the meeting had been necessary. As far as they were concerned, she was already here forever.

"Absolutely none," Donny added.

"And you wouldn't care if I asked her to marry me?"

Will thought about it for a moment while J.J. sat and watched to see where Will and the wind blew. Whatever his brother said was usually fine with him.

"Does that mean she'll still read us stories, and tuck us in, and bake really good stuff while we're at school?"

"In spades, buddy," Cody said. "In spades."

Will grinned while the others laughed. He wasn't sure what that meant, but it sounded like a "yes."

"Okay, here's the deal," Cody said. "In a little while,

Colonel Macon is going to be here. He's going to take you guys into Snow Gap and help me set up a surprise for Queen. What do you say? Think you can handle that?"

"Yes!" they cried, and this time even Donny was excited about the prospect. He liked surprises, and he loved Queen. It was about time things began to happen around here that were good things.

"Then go get changed," Cody said. "Put on some decent clothes, something that you would wear to school. I'll give you each some money when you leave with Colonel Macon. But don't spend it on yourself. This is for Queen. Today is her birthday, and she thinks we don't know it. She'll be really surprised when I bring her into town tonight and meet you guys and Dennis at the restaurant, right?"

"All right!"

The idea of spending money, even if it wasn't on themselves, was exciting, as was the fact that they were going to be in on a surprise.

Within the hour Dennis had come and gone, taking Cody's sons with him. Cody stood in the center of the big, empty house and listened, realizing for the first time how Queen must feel when they were all off on their own pursuits. It felt a little lonely, but also peaceful at the lack of noise. Will she care to spend the rest of her life this way, he wondered, always waiting for people to come home and make work for her to do?

Will my love be enough to get you through this, lady?

He could only hope.

Queen turned first one way and then another, staring at herself in the full-length mirror on the back of her closet door, and smiled in satisfaction. She looked fine.

Actually she looked more than fine, but it was beyond her fragile ego to see what an elegant woman she'd become. For the first time in her life, she looked the part of her given name—Queen. The cranberry-red wool dress did what it was meant to do. It was a showcase for her femininity as well as her style.

She tugged at the low-cut neckline and then fiddled with the sleeves that grazed her wrists, checking one last time to make sure no slip was showing. The shoes she'd spent so long picking out complemented the outfit to perfection. Best of all, the heels were high enough to bring her eye level with the man who'd stolen her heart.

She could hardly wait to see his reaction.

"Here goes nothing," she said, grabbed her purse and coat, and left her room.

She'd been surprised upon returning from Snow Gap to learn that the boys had gone to town with Dennis. The surprise had turned to excited anticipation when Cody had offhandedly remarked that they were going out to dinner tonight to discuss the project. It would give her the opportunity to wear her new dress.

Of course, she had no idea that they were on to the fact that it was her birthday. She'd never told them, and no one had asked.

All day she'd been fighting a terrible case of the blues, trying not to think of how much she missed her sisters or that this was the first birthday without them.

Tears threatened as she remembered how each year Diamond would insist on baking a cake. And then she smiled, remembering that it was always an unmitigated disaster. Diamond could sing like an angel, but she couldn't cook worth a darn.

A true gambler's daughter, Lucky would always insist that the cake must have the exact number of candles or it would be bad luck. Last year they'd laughed and teased as they'd crammed twenty-eight tiny wax candles on top of Diamond's culinary mess and completely obliterated the top of the cake. This year she would be twenty-nine years old . . . one year away from thirty . . . and it would pass without notice.

She took a deep breath. It was time to let go. The past as she knew it no longer existed.

She paused at the top of the stairs and smoothed down her skirt, suddenly nervous about Cody seeing her in something other than the familiar blue jeans and sweaters. And then she remembered his smile, and the way his eyes turned dark like a summer thunderstorm just before they made love, and knew that no matter what she wore, his favorite outfit would always be Queen as nature made her.

Cody heard her footsteps above as she came down the hallway and paused at the top of the stairs.

She'd come that far alone, and he was going with her the rest of the way. He bolted from his chair and into the hall, intent on making a big deal of escorting her down the stairs. He wanted her to know how important and special she was to all of them.

But he didn't get far. When he looked up he had to hold on to the banister for support at the vision he beheld above him.

"Oh, honey."

The way in which he whispered her name and the look on his face was enough impetus to get her down the stairs. "Do you like it?" she asked, a little unsure, a lot desperate for approval from the man who was her whole world.

Cody took her purse and coat and hung them both on the end of the newel post. He wanted to touch . . . to feel . . . but was afraid to mess up the creation.

"Like it? Lady . . . you take my breath away."

His hands skimmed the soft fabric and then across her skin, testing the differences in textures as well as the differences in his woman. He leaned forward, closed his eyes, and inhaled. "And you smell fantastic."

"It was a sample of White Diamonds. They gave it to me in the store when I bought the dress. I was saving it for something special."

"Am I that something special?" he asked, and grinned at the blush that crossed her face.

"Well, I was hoping I'd see those boys in Donny's class who think I'm such a 'babe,' remember?"

Cody laughed aloud and then couldn't resist. He whisked her off her feet, whirling her around and around in the center of the hallway, and then watched in fascination at the way her hair billowed out behind her like a fan of autumn leaves and the way the dress molded to her body like a second skin.

And what he would later remember was that not once had she told him to stop, claiming that he was messing up her hair or her clothes. She was a far cry from the perfectionist that Claire had been. He considered himself a twice blessed man.

"Cody, put me down," Queen finally gasped. "I'm getting dizzy."

"Good, then I can take advantage of you," he said, and nuzzled the curls at her neck, inhaling again the wonderful scent of Queen and the perfume.

"Advantage? I'll say. I'm seeing three of you. I don't know which of you to hold on to."

This is it, he thought. Now is the time.

His fingers curled over the small jeweler's box in his jacket pocket and, without removing the box, slipped out the ring and held it between his fingers. "Maybe if you see three of this, you won't say no," he said.

The smile on her face disappeared. Everything seemed to stop, including her heart. Twice she reached out, and twice she let her hand fall back, not believing what she saw, afraid that if she touched it, it would disappear.

"Cody?" Panic filled her voice. She was afraid to hope.

"I love you, Queen Houston. Why do you find this so hard to believe?" He cupped her cheek with his hand.

"It's a ring."

Cody grinned. "Actually, it's a rather large white diamond. Do you think your choice of perfume was a unconscious portent of things to come?"

She shook her head, unable to speak.

"So . . . you can't really read minds?"

She shook her head again and bit her lip, trying desperately not to cry.

"Then that means I have to come right out and ask, doesn't it?" His voice was rich with laughter, his heart light from the joy he saw in her eyes.

At that point, if she'd asked for the moon, he couldn't have told her no to save his soul. He grasped her left hand, solemnly separated her fingers, and held the ring suspended over the end of the ring finger.

"Queen Houston, it will be forever my honor and joy if you would consent to marry me. I will promise to love you . . . to care for—"

"Yes!"

He grinned. "Hunh-uh, honey. You made me do this the hard way, and I'm not through yet. Now you'll just have to wait. Let's see . . . where was I . . . oh, yes, caring for you. And I will. I also promise to protect . . . "

She started to cry.

"Oh, now, honey! Let's not do that!" Suddenly at a loss for words, Cody quickly slid the ring on her finger. "Look, don't cry. It fits!"

She sobbed even harder and wrapped her arms around his neck.

He sighed and held her. Women! Make them mad . . . they cry. Make them happy . . . they still cry. He was never going to learn how to do things right.

"Yes, yes, yes," Queen said between sobs. "I'll marry you, every darn one of you."

Cody grinned with relief. This was the Queen he knew and loved.

"Thank you," he said calmly as he dipped his lips toward hers. "You have made every darn one of us very happy."

Queen inhaled Cody and tears, all at the same time. Wrapped in a swirl of love and White Diamonds, they sealed the bargain with a kiss.

Cody hustled her into the Blazer, and they headed for town. Queen leaned against him in satisfied silence and was all but mute until they pulled into the parking lot of the restaurant.

"Do they know?" she asked.

Queen's hesitant question came just as he braked and parked. Cody grinned. Just like a woman. Wait until the last minute to start an important conversation.

"They knew I was going to ask you. They don't know that you said yes."

Even in the shadows within the vehicle, he saw her blush.

Cody grinned and grabbed her chin, planted a quick,

hard kiss on her half-opened mouth, and then felt his gut kick and his manhood get hard as her eyes slid shut and she leaned into his embrace.

"Hold that thought," he whispered. "We've got a party to attend."

Queen sighed, tasting what was left of Cody's kiss as she traded the warmth of the Blazer for the sharp bite of night air.

The restaurant parking lot was more than half full with skiers lingering in hopes of another heavy snow or some action in one of the other tourist attractions Snow Gap offered.

She shivered as the wind plastered her dress against her legs and suddenly wished for her old blue jeans and boots instead of the fragile stockings and slender-heeled shoes. Being sexy and being comfortable were not always synonymous.

"Oh, God, Cody. Suddenly I'm scared to death to face your sons."

"You can't be half as scared as I was, fearing that you'd tell me no."

"I haven't told you no since we met. What made you think I'd start now?"

She walked into the restaurant slightly ahead of him, leaving him with nothing but a smile on his face and an enticing view of her backside.

"Coming?" she asked as she turned at the door.

"God, I hope not," Cody said, and then laughed aloud at the shocked expression on her face. "At least not yet."

Dennis Macon looked up at the sound of her laughter and felt his gut kick twice in rapid succession. He could tell that she'd been asked. And then he took another look at the smile on Cody's face and knew that she'd said yes.

It was the final proof he needed to assure him that he'd never been in the running except in his own mind.

"Hey, boys," Dennis said. "I think we've got a winner!"

Three pairs of equally blue eyes stared. Three dark heads nodded solemnly in perfect unison. They'd known it all along. They didn't know why grown-ups made such a big deal out of the obvious. Queenie loved them. It stood to reason she would marry them.

Dennis stood up as Queen came to the table. "Let's see the ring," he said quietly.

It was what she'd been waiting for. She held out her hand, and Dennis took it, looking deeply into the sparkling facets of the stone and then into her eyes.

Queen caught a look on his face that she hadn't expected. For a moment thought seemed to become word, and for the first time since she'd known him, she realized that at one point he'd harbored a hope of his own. He leaned forward.

"Congratulations, angel. I hope you'll be very, very happy."

The kiss he left behind was swift and sweet, and Queen smiled through tears at Cody's best friend. "Thank you, Dennis. I already am."

Then it became a fight between Will and J.J. to see who would sit on the other side of Queen. Only her calm, firm control of the situation would ensure that none of her men was left out of this special night.

"One can sit on one side, one on the other," she said, begging Cody with a quick look, hoping that he'd forgive her for abandoning him so quickly. "I don't think your daddy will mind too much. He's got me for the rest of his life. Tonight he'll just have to share, right, guys?"

"Right!"

Cody's heart was too full to answer. All he knew was that his lady had not only taken him to love, she'd enveloped his sons as if they were her own. Then he realized that in her heart, they already were.

"Okay, guys," Cody said, "but later . . . when it's time to . . . you know . . . I get the ringside seat."

They all nodded and then giggled with delight at the surprise still in store for their Queenie.

Wally Morrow stood on the street outside, slid a sharp, bony finger beneath the edge of his long blond wig, and scratched. Damn, but these things itch, he thought.

He stared at the family assembled at the table inside the restaurant, saw Queen Houston proudly displaying a gleaming diamond ring for all to see, and then watched her accepting congratulations. He grinned. He'd seen what he'd come to see.

Out on bail, and in serious disguise, he pulled at the groin of his tight ski pants and wondered how in the hell men breathed in stuff like this. He felt as though he'd been canned in nylon and latex, and he feared for the future of his heirs, should he decide to have some.

"Okay, Mrs. Whittier, I've got your proof. And believe you me, it's going to cost you big time."

He scooted across the street, trying to affect a macho swagger that men who wore clothes such as these were prone to do. In no time he'd packed, paid his bill, and was in his rental car, heading out of town. He'd seen all he cared to of Snow Gap, Colorado, and the Bonner family. He still had nightmares about that crazy redhead and that wild man who'd dumped him on his ass.

But he'd done what he set out to do and drove away with a small smile of satisfaction. He'd never walked out on a case yet, and this one was going to come to a neat close. It was going to cost Lenore Whittier a bundle to find out that her grandsons were about to obtain a new mother.

"Who's ready for dessert?"

Cody's question was met with shrieks and giggles that made Queen frown. What on earth had gotten into them? And what was so funny about dessert?

Cody waved toward their waiter and then turned to Queen with a smile.

She looked at Dennis, then at the boys, and then back at Cody. Something was definitely up, she could tell by the innocent expressions on their faces.

And then the waiter came out from the kitchen, carrying a cake three stories high and blazing with candles.

"Happy birthday!" they all shouted, and then their faces fell.

She was crying, all-out sobs through a smile that barely made it.

"Oh, my!" she said, and then repeated it over and over. "I didn't think anyone knew. I've never been so happy in my entire life. Thank you, boys, for everything." She slipped an arm around each of her seat mates and winked at Donny, who was trying not to look as pleased as he felt.

"Daddy . . . if she's happy, why is she crying?" J.J. asked as he leaned toward his father and slid out of Queen's hug.

Cody grinned and ruffled J.J.'s hair as he calmly handed Queen his handkerchief. "Lesson number one, son. Women always cry when they're happy."

"Then what do they do when they're sad?"

"Cry."

"That doesn't make sense," Will said, looking at his father as if he didn't believe him.

"That's what makes them so special. You never get bored because you never understand them. Get it?"

Will sighed. "Maybe I will when I get bigger."

Donny laughed. "I don't know, Will. No one is bigger than Dad, and he still hasn't got a clue."

And then the cake became the center of attention.

"You have to make a wish!" Donny said.

Queen looked around the table at the people with whom she was sharing it. "It would be hard to wish for more than what I already have," she said.

And then she thought of something, and her face grew solemn. She felt suddenly overwhelmed by the enormity of the occasion.

She took a deep breath, leaned forward, and blew. The candles went out, and all that remained were tiny wisps of gray smoke filtering up from their burned tips as their life was extinguished.

"What did you wish for?" J.J. asked. "You looked sad. You're supposed to wish for something that will make you happy."

"She can't tell you, or it won't come true, stupid," Will said. "And it's okay if she's sad. Women are supposed to do stuff like that . . . right, Dad? Besides, she's not really sad because she's with her family."

Cody nodded. But he, too, had seen the shadow slide across her face and wondered what had happened to put out the light in her eyes. And then something Will had just said clicked, and he knew what she'd been thinking of.

He looked at her eyes, brimming with tears, and saw

the smile on her lips as she struggled with memories too painful to share. Somewhere out there were her sisters, the two other daughters of Johnny Houston, and he could tell how deeply she was missing them.

"This isn't all," he said, breaking the solemnity of the moment. "I think you've got some presents coming, honey. Dennis and the boys have been on a marathon shopping expedition this afternoon, right, guys?"

Some wrapped boxes appeared from behind Dennis's chair, which was sheltered by a rubber tree at his back.

"Open mine first!" J.J. cried.

"I'll open them all," Queen said calmly. "Your dad will cut cake and I will open presents, and then we'll all go home."

The smiles and nods of acceptance went all around the table as Dennis Macon watched with a bittersweet smile. Just at this moment he envied his friend more than he'd ever thought possible. And it wasn't only the knowledge that Queen Houston loved Cody, it was the fact that he had no one who loved him in the same way, and it was all his own doing.

Unfortunately for Dennis, he was going to retire to a motel room for the night and, in the morning, head back to Denver to Lowry AFB and the life that he'd chosen over marriage and family. But he had one small piece of himself that he was leaving with her. And because it was her birthday, no one could deny him the right.

He watched, holding his breath as she slowly unwrapped the tiny box bearing the gift from him.

"This is from you, isn't it, Dennis?" Queen asked, and grinned with anticipation as she tore through the shiny paper and the strip of ribbon.

And then her smile froze, and her eyes grew wide and solemn. She dug through the bit of tissue to the gilt she saw beneath and lifted out a pin, a perfect pair of wings—air force wings, which a pilot covets from the day he enters the academy to the day they are pinned on his chest.

"Dennis! You can't give me your wings!"

He shrugged and gave a crooked smile. "I had to, dar-lin'," he said softly. "What good's an angel without them?"

Cody looked sharply at his friend, and in that moment Dennis looked up.

"You're a lucky man," Dennis said, and reached out and shook Cody's hand. "You always were the smart one, Coda-man. All the best in the world, and I really mean that."

Cody didn't answer. There was nothing he could say. He looked at Queen, sitting behind the table, holding court with her cake and gifts and the devoted attention of her subjects, and knew that his life was full.

17

Little did Cody know, however, that his past was not quite behind him.

Lenore Whittier was furious. She'd paid an inept fool an exorbitant amount of money just to be told what she already knew. Queen Houston had insinuated herself into Cody's life to the point that he had proposed marriage. Short of murder, there wasn't a thing Lenore could do to stop it. Fortunately for all concerned, she had not considered that option.

Weeks had come and gone, and during that time she hadn't been able to come up with one thing that might discredit the woman who was trying to take Claire's place. It never occurred to Lenore that Queen had made a place of her own, that she wasn't usurping that of anyone who'd gone before her.

"I won't have it," Lenore mumbled, pacing her bedroom, which overlooked a terraced backyard, ignoring the lush beauty of her Florida home. "There must be something I've overlooked. How can a total stranger come into a family's life and take over as if . . . "

Suddenly a thought surfaced. She'd gone about this from the wrong angle. She shouldn't have concentrated her efforts on what the woman was doing now. What she should have checked on was where she had come from . . . what her background was before she arrived in Snow Gap.

Lenore hurried to the phone, flipped through the directory to find the heading Morrow Investigations, and squinted as she punched in the numbers. Even at home when there was no one to see her, she was too vain to wear glasses.

"Morrow Investigations . . . Wally Morrow speaking."

Wally kicked back on his chair and used his desk for a footrest as he propped the phone between his shoulder and chin.

"Mr. Morrow, this is Lenore Whittier."

Instinctively Wally's feet hit the floor and he swiped at the spot on his desk where his shoes had been, although the woman on the other end of the line could not see the condition of his office.

"Yes, Mrs. Whittier, what can I do for you?" Wally asked, all the while wishing her into the next level of hell. It had been weeks since he'd closed the case in Colorado, and he was still sitting on a cushion, thanks to his bout with that crazy Bonner man who'd thrown him on his ass. In spite of three different doctors' assurances to the contrary, he still swore his tailbone was broken.

Lenore told him what she wanted.

"This is gonna cost you," Wally said. "I'll have travel expenses . . . and, of course, hazardous pay. This has been a risky case."

"I don't care what it costs, just get me the information I asked for. I want it within the next three days."

"No way," he said. "I'll be lucky to just get a plane out by then. This is already the holiday season. Travel is at a premium due to Thanksgiving, you know."

"I'm well aware of the holiday, thank you. What you don't seem to understand is that this is not a holiday trip. I want my information and I want it immediately. I'll expect to hear from you soon."

She hung up the phone and missed the virulent string of curses that Wally left hanging in midsentence as the wire went dead.

"Dumb bitch," he muttered as he hung up the receiver. "She wants her miracles prepackaged and yesterday. I'll get to Tennessee and in my own time."

But the threat was for effect only. Wally had already dialed his travel agent and was mentally packing what he would need for an overnight stay in Cradle Creek, Tennessee.

Queen couldn't sleep. The feeling she'd awakened with this morning was increasing at an alarming rate. It had been there, lurking just beyond consciousness, when she'd gotten up and dressed. All through breakfast she'd felt the pressure building, and even though the boys' loud, boisterous behavior had sidetracked her momentarily, when they left for school it had come back full force.

She'd spent a miserable morning, unable to function, just waiting for Cody's return from the camp. And when he'd come through the door with a smile on his face and a weary but satisfied announcement that the first group of trainees had come and gone, she'd had to force herself not to crawl away and hide. Instead she'd listened while he commented on the various successes as well as the slight changes in the system that they would adopt for the next group of men scheduled to arrive the Monday after Thanksgiving.

She'd all but held her breath until the boys had burst into the house, wild with the excitement of a two-day holiday from school. At least they were home. Whatever she feared had yet to come.

The busywork of getting a meal prepared and served took precedence, but it was all she could do to cope. She dropped a bottle of ketchup and broke a glass, then finally left the kitchen near tears. She left Cody with the ordeal of getting the boys clean and into bed.

He wanted to linger after supper, to share his excitement about the camp and talk about plans for their future and the upcoming wedding, and she pleaded a headache instead.

Shame made her stay in her room when she'd wanted to go back downstairs and apologize, to confess her feelings and share the fear. But she hadn't, and now it was past midnight and terror had all but engulfed her.

She threw back her covers, got out of bed, and crept to the window. The curtains were pulled to ward against the cold drafts of Colorado winter, and she pushed them aside with trembling fingers, afraid to look, afraid not to. If another disaster was coming, she wanted to be upright and ready, not flat on her back and a willing victim.

She stared out into the nearly pitch-black night, remembering another day when she'd had the same feeling and ignored it. The day when Virgil Stratton had nearly ended her life.

But there was nothing to be seen beyond the perimeter of the yard. The security light on the tall pole at the back of the house could only do so much, and tonight, without the aid of moonlight, its weak beam was ineffective. Whatever was there was beyond the visible, hidden either by shadows or a span of miles, waiting for its time to come.

She shivered, suddenly needing to feel Cody's arms around her. Because of the children, they'd agreed not to share a bedroom until their marriage. Now she bolted for Cody's room. She just needed to know that if something was coming, she would not face it alone.

The hallway was cold, and she was thankful for Will's birthday gift, a long flannel nightgown. It was long sleeved, with the hem just above her toes, and the color was a very warm, outrageous shade of red. Will had loved it, and Queen wore it faithfully, abandoning it only on nights when it was in the laundry.

With her long mane of hair in its nightly braid, and her face scrubbed and devoid of makeup, she looked like a lanky child making a dash for her parents' room in fright, until one looked closer and saw the curvaceous body hidden beneath red flannel, the generous breasts beneath the tiny white buttons and lace at the nightgown's enclosure.

Her hand touched the doorknob to his room. It turned at her command and she slipped inside, closing it quickly behind her in a sudden shiver of fright.

"Cody?"

He came awake in seconds, the fear in her voice bringing him into focus, and in that moment something made him remember her odd behavior earlier in the evening. He'd wanted to urge her to confidence and then hadn't, telling himself that women needed their space just like everyone else, thinking that he and the boys had possibly done nothing worse than get on her nerves.

"What? Are you sick, darling? Is one of the boys . . . ?"

"I'm afraid."

He was out of bed in an instant, his arms around her,

his body still warm from the bed and sleep as it encompassed hers. His heartbeat thumped a welcome beneath
her cheeks as she pressed her face against his bare chest.
His pajama bottoms were brown and old and hung on
his slim hips with comfortable tenacity.

"What frightened you, baby? Did you hear something? Get in my bed to stay warm while I go check."

His voice was soft and low and wrapped around her
like a blanket. She sighed and relaxed within his embrace.
It had been right to come. Already she felt better just
knowing she wasn't alone in the dark.

"It isn't that. I'm sorry," she said, and slid her arms
around his waist. "I'm just being silly, and you're going to
freeze."

"Then come to bed with me," Cody urged.

He felt her hesitation and loved her for the thoughtfulness. She always put the boys' needs ahead of her own
desires. No one wanted her in his bed more than Cody
did, but she'd been adamant about the decision to stay in
her own room. Even though they were officially engaged,
three boys, all under the age of consent, needed to see
all the right examples, and she was determined to set her
share.

"Just for a bit," he added. "You're shivering. And your
feet are bare." He tugged at her braid in a gentle, teasing
gesture. "All those handmade house shoes you received
as presents and you still run around in bare feet."

"Old habits die hard, Cody," she said. "When you
grow up without luxuries, it's hard to remember you
have them now."

He frowned, thinking how much he took for granted.
Imagine house shoes being a luxury! He scooped her off
her feet, carried her back to his bed, and plopped her
down.

When she was warm, and he'd quit flinching at the feel of her bare toes seeking warmth up the length of his legs, he cuddled her, spoon fashion, his front to her back, and rested his chin on top of her head while he found the spot below her breasts that he'd discovered long ago. He knew if he touched lightly enough, he could feel the rush of her blood beneath his fingertips. It made him realize how fragile the human body truly was and marvel constantly at how tenaciously she'd clung to life when life had nearly given up on her.

"Talk to me, honey. Did you have a bad dream?" He stroked her body, his hands sliding up and down the soft flannel over her arms as he hugged her close. "Believe me, if you did, I would understand. Thanks to you and a little help from the base doctor, I'm more or less past mine, but could it be that you're suffering some aftereffects of—"

"It's not that."

The tone of her voice as well as the way she went stiff in his arms warned him there was more to come. He heard tears as well as fear and hated whoever had put them there.

"Then tell me, Queen. Remember . . . you can tell me anything. I'll always understand."

She sighed. "It's hard to explain," she said, keeping her voice low so that the sound of their conversation would not disturb the sleeping trio just down the hall.

"I'm listening."

"I know," she said. "It's just that it's hard to find words that fit what I feel." She took a deep breath, knowing that what she would say was going to sound crazy. "I think something bad is going to happen."

Cody grinned. "Are you telling me you're psychic? Oh, great! I'll never have a secret from you as long as we live."

As long as we live. Those words were just what she needed to hear. It made the rest of what she had to say easier.

"I'm not psychic," she said, and lightly kicked his shin for teasing her.

He felt her body tremble beneath his fingers as she continued, trying to explain what had sent her into his arms.

"It's just that . . . sometimes I get a feeling . . . I can't explain it, or tell you why. The best way I can describe it is, sometimes when I'm not expecting it, the world sort of . . . shifts. Like everything looks and sounds normal but isn't quite . . . Do you know what I mean? Whatever it is, I always have this feeling just before something bad happens. When Virgil Stratton came, I was afraid like this all day."

Cody grew solemn, thinking about her alone and afraid, and hugged her closer, still slightly ashamed that she'd endured what she had because of his absence.

"Honey, it sounds to me like you're describing an instinct for survival. I knew soldiers who used to tell war stories of similar situations. Of how they'd suddenly know when they were about to be attacked even though everything looked and felt normal."

She sighed. "Whatever it is . . . I know something's coming . . . and . . . " Her voice sank to a whisper and she clung to him, trying to let herself be absorbed by his strength. "And I'm so afraid."

"Whatever it is, we'll face it together. Remember that. You never have to face anything else alone as long as you live."

"Oh, Cody," she whispered.

He felt her relax, and a few minutes later as her feet warmed, and her breathing slowed, he knew that she slept. He held her close, savoring the feel of her body aligned with his, knowing that his life was all the richer from the gift of her love and that she'd given him something she'd never shared with another living soul: her trust.

But hours later he was still awake, staring blindly at the shadows around the room, and then, still later, at the first faint light of daybreak. He knew that what she'd told him last night had reawakened some of the same fears that he'd lived with since he'd learned that they were being investigated.

Granted the man who had been doing the investigation was gone. But that didn't tell him who had hired him or why.

Queen sighed and stretched and then turned in her sleep. When her face came against his chest and her arm slid lightly across him in sleep, he couldn't control the urge he had to grab her and hold on for dear life. What or who was trying to intrude in his world?

He held her, afraid to take guesses, afraid he already knew. She nuzzled against him, and he smiled, shoving his own fears back into the shadows where they belonged. It was morning and time to greet the new day and his lady.

He loved her awake and then made love until her eyes closed again, only this time in passion. This time when she cried it was from joy, and when she went from his bed to her own, she wasn't running in fear. She was warm from the fulfillment of love and being loved. It was a good way to start a day.

"Hell!"

It was the best and only description Wally Morrow could give to Cradle Creek, Tennessee. He'd reached the city limits in his rental car, expecting at any time to see more than what was there. But he'd been disappointed and, as he drove on, shocked to discover that what he had seen was all he was going to get.

The homes looked like something that had been dug up from the bowels of the earth along with the coal he knew was here and then abandoned . . . a slag heap of houses that were Cradle Creek.

The only thing that told him people lived in this godforsaken hole were the wispy strips of smoke that drifted skyward from the stovepipes and chimneys.

A thin crust of ice broke beneath his feet. The water below soaked his shoes as he got out of the car and started into the gas station for information.

"Shit," he muttered, and looked down at the rim of mud surrounding his favorite Cole-Haans. And then he looked closer and feared that his profanity had been accurate in another way. He could smell the odor from here.

He dug a handkerchief out of his pocket, cleaned his shoes as best he could, and then tossed the handkerchief into a garbage can as he passed. This wasn't a promising start to a trip he hadn't wanted to take, and he knew he had only himself and his greed to blame. If he wasn't always in debt up to his ears, he wouldn't have to take every piddle-ass job that came his way. And trying to dig up dirt—and, in some cases, shit—on people who seemed to be minding their own businesses would be a thing of the past.

He walked into the gas station and an hour later came away with more than he'd hoped for. He had all kinds of unverifiable information on the Houston family, which was no longer in residence.

He stared up at the hillside beyond the gas station,

peering through the thick stand of pines to the cemetery
to which the attendant had alluded. According to the
man inside, the only member of the Houston family still
residing in the town was six feet under, mixing his bones
with the vein of coal that was the foundation of Cradle
Creek.

He got into his car and drove in the direction of
Whitelaw's Bar. According to the attendant, Morton
Whitelaw would be the authority on the gambler and his
daughters. The entire time they'd lived in Cradle Creek,
they had lived next door to his bar.

"She should like this," Wally muttered, thinking of
Lenore Whittier's glee in learning that Queen Houston
came from a less than ostentatious background. "Next
door to a bar . . . across the street from whores. Hell,
she'll have a heyday."

He turned the corner and saw a string of red blinking
lights strung across a sign over a porch: WHITELAW'S BAR.

He'd found it. Now all he needed was some verifica-
tion of what the man in the station had said, and he'd be
out of here before dark. If he hurried, he thought he
could just about make Knoxville and then catch an early
morning flight out tomorrow. If not, his only option
would be sleeping in his car. And while he'd done it
before, it had not been in the middle of winter, so far
back in the hills, in a town that looked like something
out of a Stephen King movie.

From the looks of the town, people starved to death
here on a daily basis. How a gambler had made a living
in a place like this amazed him. And then he thought
back to what the man in the station had said and realized
that Johnny Houston, like all the other residents of Cradle Creek, had not profited but simply survived.

He opened the door and walked into the bar. His first

instinct upon entering was to hold his breath. But that would have been impossible, so he opted for a cigarette, although he was trying to quit. Inhaling nicotine suddenly seemed a whole lot healthier than breathing in what was inside this place.

Wally's first question elicited a response he hadn't expected from the owner of the bar.

"You want to know about the Houstons?" Morton Whitelaw smiled. He'd known his chance would come to pay Johnny Houston's daughters back for the misery they'd caused him. "How bad . . . and how much?"

Wally grimaced and started digging into his pocket. He should have known he would come across one of these kind here. In his business there were always people ready to talk if it was worth their while.

"This much and all you know."

Wally slapped five twenties across the bar and then held them beneath his fingers, staring intently into the man's pasty face until he received a nod of compliance. Only then did he move back, and when he did, he blinked at the way Morton Whitelaw grabbed the money without further negotiation.

Whitelaw began to talk, and time slipped by quickly. Before Wally was aware, the sun had begun its descent toward the treetops.

"I've got to be going," he said, putting his notebook into his pocket and settling his hat tighter onto his head. "Thanks for your information, Mr. Whitelaw."

Morton nodded. "It was my pleasure," he said, and smiled through a mouthful of stained, crooked teeth.

Wally shuddered. He knew his own limitations, but in this place, during the long afternoon, he'd seen himself elevated to the status of something between a gentleman and socially correct.

He almost ran for his car, then slid behind the wheel and locked the door. For the first time since he'd begun working for Lenore Whittier, he had sympathy for her victim. How any woman had grown up intact in a place like this was beyond him.

Why Johnny Houston's daughters hadn't wound up across the street working at the whorehouse that Whitelaw was quick to point out, amazed Wally. And it had been patently obvious that while Whitelaw talked a good story, he hadn't gotten anywhere with any of the sisters. The bitterness of rejection was obvious to one who'd experienced it . . . and Wally Morrow was a master at being rejected.

Morton Whitelaw might wish . . . and he might dream . . . but he'd never screwed one of the gambler's daughters, and Wally had known it from the start. He'd seen Queen Houston, and he knew women. She'd have sooner slit her own throat than sleep with a man like Morton Whitelaw. Not for anything or anyone.

Now the problem remained, did Wally relay what he thought or what he'd been told? None of his information was verifiable; it was all word of mouth. He sighed and shifted into gear, heading out of Cradle Creek with the sun fading fast. It played hell with business when conscience got in the way.

Allen Whittier was furious over what he'd just discovered by accident. Lenore had paid a disgusting amount of money to a private investigation firm. He didn't have to ask her why. He knew his wife too well to hope that it was simply because she might suspect him of having an affair. She was meddling, and he knew good and well it had to do with their grandsons.

He paced the floor in his den, considering his options. He could confront Lenore and make her confess. He could ignore what he'd learned and let whatever happened happen, just as he'd done for years. Or . . . he could wrap his hands around her nipped-and-tucked neck and squeeze.

He shuddered, realizing that the latter thought had seemed all too enticing, and made a beeline for the wet bar in the corner of the room. He poured a stiff shot of bourbon and splashed the liquid down his throat. It was only after he'd swallowed and the liquor hit bottom that the tears shot to his eyes. And by that time Allen could tell himself that it was the booze and not emotion that had made them appear.

His eyes narrowed. One last glance at the two cancelled checks on the desk, along with the bourbon, reinforced what he'd decided to do. He picked them up and headed out of the den. This time his wife had gone too far.

Lenore was outside, fussing with the gardener, kibitzing with the pool man, and generally minding everyone's business but her own. She saw Allen come out through the patio door and stop as he looked her way. Even from this distance she could see the angry set of his shoulders and the way he stared with eyelids barely open. Her stomach turned. She hated it when he tried to assert his masculinity.

"Lenore!"

She frowned. He hadn't shouted at her in years. In fact, she couldn't remember his having raised his voice at her ever. She wanted to ignore him, but something about his stance told her it would be better to get this over with than to let it simmer, whatever it was. She gave the pool man a parting shot and made her way toward the house, mincing through the newly mown grass as if she were a debutante instead of a dowager.

"Allen."

The tone of her voice usually sufficed to quell whatever moment of manhood he felt and send him back where he belonged. Today it didn't work.

"What the hell are these?"

He waved the cancelled checks beneath her nose. Even though she was minus her glasses and one of the checks was upside down, she knew what he'd found.

Her face flushed and then went pale. It was all Allen needed to see.

"You conniving bitch."

The lack of emotion in his voice frightened her more than any shouting he might have done.

"How dare you?" she sputtered, trying to regain her place by taking an offensive attitude.

"No, Lenore. How dare *you?* Don't you love our grandchildren? Why do you persist in tormenting their lives and their father in such a manner? There's nothing in the world wrong with Cody Bonner. I daresay the reason you don't approve of him is that he won't let you control him. And that's what you hate most, isn't it?"

"I won't be talked to like this," Lenore said, and then looked around in dismay. She'd reduced herself to having a shouting match in clear sight of the people who worked for her. It wasn't to be borne.

She pushed past her husband, intent on taking their disagreement indoors. But he reached out and grabbed her arm, stopping her progress and spinning her around until they were nose to nose, their breath mixing more in that moment than their bodies had done in the past ten years.

"You not only will listen, you will obey me," he said.

Lenore gasped as his breath hissed across her cheeks. "I won't be ordered about like a mere hired hand, and you'd be well warned, Allen Whittier! And furthermore, I've done what I've done precisely because I love our grandchildren. I don't want them put in harm's way."

"You think you'll make them happy by scaring the hell out of them? Maybe you don't remember the looks on their faces during the last court trial, but I do. Cody Bonner is an honorable and upstanding man. He's a fine father."

"But that *woman* he's taken into his employ is not!" Her ire rose along with her voice. "She's not fit to be under the same roof with our grandsons, and I can prove it!"

"How? By some sleazeball private eye you picked from the Yellow Pages?"

She flushed again, and he realized that his barb had hit home. "You did, didn't you? Pick him from the Yellow Pages, I mean. My God! How stupid and naive can you get? And I'd like to know what's so wrong with Queen Houston. She seems like a fine woman to me, and she's very good to the boys. What else could you hope for?"

"She's trash . . . nothing more than poor white trash. I won't have my grandsons subjected to her kind."

"Since when does money have anything to do with morals? I seem to remember that your father had a disgusting overabundance of the former and absolutely none of the latter."

The sound of the slap ricocheted within the shocked silence that hung between them. Lenore looked down with surprise at the red imprint on the palm of her hand and the matching one across Allen's face.

He smiled. It was a slow, threatening sort of smile that made her take a step backward in reflex.

"Oh, don't worry," he said. "I won't lower myself to responding to that, Lenore. But what I am going to do is call Cody first thing tomorrow and apologize."

"You can't," she said. "I've already booked us a flight. I thought we'd go out and see firsthand if the boys are being properly cared for. I won't sleep a wink until I see for myself. Trust me, Allen. The report was appalling."

"No, Lenore. Your behavior is what's appalling. And rest assured we'll go. That will only give me opportunity to tell him face to face what I intended to say over the phone."

He turned and walked away, the imprint of her hand still burning across his cheek, and realized that he'd never felt better in his life.

Lenore gasped. This would never do. She hadn't planned for Allen to find out. And she certainly didn't want Cody to hear an apology before he heard what she had to say first.

Refusing to think about what the pool man was thinking, and hoping that the gardener had been too far away to hear, Lenore went into the house without looking back. It would be easier to face them next time if she didn't know for certain that they'd heard.

Besides, she had better things to do than worry about hired hands. She had bags to pack and a plane to catch . . . and a woman's life to ruin.

18

Winter was back. No more hints and promises, no more mild days and cool nights. The afternoon wind whistled as it tunneled through the trees, buffeting the eaves of the house before careening down the valley toward Snow Gap.

Less than an hour ago the first flakes of snow had started to fall, and now the ground was more than half covered with the downy stuff.

Queen shivered nervously and then shook off the feeling, certain that it was caused by nothing more than the wind's mournful wail and her dread of the upcoming holiday season.

Her prediction of doom had not yet been fulfilled. More than a week had passed since she'd escaped to Cody's room in terror, and when nothing had happened she'd almost convinced herself that nothing would.

It would be her first Christmas without her sisters. Even though she was going to be sharing it with her

soon-to-be family, she still felt slightly off course and a
little bit sad, despite being extremely preoccupied with
the situation at hand.

The scent of holiday baking already permeated the
air, though the actual day was still several weeks away.
Cookies in various stages of development were strung
across tables and counters as well as on Will's and J.J.'s
faces. She had more help than she needed yet would not
have wished to trade their presence for a neat kitchen.

"Queenie, can I cut out the next batch?"

J.J.'s imploring question interrupted her thoughts.
She looked down at him, smiling at the liberal dusting of
flour all over his face and shirt, and nodded.

"Yes, you can do the next batch, and Will can mix
instead, okay, Will?"

He agreed. Baking cookies was a new experience for
both boys. Heretofore they'd been involved solely in the
eating of them. When they realized that Queen was giving their creativity free rein, it knew no bounds. Colored
sugar of various hues was scattered about the work island
and the floor and suspiciously stuck to their faces. Queen
pretended not to notice that both boys were wearing red-
and-green-sugared mustaches—a dead giveaway to the
fact that not all of the sugar was going on the cookies.

"Donny, don't eat them all," Will whined, imploring
Queen to make him stop.

She gave Donny a mock frown. He grinned and left
the kitchen, shoving one last star-shaped cookie into his
mouth on the way out.

Lord save me from hollow-legged boys, she thought.
Then she realized that when it came to feeding and raising endlessly hungry boys, she'd just begun.

"Queenie! Someone's coming!"

Donny's bellow from the front of the house sent both

boys tumbling from the stools they'd been using to elevate their height to cabinet level.

"Wash first!" Queen called. "Your dad will get the door." Then she added, mostly to herself, "Besides, it's probably Dennis."

Dennis had established a regular routine of a weekly visit on the pretense of discussing the survival camp or the new trainees in residence, though these matters could just as easily have been dealt with over the phone or at the camp itself.

Cody knew why Dennis really came. He'd become as entrenched in the warm, homey atmosphere Queen had created for his family as they had. And he loved her cooking.

The boys made a U-turn and headed for the downstairs bath. In less than a minute they emerged, still dripping, and went into the living room, leaving Queen to deal with the last batch of cookies coming out of the oven. But the sudden abandonment didn't hurt her feelings at all. She was grateful for the space and quiet.

Cody heard the two car doors slam and frowned. Dennis always came alone. And who else would be coming unannounced or without calling? Especially this far up the mountain and on a day like this, with the impending threat of a storm.

The knock was swift and abrupt. Two short, staccato raps and then nothing. He opened the door, and the smile on his face stopped short of wide and inviting.

"Allen! Lenore! What a surprise!" It was all he could say.

Donny walked up behind his father. His heart sank, and he was entertaining thoughts of escaping to his room when he realized he'd been spotted. He forced a smile on his face and went to greet them.

"Hi, Grandpa, Grandma. I didn't know you were coming. Dad, why didn't you tell us? Was this supposed to be a surprise?"

"Yes," Lenore said, as usual answering for everyone, "it was meant to be a surprise, for your father as well as you boys. I always say surprises bring the best results."

Her smile was small and secretive. Cody stood aside for her to enter and noted absently that her expression matched the weather of the day—cold and wintry.

Allen grasped Cody's hand warmly in return, hoping to make up for the aggravation of his wife and the rudeness of their unexpected arrival.

Will and J.J. came running, with smiles of welcome spread across their faces in place of the colored sugar that had been there minutes earlier. They came to a sliding halt on the polished floor as they rounded the corner to come face to face with their grandmother—high heels, fur coat, lacquered hair, and all.

Both had the look on their faces that Cody had come to recognize meant retreat. He intervened before they could act on it.

"Boys, give your grandparents a big welcome. They've come a long way to surprise you."

Lenore offered her cheek to each boy and then couldn't resist swiping at a stray bit of sugar on Will's shirt and a matching one on J.J.'s face.

"What on earth have you two been doing? Cody, they're a mess!"

"We've been baking cookies with Queenie," they said, suddenly remembering the fun they'd left behind. "Come see! We have stars and Christmas trees and everything!"

Allen smiled. "I'd love to," he said. "Just let me put down my bag and I'll—"

"I'll take it to the den, Grandpa," Donny offered. "You go with the guys. But don't eat all the green ones . . . they're my favorite."

Allen laughed as each boy took him by the hand and began leading him toward the kitchen.

"Lenore, aren't you coming? This sounds like the place to be. And from the wonderful aroma, it smells like the place to be as well."

"I want to talk to Cody," she said. "I'll join you later."

Allen frowned, suddenly unsure of leaving her alone with his son-in-law. They'd fought for three days until she'd grudgingly agreed to desist in her attempts to discredit Queen. Surely she wouldn't go back on her word. The boys' chatter intruded into his worries.

"Lead away," Allen said. "I'm already getting hungry."

The boys shrieked with laughter as they pulled him through the house.

"Something smells wonderful," he said as he unwound himself from his grandsons.

Queen turned, surprise spread across her face, and then her eyes lit up at the wide grin on the elderly man's face.

"Allen . . . I mean, Mr. Whittier, it's great to see you again."

"Please, call me Allen," he corrected her. "And now that we've settled that, how many may I have?"

She laughed and pushed the plate toward him. "With an offer like that, there are no limits."

Allen hovered over the cookies, still warm from the oven, and chose one. He quickly admired the handiwork, praising each boy in turn, and then bit into one with relish.

"Uummm," he said. "They're even better than they look."

Meanwhile Lenore had maneuvered Cody into a corner in the hall. Regardless of what she had promised Allen, she wasn't budging from her intended mission.

"Cody . . . if you don't mind, we need to talk."

Cody frowned at the tone of Lenore's voice. He didn't like what he was thinking. He stepped aside as she walked past him into the living room. He followed her in and motioned for her to sit, but she shook her head.

"No, what I have to say needs to be said standing. Unfortunately I do not come bearing good news."

Cody shoved his hands in his pockets and stood his ground, staring down at Lenore, waiting for her to continue.

"It has come to my attention that the *woman* you have hired to care for my grandsons comes from a less than desirable background."

Cody inhaled sharply. The implied slur she used when referring to Queen as "that woman" made him see red. Queen had been right! Lenore had to have been behind Wally Morrow's appearance in Snow Gap. How else would she now be in possession of any information regarding Queen?

"What you don't realize, Lenore, is that none of this is your business. And what you also don't know is that I know everything there is to know about Queen, right down to the fact that I love her and I'm going to marry her."

"No! I won't have it!"

Lenore's shout could be heard all over the house. Allen jumped, dropping his half-eaten cookie back onto the plate, and made a dash for the living room. Damn her, she promised!

Queen should have known that their arrival meant trouble. She wondered if this was what she'd sensed coming over a week before.

"Boys," she said, "let's take a plate of cookies to your grandmother and your dad, okay?"

They nodded, but the frowns on their faces were imprinting deep worry lines across their foreheads, and Queen would have liked to march into the room and shake some sense into that witch. What was wrong with her, anyway? Why couldn't she just sit back and accept the love that was due her as a grandparent and not try to meddle in the other facets of Cody's life?

Cody too had to restrain himself from shaking Lenore. "I don't care whether you like it or not. I'm past trying to work things out with you. No matter what happens, you don't like it. You don't want to try. You just want to cause trouble."

Lenore glared at him; the total lack of emotion in his voice made her angrier. "Well . . . I don't think you'll feel so positive when you read this," she said, and produced Wally Morrow's latest report with a flourish.

Cody brushed aside the paper, refusing even to dignify her actions by looking at it. That only made things worse. Allen Whittier entered the room on the run, but Lenore went on before he could speak up.

"She's nothing but white trash!" she shrieked, forgetting her proper upbringing in the fury of her tirade. "Her father was a no-account gambler. They lived in a terrible slum, next door to a bar, and across the street from harlots. Think of what she's surely seen . . . think of what she's probably done! Why, for that matter . . . they were all probably nothing but a lot of whores themsel—"

The sound of Allen's slap reverberated across the room. Cody didn't know who was more stunned—himself for having witnessed something he'd thought impossible, Allen for standing up to his wife, or Lenore for having suffered it.

And then a noise shattered the silence, and all heads turned toward the sound. Queen stood just inside the doorway with a boy on either side of her. The plate of cookies she'd been holding was at her feet, broken and ruined, just like her dreams.

Queen had walked into the room just in time to hear Lenore's ugly accusations. And in the space of time it had taken for her brain to register the unfounded rumors of her immorality, something had happened. She'd felt the room tilt. Just a bit, and just enough for her to lose her grip on the plate.

It had crashed at her feet, shattering cookie and china alike, as well as the last of her hopes. No matter how far she ran, she couldn't outrun her past. Judgmental attitudes had simply followed behind, waiting for her to let down her guard, to actually think that she could love . . . and trust . . . and not be hurt again.

She shuddered. The roaring in her ears got louder, and the room started to darken and then turn black. The last thing she remembered seeing were the shocked expressions on Will's and J.J.'s faces as their grandmother shrieked and the cookies broke.

"Honey . . . " Cody never got to finish what he'd been about to say. He watched Queen's face turn pale as she swayed on her feet, staring at the broken plate and cookies as if she'd never seen them before, and then, without a word, fell limply to the floor.

"Oh, no!" Allen's gasp was nothing more than an echo of what was in all their hearts.

All, save Lenore, made a rush toward Queen, who was lying, unconscious, in the midst of the broken glass and food.

The boys were frozen with fear. All they knew was that their grandmother had yelled and then Queenie had fallen on the floor. J.J. started to cry, and Will turned pale and backed away from the onrush of concerned people hovering over her.

"Queen, honey . . ."

But she had no answer for Cody as he knelt and gently cradled her head upon his knees. His fingers were shaking, his voice deep with concern, as he touched her clammy skin. It was evident she was in shock. "Damn you, Lenore," he muttered without looking up.

"That wasn't my fault," she said, suddenly aware of other implications. What if the stupid woman had hurt herself? She wouldn't be to blame.

"Yes! Yes, it was!" Will yelled.

His cry startled everyone. He was backing into the hallway and pointing a shaking finger at his grandmother, his face suffused with anger.

"It *was* your fault. You said bad things about Queenie. You hurt her feelings. I hate you! I hate you!" he screamed.

"There! You see!" Lenore's exclamation did nothing to calm the mess in progress. "She's already turned him against me. I told you, Allen. They have no business being exposed to her kind. They should come live with us like before. There we can give them—"

Cody erupted. "Dammit, woman. Just shut the hell up!" The look he gave his father-in-law was telling. "Allen, for God's sake, please . . . get her out of here."

It was all the urging Allen needed. He got to his feet, leaving the care of Queen to those who loved her best, and grabbed his wife by the arm, leading her from the room, ignoring her protests.

Cody lifted Queen into his arms and carried her to the sofa. "Donny, go get me a wet cloth, will you, son?" he asked as he smoothed her curls away from her pale, silent face.

Donny did as he was told.

"J.J., you and Will go get a dustpan and a broom from the kitchen and sweep up the cookies and broken glass before someone gets cut, okay?"

Tears were puddling in J.J.'s eyes as he leaned over Queen's inert body and patted her cheek with a smudgy hand that had missed getting washed. "Is she going to die?" he asked.

Cody's heart skipped a beat. Of course that's what they would think. The last time they'd seen their mother had been at the funeral services, lying in a coffin. She'd been just as still . . . and just as pale.

"No, son. Of course not. She just fainted. It's something women do sometimes, and it doesn't really hurt them at all, I promise."

"You swear?"

"I swear," Cody said. "Now run along and get that broom. Queen will be proud of you for helping, okay?"

J.J. smiled a little. Just hearing that his Queenie would approve made him rush to do his father's bidding.

Cody's hand cupped her face. "Oh, love. What else will you have to go through because of my family?" And then a thought occurred to him that was so frightening, he couldn't even say it aloud. Will you love me enough to stay . . . or will you finally be wanting that bus ticket after all?

Donny ran back into the room, handed his father a damp cloth, then sat on the arm of the couch and watched, his blue eyes wide, his cheeks red with anger.

Like his father, he was enraged at the unjustness with which Queen had been treated. He remembered weeks ago hearing her tell the bedtime story about the gambler's little daughters and what a sad and ugly life they'd had. He wasn't stupid. He'd known then that Queen was trying to tell them about herself. But it hadn't made him think less of her.

In fact, he'd come to think of her as something of a savior. After all, she'd saved her little sisters from starving to death, maybe even worse . . . and then saved him and his brothers from being taken away.

His fingers curled into fists as he watched his father pressing the damp cloth across her forehead. No one better say anything bad about her again, Donny swore to himself. If they do . . . they'll be sorry.

"Queen, sweetheart . . . can you hear me?"

Cody's voice was as soft as his touch, and yet somehow they both threaded their way into Queen's subconscious and gently pulled her back.

Even before her eyes opened, Cody knew when she came to. Her chin began to tremble, and as hard as she might, she could not stop the tears that slipped out from beneath her eyelids.

He pressed his forehead against her arm and squeezed her hand gently, resisting the urge to scoop her into his arms and just run with her and never look back. But he couldn't, and he knew it.

One of the reasons was sitting at the end of the couch, watching his every move. And from the look on his son's face, Donny wouldn't have let him get out the door with Queen. He was his father's son all the way.

"Dad, is she going to be all right?"

"Yes. Why don't you go check on Will and J.J.? I think Queen probably needs some time to herself, okay, son?"

Donny nodded, giving them a last backward glance as he left the room. On the way out he bent down and picked up a bit of china that J.J. had missed sweeping up, then held it carefully as he went in search of his brothers.

"Oh, Cody."

Those two small words held so much despair. Queen opened her eyes and, without waiting for the invitation, sat up and wrapped her arms around his neck. "I don't know why I did that," she whispered. "I never faint."

"Stop it, sweetheart," Cody said. "Don't you dare apologize. In fact, you've got a big apology coming. From the way Allen looked when he dragged Lenore out of the room, it'll be a doozy."

Queen tried to smile but didn't quite make it. Instead her mouth reshaped into a wry, bitter twist. "And she won't mean a damned word of it. Why bother? I don't need to hear it, and she'll hate me for having to say it."

Cody hugged her, then, unable to stop himself, kissed her, removing the taste of anger and despair from her lips.

"I love you, lady," Cody said. "And you've got quite a rooting section. The boys nearly took their grandmother apart, especially Will."

Suddenly she remembered the look on their faces just as she fell. It was a combination of fear and helplessness to stop what was happening in their lives.

A familiar feeling of dread began to resurface, and she remembered the terror she'd felt days ago when she'd gone running to Cody's room in the middle of the night.

"It finally happened, didn't it, Cody?"

He nodded. He didn't have to ask what she meant. He could tell by the look on her face that she was remembering.

"Yes, honey, I guess it did. That'll teach me to ever doubt your powers again, right?"

He smiled and ran a thumb across her lower lip, trying to tease her out of the panic he saw settling in her eyes.

She caught his hand and held it to her breast, needing the pressure of his touch to calm the thunder of her heartbeat. "But I'm still scared, Cody. I don't think it's over. What if Lenore tries to take the boys away? What if—"

"Hush. She can try until the moon turns blue, but it won't happen. We won't let it."

He sealed his promise with another kiss and then held her, confident that with Queen at his side, he could conquer anything . . . even Lenore, the wicked witch of the South—south Florida, that was.

Allen was shaking. He all but flung his wife into Cody's den and then slammed the door behind him.

"You've gone too far," he said. "I warned you, Lenore. Damn you to hell, I warned you."

As usual, Lenore wasn't listening. "Did you see her? She couldn't even face the truth about herself. She passed out from shock, knowing that her ruse was all over."

She began to pace the floor, thumping a fist against her palm as she conceived another plan of action. "When we get back home, I'll call our lawyer and start proceedings at once. It won't take long for a judge to see my point of view. I'm certain I'm right!"

Allen sighed and wiped a weary hand across his face. She would never change, but it wasn't too late for him. He still had some years left in him, and he suddenly didn't want to waste them any longer by living in her shadow.

"While you're at it," he said, "you'd better contact a divorce lawyer as well. I'm sick and tired of this. You lie and you manipulate, and I refuse to be a part of it anymore." At that moment he would have given anything to take a picture of Lenore's face. "And . . . you'd be well advised to rethink your position on claiming custody of someone else's children. I don't think there's a judge sitting on the bench who'll award custody of a teenager and two prepubescent boys to a woman of your age."

"Allen!" It was all she could think to say.

"Actually, you'll play hell even getting your side of the story heard, because if this ever comes to court again, I'll be testifying on Cody's behalf, against you." His finger never wavered as he thrust it within inches of her nose.

"Allen!"

"You already said that, Lenore. Surely for once in your miserable life you're not out of things to say?"

With that parting shot, he walked out of the room, leaving his wife with nothing but the lingering bitterness of his words. Suddenly she began to shake. She staggered backward, reaching out blindly behind her for the chair she knew was there, and then, when she felt the arm, dropped onto the seat with an undignified plop.

"Allen . . . "

But as he'd so rudely reminded her . . . she'd already said that. She dropped her face into her hands and, for the first time since she'd buried her daughter, cried . . . and they were true tears of remorse.

"Dad!"

Donny's desperate, wild-eyed look as he burst into the room stopped Cody's heart. Something was wrong!

"What is it, son? Did Lenore—"

"Dad . . . I can't find Will."

Queen was standing before she ever knew she'd

moved from her reclining position on the couch. The total fear in Donny's voice was spreading to her own warning system. Will! Where had he gone?

"But he and J.J. were just here . . . sweeping up the—"

"J.J. did it. He said he couldn't find Will and did it by himself."

"Oh, God," Queen said, and started up the stairs. "Will! Will!" she cried, and began opening doors and searching through closets, shoving clothing aside, praying that she'd find him hidden in the depths. He was nowhere to be found.

Her cries were an echo of Cody's own shouts as he started his search downstairs. He burst into the den, startling Lenore so badly that she didn't have time to hide her tears.

"Have you seen Will?" he shouted.

At the shake of her head, he left so quickly that she didn't have time to ask why Will would be missing. She got to her feet and ran out the door, joining in the now frantic melee of Bonners who were all but ransacking their home in search of the missing child.

"Will!" Queen shouted as she ran into her own room, hoping that he had taken refuge there. But he had not. Pressing her fingers to her lips to stop the trembling, she had a sudden idea. He and J.J. were inseparable. Maybe he knew something he wasn't telling.

"Did you find—"

Cody didn't have time to finish his question as Queen grabbed him by the arms. "Where's J.J.?" she asked.

Instantly he understood the reason for her question and turned to his eldest son. "Donny?"

Donny led the way into the kitchen, where Allen sat holding J.J. in his lap.

Queen ran to them, knelt, and then took a deep

breath, aware that she'd get nothing out of him by increasing his own panic. He'd already endured more than a seven-year-old child ought to.

"Honey . . . " He looked up at her and then crawled from Allen's lap into her arms without a word.

"It's okay, sweetheart," she said. "It's okay. I'm fine, now."

J.J. sighed and laid his head on Queen's shoulders, patting her cheek as she cuddled him against her.

"I told you, son," Cody said, stroking J.J.'s hair as Queen held him. "Your Queenie is okay, just like I said she would be."

"Honey," Queen said when she could feel J.J. beginning to relax, "Will didn't help you sweep up my mess, did he?"

J.J. shook his head. "I couldn't find him, so I did it by myself."

"And you did a good job, too," she added, looking to Cody for support.

J.J. lifted his head and smiled. As far as smiles went, it wasn't much, but it was a start.

Allen felt sick. Every bad thing that had happened to this family since Claire died could be linked directly to him and Lenore. He looked at the broken, aging woman standing alone in the doorway and, for the first time in years, actually felt sorry for her. He got up from his chair and walked toward her. And instead of walking past her, he stopped and pulled her into his arms. She leaned against him and hid her face in her hands.

"So, J.J., when did you see Will last?" Queen asked.

He shrugged. Too much had happened for him to be pinned down to details.

"Was it . . . maybe . . . when you went to get the broom?"

J.J. thought. "No," he finally answered.

"Did you see him when Donny went to get a cold cloth for Queen?" Cody asked.

He wanted to shout, to shake J.J. into remembering, and knew that were it not for Queen, he would be doing just that right now and probably ruining whatever chance they had of finding out what had happened.

"Think, honey," Queen urged him. "What was the last thing you remember seeing Will do?"

J.J.'s face lit up. Put like that, the memory came flooding back. "Getting his coat from the closet," he said.

"Oh, God!"

Cody's cry was nothing more than what Queen thought. It was getting late . . . and the snow was still falling.

Cody ran to the front door and looked out. There was nothing in sight except for his Blazer and Allen's rental car, a late-model gray Chevrolet.

He stepped outside, shivering in reflex as a burst of wind came around the edge of the house and whistled through his clothes, chilling him instantly as if he had nothing on.

He began to walk around the deck that surrounded the house, searching the landscape for a sign . . . anything. Maybe he was hiding in one of the outbuildings, Cody thought. But there was no sign of footprints that would have been easily visible in the light ground covering of snow. He looked up into the gray, overcast sky and noticed that, for the moment, it had nearly quit snowing.

Cody rounded the back of the house and then stopped. His heart slammed against his rib cage, and he felt his legs go weak.

"No! Dammit, Will, no!"

But Cody was too late to stop what had already happened. He started to run. In seconds he was off the deck and in the backyard, staring with increasing panic at the single pair of small footsteps leading into the thick wooded area beyond the house. He started to follow without thinking, and the wind sliced through his sweater, reminding him that he was not dressed for the weather.

He turned and ran back up the steps, burst through the back door of the house, and ran through it, passing the others who had assembled in the kitchen.

Queen quickly handed J.J. to Donny and ran after Cody.

"What?" she asked as she watched him shrugging into his heaviest coat and stuffing a flashlight into his pocket. "Dear God, Cody . . . what?"

"He's run away for sure," Cody said. "His footprints lead into the woods in the backyard."

Queen turned pale, remembering the dense underbrush that Virgil Stratton had dragged her through and how fast she'd lost sight of the house. Will would be lost in minutes if he hadn't stopped.

"Maybe he's just hiding," she said, hoping that Cody would confirm her supposition.

"And what if he's not?" Cody reached high on the shelf, pulled down a box, and handed it to Queen to hold while he took out the contents.

"Two-ways," he said, handing her a twin to the radio he stuffed in an inner pocket of his coat. "If I find him, I'll let you know."

"And if you don't . . . "

Cody couldn't say it. All he could do was grab on to Queen and hold her tight. "I'll stay in touch."

"Dad! Let me go with you!" Donny said as he ran into

the hall and overheard the last of the conversation.

Cody shook his head. "Remember what I'm leaving Queen here to face. She doesn't need to be alone."

Donny paused and then stepped aside. A strange, adultlike expression crossed his face as he said, "Don't worry, Dad. You can count on me."

Queen bit back her tears. "Hurry! It'll be dark soon."

In seconds Cody was gone.

19

Cody ran, trying not to think of how long Will had been missing before they'd noticed. Trying not to remember that the last time he'd followed footsteps in the snow, someone had died.

"Will! . . . Will!"

He shouted his son's name and then stopped and listened as he had off and on since he'd started the search. To his dismay, the answer was always the same: nothing but the echo of his own voice and the sound of ice cracking on trees as the wind whipped through.

"Will!"

He shouted again and then started to run, his eyesight trained on the faint trail of footprints. Because of the heavy growth of trees, there was little to no snow on the ground. Often Cody found himself following a trail on instinct rather than sight because the tracks were nonexistent. Just when he thought he would have to stop and backtrack, he'd see them again, his hope would renew, and he'd be off with a spurt of energy.

He burst through a thicket and out onto a ledge, catching himself just before he fell, stopping in midstep and flailing his arms, trying to regain his balance enough to get back to solid ground. The sole of his boot was straddling air as he stared in horror at the sudden drop below and tried to remember if he'd been following footprints or just running. He looked behind him, and the only tracks he saw were his own.

"Oh, God . . . at least I don't think he fell."

He lay down on his stomach and leaned over, staring intently downward, praying he wouldn't see any signs of a bright red coat or of a dark-headed child lying bleeding and broken below. Nothing caught his eye, but the serenity of the surroundings seemed obscene in the face of his own fears.

Cody got to his knees, letting the sudden surge of adrenaline that had rocketed through his system settle, and looked at his watch. In less than three hours it would be dark. He wiped his face with his hands and was surprised when they came away wet. He hadn't realized he'd been crying.

He dropped backward, ignoring the feel of cold ground beneath him, and braced himself by bending his knees and using a small rock at his back for a rest. When his hands stopped shaking, he unzipped the top portion of his coat, pulled the two-way from inside, and pressed down on the send button.

"Cody to Queen . . . Cody to Queen . . . do you read me? Over."

Static popped and fried in his ear, and then her voice came through. He leaned his forehead on his knee and absorbed the strength he got just from knowing that she was with him, in spirit if not in body.

"This is Queen. We read you loud and clear. Over."

"We can't wait any longer. Call Abel Miller. I'm going to need help. Over."

Queen took a deep breath and tried not to lose control when all she wanted to do was crawl away and hide from the awful truth. This was worse than she'd feared. Cody had been gone for an hour and a half. He should have found Will by now. And if he was asking for help, it must mean he was getting desperate. "I'll do it immediately. Is there anything special I need to relate? Over."

"Just tell him to hurry. I'll lead him to my location by radio later. Over."

"Cody . . . I love you. Over."

His silence haunted her. Queen couldn't look at the people sitting around the living room, staring at the pain on her face. And then the radio squawked just before Cody's voice came in loud and clear.

"I love you, too, lady. Say a prayer for us all. Over and out."

Queen dropped the two-way onto the chair beside her and jumped up, running toward the phone in the hall, fear lending speed to her retreat. She dialed, then held her breath and squeezed the bridge of her nose with her thumb and forefinger, praying that she wouldn't start crying in the middle of what she had to say. Sheriff Miller needed information to help save Will, not the sobs of a hysterical female.

Within minutes she was off the phone. She walked back into the room, saw the panicked stares of the people waiting for word, and announced, "They're on their way."

"I'm sorry . . . so sorry. It's all my fault . . . my fault."

Lenore's broken sobs tore the silence of the room. And the sad thing was, no one could deny the truth of her words.

"When Will comes back, you can tell *him* you're sorry, Lenore," Queen said.

"What if he . . . ?"

"Don't!" Queen's sharp, angry shout startled them all. "Don't say it. Don't even think it."

Allen nodded. "I think I'll take Lenore to our room. Maybe if she lies down . . . "

"You may as well use Cody's room," Queen said. "He won't be back. Not without Will."

Allen led his stricken wife away, wishing that she'd come to her senses before this tragedy had happened. If she had, it might have been prevented altogether.

"I'm scared," J.J. said, and wrapped his arms around Queen's legs.

She bent down and lifted him into her arms, then carried him to the couch to sit beside Donny. "I am, too," she said. "But your daddy is looking hard . . . and Sheriff Miller is coming with all kinds of help. They'll find Will. You'll see."

Donny blinked back tears, trying not to cry. And then he looked at Queen, saw the shimmer across her eyes, and knew that he wasn't alone.

Weary beyond belief, Queen leaned against Donny and then smiled to herself as he slid an arm around her shoulders and hugged. When the time came, he was going to be quite a man.

J.J. slid lower in her lap and closed his eyes. He was at the point of exhaustion, also. In no time he was fast asleep, and Queen sat, cradled against the comfort of one son while cradling another, waiting for Cody to put their world back together again.

Will ran, certain that he could hear footsteps pounding the ground behind him, afraid that when they caught

him they'd take him away and he'd never see his father
again. He sobbed, trying not to remember how still
Queenie had been when his father had leaned over her.
What if she was dead, too, just like his mother?

Tree limbs reached out and snagged at his clothing,
pulling and tearing. Will imagined them as wicked,
skeleton claws, trying to hold on to him . . . or tear him
apart. Panic made him strong, the limbs released their
grasp, and he continued to run as he broke free.

Once he stopped in a clearing and looked behind him,
still imagining that he heard the sounds of close pursuit.
Had he known it was only the wind, he might not have
run so far or so fast.

He ran until his legs were shaking and the cold air
he'd inhaled burned his lungs so much that he had to
stop. Then he leaned over, gasping for much needed
breaths as he grabbed hold of his knees and braced himself to keep from falling.

As the first spurt of panic subsided, he began to look
around, and another sort of panic set in. He had no idea
where he was. This was a part of the mountain that he'd
never seen. Tears shot into his eyes, but he bit his lip to
keep from crying. He was lost!

At this point it would have been hard for Will to express
what he was feeling. He needed to cry . . . bad. Tears
burned the back of his nose and thickened in his throat.
But that would not help him out of this situation. There
was only one thing he knew to do. With that in mind, he
straightened, took a deep breath, and started walking
back the way he'd come. At least he wouldn't be lost so
far from home.

One minute he was on firm ground, and the next
thing he knew, it gave way beneath his feet. He felt himself falling. For a moment he had the impression that

the mountain had simply opened its mouth and was now swallowing him whole. He reached up and grabbed at grass and earth as he passed through the hole, but there was nothing to hold on to. The sky receded as he fell into a darkness that engulfed him. He screamed as a burning pain jolted his body. A patch of blue sky, the same color as his daddy's eyes, was the last thing he remembered seeing.

Dennis Macon pulled over to let the patrol car pass, its flashing red and blue lights a signal that urgency was needed, and then frowned as he saw three more just like it close behind.

"What in the world?" he muttered, and looked over his shoulder, just to make sure they all had passed before he pulled back onto the road and continued his trip with increasing dread. Something told him that all was not going to be well when he got to Cody's.

He rounded the last curve in the road that led up the hill toward the Bonner home. Fear squeezed the breath from his lungs as he realized he'd been right. When he saw the flashing red and blue lights, he accelerated, making the last hundred yards in a flurry of snow and leaves.

He stopped in a skid, jumped out of the car, and burst through the door without bothering to knock.

Queen looked up. The concern on his face was enough to send her into his arms.

A silent groan was all Dennis could manage as he caught her in midflight. He pressed a quick, reassuring kiss at the corner of her temple and then pushed her back enough to see her face.

"Angel . . . what in hell's going on here?" He watched her lips tremble as she struggled to maintain control.

"Oh, Dennis . . . Will is lost on the mountain. Cody's been looking for over two hours. He had me call in Sheriff Miller. I was just filling him in on the situation."

"Hell," Dennis said. "How did this happen?"

"It's a long story. Cody can tell you later . . . when he and Will get back."

Dennis heard the panic in her voice as he listened with half an ear to the sheriff and the quick decisions being made regarding the intent of search. Then he caught Abel Miller on the exit.

"Sheriff! I have an entire team of men at a survival training camp. By air it's less than thirty minutes from here. The air force is at your disposal if you want it."

Abel Miller nodded. "I'll take all the help I can get. It's going to be dark before long. That boy and his father are going to play hell not freezing to death." Too late he realized what he'd just said and tried not to look at the stricken expression on Queen's face. "Sorry, honey," he said. "Me and my big mouth."

"Just find them, Abel," she said. "Just find them."

Dennis didn't waste time. He headed for the phone.

Queen listened to him giving directions and orders and knew that she was seeing Lt. Colonel Macon in action, not Dennis, the family friend and best friend to Cody.

"I need to borrow some clothes," Dennis said. "I didn't come dressed for hiking."

Queen waved him upstairs. "Take anything of Cody's you want. You two are close enough in size that everything should fit. Donny, go with him. Help him find what he needs."

Lenore and Allen slipped downstairs and retreated into the den after being ousted from Cody's room. Allen knew that the only way he could help was to keep Lenore under control.

"Queenie, I'm cold," J.J. said, and started to cry.

Queen knew he wasn't crying from the cold. He was crying from the fear.

"Come on, honey," she said. "Let's build a fire. That way Daddy and Will can smell home before they reach it. Okay?"

He nodded. The idea of smoke drifting into the air as a signal was intriguing enough to make him stop crying.

Queen gave Abel Miller a look he couldn't miss and then walked away. He was trying to decide whether it had been an order or a plea and then realized that either way the results needed to be the same. They had a little boy to find and not much time in which to do it.

"Let's get moving, men. Bonner's got a radio. Check your frequencies. Make sure you're all on the same one. He'll guide us in."

They left, taking hope with them, leaving Queen with nothing except a heart full of prayers and faith that they would be heard.

Minutes later Dennis came downstairs dressed in Cody's clothes. For a moment Queen imagined that Cody had come back, and Dennis knew it. The look on her face made him sick. When she realized that it was him and not Cody, the life had completely gone out of her eyes. He tried to give her a comforting smile.

"Hear that?" he asked, pointing to the ceiling.

Queen cocked her head and listened. "Helicopters . . . They're already here, aren't they, Dennis?"

"The flyboys have landed, angel. As John Wayne would say, 'Hold down the fort, pilgrim . . . I'll be right back.'" He grinned. "Or words to that effect."

She smiled. It was the first time she'd felt like it all day. Surely this was a good omen.

✿   ✿   ✿

The euphoria that Cody had felt when the first of the searchers arrived, and then the added hope that came with Dennis and the survival team, set with the sun. They'd found no sign of the child and were now hampered by the darkness.

The moonless night was an impossible scenario for a search. Cody kept remembering his own near miss in going off the side of the mountain, and that had been in broad daylight.

Camp had been set up in a clearing halfway between the top of the mountain and Cody's home. Cody was certain that Will was somewhere in between, and that the reason he hadn't found him was that he was either unconscious or hurt. He couldn't think past those options. Imagining life without all of his children was impossible.

He paced the interior of the tent, hunching within the confines because of his height, unwilling to look at Dennis and see the concern on his face. Unable to talk about his own fears, he could only wait for daylight and pray that when it came, Will would be found. A child . . . unskilled in survival techniques . . . would not live more than one night in this weather. With Cody's background, he knew that better than most.

"Did you eat?" Dennis asked.

Cody shook his head. "How can I eat knowing my son didn't?"

The question was heartbreaking, as was the tone of Cody's voice. Dennis sat cross-legged on his sleeping bag and stared at his own hands, helpless to make things better.

"Okay, but lie down and try to get some rest, will you?"

Before Cody could argue, Dennis held up his hand, staying the interruption he saw coming. "I didn't say sleep, I just said rest. You owe that to Will as much as yourself. How are you going to keep up your strength if you won't eat or sleep? That won't do either of you any good."

Cody dropped onto his sleeping bag and then lay down, unwilling to admit even to himself how weary he actually was. He was sick at heart and scared half out of his mind, and they thought he would be able to sleep?

He folded his hands beneath his head, stared up at the tent, and then closed his eyes, knowing that all he was going to see were horrible images of Will lying in the underbrush of the mountains. At that moment, if he'd been close enough, he could have wrung Lenore's neck and not regretted it one bit.

"Oh, God," Cody said. It was both an expletive and a prayer.

"I know, buddy, I know," Dennis said, and rolled over and doused the light.

Darkness engulfed them. Soon all Cody could hear was the constant howling of the wind outside the tent and the soft, gentle sound of Dennis's snore. He swept his hands across his face, wiping the tears that ran in profusion, and wished that he had Queen to hold him, to tell him that everything was going to be all right.

He needed her strength and courage now, more than he'd needed water in the Saudi desert. Then it had been his own life at stake; now it was a child's . . . his child's.

Will hurt . . . and he couldn't see. At first he thought he was blind. And then he realized that it was just night that had changed his world. He vaguely remembered being able to look up and see a sliver of sky above him, but now he could see nothing, not even moonlight or stars. He covered his face with his hands and, as he did, for the first time realized how truly cold he was. His fingers were numb, the ends tingling and burning as if they were asleep. As he traced the angle of his aching leg, he realized that it was all wrong. He knew that it must be broken.

"That means I can't walk," he whispered to himself, and then shivered uncontrollably.

It was at that moment that bits and pieces of what he'd heard his father say about surviving in below freezing temperatures came back to him.

"Body heat escapes through the top of your head. Your face, hands, and feet are the first to suffer frostbite. Move around to establish a good flow of blood to your body."

And then his heart pounded, skipping beats as he listened to his own voice echoing back at him from the depths that held him captive. He jerked with fright, even though he knew it was only himself that he heard. The pain that shot through his leg made him cry aloud, a wild shriek that frightened him even more than the pain that had caused it.

"Daa . . . dee . . . ! Help! Someone . . . help!"

He tried to still his own breathing enough to listen, praying that he'd hear a familiar voice calling back an answer. But all he could hear was the blood rushing past his eardrums. He groaned, closing his eyes and trying to think of something besides the pain in his leg. The thought of Queenie and the fun they'd had only hours ago while baking and decorating cookies came instantly.

A sob tore up his throat as he thought of her . . . and home . . . and the soft, sweet smell of his own bed. Of how warm the covers would be and how safe he would feel knowing Dad and Queenie were there to protect him. Now his grandmother's threats seemed silly compared to the fact that he was cold and lost. He couldn't even contemplate the possibility that he might not be found.

He moaned and shifted, trying to find a comfortable spot between the small rocks upon which he'd fallen. Then he pulled his coat up around his ears, stuffed his hands inside its arms, and tried not to think of his numb feet and empty belly.

Queenie! Come and get me! Please come and get me!

He fell into a fitful doze with that thought on his mind and the image of her in his heart.

Queen sat slumped in the chair she'd pulled in front of the fire, sleeping in fits and starts, awakening now and then with a jerk only to find that everything that had happened wasn't just a bad dream, but a horrible reality.

J.J. lay on the couch, wrapped in Donny's arms, where they'd finally collapsed hours ago into an exhausted sleep. Queen hadn't had the heart to move them to a bed. She sensed their need to be as close to her as possible.

Queen sighed in her sleep and reached down to pull up a blanket that wasn't there. And then her hand stayed, and her breathing became rapid and shallow. Her eyelids twitched and jerked as she traveled through the course of her dream.

Suddenly she woke, sitting straight up in the chair and gripping the arms with her hands until the knuckles on her fingers turned white. Her blank, wide-eyed stare saw nothing of the dying embers of the flame into which she looked.

Instead she was looking into the heart of her dream, seeing the truth of what was really there. And when it was over, she shuddered and blinked, suddenly aware of her surroundings, finding it difficult to distinguish where she was from where she'd been.

"Oh, my God," she muttered, and staggered to her feet. "I've got to tell Cody! I've got to tell Cody."

She ran through the house, trying to remember where she'd left the two-way radio after the arrival of Sheriff Miller and his men. She entered the kitchen, where the dim night-light over the stove shed a weak yellow glow across the corner of the room. And then she saw it lying on the end of the counter and grabbed it with shaking hands, aware that what she was about to do would take more trust from Cody than he might have to give.

She closed her eyes and said a prayer, then took a deep breath and punched the send button on the radio. The static was a loud, unwelcome presence in the silence of the room.

"Queen to Cody. Queen to Cody. Cody . . . please come in!"

Cody thought he was dreaming. He heard her voice so clearly above the wail of the wind that for a moment he imagined she was here beside him. Then he remembered his surroundings and realized that he must be hearing her voice over the radio.

He dug for it beneath his covers, unintentionally waking Dennis, who swore as he tried to unzip his sleeping bag and then fumbled in the darkness for the lantern switch.

A luminescent glow filled the tent just as Cody's fingers curled around his radio.

"Cody here! What's wrong?" The question was instinctive. At this time of night, after everything else that had happened, it couldn't mean anything good.

"Cody . . . I had a dream. Over."

He sighed. "I'm having some bad ones, too, honey," he said quietly, aware that Dennis and probably every man in camp whose radio was on was listening to their conversation. But he didn't give a damn. In his shoes they would be doing the same.

"No!" she said, almost shouting into the receiver. "You don't understand. In my dream . . . I saw Will. I heard him! I think he was trying to tell us something. Over."

Cody frowned. "I don't get it. What do you mean? Over."

This was where his trust would be imperative, and Queen knew it. But there would be nothing gained if nothing was lost, and she was willing to lose a lot to get Will back.

"Cody . . . I think you've been looking in the wrong places. Over."

"Hell . . . there are no places left to look!" he shouted, and then buried his face in his hands and took a deep breath, trying to calm the sudden spurt of anger and fear that nearly gutted him. "Sorry. Please explain what you mean. Over."

"I heard Will calling. It echoed. His voice sounded far away and hollow. And it was so dark. I couldn't see him. But I could hear him cry . . . I could even hear him breathe. Over."

"Hell," Dennis muttered as goose bumps skittered across his skin beneath the cover of his shirt and coat. She was even getting to him.

"What are you trying to say, Queen? Over."

"I'm telling you that when morning comes . . . don't look on the mountain . . . look inside. Cody . . . I think Will's inside the mountain. Over."

The radio fell from Cody's hands. He swallowed twice,

trying to talk, and then started to shake. Dennis reached out and picked it up, pressed the send button, doing what Cody could not.

"Hey, angel. Dennis here. We heard you loud and clear. And what the heck . . . we have nothing to lose and a lot to gain. Thanks for the call. See you soon. Over and out."

When there was nothing between Cody and Dennis but the faint lantern light and the shadows, they stared into each other's eyes, unwilling to admit even to themselves that finding the exact place on this mountain where a child might fall . . . or crawl into . . . was nearly impossible.

"What do you think, buddy?" Dennis said.

For a long moment Cody didn't move . . . didn't speak. His eyes narrowed, and the skin on his face seemed to shrink across his bones from the tension inside him. And then he turned and looked at Dennis.

"I think she hasn't been wrong yet. That's what I think. Turn out the damned light. I've got to get some rest. Tomorrow's going to be a bitch."

Queen laid down the two-way radio and walked to the stove, turning on the gas beneath the kettle to heat some water. She was freezing. Maybe if she made some coffee, she wouldn't be so . . .

She stopped, reached out, and turned the gas off with a jerk, then walked out of the room, the tears so thick in her eyes that she had trouble finding her way out the door.

It was the thought of how cold she felt that made her realize she wasn't feeling her cold . . . she felt Will's. And being warm when he wasn't seemed selfish, even obscene.

She went back into the living room, pulled the comforter back over the boys, who still slept in a tangle on the couch, and then bent down and put another stick of wood on the fire.

The wind rattled a window on the other side of the house as she crawled into her chair and sat, watching as the dying embers took on new life at the fresh fodder, licking and eating their way into the heart of the wood.

Queen stared at the flames and never knew when her eyes closed. Her head slumped against the arm of the chair, and she slept. And when she woke, it was morning.

20

By morning the wind that had buffeted them all night had calmed. They broke camp before dawn. The search started at daybreak to the tune of a cloudy sky with alternate glimpses of sunshine. The men had nothing but coffee and cold rations for sustenance, but not one of them voiced a complaint or wished for warmer clothes and a full belly. No matter how uncomfortable they were, they knew that somewhere there was a child who was in much worse straits.

Also to their credit was the fact that not one man had blinked an eye at Cody's announced change in procedure. And when he told them of the possibility that Will might be underground, or had crawled injured into a cave, unable to travel, not one of them asked why.

It didn't take Dennis long to realize that the whole search party had heard Queen's frantic radio call to Cody last night. No matter what their opinions on the subject might be, ultimately it was Cody's son who was lost. If he believed it possible, who were they to question him?

Spaced some fifty yards apart, with two-way radios as the communication of choice, they began a wide, fanlike sweep down the mountain. Only this time they would pause at the designated signal, shout Will's name aloud in unison, and then stop and listen before moving on.

The process was agonizingly slow. Cody wanted to scream with frustration at the snail's pace with which they were moving, yet he knew that going any faster might mean the difference between hearing Will's cries for help and missing them. There was no doubt in his mind that Will was still alive, because Queen had told him so. All he could do was go on as planned.

Two hours passed, with the searchers moving, stopping, calling, listening, and then starting all over again.

Dennis saw Cody's intensity increasing. And at the same time he felt the same agonizing disappointment each time they called Will's name and received no answer.

Cody focused entirely on what he might hear, not what he saw. The farther down the mountain they moved, the more convinced he became that Queen had to be right. If Will was alive and aboveground, he would already have been found. There was no other explanation for the fact that his son seemed to have disappeared from the face of the earth—or, in this case, the face of the mountain.

It was time to call Will's name. Again they stopped, and the signal to do so was passed along the long, single chain of men. Sometimes they could see only as far as a man or two on either side of themselves. But it was far enough to see.

"Will . . . Will . . . Will . . . Will . . . "

The silence that followed was eerie as each man

strained to hold his breathing to a minimum, hoping for the miracle that had yet to occur.

Cody ached in spirit and in body. The urge to drop to the ground and wail in unrelenting grief was almost overwhelming. Yet when he thought he couldn't move another muscle, he'd picture Will's big blue eyes, and the way his unexpected smiles would brighten an entire day, and knew that he could take that next step. He *had* to. What if Will was about to give up, too?

And then it was his turn to shout Will's name aloud.

When he heard a cry, he thought at first he was imagining the sound because he'd so badly wanted to hear it. And then it came again, more urgent . . . more frantic . . . and Cody's heart jerked against his chest as he shouted for the men to wait. He'd heard Will's voice.

"Daa . . . dee! In . . . eee . . . bod . . . ee . . . Help!"

His call seemed weak, as if the place he was in had eaten most of it before it escaped through the opening above. Cody shivered in response to the image his mind had conjured.

Will sniffled back tears and shouted again, and as he did, he realized that his voice was weak because his throat was terribly sore. He swallowed. Then, just as he opened his mouth, he stopped in midmotion, forgetting to breathe as he cocked his head and listened.

Someone was calling his name! A whole lot of some-ones! But what if they couldn't find him?

He started shouting . . . screaming . . . afraid to stop and listen and hear that the voices had moved on, that he was left behind in the dark and the cold . . . again.

He looked up. The piece of blue sky was still there . . . taunting . . . reminding him of how often he'd looked up into that same sky and never considered his luck in being able to move freely about beneath it.

Cody hit the ground on all fours and began crawling, turning first one direction, then readjusting by degrees as he tried to zero in on Will's voice. But it was so difficult to tell where it was coming from.

The men came from everywhere to converge on the area and repeat Cody's behavior, listening carefully and trying to follow the sound of the boy's shouts.

"Over here . . . over here!" a young lieutenant shouted, the first to see the small, narrow cleft in the ground. As the men merged on the area, it was painfully obvious by the way the ground was disturbed around it that Will had tried to catch himself as he went in. Grass was uprooted, small rocks and pebbles dislodged.

They moved aside as Cody burst through the ring of men. In seconds he was flat on the ground, prone above the narrow opening, peering down into the slit, trying to see into the darkness.

Will gasped as the sky above him disappeared. He stopped shouting, frightened by the sudden darkness, until he heard a familiar voice calling down to him. It was then that he figured it was all right to cry.

"Will! Son! Are you down there?"

"Daddy . . . Daddy . . . I fell. I can't get out."

"Oh, thank you, God!" Cody's soft whisper was heard by the men, but they knew that it hadn't been meant for them. They, too, were saying their own prayers as Will answered his father's call.

"Okay, Will. Don't you worry. We'll get you out. Now tell me . . . where do you hurt?"

"My leg. Daddy, I can't move my leg. I think it's broken."

"Give me a flashlight," Cody shouted, and reached behind him. The object he asked for was slapped firmly into his hand.

He flipped it on and then leaned down, his gaze following the narrow beam of light as it traveled toward his son. Will's face suddenly came into focus, as did the fact that the only way to get Will out was straight up.

"It's me, son. It's Daddy. I see you. Don't be afraid."

And then he turned his head and stared straight into Dennis's face, his words low so that Will couldn't hear.

"We can't use the harness. There's no way he can maneuver himself into that alone with a broken leg. And there's no way in hell I can get down to him. It's too small."

"Damn," Dennis muttered, looking with dismay at the narrowness of the opening through which they needed to work. No grown man could possibly fit through it.

"Just a minute, Will!" Cody shouted. "Don't be afraid. I'll be right back. Sheriff Miller is right here, and he's going to talk to you while we figure out what to do, okay?"

"Okay." The trust in Will's voice was implicit.

Cody got to his feet and walked a few paces away from the hole as the men took turns shouting down words of encouragement.

"If we can't go down after him," Dennis said, "then how do we get him up?"

Cody thought. And then what he decided depended entirely on Will being able to cooperate. He dropped back to the opening.

"Will! Is your leg all that hurts?"

"No . . ."

"Oh, hell," Cody muttered. "Okay, son. Tell me exactly what parts of your body you can't move."

"Oh, that! Only my leg. My throat hurts . . . and, uh . . . my ribs are sore. But I can move my mouth and stomach okay."

A smile broke Cody's grim expression wide open. He rolled over on his back and laughed. "Ask a kid a specific question . . . he'll give you a specific answer. All I've got to remember is to ask the right questions."

He rolled back over and shouted down to Will, "I'm going to drop you a lift, son. All you have to do is put it over your head and then beneath your arms. You'll wrap your arms around it and hold on real tight while we pull you up. Think you can do it?"

Will's voice rose two octaves. "Is it the kind like the navy seals use to fish people out of the water? One of those deals?"

Dennis chuckled. "A true son of the military."

"Yes," Cody said. "One of those 'deals.' Can you hold on tight enough so that you won't fall?"

"Sure. Just let 'er drop."

"Oh, hell," Cody said as he stood and signaled one of the men who was carrying rescue equipment. "Sure, Dad. No problem, Dad." He swiped a shaky hand across his face as Abel Miller walked by and gave him a slap on the back. "Thank God for the resilience of kids," Cody muttered.

In minutes the rigging had been completed. The men now formed a chain as they lowered the lift by the attached rope, all equally eager to be part of the process of raising Will Bonner from the dead.

"Got it!" Will shouted, and eagerly grasped the horse collar–shaped object that had just landed in his lap. In seconds he'd shrugged it over his head and positioned it firmly beneath his armpits. He wrapped his arms tight around it, tested it once or twice to make sure he had a firm grip, and then shouted, "Pull away! I'm ready."

Cody was flat on his stomach above the hole, the flashlight an extension of his arm while he leaned as far through the opening as he dared, needing to watch his son's progress. He said a slow prayer, took a deep breath, and then turned to the men, who were waiting for his signal.

"Let's get him out of there," Cody said. It was what they were waiting to hear.

Will groaned as movement sent pain racking through his body.

"Are you all right?" Cody shouted, at the same time motioning for the men to stop pulling.

"It's okay, Daddy. Just get me out."

Cody signaled again, and the men resumed pulling on the rope.

Will hunched over the lift, tightened his hold even more, and bit the inside of his mouth as his feet left the floor of the minicavern. Twice as they pulled him up, he bumped against the narrow chimney, and twice he groaned aloud, certain that if it happened again, he would pass out from the pain and then fall. But somehow his daddy's voice, and the fact that daylight got closer and closer, kept him from losing his grip on the lift and on consciousness.

A scant minute later Cody's hand connected with a thatch of dark hair and then brushed over the bright red jacket. Realizing that he had touched his son, and now had to move back to give the men and Will the space in which to maneuver, was unbearable.

And then suddenly Will's face broke above the surface, and that was all Cody was waiting for. He jumped to his feet, then bent down and, with the strength of giants, pulled his son into his arms as the mountain gave up its prey.

There wasn't a dry eye in the crowd as the men cheered wildly. This was a good end to a bad beginning.

Cody's belly turned at the sight of the awkward angle

at which Will's thin leg hung beneath his torn and muddy jeans. "Get me a stretcher," he shouted, and in seconds Will was flat on his back, his leg being positioned so that it would not move until they could get him to a hospital.

"Daddy . . . is Queenie all right? I saw her fall."

"She's just fine, son," Cody said as he bent over the stretcher while the others worked to secure his son. "In fact, she's back home just waiting to see you. They all are."

The smile slid off Will's face. "All of them?"

"It's okay, Will. Your grandmother is sorry. Probably more sorry than anyone there. She never meant for you to be afraid. Do you understand?"

"I guess," Will said, and turned away, unwilling now that he was free of one burden to face what had sent him running from home in the first place.

"Wait," Cody said as the men started to lift Will's stretcher. "There's someone else who needs to hear his voice."

He took the two-way radio from his inner jacket pocket. "Cody to Queen. Cody to Queen. Do you read me? Over."

"This is Queen. I'm here. Over."

Her breathless voice and frightened tone told Cody that she'd spent a night in hell with him, only miles apart.

Cody laid the radio against his son's cheek and pressed the send button as he nodded for his son to speak.

"Queenie . . . this is Will. Are you all right?" And then he added, "Over," at his father's silent reminder.

She started to cry. After all their fright, and all their worries, the first thing he wanted to know was if she was all right.

"Yes, Will, I'm just fine. Hurry home, sweetheart. Donny's eating all your cookies. Over and out."

Will grinned. "Better hurry," he told the men. "Donny's got a hollow leg. Queenie says so."

Cody found it much easier going down the mountain with a lighter heart. Within the hour the roof of his house was in sight. And when they broke out of the trees and into the clearing, the first thing he saw was Queen, standing on the deck in the cold morning air. With her fiery hair and the smile on her face, she was like a bright beacon to come home to.

And then she was running down the steps, covering the distance between them in long, even strides.

Cody caught her in midflight and wrapped his arms around her, burying his face against her neck and whispering things meant for her alone.

"Needs more icicles on this side, J.J.," Will said, and pointed toward a bare spot near the wall.

J.J. nodded, following his brother's directions. Although Will was home and safe, for the time being he was couch-bound with the cast upon his leg. His share in the decoration of the family Christmas tree consisted of directing the entire proceedings from a reclining position.

Donny was of the opinion that Will was getting bossy, but he was so glad to have his family intact that he had yet to complain. J.J. was glad to have his mentor back in place and his world in order.

Will sighed as J.J. carried a fistful of shiny aluminum strands toward the back of the tree and wished that he could stand long enough to help. It was the first time in a long while that they'd put up a tree, and he was missing out on all the fun.

The Christmas they'd been with their grandparents

they'd had a tree, but it had been a designer original. No hands-on decorating for Lenore Whittier. And the theme of her tree had lacked the warm improvisation of this one. There was no way that pink velvet bows and white satin balls could compete with blinking lights, four different sets of balls in four different colors, and Queenie's surprise—special oven-baked ornaments in the shape of gingerbread men, one with each member of the family's name swirled across the fat belly in red icing. All in all, Will thought it was a marvelous tree.

"Your grandparents called," Queen said. "They wished you all a Merry Christmas."

"Yay!" J.J. cheered, and Donny gave her a thumbs-up sign to indicate his own approval as he glanced beneath the tree at his grandparents' presents, which had arrived by special express days earlier.

Queen noticed that Will had little to say regarding the message and knew that it was going to take time before he could fully forgive his grandmother. Of all the boys, he'd taken their threats the most to heart . . . and had suffered the most because of it.

The Whittiers had been at Will's bedside, as had Cody, when he'd awakened with the cast on his leg. At first he couldn't figure out what was different about his grandmother.

She'd apologized over and over, and he remembered that she'd been crying. It was only later that he realized she wasn't wearing all her makeup. She had looked old . . . and, somehow, almost safe.

Will shifted on his chair and then smiled as Queenie came into the room carrying brownies and hot chocolate.

"Me first," he said.

"What else is new," Donny muttered, and then winked as Queen gave him a look he recognized meant business.

"Will . . . when we get finished, want to put the star on top?" Queen asked, setting down the goodies.

Will's face lit up like the lights on the tree. "Oh, yes . . . but you can't lift me that high," he said, and then slumped back onto the chair with a sigh.

"I can," Cody said as he came into the living room, bringing a burst of cold air with him.

Queen smiled. Her heart broke rhythm just once, a reminder to herself that his mere presence still made her weak in the knees.

Cody grinned and winked, recognizing a look in her eyes that he would gladly address later that night.

Queen stared at him in all his magnificence, his black hair frosted with a peppering of the snow that was falling outside, his eyes bright and glowing with life and laughter.

He set a small box on the table, shed his coat, and then grabbed her, covering her mouth with a quick, passionate kiss, knowing she couldn't object if she couldn't talk.

"Yuk, mushy stuff," J.J. said, tossing the entire handful of icicles toward the empty spot on the tree.

Will smiled and reached for a brownie. Donny stood beside the tree, staring pensively at the couple across the room, remembering a time long ago when his mother had been alive . . . remembering how empty their lives had been when she died . . . and now, with the arrival of their Queenie, how full and happy they seemed once more.

He sighed and then grinned. It wasn't everyone who found a savior at a bus stop. He considered himself pretty darn smart for having recognized her worth.

"Queenie, tell me again about the dream."

Will's plea was a repeat of the same request they'd all heard over and over.

She smiled and ruffled his hair. "You've already heard it a hundred times," she said.

"But I want to hear it again. Did you really see me in the hole?"

"Yes, I believe I did," Queen said. "How else would I have known what to tell your daddy?"

J.J. listened intently, already drawn into the magic of the story.

"And did you really hear me crying? Did you hear me say your name?" Will asked.

There was more to Will's question than just the need to hear the story of his rescue again and again. Cody heard his need to feel connected . . . in that special way . . . with that special someone. He understood that need, because it was a mirror of his own.

"Yes, darling," Queen said, and knelt beside Will's chair. She cupped his face and smiled, loving the blue eyes and black hair and his face, so similar to another's— the man she loved with all her heart. "I heard you call, but I didn't hear you with my ears . . . I heard you with my heart."

Will sighed. It was what he needed to hear.

"And I think I hear a kiss coming," Cody said. "Must be for me . . . my lips are still cold." Teasing was the only way he could hide his emotional reaction to her comment.

"Cody . . ." Queen laughed, stepping just out of his reach as she looked down at the small box beside his coat. "Presents already?"

The blue sweater she'd been knitting secretly, the one the color of Cody's eyes, had been wrapped for days, just waiting for Christmas morning to arrive.

Cody's eyes lit up. "I almost forgot. I thought we needed a new ornament for the tree in honor of our new family. What do you think, guys?"

He needn't have asked. They'd adopted Queen as theirs long before he'd admitted he'd fallen in love with his sister who wasn't really a sister.

He handed Will the box. "You open it, son. It's for the top of the tree. I remembered our old star as looking pretty ragged."

"Great," Donny said. "I'd just promised Will I'd let him do the honors. Now that you're here you can lift him up. That cast weighs nearly as much as he does."

Queen knelt beside Will's chair, watching as he lifted the lid and sifted through the tissue paper inside.

"Look! It's an angel," he cried. He held it up and turned it from side to side, admiring the delicate white fabric of the gown and the fragile, ethereal wings rimmed with a tiny gold thread. "And she's got red hair . . . just like Queenie."

Queen stared at the doll-like ornament, blinking furiously against the sudden onset of tears.

Cody leaned down and picked up his son. "Put her on good and tight so she doesn't fall," he said as Will worked the angel over the top of the tree.

"There." Will was finished.

Cody set him back down on the couch and then stepped aside, squinting his eyes just enough to admire the way the angel seemed to hover above the treetop as if in flight.

Queen slid beneath his arm and laid her head on his chest as he hugged her gently. "It's beautiful," she said. "Thank you, Cody. Thank you for making me feel so loved . . . and so special."

"Look at her, Mom. She's shining."

J.J.'s innocent cry stunned them all. Unaware of what he'd said, he danced around the tree in a childlike frenzy, admiring the way in which the blinking lights reflected off her wings and her hair.

Queen was in shock, afraid to let her joy show . . . afraid that the others might be offended by what J.J. had done. But she needn't have worried. Donny just winked and then turned away, busying himself with brownies so that he wouldn't have to admit to the lump in his own throat. Will considered what J.J. had said. Without speaking, he simply slipped his hand in hers as she stood beside him and squeezed once. It was enough.

Outside, the snow continued to fall, covering trees and earth alike in a heavy white blanket of cold beauty. Inside the house, a fire burned brightly in the fireplace, love and laughter filled the rooms, warming their hearts as the fire warmed their bodies.

Cody took her in his arms, pressing his cheek closely against the soft warmth of her own.

"Welcome to the family, my love. Welcome home."

Epilogue

Lids rattled on the pots as wind rattled the windows. Queen walked from stove to cabinet and back again, stirring patiently and checking to make sure that the evening meal would be ready on time.

She could hardly believe that it was their second Christmas as a family and, within days, the first anniversary of their wedding.

With four males in the house, it had been a whirlwind year.

A small squeak and then a squawk turned into a definite wail as Amanda Bonner woke from her nap and for one of the few times in her very young life did not see a face hovering over her cradle. She was certain that she'd been abandoned and thereby proceeded to make her presence known.

Cody beat his three sons into the kitchen by inches, scooping his daughter from her cradle before she had time to finish her third yelp. Queen smiled and shrugged. It was hopeless to assume that this child wasn't going to be spoiled. If Cody didn't have her, Donny, Will, or J.J. did. She would never know what it was like to be lonely, but she would certainly know what it meant to be loved.

"Is she hungry?" Cody asked. "I'll finish supper if you need to feed her." He cuddled the tiny scrap of humanity that he and Queen had created and tried not to gloat at the beauty of their child.

"She has your hair," Queen said, amazed that a man of Cody's size could be reduced to mush by one so small.

"But she's going to have your eyes," Cody said, aware that the baby blue eyes Amanda had been born with were already changing to a deep forest green. It was a perfect blending, as was everything in their lives.

"Yeah, but she has J.J.'s personality," Donny said. "Totally rotten."

"Does not!"

"Does too!"

Cody rolled his eyes. "Guys . . . for Pete's sake, cut it out."

Queen smiled. She loved this rollicking mess of men and muscles and wondered where she and Amanda would fit into such a male-oriented world. If she knew her Bonners, she suspected it would be somewhere around the top of the pedestal.

Because of the weather, the radio on the shelf above the desk was picking up many unfamiliar stations. Cody said they were picking up skip, but whatever it was, it was music, sweet and familiar.

Queen listened absently, thinking how long it had been since she'd heard that particular station, and then realized what she was hearing was a live broadcast of the Grand Ole Opry out of Nashville.

"Oh, my," she said, and had a sudden hunger to see her family.

She sighed with regret when she realized how long it had been since she'd tried unsuccessfully to find Diamond through Jesse Eagle's music label. All three sisters were so lost from one another.

An unusual and intense longing overwhelmed her, and as the announcer began to talk, she turned away so that they would not see her tears.

Cody noticed Queen's face change expression. It had been months since he remembered seeing that longing . . . that far-off look of remembering. He silently handed Amanda to Donny and walked up behind Queen, intending to give her a hug, when she actually bolted out of his arms and made a beeline for the radio, turning up the volume while waving for everyone to be quiet.

They stared at her odd behavior and then watched in amazement as Queen began to smile.

" . . . live from the Grand Ole Opry in Nashville, Tennessee."

A woman's voice filled the room, and even though Cody had never heard the song, a chill ran up his spine at the familiarity of the voice.

It wrapped around them as they listened, lulling them and then, when they thought it had passed, yanking emotion from them in unsuspecting fashion. And all the while Queen was laughing and crying and dancing in a little circle beneath the shelf.

"Oh, my God! My God . . . it's her! She did it! She really did it!"

She kept repeating it over and over until Cody started to suspect what she was talking about. "Honey . . . ?"

The song ended, and the wild sound of applause was drowned out by the announcer's exuberant shout. "And that, ladies and gentlemen, was Nashville's own Diamond Houston with her latest single."

Cody started to grin at the look of pleased shock on Queen's face.

"It's my sister!" she shouted, pointing toward the radio.

"Wow!" Donny was duly impressed. "You mean that you have a famous sister?"

"So it seems," Queen said, and nearly danced into Cody's arms.

"Well then," Cody said, hugging her tightly against him, feeling her trembling and her joy as his own, "I believe we need to rethink where we're spending Christmas. What if I see about tickets to Nashville? If Queen can contact her sister and let her know it's okay, I think she deserves this Christmas with her own family . . . what do you say?"

The two younger boys were silent. Finally Will was brave enough to speak up.

"I say it's fine as long as we go, too. After all, who'll look after her if she goes alone?"

Queen laughed. "My God. He has it, too."

Cody grinned. He knew what she meant. That overprotective streak of his was definitely a dominant gene among the Bonner males.

"I wouldn't go without you," Queen said. "Remember, we're all one family now. And Diamond will be so excited. But Cody . . . how will I contact her? I lost Jesse Eagle's address. I don't even know if they're still together."

Cody grinned. "If she's that famous, she can't be hard to find," he said. "Just give me a phone and a couple of days."

Queen laughed, then took Amanda from Donny, watching as her earlier excitement caught fire and swept the room. Suddenly she had a vision of the woman she'd been when she left Cradle Creek nearly two years ago. That woman no longer existed, and it was due solely to a twist of fate.

Despite her dislike of Johnny's way of life, she'd taken quite a gamble of her own. She'd done something she swore she'd never do and found herself happier than a woman had a right to be. All in all, getting off that bus was the luckiest thing that had ever happened to her.

Then she smiled. Who would have thought that luck would make a difference in my life?

And just for a moment she had a vague understanding of her father's unrelenting need to search for luck of a different kind. He'd chased impossible rainbows, but she'd been looking for an anchor. And she'd found it in Cody.

Queen had all she needed. Her family . . . and her man.

And then she had to laugh at the thought that came next. With any luck, after the kids were asleep, she would have him . . . in spades.

Tame the Wildest Heart by **Parris Afton Bonds**

In her most passionate romance yet, Parris Afton Bonds tells the tale of two lonely hearts forever changed by an adventure in the Wild West. It was a match made in heaven . . . and hell. Mattie McAlister was looking for her half-Apache son and Gordon Halpern was looking for his missing wife. Neither realized that they would find the trail to New Mexico Territory was the way to each other's hearts.

First and Forever by **Zita Christian**

Katrina Swann was content with her peaceful, steady life in the close-knit immigrant community of Merriweather, Missouri. Then the reckless Justin Barrison swept her off her feet in a night of passion. Before she knew it she was following him to the Dakota Territory. Through trials and tribulations on the prairie, they learned the strength of love in the face of adversity.

Gambler's Gold by **Barbara Keller**

When Charlotte Bell headed out on a wagon train from Massachusetts to California, she had one goal in mind—finding her father, who had disappeared while prospecting for gold. The last thing she was looking for was love, but when fate turned against her, she turned to the dashing Reade Elliot to save her.

Queen by **Sharon Sala**

The Gambler's Daughters Trilogy continues with Diamond Houston's older sister, Queen, and the ready-made family she discovers, complete with laughter and tears. Queen Houston always had to act as a mother to her two younger sisters when they were growing up. After they part ways as young women, each to pursue her own dream, Queen reluctantly ends up in the mother role again—except this time there's a father involved.

A Winter Ballad by **Barbara Samuel**

When Anya of Winterbourne rescued a near-dead knight she found in the forest around her manor, she never thought he was the champion she'd been waiting for. "A truly lovely book. A warm, passionate tale of love and redemption, it lingers in the hearts of readers. . . . Barbara Samuel is one of the best, most original writers in romantic fiction today."—Anne Stuart

Shadow Prince by **Terri Lynn Wilhelm**

A plastic surgeon falls in love with a mysterious patient in this powerful retelling of *The Beauty and the Beast* fable. Ariel Denham, an ambitious plastic surgeon, resentfully puts her career on hold for a year in order to work at an exclusive, isolated clinic high in the Smoky Mountains. There she meets and falls in love with a mysterious man who stays in the shadows, a man she knows only as Jonah.

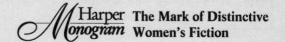

SHARON SALA, an Oklahoma native, lives with her husband of over twenty-five years on a farm north of Prague, Oklahoma. *Queen* is her eighth published novel, and the second in the much-loved Gambler's Daughters Trilogy.

YOU COULD ALWAYS COUNT ON QUEEN

Of all gambler Johnny Houston's remarkable daughters, big sister Queen has shouldered the responsibility of caring for the family since she was a child. Now that they're all grown up, the flame-haired beauty finds herself free to pursue her own dreams. Far away from the Tennessee hills, she enters a new world full of surprises—one of which is Cody Bonner.

BUT QUEEN NEVER COUNTED ON LOVE

Handsome widower Cody Bonner has his hands full raising three boys, though he wouldn't have it any other way. But when Queen comes into their lives, he soon realizes he wants more than just a housekeeper and mother figure for his sons. Cody reckons it will take a lifetime to show the depths of his love for her, if only he can convince the lady to give him the chance.

Harper
Monogram

The Mark of Distinctive Women's Fiction